HIGHER LEARNING

A Novel

HIGHER LEARNING

A Novel

by
Marianne Shapiro

The descriptions of people, places and events
contained in Higher Learning are fictional.
Any resemblance to actual people, places or events
is strictly coincidental.

Book design by
Carol Pentleton / The Digital Artist
http://www.thenewplace.com
carol@thedigitalartist.com

Cui prodest?

CONTENTS

April 1944
PROLOGUE

Will's P-51B Mustang had been flying escort with four others all the way from the airfield in England without encountering so much as a speck of Nazi armor. It had been an unusually cloudless day at Coltishall when the squadron took off, but the forecast had been for clouds over the Continent. Their bomber support mission was to take them over the Low Countries into Northern Germany, a run Will had made several times since coming over on loan from the 99th in the Mediterranean Air Command. General Davis' trial balloon, the joke went. Will had been in some tight scrapes too, including a couple of hairy dogfights with the Luftwaffe.

No menacing Focke-Wulf 190s to be seen so far. As dusk gathered and the plane's engine droned on, Will's thoughts turned for the thousandth time to his family in Alabama, where he'd left them after flight training at Tuskegee Field. His mind's eye caressed his wife and five-year old daughter as they sat on the front porch of their house near the Institute. He could picture the campus bathed in the late-autumn glow, students with serious faces, wondering when the war would end.

Will's daydream was brutally interrupted by the sound of bursting 88mm anti-aircraft fire which seemed to come crashing from everywhere and nowhere. It was too late to take evasive action. In the split instant of realizing the onset of a flier's worst nightmare Will's fighter was aflame, losing altitude, threatening immolation to man and machine.

Training and instinct both came to his rescue instantaneously. Almost in a single movement Will's hands undid his straps, tore off his helmet, and pushed up the hood of the cockpit. Then they grasped the edges of the cockpit, and Will was out and away, falling, reaching for the ripcord, jerking it with his right hand, and the next clear consciousness was of the heavy jolt of the straps jerking him hard between the fork of his legs, and his parachute billowed out. Will started floating down through the clouds. It took only a few minutes for the Dutch landscape, with its green-orange melange of patchwork plots and irrigation ditches, to swallow up the aviator's body.

Like all the other pilots he had been force-fed more than his fill of briefings on survival procedures, but this was no simulation. Every moment yawned like an eternity as he hurried to do what he had been taught. Luckily the spot where he'd landed was lined with hedgerows. The parachute was now an unwieldy mass of folds. Will quickly gathered it up and stuffed it under the nearest foliage together with the rest of his gear, then he looked around warily and contemplated his next move.

There was a great chasm of silence. What had seemed to take only a few minutes had actually been time enough for dusk to change to dark. A wet wind was blowing on Will's face as he reached mechanically for the revolver that ought to have been at his right hip, only to realize that he had inexplicably not brought it with him this time. His eyes had grown accustomed to the dark. About two hundred yards in the distance he made out a row of hedges which formed a protective defilade on the rear side of a lone farmhouse that faced a dirt road no wider than a bicycle path.

Will bent down and rubbed his ankle. It was only a light sprain, and he knew he'd have to move quickly, bad ankle or no, toward the farmhouse that held out some chance of concealment if not refuge. In a matter of a few minutes he had stumbled up to what seemed like a utility door, a massive oaken affair kept shut by a latch painted green.

Suddenly he heard a little noise as though someone had shuffled his feet on gravel, and when he jerked his head around he saw the old man. He was sitting on a stone between the farmhouse and the hedges.

"I'm American," said Will, as if his clothing and the color of his skin were insufficient evidence of who he was.

The old man looked up slowly but said nothing. Will tried again, this time in his well-rehearsed French, "Je suis americain. Aviateur. S'il vous plait, je veux me cacher."

Suddenly this stalemate was interrupted by the sound of the

door unbolting. A younger man's tousled head popped out. "Get in here fast," he barked out in what could have passed for normal American English.

Will's body raced ahead of his mind. He was inside the house instantaneously. The old man had come in after him without a sound. "My name is Mark," said the speaker, who was clearly in charge. He was dressed in a navy blue flight sweater and dark grey moleskin pants with leather piping. The ruddy serio-comic face reminded Will of Breughel. "You're probably wondering about my English. Before the war, I was a merchant seaman on a freighter. We made regular runs between Rotterdam and New York." Then pointing to several men seated around an enameled-top table, he introduced the rest of the company, all of whom bore New Testament names and looked pretty much the same age except for the one called Peter, who couldn't have been older than a college student.

"We call ourselves the Apostles," added Mark, as if in answer to the inchoate question that had just then tweaked Will's subconscious, "for reasons that have to do with the Gestapo, not religion." He gave a stiff little laugh, reproving himself for the staleness of the in-joke, and then asked Will for his name, rank, and serial number. The information was duly entered in a miniature notebook, which disappeared into Mark's fob pocket.

"I've got to make it back to England. Can you help me?" Will had still not fully recovered from the abruptness of his plunge from the heavens, but his survival instinct did not slumber for an instant.

Mark was clearly struggling with his own emotions. He looked around the table. "Look, we want to do everything we can to help you, but first we must formulate a plan. We've helped others before you, but every case is different. The situation changes constantly." The other men kept their silence, obviously deferring to their leader.

Will's ankle was continuing to throb. The cumulative effect of stress, fatigue, and pain had made him feel the pangs of hunger for the first time since Coltishall, which seemed galaxies removed from this new time and place.

"Can you at least give me something to eat? I'm really in your hands now."

Mark said something in Dutch, and one of the Apostles got up to go towards what looked like the kitchen through the half-lit doorway. He returned with a steaming bowl of a thick broth in a wooden crock and set it in front of Will, who lost no time in attacking the food. It tasted like a mixture of root vegetables. While he ate, his hosts began an animated discussion sotto voce.

Mark's voice soon rose above the murmur. "We've decided to move you right away to a safer place. Peter will be your escort. Go with him and do exactly what he says."

Will slurped the remainder of his meager meal and got up to leave. Peter had already approached him; a half-smile lingering on what Will now registered in a flash of clarity was an oddly incongruous young-old face. Peter turned out to speak good English too.

"I think we're going to be able to get you safely back to England," were his first words. "Let's go right now. It won't be that easy."

Will's watch, keeping perfect time in defiance of all probability, told him it was eight o'clock. As he and Peter exited the farmhouse, Will noticed that a cold drizzle had begun to fall while he had been inside, and he was glad that he hadn't ditched his flight jacket along with his goggles and heavy outer footgear.

They set out on foot, Peter leading the way. The road was stippled with wet clumps of flowers and shrubs. A glowering sky provided cover for a journey that Will reckoned took fifteen minutes before Peter stopped at a nondescript structure that could have been a utility shed. It was set back from a cluster of dwellings, and Will noticed only one window, immediately next to the door. A loud knock followed by two rapid softer ones produced an immediate response, and they were inside.

Will had some difficulty in adjusting his eyes to the darkness. Slowly he made out the shapes of three men. Their uniforms and holstered pistols were superfluous accoutrements. It was something about their bearing... Will knew. A primeval dread suffused his being as he realized that his apostolic guide was no longer in the room.

"Was könnte die Lebenserwartung eines flüchtigen Negers sein?" were the last words he heard.

Monday Evening, April 5, 1993
MURDER GOES TO REDFERN

The Redfern University swimming pool has been crowded all day, bursting with racers breaking out into each other's lanes, the concrete walls of the pool hall streaked with dives and splashes. But dusk is falling almost all at once, lending the humid air a chill despite its constant temperature, and swimmers are evaporating to the locker rooms, their dull shouts and slams already barely audible.

Selena loves that bit of time by herself with the delight of someone naturally sociable needing a recharge. The thought of tonight's party brings pleasurable feelings, so a half-hour is all it takes for her to unwind. She even likes the echo of occasional odd voices and when they die out she hums a little nursery tune, enjoying the magnified sound. Now to remove and toss her cap and goggles, letting her hair swirl around in the water against the rules.

No one else here at all, and no one waiting to pester her later—not even Hilary, whom she'll deal with later at the party. Selena does a few laps of a side stroke people never do anymore because you can't get anywhere fast with it, then turns luxuriantly onto her back. She blinks a little and takes in the solid columns of a woman's legs placed solidly apart, her middle and waist looking funnily tubular, foreshortened as Hilary would say, but still the figure looks tall as it stares down at Selena in the stingy light. And Selena goes right on floating on her back above the wavering black line. The woman's head is a squared-off egg in its bathing cap, the chinstrap holstering it with the eyes obscured by goggles. Selena squints up at her; is she going to say something?

The hell with it. Selena crashes into a speed crawl, kicking up huge arcs of water between herself and the staring female, willing her to go away, pad back down the deserted concrete corridors, then up and out. But the woman's broad face is highlighted by the meager pool lights, and evidently she is immersed in a great view of Selena, whose momentum is hampered by that goldfish feeling. No privacy ever. Selena finally pulls up, and with a huge splash, white light blinds her and a hammer slams her just above the heart. She swirls back down and tries to skim past her assailant under water as if taking an ocean wave. Any screams of fright and of battle would be blocked by two huge hands, so for a few seconds she acquiesces in her end, somehow fearful only of the echoing turbulence. The hands are now bearing down on her head and will not be satisfied, but with the last of her strength she kicks out, rocking the huge woman as the waters shift, feeling herself still conscious though in eclipse. Then one of the hands slips in the oily water, sending her spinning and smashing into the concrete edge. Pain echoes through her body, but she can't really take it in, even as her tears stream and the impact helps her to nose upward, coughing and sobbing. She half-swims, half-crawls to the edge, hoists herself up and out, but by the time she can even focus the woman is gone, leaving nothing of herself but a train of little puddles on the concrete.

It's all over so fast that already Selena can hear well enough to make out the tranquil murmur of water draining back into the pool. A wave of dizziness makes her flatten herself against the wall, her breath coming in jagged gasps. Then she feels her muscles bracing with the physical return of confidence.

Her eyes feel swollen and sore, searching uselessly about her as if the attacker were waiting patiently in some corner. Was it female at all, this giant figure of a matron? Selena has no doubt that she will try to strike again. Still standing nearly motionless at the deserted poolside, Selena feels surprised by the calm that has succeeded her terror. There is something almost comforting about having faced the worst and seen it through. Concentrate and answers will come, as usual. She fastforwards to a core list of possibilities but is it possible that any of them would stop at nothing? An uneasy idea begins to form in her mind, and to put it aside she moves slowly, as if offering herself once again, toward the locker rooms. It is not likely that the creature will make a second attempt on her there, lacking the protection of water.

Still enough time to get back to Blight House and change. For tonight's party counts too much to be missed, and Selena is not one to move her plans around in deference to fear-and-trembling. The incident will be reported to the police, as she fully intends to do, during the lull, which usually comes at the halfway mark of those parties. And then she will calmly present her views on the identity of the Abominable Female. A far-out but sadly plausible theory which she is now assembling even as she takes on speed, at a clip if not a run.

FROM THE DIARY OF SITA AMANPURI

My own true and most secret darling,

I deem this madness of mine subversive of my most profound being. Yet I could no sooner resist it than fate itself. It was fate was it not? that placed us in each other's path. Such is her inexorable force that you will never access the source of her gift to you, a man content to go through life in servitude to the whims of others!

I know He wants me! His attraction to me has grown more obvious with each day, each week, each month, despite all those endearing subterfuges. And now I've got tenure! Yes, there is a rapacious ego and will there, only proper to match His bodily splendor. (O to dissolve against that unyielding physique). But I have known with all my senses that they are only crying out to be dismantled by the fated life-partner, and that I am she.

Today He looked at me long and melancholically. I sensed that He sees in me a kindred soul, one to touch very deeply but also, perhaps, to manipulate. I must watch my speech and my actions with Him...but does he know at all, what homage I pay him?

It is no longer possible for me to await your capitulation, my Torment. I am not in the least deceived by your cold social manner towards me. Of course you efface yourself as ever, seeming to give the whole bounty of your time and emotion to university matters. That is simply your way of getting through life.

But whence that insensate attachment to the Fenn girl, which He sees, fit to exhibit even in my presence? Could it be for real? LuAnn and I certainly agree about HER. I can only presume that He is employing the utmost discretion, for favoritism toward me would indeed produce a most negative effect. And she is almost a relation of his. With me, of course. He must be discreet above all, for it must never appear that my swift rise in the University is due to His special favor. Discretion and gallantry are the sole reason why His name has never been linked to that of ANY woman under the SKIES as far as I know. (Could it be men????? No, I think not!, though the atmosphere of the gym and the locker room were perhaps conducive. But no.)

I have understood this with my common intelligence. But intuition must triumph, which only a woman can follow, undaunted, to the fullness of love. I would eschew all further appearances of indifference if I were you; they are no use against me. How glorious it will be to teach you pleasure if you are actually that ignorant at your age! Tonight yes, at the party, in the midst of uncaring revelry shall wait one last time for the perfect moment of revelation. I shall speak my heart. O madness.

New Campaigns kick off with a gala fundraiser, and this one was now in full swing. This time the target amount was $450,000,000. Outside the Admin Building's elegant reception hall, the buildings of the main quad still looked darker than the sky, while a mellow festive mood reigned within. The decent woodsy greenness of the great room, hardened only slightly by the glitter of a ten-foot crystal chandelier, set everyone off in their own personal glow. Little knots of guests formed and reformed around the standard-issue Redfern U. buffet, smiling and gesticulating like happy peasants in an opera. But a keen eye noticed two members of the party making for an exit in single file. They looked unhurried but were not. Both had already had plenty to drink especially the man, who virtually bulged with avid concupiscence. Alcohol and excitement had formed beads of perspiration on his forehead and just below the nose.

Selena moved sinuously after him. Her face wore an all-knowing expression that was belied by her probable age; but then parties like this one were her habitual staging ground, and the desire she generated was part of it.

He had to get back to the party; she had all the time in the world, or so it seemed. Her myopic gaze was fixed elsewhere; her halfsmile anticipated the exercise of a power that had never yet failed her. His popping eyes registered pure lechery.

He knew exactly where they were going. Spiraling down the stairs, they ended in an empty concrete cubicle whose window was a mere black square.

"I want to see it first," she said.

"Later, my dear, later."

"Now!"

The man sighed a flabby sigh and reached into an inside pocket. He pulled out a bankbook with a red plastic cover that read SCHWEIZERBANK ZÜRICH, dog-eared at the edges but containing page after page of gradually rising seven-figure amounts — wire transfers to the dummy account. Two names she could not recognize headed the columns of figures.

"Ha. Just as I promised," he said. "Ha! black and white. There you have it. Now enough."

"This is a wow," she breathed. "There's more here than I might ever have myself...it's unbelievable. Are you serious about how you got it?" She kept on flipping the pages. This discovery was worth every moment of the effort it had taken to get her here tonight. He tried to peer over her bare shoulder but she elbowed him away, her great eyes riveted on the bankbook.

"Why NOT serious?" His voice carried the petulance of a customer who could have been as well pleased at a different shop. "We were, as I have said the sole facilitators. Everything passed through us. Very simple: persons in power needed our cooperation and they got it. The most serious thing possible."

He began to run a line of clucking kisses along the shoulder, which she overlooked, still staring into the book.

"Something more concrete would help," she said.

"Something more concrete after, darling." His mouth had formed an O, and she could hear his breathing come shorter and faster. "There is an abundance of documentation. Journalistic articles. Memorandums of the meetings. Papers, to the sky. Now enough of this!"

He eased her onto the floor, raised her adhesive black skirt, planted a hand on one breast. No time, never enough time! Seconds later, Selena gave a triumphant little laugh.

"A professor in the classroom and a lover outside, mmm? I think maybe you're the opposite, after all!"

A sort of Maginot Line had formed the guests into two camps that transcended their common aim of fundraising. One boasted Juliana Redfern Slote, the Surviving Descendant of the founding family, held together tonight by a fully visible skeletal structure. She was attended by General Ethan Fenn, her equal in bones and a much bigger giver. Their crowd of oldsters moved gradually to one side, politely making way for glittering new money that was pushing, pushing, pushing the boundaries. Glittering trophy wives and paunchy husbands with year-round suntans, looking pleased as punch to have "one foot in the life of the mind," as one put it, mingled with more spiritually dressed, abstracted types in monastic black.

"That blonde looks too old to be bulimic," a raw voice called out from the bar. It came from an emaciated woman in her upper sixties, mummified in black, her eyes frozen in the perpetual amazement of the most recent face-lift. "But that husband of hers—she probably makes him stick his finger up his throat, he's got an ass like a six-year-old." The little man next to her held a finger to his lips, grinning, and she tilted slightly as he guided her over to the wine-and-cheese. Within earshot, Sol and Krysti Goldfader craned to get a look at the bulimics. They were undercut by the Urban Developer Alan Sakulin, an eager, beaky man still in his forties, who had already coughed up the mil and a half for the Alan and Sharon Sakulin Professorship, now in search of the first occupant, superstar Palter Van Geyst. But Van Geyst, ever the elusive one, seemed to be keeping just two moves ahead of his patron. He was there and yet not there in his inimitable way, some few reporting glimpses of him. Sakulin made do for a while with the Fishbanes, Armin and Graziella.

Armin F., the Tefflahn Professor of English, Modern Media and Massage, and Chairman of Comparative Literature, held his own group in a narrowing gaze. His selective memory had long ago spliced him into the ranks of Most Desirable and Marked for the Top, and his own confidence had gleaned him a respectable number of believers. Armin's New York edge had once helped his elders tolerate him as a Maverick, and the same brashness and entrepreneurial arrogance continued to overawe them when he became their equal. Redfern had rewarded him with an Easy Chair for his innate gifts of impresario, travel agent, toastmaster and moderator, for his immaculate blazers, his whorls of moussed silver hair. The melting dark eyes remained the only sign that emotion ever stirred under those glossy suits. Now Armin's carrying tones, where Harvard met the Bronx, quelled the guffawing and trilling sounds around him to a virtual murmur.

"And I said to Chuck, said it right out, that if it cannot be Marvella for our Rumpe Professor, it must not be anyone at all," he sang out. "The time to make a real argument is now. Hang the money; we know he's got it. Plus our Department carries half the students by itself."

"How you could, Armin," crooned Sita Amanpuri. "You KNOW enrollments don't count." Her deep-set eyes smoked out of their pencilled rims, and her mouth betrayed the crooked lift of a corrected harelip.

"'Course I know, but does Chuck?" This produced a blanket of laughs from everyone but Graziella, very ripe in her turquoise taffeta bubble. Armin watched crossly as she raised an arm to adjust a loose strand of her red hair, exuding a slight whiff that seemed to Alan Sakulin especially European.

At the very center of the reception hall, turning in both directions to embrace guests from both sides, ecumenically, stood the University President, Grigol ("Chuck") Chavadze. He was a jolly bear-like man, broadly smiling under a prodigious moustache. The moustache could have looked pasted on, except that its grizzled expanse was matched by the same kind of black hair tinged with grey, too tightly fitting to be luxuriant but thick with Assyrian curls. In evening dress, Chavadze resembled the sort of expensive headwaiter routinely spoiled by society clotheshorses. In fact, he looked like a pet until you got close enough to notice how clever and quick was his size-up stare and how the merriment could write itself and erase itself in an instant, leaving the same face behind. A winding history of survival and compromise had etched itself onto those features and showed deep in the crinkles of his friendly grin. And the open-armed embrace was for everyone potentially, for the whole treacherous world bazaar Chavadze inhabited without prejudice.

During the year and a half of his Redfern presidency some old hands had nicknamed him The Bear Hug, observing that his lively demeanor and stage ethnicity just didn't go with Redfern's laid-back atmosphere. His background was a zigzag itinerary that whisked him from Professor of Something Obscure—Georgian military history, was it?—accelerating to administrative moneyman, first as provost of Texas Megatech, a huge drab multiversity situated at the wrong end of the country, then a quantum leap to President of the New York National Museum of Art. This job came complete with palatial digs and a new, cleanly chiseled second wife, both of which he'd retained.

Chuck's effect on the Museum, the first ever RELEVANT museum, was now legendary. Under his leadership the Museum had constructed an adjoining office tower, designed by the internationally acclaimed architectural firm of Olney Mee. The size of the Museum's capacious gift shop doubled, and a nouvelle cuisine restaurant opened. End-to-end blockbuster exhibitions splashed their logos onto giant banners that billowed under every breeze. At a time when any museum not busy expanding was automatically considered to be in dire straits, the National had transformed itself into a Mecca for Japanese tourists, for would-be lovers seeking soulmates, for the sort of connoisseur who would never have looked at a work of art without a price tag under it. When "Meet You At the Museum", spearheaded by the mercantile talents of Chavadze, came to the attention of the Redfern administration and trustees, he won the presidency in a close but decisive series of ballots. Tirelessly touted for his compassion and his flair for "bringing us together," he had won over the rigid objections of the Redfern Old Guard, to do what he had done for the Museum: raise money, lots of money, NOW. No more of that classist gap between Old Money and New Money: the only meaningful distinction was between More Money and Less Money.

In his own words, Chuck was a "bricklayer, not an architect," and management was his style, not command. Persuasion, not strong-arm brutality. Accordingly, his very Inaugural had oozed inclusiveness. The new Redfern logo, OUR PRODUCT IS EXCELLENCE, was born the same day as the New Curriculum, which meant No Curriculum. OUR PRODUCT IS EXCELLENCE appeared on souvenir posters, pompons, T-shirts and a broad range of other products, which did brisk sales at the New Bookstore as well as at the stands of Biscottini Stadium.

Redfern's New Spirit climaxed at the moment when the incomparable Marvella's keynote speech blew her audience away, swept them before her just as she was to sweep 1993's literary prizes. Her finale "I have known all the pain...I have known all our pain...but in YOU the journey is!" brought real tears to the President's eyes as he rose, first among thousands, to applaud. Marvella Jilkes, Celebrated Black Woman Novelist and Poet, prime among her peers, making an appearance at Redfern's little inaugural, and even...just maybe, but no... it was too soon to conjecture that she might soon lend her name to the Redfern Department of Comparative Literature. So far, that was nothing but an unsubstantiated rumor.

Although he kept his best New York perks as Redfern's president, and despite the investment Redfern had agreed to in rehousing him and his famed collections of Caucasian swords, Persian miniatures, military maps among walls hung with brocade and flocked velvet, despite the Japanese garden they'd added to the Presidential mansion, now banked in bonsai-lined walks and mapped with lily ponds and red bridges, in sum, despite all the allurements the locals could muster, Temperance, Mass. still couldn't turn into New York. And the New York friends, the media moguls, the artists who sold, the long-lived dowager queens, the authors of scandalous psychobiographies and swappers of annual awards, couldn't see for the life of them what this job held for Chuck. The general bet was on a speedy onset of boredom and a quick new move.

Upholstered tonight in administrative pinstripes rather than elitist black tie, Chuck turned now to the man standing on his right and raised an arm in good-natured protest. "You can't be an American, Garso, unless you stop smoking!"

At first glance it seemed that one of Chuck's military prints had come to life and stood at attention. The man wore the crumpled darkish jacket, long divorced from the pants, of a hardened traveler in a tough world. His trousers were of a second incompatible darkish hue, tightening at the knees and flaring at the ankles. The heavy, scuffed shoes, too large for his compact height, clinched for anyone in the know the guess that this outfit was the Soviet getup par excellence from Siberia to the Black Sea, which had not kept pace with politics in an era of change. Yet the muscular body straining at the outfit showed nothing of the earthbound fatigue often exhibited by wearers of such clothing. The man had already made himself at home, though he had arrived barely a day ago. Elbows at his sides, he flashed everyone a younger, fitter, taller, sexier version of Chavadze man ready to present arms or chugalug a whole carafe of vodka or bet his wife away at cards, if necessary. Now he dropped his cigarette on the floor and stamped on it once, twice, three times.

Chavadze's arm moved up around the man's neck and lounged there like a furpiece. "Our Poet in Residence!" he proclaimed. "Our Redfern Poet, for the whole week. God has brought us a true inspiration. AND he can drink anyone under the table."

Giggles and cooing from the attending company, and from an Old Redfernian, a muffled snort. But the spoilsport made no headway. For Garsevan Yashvili belonged body and soul to the world of local color, a world that cruise passengers longed for but generally seemed to miss by a hairline, a world of enchanted, landlocked never-neverlands like the Caucasus meeting place of gods and men. Ladies clustering around Chuck and his Georgian friend imagined Garso bedecked in generic gypsy scarves and beads, moving catlike among mountain tribes blazing with desire, of course, then sunk in despair. One even recalled a fact learned in Mythology for Wives: Medea, who murdered her own children for revenge, had been a Georgian princess.

And an ex-Soviet to boot, a redeemed soul! They longed to hear his accounts of frightening experiences, unspeakable sacrifices, blizzarded mountain treks.

"Do you compose in Russian, Mr. Yashvili?" A solidly built lady trustee offered her eager smile. "Then we'll hardly be able to read you. But some of us took Russian For Wives—well, you never know!"

Garsevan Yashvili's tongue clicked impatiently against brilliant teeth, some flashing gold and even steel. "Madam Slote, in Georgia we are all forgetting, gradually, the Russian language. Never soon enough for me! But no one is forced into it anymore. Now, in absence of Central control, we enjoy the play of our individual traditions. They are older than Russian ones, so everyone remembers. Every child walking down the principal street of Tbilisi, our city, everyone knows that Avenue Rustaveli is named for our poet, the composer of 'Knight in the Tiger Skin.' No one of us would write now but in Georgian, or live, but in Georgian." The little group marveled at history in the making before their eyes. "But Mr. Yashvili," the same Old Redfernian ventured, "I trust that you take account of the civil unrest in your country. Isn't it—well, partly, the result of the dissolution of central control?"

The bubbly little circle felt mortified. Not too many were keeping up with the TV news about the Georgian planes shot down by insurgent minorities, of the city besieged by new nationalist troops — was it the capital? The Old Redfernian went doggedly on. "I've got a book at home that says Georgian nationalism is being used as a rallying call for a gaggle of warring Mafiosi."

Yashvili, unruffled, disengaged himself from Chavadze's encircling arm. "We Georgians are, alas, the crucible...is it correct, crucible? of conflicting systems and thought across the ages. But this is what poetry means for me personally: the shock of ideas in the music of words." This intellectual blast brought on a moment's lull.

"Garso, never mind Georgian language now. No one here understands it. Recite something in English, just a little fragment. For an old drinking friend." Chuck raised to his lips the same sour glass of white wine he had been nursing for the past hour. His left hand slapped Yashvili on the back so hard as to erase his scowl. This was a really hands-on President. "And hurry up please, the party is nearly over."

Yashvili's chin rose an inch and his rebel's dark stare swept the group. "Very well, my friend. I will speak."

The group immediately gained new, bemused faces. Even the University Provost, Seymour Gorellick, a bagged-out blend of worry, indigestion, and greenish fatigue, a man not given to poetry, moved in to hear. Maxime-Etienne Lamamba of Radical Rereading flirtatiously riveted his eyes to Yashvili's.

LuAnn Rossiter's whole generous body emoted in the language of intense compassion as she hove in view of the action. She was a large, broad-beamed woman topped by a glossy pageboyed head, and her speech remained a soft Texas drawl as she trod on the sandaled foot of Sita Amanpuri in her red-gold sari. Even Roberto Ricci, the Professor of Italian, towed over his wraith of a wife.

"O breast-giving falcon, my only love,
I am one with you again,
All in one heart.
And may alien chickens
Cluck the father's false land."

Garso had just gotten going but the group took his pause for an ending and the buzz ensued, just as Chavadze had expected. Years of stunned attendance at Redfern cultural events had primed everyone to swing immediately into antiphonal bursts of praise.

"A most powerful new statement," Gorellick mouthed. "Proud to be here tonight."

"The chickens — an image right out of the land..."

"Are you published over here yet?"

"Is this part of a sequence? a cycle?"

"Where's Van Geyst? He'd have to go for this!"

""You might well ask: where's Van Geyst, indeed?"

"Are you on disc?"

"Ze triomphe of ze genuine unwritten voice," Maxime-Etienne proclaimed. "I, too, am in combatte wiz ze law of ze written word."

Sita Amanpuri, newly tenured, showed her pluck. "A disgraceful remnant of colonialist arrogance," she muttered, her long neck turtling out of her sari.

"But such a daring dis-play-ussment of the Fawther Figure," LuAnn protested.

"I, for one, cannot condone this falcon sort of thing. It is a trite macho pose," bellowed Mumtaz Mahmoud, turning up the volume. "Phallomatrism, that's what!"

LuAnn was not for nothing the Chair of Femmes Against Mastery (FAM) and Director of the Bolingbroke-Redfern Womancenter (BREW). The tallest and bulkiest by half of the three FAMS, she tossed her glossy pageboy and, moving fast for so much woman, hauled the others off with a scolding. In a twink she was back in the midst of Yashvili's admirers.

"Ah wanna tell yuh," she said, laying a commanding hand on his arm, "how stimulatin' yowah poem was to us."

"You embarrass me, Madam Rossiter, but even an embarrassment from so splendid a lady is an honor." Garso's powerful arms outlined themselves in their shiny dark sleeves as he encompassed the hand in both of his. He had instantly acquired the American habit of remembering everyone's name. "It is Texas, not? your country. Also, I think, a place which is not so politically correct." A downscale titter made its way around the group.

Student servers were threading nimbly through the crowd with trays of tired sandwiches, and LuAnn helped herself while deciding on her answer. "Ah do mean this," she said after a moment. "Ah say it an' ah mean it. Theah is NO SUCH THING at awl as Political Correctness. Not any more than—than Unahdentifahed Flyin' Objecks. Whah, people goin' on about Thought Police, about this or that bein' forbidden, theyah simply lookin' for attention themselves. It's jes' that Whaht Male Oppressionist Thinkin' is bein' challenged, is awl. That givin' an' carin' matter, not jes' fight'n' an' egos. That new voices are takin' ovah th'old. The kids heah, f'rinstance, are sick 'n'tarred of the ole stuff. We need to talk theah language if we wanna reach out to them."

"Bravo, Madam Rossiter, bravo," said Yashvili, amused.

"Now LuAnn, baby." A taunting male voice, English. Tony Banter was LuAnn's customary foil at parties. "The so-called Great Books aren't all evil. Don't you turn to the dirty parts first?"

"Ah repeat," she said, keeping a gimlet eye on Chavadze and Yashvili. "Theah is no Political Correctness on THIS campus, anyhow. The effot to avoid offense, whah, yes. To take West'n' Civilization down a peg. To de-bunk musty ole mastuhpieces. Ah'm fed up with stories 'bout some man travelin' an' comin' home again. Mastuhpieces, hmf!"

"Ah, ze masterpiece, ze enemy!" Maxime-Etienne Lamamba sighed. The rumor he had floated that he was descended from a line of Senegalese princes was still making its implacable rounds, spurred on by well-timed denials. "Of a certainty...of a certainty."

"Absolutely right, LuAnn." Tony Banter chuckled. "Naughty LuAnn."

The laughing core began to dissolve, and LuAnn linked arms with Yashvili in a triumphant recessional, keeping her squared-egg of a head demurely lowered to produce the effect of gazing upward. The other FAMS would have to be on their own for a while. Her maternal eye spotted Mumtaz getting a fresh drink, more eats; but Sita Amanpuri was nowhere to be seen. So much the better; enough to do without having to nurse them into the bargain.

The moment of truth now past, Sita Amanpuri stands drowning in chagrin with two chill blasts of subterranean air striking her at right angles. The red sari swirls around her majestically, its brilliant gold embroideries catching the light of a fluorescent bar and lending her a special air of bereavement.

She has played all her chips on Red and reaped Blackness. Months of repression and patient torment, all to end in No—no chance, no attraction, no hope. And as if to underscore the negative with even more superb cruelty, He recoiled from her confession of love in panicky haste, pleading nothing more urgent than Duty! The shrinking of his body burned her longer and harder, but the sheer triviality of his excuse is what's making her blow off steam right now.

"I've got duties here, Sita. Have to get something from the cellar. Romanee Conti. Collect yourself." And Keith is history, hurtling off on some petty errand. Abandoned in this maze of concrete walls and doors and stairs, all exhaling their revulsion—and quite disoriented, to boot. Sita had never seen the Underground Campus before in her life.

Turn left or right? Skimming the stairs in Keith's wake, she had barely noticed her direction, had sensed only the wavy trace of some other presence in the maze. Her overflowing urgency had cast aside the possibility that Keith was not alone, and now someone, anyone, might have taken in the whole thing. Imagine if it was Chavadze himself, or Berto Ricci, or worst of all, LuAnn Rossiter! Sita stared at the quarter-pie angle formed by the two long, identical corridors, at the closed metal doors set into the walls. Both ways probably forked again and again, linking everything to everything.

"I've got duties, Sita. Collect yourself."

She conceded that this was in fact the wiser course, and began to plot her escape. From a distance, thank goodness, she did hear a metallic slam. Someone had turned up of whom directions could be asked—perhaps Keith himself, hurrying back to voice his contrition and surrender to her superior force. It was certainly his step she heard and even, she thought, his pause. He must see her clearly enough. But without approaching her, he—for surely it was a he—suddenly made his way out to the street level through an unmarked stairway door. By stealth, as she might have expected, and what's more, giving her a wide berth where she stood in her glittering sari. Elsewhere bound, and probably feeling the shame that was coming to him. But was it not finally shyness that had overwhelmed his desire for her? This flight of his, ignoble though it was, already seemed to her little more than a false start, a mere aberration, a glitch in the maturation of their inevitable amour. And she'd see herself back to the party via that very door, thank you very much. Further opportunities were sure to follow.

The call came in to the Temperance Eleventh at 6:57 p.m. following a routine succession of drug busts and domestic violence breakups. Just then, no one much was in. Florio and Vakkonen were mediating a bout of domestic violence and Mike Haley was on the desk. That was the whole reason why, of all the policemen in a town of two hundred thousand, Simon Blank was to have this case set on his shoulders, like Atlas stuck with the job of holding up the world while his coevals cavorted.

"I can hear you," Haley was saying into the phone as Simon gave a waking start. "I know you can't talk loud, Mr. Chambers, I mean Professor. One of us or both'll be right over. Yeah, the side entrance."

Haley, as Simon observed, was being extra polite. He hadn't registered at first who was calling, though it was a name he knew. The weak, bitter taste of Styrofoam coffee in his mouth, he was just noticing, had mixed with the worse taste of sleep. And he hurt where his belt was too tight. At thirty-six, Simon could see around the corner to the home stretch before retirement. One hand went to his spreading bald spot, and his feet plunked onto the floor from the wobbly chair where they were resting.

"Wha...what, Haley?"

"You're going back to school—I mean Redfern," Haley growled, not without sympathy. "A Redfern girl has been killed. Get Granita. It's your assignment; you'll need just one other guy. You can pick up Granita at Ruby's." He swung his swivel chair back to face a huge pile of untidy paperwork on his desk. "Go, Simon! Boola, Boola."

"Wrong college, stupid," Simon heard himself answer. "Boola Boola means Yale"" It was freezing outside, and though he had heard Mike Haley clearly, all of his reactions were lagging behind this news.

"Whaddever. You better move. There's a big party going on there now, must have happened during the party."

Simon felt a stab of loathing for desk jockeys and a simultaneous yearning to be one. On the way to pick up Granita, as he swung the unmarked car around the wide turns necessitated by Temperance double parkers and semi-stupefied wrong-lane drivers, he felt lucky to know at least some scattered factoids about the university—a few rules, names, customs. This murder had happened right on campus, the first Redfern murder he could remember.

It took just a couple of minutes to excavate Granita from his special booth at Ruby's. Phil Granita was a veteran cop and a completely good guy, and it was going to be fun to watch him operate at Redfern, even though Simon would probably have to explain every little stupid twist and turn of the ropes.

"Probably a six-oh-one," Simon told Granita in the car. "The call came from a Keith Chambers. He's the special assistant to the President—you know, Chavadze. You gotta know who that is, always on TV" The old president of Redfern came to his mind, now dead of golf-related heart failure. "Anyway, Chambers called from the party. There's an enormous crowd there, that'll help us. It's two crowds, because they've got a demonstration going on too. He couldn't tell me any more. No time."

Phil settled back in his seat, grunted. "Fucking cold night for a demo. Where the hell did he tell us to go?"

"Admin Building, next to the Fulfillment Center. We'd know from the noise, we'll see all the people, but anyhow it's right in the middle of the campus. Everything kind of radiates from there." Everything radiating from the Center, hell: the campus has maybe thirty Centers now, who'd know one from another?

"You mean a student party? Hundreds of 'em to plow through?"

Not students, Simon thought impatiently, they've got nothing to do with anything. "That's not what I mean. I mean, students'll be there tonight because of the demo, but I'm talking about a society party, for the biggest donors. It's their New Campaign. They want to raise four hundred an' fifty mil."

"Who's Chambers? What does he do?"

"You know what Marlin Fitzwater did for Reagan?" Simon tried hard to be clear but didn't understand much more about deskmen than Phil did. "Or Jordan for Carter? Now you put that together with whatever the White House Chief of Staff does. You add a big dash of speech writing. You allow that sometimes he can be a White House Special

Prosecutor, and then you have something like Chambers' job. And he probably does run interference from students to boot."

Simon wondered what he could expect in the way of cooperation. He didn't actually have the feel of Redfern anymore, and the run-of-the-mill cases that seemed to run his life had less class to them. He was going to need a lot of help.

With plenty of large-scale urban problems to keep the police busy, Temperance was no mere college town. A former manufacturing center, it was now fallen like sister towns all over New England. Scattered ruins of her vanished productivity stood hollow-eyed along the canals that ended at the Sound. There, rows of empty warehouses and factories reproached the citizens with neglect, while downtown a kind of Gotham City movie set waited to be carted away.

Even the residents of the snug eighteenth-century and Victorian core, many of whose houses had been spiffed up by the university and repainted in subdued Yankee colors, lacked the civic pride it took to plant in spring and plow in winter. Now the same snowfall, late for April, was going through the usual wet and dry cycles in a townscape where the artist had forgotten to paint in the people. But Redfern University positively glowed now in a soft twilight enhanced by fake gas lamps that made the shuttered Federal-style houses enfolding the green quads look patrician, not sour and shut. Everything seemed sanely constructed to a human scale.

Old-timers liked to remark proudly that Redfern "wasn't Harvard," which was overwhelmingly true; more of a "people place" was the way new-timers put it. Through a savvy combination of admissions know-how and notoriety as a college where students designed their own courses and programs (The "New Curriculum"), Redfern had managed to fill what had started as the neediest cashbox in the Ivy League. By now it had made the *Times* List of Hot Colleges five years running.

All the same and in spite of its approachable down-and-outness, the campus had not quite begun to blend with the rest of Temperance. The university had its back turned on the pursuits and hobbies of ordinary people, steadfastly rejecting the possibility of togetherness in pleasure which entrepreneurs of the business community hoped would eventually come about if they kept steadfastly on trend. Meanwhile, the Gotham City malls and restaurants got hardly any Redfern business. Yet Temperance, too sleepy to protest the Redfern package of low wages and long hours, had suffered very little of the town-versus-gown antagonism that beset similar places housing Ivy League universities. Unruffled by worker unrest, Redfern just slouched along, shrouded in a defensive modesty, which belied the fact that it had long been a leading Temperance slumlord.

Simon and Phil drew up to a discreet spot about the equivalent of two blocks from the Admin Building, a little parking lot for ten cars reserved, as the sign read, For Human Resources Personnel.

"Human Resources, huh?" Granita snorted.

"Yeah, people you can't put to work anywhere else." Simon had seen lots of other Offices of Makework in his line of duty.

They kept to the lines of scruffy tall bushes that passed for hedges, and in seconds heard the noise. You could divide the sounds into two kinds. One reminded Simon of nocturnal birdcalls, the guffawing and trilling of festively dressed folks past their prime and scattering to find their cars. The other, more menacing racket came from a formless mass of students shouting and screaming, maybe sixty of them, some waving signs you couldn't read in the dark. Despite the profusion of decorative gas lamps, nothing was much clearer than it would be on a Temperance Halloween night with everyone saving on energy.

No one noticed Simon and Phil moonwalking through the bushes with their unmistakable cop's tread. The suits, too, could belong only to policemen—the way they flapped around the coat-ends but hugged your butt. Still, for all anyone noticed, the two might as well be waiters or barmen

"You always get it right, Martha!" A willowy young man, one of the diehards, a Harvard green canvas book bag slung over his dinner jacket, smiled a dolphin's smile at the little mink-coated woman he was escorting down the shallow steps of the Admin Building. "That's perfect: much ado about nothing. No student would even know the line, though; they wouldn't even know about the play." Martha tittered up at him, tightening her blue-veined little claw of a hand on his arm.

Three female students were positioned on the steps, all wearing oversized tees and lettered signs: "End Redfern Apartheid" "Out the Ins" "We ARE A Position," " Soul Food Lunch Now." They were surrounded by an expanding spitball game. Simon saw a spitball bounce off an old sport's nose. "Nothing's changed here, didn't I tell you?" the Old Redfernian joked.

The demo was creating an obstruction, but there was something oddly scattered and small about it. The chains on students' legs didn't clank, and they swallowed the ends of their shouts, which went mostly unregarded. Partygoers just negotiated calmly around them on their way out, raising their voices over the din.

Simon and Phil were to meet Keith Chambers at the tiny door of the side entry. Sure enough, his soldierly figure stood tall in the faint light of a single bulb, just at the boundary door between the festively lit Admin lobby and the concrete downstairs labyrinth of the basement. Keith was never late, and he never had to make an effort not to be. His stance had something deceptively casual about it, the length of a former athlete almost lounging against the concrete wall. Smooth brown-grey head, grave profile, regulation blazer, a civil halfsmile.

"You'd better come in after all," he said as if they had come uninvited, squaring his shoulders, Outside, the buildings were still darker than the sky and they were met full-force by the party and instantly elbowed by a zealous student waiter with black tie askew. She was female, as Granita noted with a sigh—a tall, dark girl with deep-set features and a mane of electric hair, scraped and tied back from her face for the job.

Keith ushered them expertly through the extra-thick glut of people around the tired remains of cold ham, cold turkey, university cheese cubes, bunches of wrinkling grapes. Keeping his ears perked up, Simon watched his partner slump into defensive indifference.

The three stood awkwardly awaiting their cue. Finally a beeper in Keith's blazer pocket went off, and he extracted the slimmest possible cellular phone. "Okay, we're coming now." Granita followed in Simon's wake, hating every minute.

Shepherded by Keith, Simon and Phil sloped along to the end of the reception hall and now, even through the thick mahogany doors, they could discern a different kind of crowd noise. Security personnel, distributed at fifty-yard intervals, were barking into walkie-talkies, and all the while cohorts of students kept on coming, some chained to each other and dragging their chains on the ground. Others carried signs reading "No More History," "Sex in the Classroom! Yes!" and "Academic Death Squads Out." A girl in granny glasses and cutoffs solemnly handed out dildos from a box.

The event seemed to be under control, coming and going in little waves like the canned laughter on a TV sitcom sound track. Not like the demos they'd been called to in the last couple of years. This one almost had a kind of genial look, like the second-hand togetherness that holds sway just before a rock concert while the first few hundred fans muster up. Meanwhile the very last stragglers were exiting the party, trading smudged goodbye kisses and shoulder slaps.

They found themselves tramping down steepening flights of concrete stairs. And now a second, underground campus stretched out before them. This labyrinth supported the gracious, genteel Admin Building. And how many others? Under the sickly light of naked fluorescent bulbs, a welter of narrow corridors, indented by closed doors. The concrete seemed soundproof. Neither their steps nor any overhead noise—even the stirrings of air reverberating in the tunnels were inaudible.

"This basement reaches forever," Granita said.

Two paunchy policemen pacing: would Simon be just like Granita in another twelve years? But Keith never slackened, just went right on striding through the maze as if he lived there. More turns, more dead ends.

Once Simon had seen a blackened engraving of such a place, deliberately smudged over and engineered so that the image looked turned inside out. Inner stairways swerved so as to circle suddenly outside. Enclosed spaces ended in dizzily exposed precipices. An undecidable number of levels and stories kept on changing, like those California freeways that soared into the air then stopped all of a sudden, so all you could do was turn around and go back. The engraving belonged to a series called, as Simon found out, "The Prisons." Of course there was nothing they didn't know about prisons in the eighteenth century.

The men puffed to keep up with Chambers. A sound like rushing water, probably some ventilation system. Simon could not begin to guess the size of the rooms behind those doors. The Redfern underworld reached way beyond the limits of the aboveground campus, forming connections among the separate buildings. At rare intervals the policemen could sense the party as if through a hearing aid which flared up in sudden angry crescendos.

They came to a door that had been propped open some three inches with a bottle of red wine. Inside the ten-by-ten space, harsh reflector lights blazed. Blinking the dappled spots away, they saw three people working bent around a rectangular table. Everything seemed to grimace at them as the forms gained outline and direction.

"These are Sergeant Granita and Lieutenant Blank," Keith said tonelessly to no one in particular. For a moment he looked embarrassed at having reversed the precedence of police rank. He closed the door, picking up the wine bottle, and stood turning it in his hands. They were strong capable hands with blunt fingers, and he held the bottle the way you'd play with a just-caught ball. To put off the moment that he knew was coming but had never gotten used to, Simon wondered how old Keith was, and why a bottle of wine had propped that door open. He let Granita go first, but then, inescapably, there it was.

She had been twenty years old. Her waist-length hair was long and of a brownish gold color, draping over the edges of the table like a mermaid's. The body still seemed to be dressed, but on second glance it was more punctuated than covered with patches of clinging black material. As if a painter of voluptuous nudes had posed it for welcoming allure, it had its arms relaxed, one coyly shielding the breasts but with splayed fingers, the other hanging over the edge of the table. The legs described a generous V.

From where Simon and Granita stood blinking, nothing else of the body could be discerned. She had been slender enough to wrap herself in that hair, swirling strands of which obscured most of the face as well. It occurred to Simon that she must be very uncomfortable. Her torso seemed to him scantily swathed in tight black bandages. The twists of what had once been an adhesive black cocktail dress strained against the curves of hips and buttocks. A matching but much narrower black twist, maybe two inches wide, was tied jauntily around the visible part of the neck, as on a gift box. Too tight, Simon thought, but otherwise efficient. Several inches of its length streamed down each side of the knot.

"Where the hell did you get that table?" Phil Granita growled at no one in particular. "Did you have it ready for her, by any chance?"

"These gentlemen are from the Police Department, Lieutenant Blank and Sergeant Granita." Keith Chambers gestured at the policemen, then at a campus security guard and a gleaming white-coated pathologist. The indelible halfsmile had returned to his face, weirdly appropriate to the setting.

"You moved her." Simon spoke quietly, merely registering this enormity. I still can't see what happened, he thought. The damn lights here. Everyone in our way. This stifling room, what do they use it for? The maze we came through to get here. "You moved her." He heard the rushing water sound again.

"A mistake was made," Keith Chambers conceded in a voice of restrained despair, no one else bothering to answer. "Gentlemen, she was lying on cold concrete," he added, voice softening. "Nothing you'll need to know was changed."

As if following secret orders, everyone around the body straightened up, and the campus cop backed away from the table in confusion. The pathologist, of indeterminate gender, age, and appearance, turned to the policemen and said: "Look." How had this person arrived at the scene before the police? "You'd better look."

Simon and Phil clubfootedly approached the table, the kind used for buffet spreads at corporate parties like the one upstairs. Buffet table, wine bottle holding the door. Simon couldn't understand why he felt so ashamed.

He brushed away the longest thickest swathe of hair, and the face belonging to the body came into evidence. It had very large, probably nearsighted eyes, round, open, perpetually astonished. The angle of her head made it look as if she were trying to peer over her own brow. But the red lips were savagely drawn back in a rictus that could mean fury or sex, arrested at midpoint. Looking away, Simon noticed the dried pasty spots trailing from the point of the V formed by the legs, unequally distributed, running along the thighs. The body was naked under the twisted black dress.

It had been identified within a very short time, maybe minutes.

"This is Selena Fenn," Chambers resumed his job of making introductions. "Her purse was right by her; you'll examine it in a moment, but we at Redfern all knew her. Most anyone could tell you who she is." Now his voice made a point of not breaking and he ostentatiously squared his athletic shoulders. "Selena was in her senior year here and she was very well-known. You will learn all you need to about her background. Her parents died in the Van Horn cruise shipwreck when she was seven, so her grandfather Fenn has done the best he could to pinch-hit for them. He brought her up to be one of our very best. She comes into her inheritance at twenty-one, just a month away. And you may as well know that she is my dear godchild. Was."

For the first time Simon could look into Keith Chambers' eyes. He was taken aback by their mild, open blue-grey, which refracted everything you fed them, like sunglasses with mirrored lenses.

"I also want to say that there is no conceivable thing we will not do, nothing we would not undertake to help you find who did this."

"Strangulation," the pathologist said. "Manual strangulation is what it looks like now. That's all I can say at this time. Obviously other effects to the body. We need to evaluate them in the context of our resources."

He caressed Selena's gracefully sashed neck. "There are throat injuries," he said, and scissored the black crepe necklace off with one snip. The policemen stared at raw, mottled reds—blue-reds, scarlet, and violet, in spots and in lines, radiating from one spreading red starfish. If it was the work of hands, they had been large and devastatingly strong.

Granita stepped back, stumbled over a spike-heeled black evening shoe, noted its mate not far away. "What, what about the purse?"

It was duly produced, had in fact been visible all the time, but Simon and Granita were off their game, not sure whether it was the abuse of Selena's body or the incongruity of the Redfern setting that had them stumbling and stammering. The black satin evening bag held a bright red lipstick, a much-used powder compact. No wallet would have fit into it, and there was no loose money, but a little black crocodile date book obligingly dropped out. Simon put it in his pocket, shrugging at Chambers and wondering if Selena had taken off her shoes herself.

"Was she invited to the party?"

"Of course she was invited," Keith said with a touch of indignation, as if he had expected the policemen to have a better grasp of Redfern ways. "Selena cared about Redfern, really cared. She would want me to continue as we began, with our Campaign. More than ever, now." He paused to explain with a show of patience. "In the event of her death Selena's inheritance was to go to Redfern, just as she would have wanted it. And she was going to be a very rich young lady. Very. But who was to imagine.... You may think it callous of me, gentlemen, to refer to such things at this time. But you'll need to know the facts..." He swallowed, keeping his mild blue eyes apologetically s on the policemen.

The pathologist gave Selena's head a turn to the right, then the left, then said abruptly, "I'll make the calls now." He turned back to open and close the head's mouth.

The campus cop was allowed to go. Once the fingerprint people, the scene-of-the-crime officer and the photographer had completed their work, there was no excuse for him to remain, but he hung there for a moment, thinking there must be something left that would put his mind at ease. It was unfair how much explaining he would have to do next day at Redfern, since it was Keith who had found the body.

It was Keith and his squads of flak-catchers, besides, who had helped cut the number of campus cops down to the barest minimum. There were so few left these days that intruders were held at bay by not much more than a few pairs of crossed fingers.

Keith led the way back exactly as they had come, but neither policeman had any recollection of the layout of staircases, halls, or closed doors. A few shocking little bursts of party noise came at intervals from the air vents. "What are all these places for?" Simon asked.

"This is our Underground University," Keith answered, "That's what you'll hear most people call it. Redfern is currently dealing with every kind of storage and space problem. So you'll find many of our records down here the faculty personnel files, for example. We couldn't put up with the idea that written files might have to be destroyed just for lack of space. Under this building you would find the history of our faculty—of course it's all reproduced on computer elsewhere," he assured Simon. "And here, as it happens, the complete files for our administrators going back twenty-five years. We feel justifiably proud," Keith had eased back into his social introducing mode, "justifiably proud, of our precise records. I bet if Jesus Christ came riding into Redfern on an ass, we'd start a file on him."

Again the same puffing trip down endless corridors. "What else do you have in this Underground University?"

"These are storerooms for records, as I said," Keith's bland voice resumed as if used to endless repetition. "But also for imperishable provisions for Cafeteria Facilities; for extra computers—you know we give one to every faculty member—for photocopying, fax machines, for Presidential projects. Oh, and Graduate Teaching Assistants have their offices in the Underground part of Pelfe Hall. The design makes it possible for them to be right at hand wherever they are needed."

"You were a professor, right, when I was a student here," Simon said, consulting some corner of memory. "What do they call you now?"

"I was an Assistant Professor," Keith spoke in uppercase letters but kept his polite smile. "What they call me now is Dean of Student Life and Relationships. It comes with an office next to President Chavadze's and a hell of a lot of extra work. I do some of everything. And people expect everything of me, too." A wry sigh, looking for commiseration. "I told you Redfern will do whatever we can to aid your investigation. That of course means me, as usual. I'll be your guide to the Underground University."

"Then start with one thing, please," Simon said. "How come a bottle of wine was propping that door open? A goddam wine bottle." Phil Granita perked up; the question at least touched on a more familiar world.

"That's pretty simple," Keith answered, speeding up a bit. "The little room next door is the coolest one, even in this cool basement, so it's our wine cellar. We obviously needed to keep that door open." Due to Keith's unruffled straightforwardness, the mottled scarlet on the dead girl's throat became a muted recollection, even as Simon marveled at the man's callousness. "Tonight is the first night of our New Campaign. We have a number of extra-special bottles on hand."

The hell—no one had even mentioned the sex, the spots on her legs. Are you dead from the neck up yourself? My dear godchild...

"You have to understand," Keith said pleasantly, as if reading his mind, "that we are in business as a university." He revved up for another Redfern plug. "We're slotted into an ever-widening sphere of relations.

Among other things that means wining and dining our most valued friends."

"What was the demo about?" Simon asked.

"It's some kind of freak. You'd almost think people actually intended to sabotage the donors' evening, in a way. Look, I don't have to tell you that demonstrations are now standard fare at every institution of higher learning. But not Redfern... if only, quite simply, because no one has to go to those lengths in order to get a hearing. We are right at the top in responsiveness, in sensitivity. We were the first, too, as you may recall, to have an Open Curriculum—without any course requirements, no coercion whatever, nothing to stem the flow of ideas or inhibit free choice."

"What about the money, Selena's money?" Granita asked abruptly. "Redfern U. gets it if she dies? Who decides how to spend it?"

A twitch appeared at one corner of Keith's lips. "The Trustees, in consultation with the President. We can expect something of a free-for-all, I'm afraid. Things are tough here, getting tougher and tighter every day, and we are not without our internal rivalries..."

"I get that. Now who else knows about the Fenn money besides you? I mean anyone and everyone."

"I assure you, Lieutenant, that no one else has a grasp of the... amount... but her grandfather, General Fenn, and the fellow who's provost these days—Seymour Gorellick. A man who knows how to keep his counsel. He would certainly never, never prattle about anything of this magnitude. I will give you the figure as I know it."

And Keith Chambers leaned down to whisper magic numbers into Simon's disbelieving ear.

"You're not planning to leave town soon, are you, sir?" Simon asked Keith, trying to sound casual.

"Not unless you count Alan Sakulin's house as out of town. I ought to have been there right now. Follow me up there if you think you must. He's one of our most respected benefactors. You'd have to tell General Fenn sooner or later, and you'll find him there as well."

Keith bent and picked up some bits of the last party rubbish from the polished parquet floor—a piece of squeezed-out lemon rind and a scrap of paper with a design of black scallops on it. He grimaced as he rubbed his thumb and forefinger together, at a loss as to how to dispose of the filth.

"I'll take it for you, sir," Simon offered. He had quite a pile of debris waiting in the brown unmarked. "Makes no difference to me."

The policemen walked back to the waiting car and called into the station.

"There's something here I can't understand," Phil said after the call. "That doctor—first of all he got to the scene before us. Then, he goes and phones the Chief.... How do I know? The Chief just finished givin' me a crocka shit. Said to forget they'd moved the body, to go on land lines." Landlines meant the ban on carphones that made certain no one, but no one, could overhear a police conversation whatever gadgets they were carrying. "The Chief is having a litter over this case."

At least someone seems to care.

"The Chief is home in bed," Granita went on, "lined up next to his old lady, and we have nothing to do either," he snorted.

"Yes, we have," said Simon, "We're going to Sakulin's house."

"Sakulin?"

"The developer, the big donor. Where the party diehards and bigwigs are caucusing right now. Chambers is over there already. There's going to be confrontation," he promised Granita, "We're gonna be real spoilers."

MOVERS AND SHAKERS

They had Temperance to themselves already though it was only going on ten. Careening around the narrow Yankee streets of the innermost town, they sideswiped a stationary bakery van, shared a nervous laugh. The streets broadened out into spiroform roads climbing a rounded hill. In its flanks nestled houses surrounded by landscaped yards, then bigger and more widely spaced houses set into green acreage. Some had fake Tudor fronts; others loomed stonily behind high metal gates.

Sakulin's spread was enormous for the Temperance scale. Of all his houses this stucco mansion was by far the least open-heartedly lavish, for Alan Sakulin had built with "sobriety" and "tasteful informality" in mind. These watchwords meant no pool (Temperance was no L. A.), no formal French gardens, no gazebos, just a curving treelined drive that attenuated the steep rises of the hills. The upper two stories looked dark, but from their parking space the policemen could discern a few heavy-moving presences in an ample ground-floor space just light enough to show that someone was at home entertaining.

At forty-nine, Sakulin had traveled so far from his Redfern days that he remembered only the most obvious trappings of the gentlemanly atmosphere he had once adored, and he played at recreating it much more expensively, like a Ralph Lauren addict. In fact, he still sometimes made purchases at the surviving Temperance clothiers, Waterhouse—scene of his first fitting ever—just for old times' sake. The Temperance house was never closed, always kept a skeleton staff, and when Alan was in town he loved to spot old landmarks on his walks. Once in a while some passerby would remind him of an old teacher—like Knox Lydgate, whose Homer course had clued Alan Sakulin into the hierarchy of fathers and sons that ran the world. But other, bicoastal charities often mattered more, since Alan often found Redfern wanting in excitement these days.

The most with-it thing that seemed to be going on just now was the excitement of the superstar nailed by the Comp Lit department. Palter Van Geyst, the Sakulin winner from the first handshake, was genuine international world-class stuff. What luck that he happened to want the peace and quiet of a small private campus. And pretty decent of Armin Fishbane, too, to move over for a once-in-a-lifetime genius mind like that—not to begrudge Palter his huge student following, his pivotal influence on insider decisions, his negative charisma, his... central stillness, his total sufficiency unto himself.

Berto Ricci was another ace in the hole. The endowment of his Chair in Italian Studies had been announced in the same year as Fishbane's Chair in Comp Lit, English, Modern Media, Law and Medicine. The evening was remembered still as a culinary triumph,

Unbeknownst to Sakulin, campus watchers trying to understand the meteoric rise of Ricci often decided that it was due to his wife's cooking. Or because he "did" something "nonconfrontational" and was "so amusing." It just happened that in addition to those sterling qualities, Ricci was a close friend of at least one big Redfern donor, but this fact was never mentioned as having greased the wheels of his success machine.

Now Chavadze and Ricci stood wifeless together in a corner of the library (also known as Sharon's "drawing room") looking as if they were planning to elope. They moved in slo-mo lockstep through a French door to the terrace. Chavadze felt a chill wind at his back, but did not turn around. The two looked at each other eye to eye, each encased in a suit that was polished to a regimental gloss. They both had broad shoulders and stood with their legs apart, hair waving elaborately back from jutting foreheads. The chubby wreaths around Ricci's neck advanced and retreated as he reknotted his tie.

"Chuck, I must to tell you," Ricci said, shifting bellyweight to his other polished elevator shoe. "This perhaps is not a good moment, but we have little time. Alan has assured me that he wants to help with the Center. Nothing has changed, he's solidly behind us." He moved his chin very slightly in the direction of Sharon's drawing room.

"You are wearing a very sober face," Chavadze remarked, "for a bearer of such good news."

"Not everything I have to say is so good. Machiavelli has told that if you have an unpleasant message you must deliver it all at once, that is, to devastate at one time before anyone has the time to respond in serial fashion. But I have trouble doing this."

"Machiavelli said that about killing," Chavadze spoke sharply, "not talk." Still he looked around him with the circumspection of a man who knew how complicated a transaction could get.

"Very diverting, as usual, Chuck. Here is what Alan says. We managed the Biscottini Stadium, fine, but this is different, the times are other... He tells me of his intention, but he is also afraid. Everything is infinitely more complex." Ricci salivated at the memory of his last coup. It was exactly two weeks after the announcement of his lavish new Chair that the construction of the stadium and sports center had begun, and already they were rooted in the Temperance civic mythology.

"Chuck. You know we have never been in the slightest disagreement. You know how well we have always understood one another. But Sakulin is a complicated man, and now he has more partners, he is even less alone than ever." As Ricci fixed his most doting gaze on him, Chavadze absorbed everything, leaning amorously forward. But his lion's stare clouded over with a self-doubling concentration, as if a movie with subtitles were running in his head.

"Don't worry, Berto," he said, "you know you can tell me everything."

"The partners want assurances of a clean break with the past," Berto said. "They need it for another reason also. There is some sort of investigation going on, a nonsense, but you cannot ever be certain, Alan does not even know who is making all the fuss, it is only something which came to him from newspaper friends."

Both men had missed their dinners, as many times before, but now Chavadze sagged from something more than hunger. Ricci saw his moment. "My dear, dear friend," he said. "My Chuck." Then, "We can see this through together and have our Center too, eventually. How is Redfern different from Texas Megatech in substance?"

Chuck looked glummer. "It's the time, as you said, not the place. No one has anything to do lately but indulge themselves in endless investigations and breastbeating. But let me tell you something," perking up. "Every one of them, every exposé, trial, fracas, TV extravaganza, shows you nothing more than how easy it is for people to get used to—irregu-larities. I don't mean just that once it's off the news it's over. I mean that the whole public experience of self-accusation," he warmed to the topic, "actually licenses whatever it seems to condemn. Watergate has made all kinds of political action look okay, once someone got punished. This is a kind of American ceremony, Berto," he went on with a confidential sad-ness. "They want everyone to acknowledge the presence of this or that sin, to give it attention... But can you imagine anyone believing in the possibility of a real ending? These investigations are rituals—then after, everyone is happy again."

Ricci's fleshy lips grimaced, a lowercase O. "Ha! According to this ritual, first you will pardon me, and after, I will pardon you," he said. "Now let me get to the point. Chuck, dear friend, you have a great future before you, no don't protest, a future of true magnanimity. But I am only a professor, a little man. Maybe like an 'igh-school teacher in Italy. But God's sake, at least we understand each other. Now look 'ere: I need more."

"How much more?" Chuck was on old ground, almost relieved. "What in the world have I not done? The house, everything in it, the boat, the Chair..."

"You cannot count the Chair. You do not forget 'ow it came to me. And not to put too fine a point, when the president throws that first ball in the beginning of each season at the Stadium, he should also keep in mind..."

"I am not alone, Berto. Our lives at Texas Megatech were as entwined as the arms of lovers."

"That sounds like Yashvili," Berto said. "And it is pointless, also, to renew our grief of that time. But you were the Provost, not me. You had final responsibility. Your Committee found me blameless. Sakulin's partners want to dig into that extinct volcano before they produce, and I can hardly stop them. But I will try with my whole heart, though I have so much less to lose than you. I ask only for that little encouragement which keeps every man going in a hard world. On a regular basis, so that we never have to talk about it again."

But Chavadze knew they always would. When they agreed upon a sum, he had already figured it into the annual budget, and when Ricci added "no teaching at all" to his list of new perks, Chavadze was briefly happy for the students who would be able to miss Ricci's sententious droning. They would make room and funds for a new young recruit to do the work. Meanwhile Ricci scrolled down his list of small favors owed and found a meaningful name that would fit the new job. A dynamite type, a young firebrand, Bisticcio's star student.

The notion that tonight had reactivated the relationship for good continued to trouble Chavadze all evening. He remembered a scene from the punishment of sinners in Dante's *Inferno.* Somewhere close to the end of the first book, near the bottom of hell, two traitors locked in the mockery of an embrace. Dante's irony was that the two could never be rid of each other till the universe ended. One has his teeth sunk into the other's neck, the other enfolds him for eternity.

Sakulin's rump session had splintered by now into the usual two-some of quarreling factions. Sakulin is in charge of one, ensconced in his favorite wing chair. The other has as its backbone General Ethan Fenn, who would have presided in exactly the same fashion had no one else been there. He seems barely to tolerate the oversized armchair into which Sakulin almost hysterically urged him. He holds a tumbler of straight Scotch in one hand, the other lies austerely in his narrow lap.

The General has turned eighty this year but no official celebration has been sanctioned: he shuns the limelight just as he had when he was in charge of C.I.D. in Tokyo under MacArthur. He still takes the shuttle into Washington once a week to participate in some more-than-formal meetings at the State Department, whether the current Administration is Democratic or Republican. It was in Fenn's glory years that the War Department became an unprecedented power center in Washington, and to this day he receives and transmits firsthand knowledge of the capabilities of the British and German intelligence bureaucracies. The General still displays the qualities of a privileged man who long ago voluntarily gave himself over for the national good—a yardstick by which members of the American establishment can judge themselves and the world.

It had surprised those nearest to his command that this steely man, whose personal dealings were filtered through a steadfast though reserved anti-Semitism, had proven tireless in his efforts to persuade the government to take its first steps toward desegregation of the army. Old-timers would slide unprompted into the anecdote about how Roosevelt would greet his arrival at the Oval Office with the straight-arm Hitler salute. Yet he had won and retained the complete trust of all the prickly personalities involved in the reconstruction of postwar Japan.

Compared with all this, what were the challenges of Redfern trusteeship? Yet the Fenn bunch shrinks in size and influence even since last year, on account of the new people like Sakulin and Chavadze, whose appointment the General had vigorously opposed. Now Fenn looks about him, narrowing his eyes as if seeking someone like himself for an evening's entente.

The impassive, soothing voice of Palter Van Geyst was holding forth, barely audible amid the somber brocade drapes, when a panicked butler ushered in the policemen, wildly shrugging and rolling his eyes behind their backs. The others were riveted to Van Geyst, frowning and straining to hear. He had almost shed his Dutch accent—just a little weighty on the ds and ts, just an extra drop of gas in the h-sounds. It was all so simple, but so complicated, too.

"The exhilarating freedom of nihilism that comes from the unac-countable exercise of power," Van Geyst was saying, "has exposed the weakness of our moral effort to construct a human history." He delivers this deadpan, the way you would compliment Alan on one of his new Crystal-Age paintings. "That, to my mind, translates into the question 'Does might make right?' In a sense, the answer is yes."

Palter's lined sixtyish face bears not a trace of bullyishness; in fact when he says things like that about power and history it looks more amiably beige than ever, and he smiles that old schoolboy's smile. His one suit has acquired the shape of a body though no body can be discerned underneath, even when the suit shifts weight or leans forward so that one of its hands can close around a pen or a glass. Tonight Palter is neither eating nor drinking.

Disembodied genius, thinks Sakulin, no closer to Palter's mean-ing than he had been half an hour ago but coasting on an intellectual high. Sakulin dimly recalls some German thing he'd had to read for a student paper, something reminded him of, was it Nietzsche or.... But of course what Palter was saying was all new.

When Palter means to sound more intense, he lowers his voice a little more. "Any version of human history you can think of is driven by an agenda, by a will to power. What does the person want? There will always be a precise objective. Let me provide just one example," his benign smile widening. "Rousseau tells in his Confessions of an incident in which he participated as a young man, when he was a guest at the country house of a prominent lady. One of the lady's ornamental ribbons, the sort she would have wound into her neckline, went missing. Jean-Jacques reports that finding it accidentally, he pocketed the ribbon, and when in due time, one of the lady's maids was accused of stealing it, Jean-Jacques kept silent, taking note of everything that was said. He experienced the whole scale of her emotions with extreme sensitivity: the lady's wrath, the pleading confusion of the maid, her grief at being sent away. All of this became part of his own experience, and in so doing, was transformed."

Sakulin interrupted. "But look, Palter, he did steal it, right?"

"So he tells us."

"Then that's the simple truth."

"Not simple. It is not this mere event, which anyhow he reported himself—took responsibility for—that counts here. It is the feeling he wanted to bring out in himself that caused the entire affair. And who knows what happened? It is a reality only within the world of this fiction that Jean-Jacques is making. My point is," as everyone wonders what it could possibly be, "that events happen only to be profited from and forgotten. The language that claims to report events—to tell their truth—is no more than non-sense," Van Geyst says, pointedly uncoupling his last two syllables. "We are all left in the tragic position of having to make sense of it. And then we discover our only ease is unease, that for Jean-Jacques a single true account of 'what happened' is forever lost. There IS no true version. Nothing that will survive the course of time and the transference of power."

They all heard the quotation marks of scorn but couldn't guess where they applied. For Van Geyst was looking at the little semicircle with the patience of a country doctor on a slow round.

"But he did steal the ribbon," Sakulin persisted.

Palter's withering schoolboy face grew even more eager to please. "Remember that this is only what he SAYS, the product of a reality that exists only in his mind."

"Still that is the best account we can get, I'd say," the Old Redfernian remarked, revving up for a rally. "What agenda, as you call it, excuses the evil behavior you're talking about? He's not thinking of anything political. More like something criminal."

Van Geyst took on an expression of terminal patience.

" 'Best' is a purely relative term, and so are terms like 'pure' and 'excellent'; that is perfectly illustrated by the story. Even by the fact that it IS a story. The final result is nothing but empty language which we fill with artificial meaning, called knowledge."

"Excitement, you can see what I mean," mouthed Gorellick to Sakulin beside him. "We've got real excitement here. Everyone wants to know what a guy like Palter will say next."

"I'm bound to say, myself," said General Fenn, "that your story sounds like utter baloney, Van Geyst."

"A blast, makes you rethink it all," said Sakulin, nodding his head over and over, like someone being interviewed on TV and desperately signaling that they have nothing more to say, though the mike is relentlessly stuck under their face. "I mean, wow."

"Mind you," Van Geyst leaned back a little, "there is no power in the world that can call itself, actually, knowledge."

"You are equating power and illegitimacy, it seems. Power sometimes goes to the best," Fenn persisted.

"The point, General, is not whether power is legitimate or not. It just IS."

"Sure," Sakulin followed up. "You get things on people, you fix their parking tickets—that's clout." He tried a laugh.

"Knowledge IS power," Van Geyst said quietly, disregarding the children. "Certainly, we make statements that mean to be true; or statements that mean to be fiction. But they are all fiction."

"We're real, though," Simon spoke up from the entry archway. "Sorry we have to disturb you, gentlemen, but a student has died at Redfern. Mr. Keith Chambers found the body, he told us, in the Underground Campus, or whatever you call it."

Sakulin looked Simon right in the eyes. "When?"

Simon was reminded he didn't know. "The only thing we can say now is it might have been just before or during the party. Mr. Chambers told us he found her when he went to get some bottles of wine from some special cellar. There was a student demonstration going on and they were trying to get into the Administration Building; we saw some of that ourselves." How quickly that demo had just petered out for no apparent reason!

"I'd better find out who you all are," he said. "This is Sergeant Granita, I'm Lieutenant Blank, and I've been assigned to this case," shifting feet. "No time can be established until the pathologist's examination is complete—that means tomorrow—and even that might not tell us so much. This is not a mystery story." The lame finish came out as Simon counted the faces before him and wondered how many of them had been at the Admin Building an hour or so ago.

Sakulin frowned in his chair next to Palter's. With his pumped feet still propped on a hassock almost as high as his wing chair, Berto Ricci, frowning, retracted his pug snout and loosened the tie around his overflowing neck. Keith Chambers chose that second to reenter the library, wearing his blandest expression. Several Big Givers melted into their sofa pillows, avoiding an imaginary camera. So did the Old Redfernian, who had come in specially all the way from Palo Alto. Fenn, a study in right angles, seemed to be mulling over his next set of orders.

At last Chavadze broke the silence. "I'll go there with you now," he said stoutly. "Every Redfern student is my personal concern. If, God forbid, there is reason to think for a moment that this.... tragedy was brought on by... that is, if there is some unnatural aspect to it, we will all stand up to it together..." The Old Redfernian, now a mover and shaker at Stanford, watched admiringly, head tilted. Chavadze was justifying his rep for crisis management, right before his eyes.

"We think the student was murdered," Simon Blank addressed himself mainly to Chavadze "By strangulation. Mr. Chambers can tell you everything he knows," he added wryly, "on the way."

Keith braced grimly for later. Chuck would have a fit about not having been told sooner, just as he would have anyhow if Keith had told him right away.

"Are we needed here, Lieutenant?" This was Van Geyst's usual even voice.

"Doesn't matter what you do," growled Phil Granita, for Simon.

"The name. We ought to know as soon as possible," Chavadze

asked.

Chavadze's eyes followed Keith's around the room to the chair where the General sat looking like one leg of a swastika. Keith took a breath. "It's Selena," he answered. Again, to Chavadze's bushy raised eyebrows. "That's right, Selena Fenn." Without a word, General Fenn was seen to rise, straighten up, and leave the room, carefully opening and shutting the heavy mahogany doors without a slam.

On the way to the Presidential car, Chavadze meditated on a number of possible results, wrinkling his nose as he assessed the damages, among them the devastating effect this catastrophe would have on the New Campaign. Was there now going to be a run on the College, parents of female students snatching them out? Would Redfern be deluged with disastrous media attention? Would it become the scapegoat of armchair education reformers?

Keith, in turn, had never agreed at heart with the abolition of dorm rules that had accompanied the New Curriculum into Redfern. Gone were all restrictions: no more curfew, everything permitted, any guests you want in your room, whatever horrors you went in for being perpetrated right, left, and center. He spent a considerable amount of time these days imaging forth those horrors.

Yet his early reaction to the discovery of Selena's body was to compose a memo, to be distributed posthaste, saying that the relaxation of rules had nothing to do with this or any criminal behavior. He reflected with distaste that Selena would probably be receiving mummifying fluids intravenously by now, and that he, Keith, would eventually have to help with the details, there being as usual no one else around to take on the really repulsive jobs. Keith's body, preserved in its own aspic of muscle and veins, housed the morals of a maiden lady. And he hated bodily fluids.

For the moment he stopped contingency planning and fell to blaming people like his subdean, Marlayne Sorley, and the whole slew of personnel who were there to promote the New Redfern. AND that jester Ricci with his porcine face, and the upstart Fishbane, and those FAM women, and the enigmatic Van Geyst—he thoughtfully reviewed them all, feeling sorry for Redfern and for himself.

Then they were there. He got out of the long black car and opened the door for Chavadze, like a chauffeur.

Though Keith's duties at Redfern had turned more and more commercial—fending off the complaints of alumni that their children were not getting in; running interference for Redfern sports coaches whose teams were not winning; keeping a smooth veneer on meetings—he still had the rare privilege of day-to-day executive independence. At a time when everyone in Redfern's pay seemed to need organized support, Keith unabashedly functioned on his own... Every complaint came to rest on his desk, where it aged like old cheese and was thrown out. People tolerated this treatment because it reassured them of his stability and his dogged, unshakable loyalty to the institution.

Keith's character had cemented by age fifteen, and he still inhabited the physical structure of age twenty, for him a blameless age. He had played football for Redfern for two of his college years, but evaded the legendary sex life that went with team sports. There were still traces of ingenuousness in his pale eyes, a slight crinkled when they smiled, which was rarely. Later, no one could understand just why, having slotted himself easily into a vacant teaching job, he couldn't stay a Redfern professor forever, but temptation got the better of him and he was painlessly transferred into Administration, from one parish to the next.

Keith alone could vividly remember the time before the deluge of the sixties counterculture—before a prof could make real money, before the job crunch started, and at the same time Redfern became Big Business. There were no women then; Bolingbroke College, a little brick settlement well east on the Redfern peninsula, housed, fed, and taught the girls. Though he harked back to those fabled days, Keith he could fastforward his mind right into the present without a hitch. He hadn't faded away, only modernized.

Keith knew that what the warring interest groups in his charge wanted REALLY was just plain attention. The efficient way of dealing with them was therefore simply to divide his time among them, and make sure they knew he liked them all. He lacked Chavadze's discount charm, but he did have the same deeply rooted awareness that the only thing no one could tolerate was being disliked, hence ignored. If the Dean of Relationships went on mouthing the formulas of respect and affection, he was almost never expected to follow up with money. How easy it was for "special interests" to take reassurance for power!

Entering the Admin Building for a nocturnal emergency session,

Keith and Chavadze noticed the last demonstrator—male, T-shirted, a mass of black curls under a pirate's bandanna—and read his sign, which said: "REDFERN PROFFESORS SOCK."

Keith blocked the demonstrator's path, a smile hovering on his lips but not his eyes. "What the heck is all this about tonight?"

The boy looked down at his sneakers. "It was assigned for us," he said. "The Dynamics of Political Action, YOU know," it came out "joo." "Mr. Lamamba's course. To understand what means protest, by disrupting the ritual of the oppressor." Didn't professors even know what their friends were giving students to do?

"Comp Lit 99," the kid almost whined with impatience. "We make our own signs and we come down and protest. Oh come-OOONNNN." He lowered the sign and trudged off with it under his arm, his head moving from side to side.

So it seemed that the demonstration was not a cover for the murder after all.

The two top Redfern executives sat together in the nocturnal Presidential Suite at the huge doublesided partners' desk, in urgent conference mode. Chavadze smoked one of his secret Gauloises, a secret, incorrect indulgence he kept even from the redoubtable Peggy. When he'd picked those furnishings for the office, he thought, I must have been pretending that the world is not a misery.

From the rinky-dink local channels to Morgan Broadside and the rest of the network commentators, to CNN, who would beam it to Alaska, Egypt, the Cameroons, Redfern would soon be world-famous for murder.

Keith tapped the palm of his hand with a closed ballpoint pen. His gaze held no hint of emotion.

In Keith's neighboring suite, the telephone rang.

Chavadze moved heavily around the partners' desk, facing a large, unopenable picture window. Across the low buildings, a stereo playing rock, with its speakers turned outward, boomed a relentless bass. Was she raped, thought Chavadze, taking in the beat.

And how tiny and cramped this campus is, like a string quartet for a symphony conductor. But you still had to dream up the concept, write the program notes, conduct the performance, instruct the audience from the podium, and throw a party before or after every performance.

Keith was back. "The Chief of Police assured me once again, Chuck, that everything will stay confidential. He did call me right back, didn't he?"

"Fenn knows," answered Chavadze.

"You don't expect Fenn to blame Redfern, do you?" Keith took a few more pokes at his palm with the pen.

"Blame Redfern.... I still cannot encompass this. No one would want to kill Selena."

"If anyone did, IF, mind you, it will turn out to be someone outside Redfern. That's for sure. Someone left one of the entrances to the Underground University open. God knows Temperance has any number of persons who'd be trying to get inside. There's a release on my desk from Democratic headquarters, for instance. It says that Governor Pelham has had an extra thousand patients dumped from Clearwater this year alone. You recall Old Crazyhorse, I think, Chuck."

Chavadze certainly did. This was yet another diversion that Redfern students had blown up into a cause. Last winter a homeless man had taken to sleeping on the grating of a two-by-four air vent on a Redfern street. You'd have to step over him at night, though he and his market cart of bundles would disappear punctually at seven in the morning. Students in the two-story dorms that lined the street were as deaf to his noise as to the stereo bass. Sometimes they fed him leftover pizza or brought him coffee from the dorm. But in time his residence on the warm grating brought Old Crazy to the attention of Redfern administrators. Neither Redfern's fifty-strong Community Relations Task Force, nor its Human Resources Conservation Board, Red Heart Giving Program, or even the Redfern Way, which dispensed spoiling food to the truly needy, could agree on what should be done, except that no matter what, Old Crazy must vacate the Redfern grating. Every night three security men traded duty to make sure he would never come back. It felt silly parading around a grating, but those were their orders.

Students formed protest groups and even stormed Keith's suite; editorials in the Redfern Rumble railed against this newest instance of capitalist cruelty, but the Redfern administration was unanimously united against Old Crazy, and closed him down. Which showed how quickly and resourcefully they could act when they really had to. "No domestically challenged person seeking aid will be referred to by demeaning nicknames on our campus."

Could Old Crazy be back? Not a hope.

"Ricci," Chavadze said, his lips barely moving. "You remember."

Keith panics at this casual mention of the unspeakable, the threshold of a gaping cave he cannot bear to enter. The time he found Ricci and Selena—and on the floor of his own suite, yet—he could only splutter and stammer his disgust. Now he remembered her tossing back the mussed braid of her golden-brown hair, slowly putting on the jeans and shirt that had been her only clothing as if she were taking them off, slipping her feet into Docksiders. She turns back at the door and smiles the smile that says she sees right through him and appreciates the restraint it takes for him never to raise a punishing arm. "So long, Keith dear. Don't even try to understand."

Now Keith's dowager Plymouth cruised the rows of inward-turning storefronts, as he reflected with surprising calm how harlotry had become second nature to her, but now it was all over, fate had put paid to it. The cold clarity of the night purified his wavering, waffling impulses of pity, leaving the silent mover in full control of the detachment it took to do his job. His moral stand had been contemptuously ignored, and at her peril. Powerless against hormones, ruled to the finish by the obscene imperatives of sex—very well.

The Dean of Relationships bridled at the wheel, switching to low beams so that no oncoming driver could see his face, which streamed with tears.

The nearly empty streets seemed to flow red with female vitality, females everywhere hugging themselves further into their own brazen bodies, even the slender ones—as we know—made of the same clay-like earth, all the same. The only woman on the streets at this hour accosted him at a red light, and the temptation to run her over was almost more than he could stand, burning rubber as he swerved away. A girl like Selena, no more. His whole soul sighed with relief for her as much as for himself; one less bestiality would take place this night.

But Selena had been uniquely placed in his care; he'd had no responsibility comparable to the one now gone. This gnawed at him so that his strong body felt flaccid and disjointed, his pale eyes clouded with loathing in the mirror. Keith tried the usual mnemonics that traced him back to his proper self, rehearsed the beginnings of memos and the answers Chavadze would need for routine questions. The holding action only staved off what was usually waiting, the relentless bilge of trash images on the television screen, the obscene noises of goodnights from the street as the campus building quieted down, or seemed to.

But the neighbor, a single man, had picked tonight to have company. The self-mutilating sensuality of those women was recognizable. In the dimly lit calm of his little living room, Keith could hear the horrid laughter, even a bottle crashing to an uncarpeted floor. He could all too easily image forth the savage embrace. A shout rose from his throat, then he stifled it, jamming a hand onto his mouth. He raised his fist to smash the creatures, but his reason got the better of him and it hit the wooden arm of his chair. The sound of his own cry of pain propelled him up and out, and grew into a bellow.

"You goddam animals cut that out. CUT THAT OUT or I'll...or..."

He shouted until he was hoarse, long after giggles turned to silence next door, shouted until he felt his lungs burning and his face hot with the redness of the nightmare tunnel walls. Then the comforting memories of Selena took over in peace, and he kept them running in focus until bedtime ablutions—longer than usual—were done, and he was restored by the urgent reasonableness of his purpose: to keep this fall and disgrace from Redfern, whatever its anatomy held within.

It was going on midnight now, and Simon Blank let the sergeant drive while he read Selena's pocket diary. Assuming as he now did that the throat injuries on the body would amount to murder, he tried to link them to the evidence of recent sexual intercourse. "Someone did her two ways," he said to Granita.

"Could've been two someones."

Selena Mortimer Fenn, said the curling vertical script, the kind used on party invitations, with a circle dotting the "i". Then MY BOOK: REMEMBER!!!! Flipping through, fragmentary notes: "Cultural Revolution Paper 4/10" or "Party, Keith pickup, 4/5, 5", or "Get fridge fixed." There were almost no references to other people. On the inside front cover, in heavier black marker—HANDMAID. Just HAND-MAID.

"Confidentiality. Our responsibility to our students," Keith had told the policemen, "includes full protection of their privacy."

"Getting her student file, just to look for clues, can't hurt her much, can it, right now?" Simon asked with a tinge of sarcasm.

"But it may hurt others. You've got plenty of other things to do," he observed with a touch of irony. So all they had in hand now was a little black book that made them both feel like cops in a B-movie.

"Write to Marcus," Simon read out loud. "Looks like she had at least one friend. Or no, she wrote 'call', so maybe this Marcus is in town." He turned the pages more slowly.

"Whaddaya think about this Chambers?" Granita said.

"I think he doesn't care about anything except Redfern. He's going to obstruct us every step of the way unless he believes it's for Redfern's good. He figures that now his dear godchild is dead, his job is to show that some outside person did it."

Granita swerved away from a double-parked van full of TV sets. "I need coffee."

"No," Simon said, "You—and I—need a beer. And we need to get it where the campus security goes."

They drove through the few streets rimming the far end of the campus whose shops sold Indian bedspreads or New Age books or recycled cutoffs, and pulled up at a little sawdust-floored bar, where they sat and squirmed on stools too small for them. The wall directly in front of them was mirrored, giving them an unobstructed view of two overweight, unshaven policemen.

Simon went on reading the agenda. "Honors thesis McFarquhar." Could that still be her?

The one "grownup," Simon could recall from his Redfern days with unblemished pleasure, was Willona McFarquhar. His recollection of Willona even made the lukewarm Bud taste better. You could face an army of Redfernian types with someone like her on your side. It was Willona who alone had sympathized when Simon, a scholarship student, had announced that he was going in for police work. He saw her again in her stylish suits and shirts, her hair swept up off her face, a handsome face that hardly ever smiled.

"You're a born investigator. Maybe you're no candidate for the new James Bond, but it's a secure future." No pretense of anything transcendental, no need for high-flown reasons. You could be straight with McFarquhar.

Granita took huge gulps of his beer, staring before him. On the way to the toilet Simon spotted a campus security guard at a table alone. He was black and in full uniform. Simon was guiltily reminded of railway porters in his childhood.

"Sorry to bother you," he stopped at the table full of empty beers. "My partner and I need your help. We're from the Eleventh Precinct," showing his badge.

"We heard," said the campus guard. "We're gonna hear for the rest of our lives. And they know better, too. "

"They?"

"You may as well sit," said the guard. "We're all gonna be talking. Dean of Everything gonna spend his time on us. Trouble is, they know more than we do. About the Underground University, f'rinstance. None of us really gets a chance to ever learn 'bout the whole place. Everyone just gets a part an' gets to stay there a few hours a day. They're the ones that know..." His tone was entirely matter-of-fact.

"We can't see why you didn't have orders to keep every entry triple-locked. Mr. Chambers says there are five."

"Ever'thin' was locked," the guard raised his voice. "Me, the others, no one ever let the doors open except for people with cards. Doin's at Redfern concern just people with Redfern cards. My name's Marston Hall," putting down the beer, "I've been a campus guard for fifteen years. Jus' let them say we were asleep on the job or anythin'. Mind you, I'm not sayin', not even thinkin' that anyone wants to pin this on us, if anythin' they'd be afraid... Pays to be black sometimes."

Simon avoided that angle. "You're saying that no one could ever get into the underground university without showing their cards?"

"None of us was off the job, either," the guard said. "Not even to take a leak. Mr. Chambers and even Mr. Chavadze saw us specially, all five, yesterday morning, one after the other. They warned us that the Administration Building would be extra crowded. An' that doesn't count all those Deans. Same ones who run in an' out all the time makin' faces like the earth depends on they're there. Ever'one I saw down in the undergroun' the same as the people hangin' out the rest o' the time. They show up at any time even in the File Room. Look, anyone would lose track of who comes in and goes outta there. You're supposed to sign a paper but none of 'em do. In an' out, in an' out. Specially in the File Room. Seems like someone's always takin' somethin' out, puttin' it back," he droned. "You get used to the idea that only outside people need talkin' to about it, an' I could swear no one gets by those locks. No one."

"They're thinking it might be Old Crazyhorse."

"You make me laugh, a poor guy like him. Or—lemme guess—a loony from Clearwater, right? Spin doctors gonna make someone out of God's own clay an' set him up as a murderer."

"What about the paper files? Do you have to check, make sure they're returned? That's a lot of responsibility, Mr. Hall."

"You can't," Marston Hall said. "There's just too much activity. Even if I was—quicker on the uptake, if they had younger men doing my work, it would be plain impossible to keep track of their borrowin' and returnin' those files." He shook his head slowly. "They say f'rinstance, one day, that Mr. Chavadze needs it, well, we can't know how long."

So the files could be stolen or tampered with. But if everything was also on computer, why would anyone mess with old paper? On the other hand, the excuse "Chavadze needs it" struck him with surprise. Why would a University President send for a humdrum personnel file?

Marston Hall went on. "They do it all the time. Matter of fact, just today, about four I guess it was, I'd punched in an hour before, I saw someone'd left a file door open—one of the cabinet doors was just sort of hangin'."

"No one could get in from outside, that's the bottom line," Simon reported to Granita. "This is the kind of key they use, like a hotel room key." Simon turned a perforated card around in his hand. "It can't be reproduced. It has to be changed all the time. There's a sorta electronic message printed on it. You go in, shove the key into a machine, the door opens. You go in, it shuts."

"The campus police wouldn't deal 'em out to anyone else, would they?" Granita asked.

"Maybe Selena felt like visiting the file rooms. New kind of thrill. An' you could get a nice drink of wine."

"Let's go back."

The series of doors was heavy but noiseless, like rubber. They tried room after room. It was a matter of minutes before they spotted the one with the open cabinet. Phil picked up a brown manila file that had been wedged under the cabinet with its margin showing diagonally. The tab said Roberto Ricci. It contained absolutely nothing.

"There's no reason to stay here," Simon said. "We can't connect any of this missing file business with ...her. Someone wanted Ricci's file, so what?"

"Chambers said he found her in that room next to their wine cellar," Granita answered. "And why did whoever wanted the file leave the cover for us to find?"

The night was slow to end, and Keith Chambers shifted in his narrow camp bed, dreaming the same horrible dream, then shook himself awake. No escaping the blurred outlines of Selena and that swine Ricci, leaving the party together. Suddenly he stopped rehearsing that moment and lifted his head and gazed straight ahead, almost laughing aloud his rare dry laugh. At the moment of Selena's slinky walkout Keith had been stuck with the Poet in Residence, Yashvili, he of the falcon and chickens. One of his more absurd jobs this week was still finding more for Yashvili to do.

Redfern had never had a Poet in Residence before. The Fulfillment Center's Tell-Alls were the closest thing Keith could think of to Yashvili's poems. Redfern was getting to be quite a place for readings, though. Marvella Jilkes' seven hundred-page autobiography was the latest ("a work ever in progress", as Marvella put it, "for a chronicle of myself can never end."). Thank goodness this Poet in Residence was going to be around only five days, and so far it had all gone smoothly.

Yashvili's descent from the little commuter plane at the Temperance airport had come off without a hitch. Even on Monday morning, with so much to choose from, the local news had found time for Chuck's welcoming embrace of Yashvili, their flashing exchange of salutes, Chuck even seizing Yashvili's little bag and striding off with it. Now if we can only keep Marvella here, Redfern will be all over the map. As Alan Sakulin put it, "With one big fish we'd get a million more bangs for our buck."

Values Clarification and Euphoria had already sent her glossies to the Rumble and the Temperance Trib with a breathless bio that retailed Marvella's rise to fame—from beginnings as a whorehouse madam to the test of her character as a crapgame shill, to her sudden catapult into literature. The new catalogue already listed Marvella as the Oleaginus Rumpe Professor. Keith vowed to stay on top of Gorellick till it got done, and he drew himself up, still prone, to his full height in bed.

A redeemed Soviet and a major, major black novelist, both at once! But the excitement of this possibility had almost made him forget what his mind was already recasting as "the events of the previous evening." He'd not been very sensible though, he realized that; all he'd had to do was keep closer watch to make certain that the orchestration he had mapped out never varied.

The General would never, never forgive—or at least, not for quite a while—but would Keith pardon his own mindless surrender to the moment? Swamped with revulsion for the musky viscosity of sex and the whole scabrous lot of imaginings that stick to it like spiderwebs, he searches the night for any remainder of the ghastly noises. Bestial maniacs varnished over by a sloppy coating of civilization, it is they who will never attain forgiveness.

The Redfern team picture on the opposite wall, vintage 1956, reproached him with its purity as Chambers dropped off.

MOON GODDESS

Hilary Slocombe found no rest on her side of the wide and luxurious bed that dominated the little dorm room. The steeple clock had chimed ten, eleven, and twelve, but the comfort it usually offered her did not come. Every sound in the entryway was augmented through the radiator vent, none the sound she waited to hear. Selena would not come. The jealousy that stalked Hilary like a shadow loomed over her, receded, then jumped out at her again. So much in love, and yet...you never knew Selena, that was part of her fascination, always something to discover, some carefully shaded new side.

The guy across the corridor had borrowed the computer printer. Now he knocked at the door wanting to know if they needed it back.

"I've got an all-nighter coming," he said. "Fishbane on Situational Ethics and the Self. The man's a genius. Paper's due tomorrow."

"Keep it," Hilary mumbled. "Tomorrow night, doesn't matter."

She had very little use for the printer, for Hilary was a sculptor, one of the "creatives" who boosted Redfern's reputation as a place for students impatient with conventional academic requirements.

An unconventional student, for sure. Keith Chambers' squad of admissions subdeans, checking out her application, had just about squealed with delight. Or at least some of them.

"A woman like this speaks volumes for geographical diversity," said Sypher.

"A sculptor—how absolutely intriguing," said Garnix. "I can see it: a feminine Colossus, striding over our heads," said Nill, turning pink and inhaling through his nose. "If we could only really find out what she looks like!"

Not all had seemed enthusiastic about the Colossus.

"Do we need students who are driven by some bourgeois concept of mastery?" Sita Amanpuri's syncopated contralto intoned. As a newly tenured Comp Lit "person", she still weighed and measured her words, but knew that she would always owe any advancement to LuAnn Rossiter's persistence in taking care of her own. For Sita, whose job it was ostensibly to teach East Asian Civ, was not conversant with any East Asian Civ in any language under the sun.

"This applicant, it seems to me, corroborates a dangerous new stereotype of women, one that is limiting, restrictive, even possibly demeaning." Everyone looked at Sita, deliciously intimidated as they always were when she laid down the law on the West.

"I will make myself clear," she went on. "This application says in almost as many words that the student wants to study examples of artistic genius, all kinds of large-sounding things. What does that mean as regards the FEMALE imagination, OUR problems, OUR desires? What are all those Masterpieces she wants to create, what are they to WOMAN but a set of fetters on her own bodily creativity? Redfern has come to signify freedom from these constraints of so-called genius, and above all, MASTERY. Look, her Personal Essay shows all those biases. On top of everything, she wants to learn to work in bronze. You do understand? Bronze!"

Mumtaz Mahmoud, newly elevated to FAM, joined the snickers and chortles. But Sita grew suddenly serious. One huge dark eye, set into her better profile, kept casing the table.

"It is difficult for me under the circumstances, very difficult indeed, to endorse such an application."

This had been a long speech for Sita, but she was hot that day, fresh from a Symposium on Erogenous Xenophobia where she had represented Redfern. The weather in Florence had been glorious.

"Granted that we are talking of nothing more than a naïve belief," she said, "four years of college may not be long enough to correct it."

The discussion took on a note of high seriousness. "The idea of WOMAN indulging in the praxis of sculpture," said Bonza Leier (Video Studies), standing to be heard, "is problematic enough. No art carries the burden of more oppressive, repressive, images of woman. Now this applicant wants to follow in the noble tradition"—emphasis, pause, more snickers, "right, the noble tradition, of folks like Mr. DaVinci and Mr. Cellini and Mr. Matisse. Not with MY help!" Bonza wound up, thumping her file of applications on the table several times. She sat down wreathed in general approval. Her frizzy yellow hair stood up all over her head, making her look more vague than usual—like a shaky snapshot.

"That's Bonza for you," said Sypher, who had come aboard only three months ago. Everyone laughed again, a downscale trill in relay.

"People, people," urged Marlayne Sorley, the Dean of Values Clarification. "We're blowing our time. Who among us even HAS any time at all?" Groans all round, you-betcha noises. "Let's go on, there are thirty more applications to discuss in the next half hour."

"Goodness knows it's time," from Sypher.

"I'm about set," from Garnix.

"All ready?" from Nill.

"Let's take her," someone from the Office of Students Teaching Students spoke up. "Anyone who can sculpt in bronze could—be of help in Supplies and Storage, they always need movers. And this one says she needs Financial Assistance."

That last was the reason the Dean of Values Clarification had thought it best to reject the application. But rapid negotiation between the man from OSTS and his counterpart from Buildings and Grounds ultimately saved Hilary.

The meeting, as it happened, also generated Femmes Against Mastery. Now FAM was an omnivorous three-year-old, perpetually crying for attention.

"It's up to us few," Mumtaz had confided in Sita, "to at least put in a word for woman at Redfern."

"It's jes' the most sayulf-evident thin'," LuAnn decided, "the mos' cryin' need. Refashionin' woman at Refuhn. What we have heah is nothin' but cultural repression—plain ole androcentric repression."

The founding members soon amassed a serious following and

branched out to other campuses. LuAnn Rossiter, its head, came to spend far more of her time E-mailing, phoning, faxing, wiring her counterparts at other universities throughout the world than doing work that was entirely uncongenial to her ability and temperament. Key people they were, too, like Vassiliki Fink, Sherri Tooley, Jeudi Bloomentochter, Aviva Har-Shalom, and even Megan Mehan, who taught her own witchcraft at Harvard.

Mumtaz had made it into FAM on the ground floor. Her book-in-progress, IN A SHEEP'S EYE: Woman's Unveiling in a New Eden, was going slowly despite the signing of a fat contract that had scrupulously set aside all movie rights for the author. The little advance had already been spent three times over. Redfern couldn't subsidize travel to half the meet-and-greet conferences you still needed to attend in the normal run of a year until you got tenure, so Mumtaz had to scrimp and save. Just like being a fifth unmarried daughter back home, she thought, then remembered what that was really like.

Yes, FAM was the way to go, and it never ran low on funds.

LuAnn seemed to be taking care of Gorellick, the Provost. Mumtaz could never understand how she did it, but the steady cash flow continued despite Redfern's perennially advertised need to economize. Hardly a week passed without bringing some fat new memo in the junk mail concerning excessive phone charges or instructing everyone to keep turning their lights off when leaving the office. None of this affected the FAM budget, which had recently reached three mil and counting.

FAM was a public force to reckon with. But Hilary and Selena were lovers, and they cherished their privacy.

Hilary, listening to the sparser night sounds, had hardly moved when one chime was followed after a moment, it seemed, by two—then three, the hour when fear rules the world.

My life will never be what it was before Selena, never.

There had really been hardly any except for her work, which alternated seamlessly with food, sleep, and chores, near or far. Hilary had managed to get back to Redfern from home in time to be a student waiter at the donors' party. It had been a matter of some eleven hours, but the mosaic of flights from Montana fitted together perfectly. Families just surface when they need you, and on this latest trip she had realized that she did not need one herself at all.

But her instant reaction even to Selena's name would never change. It was a surge of the whole body, capable of producing any result Selena wanted according to her whim of the moment. They had divided their time more or less accordingly, for Selena was nothing if not organized:

"You'll never get anything done if you let me distract you. Here's what we'll do: work three hours and if you can even get that right side started, then we'll play."

This scheduling, the most effective known cure for Hilary's slap-dash habits, had eventually led to the completion of several pieces that astounded even those of the art faculty who were most stolidly devoted to equalizing the students. They sat back as one and just let it happen, none of Hilary's teachers singling her out to remark that they'd seen the story in the Temperance *Tribune.* Nor did they congratulate her on that most amazing of artistic triumphs: a sale, just last year.

Her "Victory," a self-absorbed beauty growing more and more like Selena, stood with all the other student work on the floor of the arts center Underground University basement, draped in a tarp. She was the work of Hilary's hands alone, a classical beauty looking out of her depths amid the Earthworks and Installation Pieces that lay scattered at her feet, making odd troughs in the studio floor.

Hilary did get by Sypher, Garnix, and Nill but was blocked immediately at the next stage by the Dean of Values Clarification. He responded by circling the phrase "individual and individuality" with a comment in purple marker: "This is a Red Flag phrase today, which is considered by many to be Sexist and Racist. Arguments that champion individuals ultimately privilege 'individuals' belonging to the largest or dominant group."

Three chimes and still Selena did not come. Hilary was no stranger to misery, but the previous evening had witnessed a certain extra bitterness between the two, which had left her with a feeling of something concluded. Between trips to and from the kitchen with trays of hors d'oeuvres and drinks, she had only managed to catch glimpses of Selena flitting about among her close acquaintances, doling out smiles and waves.

"It's all acting anyway, darling," she explained, "why not go along with it? More fun that way. Mix, circulate, listen. You can laugh at everyone even more afterwards."

And she sailed off, giggling idiots, her hair flowing behind her.

Tonight the prospect of later hadn't helped to soothe the anguish of knowing how far she was from what she wanted, which was, quite simply, total possession. A numbing anger made her stand petrified in the midst of the crowded floor with the wineglasses oscillating on the tray, her heart pounding against her ribs. Perhaps it was the trip home that made the difference this time, or the absurd waiter's tuxedo she was wearing, but an access of rage prevented her from stoically resuming her duties, leaving ill enough alone one more time.

Three a.m. saw Myron Wiener, in his campus cubicle, working on footnotes to his book. Academic writers usually put those in last, but Myron knew he would have to do the opposite. He had decided to write the notes first. How better to be sure everyone got in? This would be a real departure: a book generated by acknowledgements, driven by debt and fear.

He worked in a tizzy of paper despite the efficiency of his computer. It was impossible for him to visualize how everyone and their works would look on the page unless he printed out every version. So the squeak-and-grind of the Redfern-issue printer wheezed on down the empty corridor of the Underground section he inhabited, like a nocturnal animal.

If he went along with the prevailing fashion in Fielding Studies, citing Mortmain on the feasibility of discovering more genuine autograph letters at this late juncture, well, then he could assert that he himself had found some. But wouldn't he also have to defend the importance of the Letters by turning against the sheaf of Redfern colleagues who disparaged the "autograph hunters?" Including, of course, Palter Van Geyst. What was Fishbane's real feeling about Van Geyst? Desperate to understand this, Myron tossed another two pages of printout across his cubicle. He had lost his compass, he knew, in the fruitless effort to dope out the skein of relationships among the people who would casually determine his destiny.

He leaned back in the creaking swivel chair, imagining the completed Book. Not too fat to entertain Fishbane, not too slim to outrage Knox Lydgate; just the right treatment of women—no, WOMAN, for LuAnn Rossiter, with postcolonial diatribes for Sita, and for Ricci, flattering comparisons to some Italian novelist nobody reads.

Myron sat bolt upright, running his little fingers again and again through what was left of his hair. A cold fear was running over his body. He thought of the incident in the Campus Can last week, when he had been confronted by LuAnn and Sita Amanpuri and asked—oh so coyly— how the book was going.

I've done nothing yet, absolutely nothing. But all I need is more time. How long can it take to get two hundred pages into a computer? Does it matter what I say as long as those notes show me where to go? Notes first, book later, really original. I think.

Haven't even unpacked everything yet, after years of being here. Myron had given up hoping to see a friendly face or hear a word of encouragement in the course of the day. His hope rested entirely in the possibility of squeezing through, past where they can catch you—of making himself small enough to fit the smallest mouse hole. Then he could unpack.

It was later than he thought; the meeting was scheduled for tomorrow morning.

Tuesday Morning, April 6, 1993
ALL IN A DAY'S WORK

Armin's tie puffs luxuriantly from a tiny knot just under the flared white collar; the built-up shoulders know just where to stop. The silvery hair springs in those abundant whorls expertly controlled by the blowdrier. His full red lips curve into a ready grin. Scan for icebergs as he might, nothing floats this way just now but fun.

He will soon belong to an inner sanctum where faculty and administrators meet, the top echelon who never, ever, have to see a student. Meetings were a piece of cake. Armin loves those tenderly mediated encounters with other Redfern movers-and-shakers; the creamy conversations and unspoken understandings, all cocooned in an atmosphere thick with consultation. He rewraps the oversized fifteen-ply cashmere tweed topcoat and buttons the top button, feeling outdoorsy now even though he is a confirmed indoor cat.

He likes to count up his career by decades, which span the years from postwar expansion to nineties retrenchment. The Fifties meant gentility and serenity, crashing the snobbish faux-Britain of English Departments before the creation of blessed Comp Lit. The Sixties meant riots and demos, relevance, and the End of Work. The Seventies meant Less-Is-More, the perfect T-shirt, a return to nature and, alas, Women's Lib, as he still called it. The Eighties meant divine Conferences.

Armin knows that the Golden Age of conferences is long past, a casualty of the recession. Useta be, you could string 'em together for most of the year: Paris, Milan, northern Spain. These days the only available high has to come from inside Redfern. He scrupulously avoids doing research ("the grind"). As far as teaching anyone anything goes, the Old Fatheads who ran the Department in his early years had kept it light. But even way back then, he had known he would always hate that too, every moment of it.

He turns the final corner under the jolly, gentile sky. An edge of worry creased his bright, well-pressed mood.

"But sir—" Emil Wahnsinn, that odd Teutonic, never seemed to catch on like the other T.As. "How can I take the course on Renaissance medicine and gynecological law? I have never known anything of these things; I could not possibly do justice..."

"You'll... be... fine," Fishbane said with the right emphasis, training a gimlet eye on Emil. "Look, stop calling me sir. That's entirely superfluous."

Emil had scuttled as fast as anyone that tall and thin could scuttle and prepared for an all-nighter with RENAISSANCE GYNECOLOGY: A MISCARRIAGE OF JUSTICE 1450-1550 by Vassiliki Fink. This was Fishbane's choice of text for the next lecture, illustrated in lurid full-color. Emil did not see what it had to do with Literature, but it is not his place to wonder.

NOW what? Who was this potty little figure emerging from a crouching stance in the shrubbery? Who was that round, yet quick enough to surface all at once like that, between Fishbane and the Pelfe Hall door? It was impossible that anyone could have invited Myron Wiener to the meeting; it was inconceivable that Myron Wiener would even know there was one. Yet it was Myron who arose before him now, slightly lurching on his size-seven Wallabees. Myron had to crane his neck to catch Fishbane's eye. His back hurt; he had lurked in the bushes for an hour, semi-seated, clutching a book for dear life in case anyone else happened there who knew him. As Fishbane's dapper figure cantered in his direction Myron blinked, feeling the impulse to attack before being attacked.

"Have you heard anything yet, Armin?" Myron forced himself into a confidential stage whisper but it came out croaking.

"Myron, is that you? That was really good chicken the other night, Myron. Really good, shows what you can still do with the simple things. Tell Vera we enjoyed it a lot, Graziella and I."

Fishbane tried to look as if he considered the apparition from the shrubbery perfectly normal, so the twosome attracted no special attention from the thickening little groups now entering Pelfe Hall.

"But I mean, has anything come back, you know, Armin? Anything from Meinfield, f'rinstance? Did Dillotant receive your request at all? It seems so long since our last conversation about the file. It looks like my dossier must be complete, but I want to say that I will be happy to furnish any further materials you may require...."

Fishbane cut short the babble. "We've got everything, Myron," he intoned, "everything we need. There's nothing more—except you go right on doing your work. Just do your work, Myron, and do it with dignity. Everything will take care of itself in due course."

This little schmuck, here, now! Not an inkling of what was...well, appropriate. No tact or people skills at all. Worse than Benny who married Reva's daughter Ida and settled into a career of mooching and sponging. Fishbane taking in the twenty-foot radius from the shadowed spot of this dialogue could see no one, thank goodness, but two jocks, reversed baseball caps on choppy hair, same height, loping past Pelfe Hall with their Frisbee. Another world.

A world of coeds and frats where you lived the traditional campus dream: not Fishbane's own, which was to conquer WASP America but the campus that was home to the greatest guys ever, filling in the social skills that would far outclass anything they had memorized from *Cliff's Notes*. And the girls in angora sweaters, barretted blond pageboys, lipstick, carrying those little boxy makeup bags that held everything they needed for a dirty weekend, were no more... those headlight boobs... now THAT, he reflected, was once—and not so long ago either—the endpoint of a young man's quest for...himself.

But this Wiener is still here! And he always catches you alone; no one but us two Bronxites. Wasn't it enough that he and Graziella had actually made the time to go eat that chicken dinner, that the child— Jason? Lisa? Matthew?—acted up the whole evening, that there was (naturally) no one else there to talk to, that they had to dance around The Topic for three hours, but no, here he was getting hijacked by Wiener on a perfectly jelled bright-blue and gold morning.

It came to Fishbane of a sudden that what was wrong with Wiener was that he just didn't stand for anything, that he had no constituency, didn't have the guts to take sides. In fact, he was just the kind of jerk who could get identified with the wrong party and not even know it. You could belong to no one like Fishbane, and seem to belong to everyone. Or you could belong to no one like Wiener, and no one would want to claim you.

How had Myron ever gotten into Redfern at all? By slipping between the cracks into the Assistant Professorial rank and file of an austerely divided Department, with Fishbane in Marrakesh at a conference. The real culprit, as everyone knew, was the Alan and Sharon Sakulin Professor, genial and inscrutable Palter Van Geyst, who'd shrugged Myron right into position as a fill-in.

Still there! The guy virtually stank of fear. Up close you could hear him making a popping noise now, like the "plup" of a baby sucking milk.

"So, how's the book coming, Myron?"

It was none of Wiener's business whose letters of recommendation the Department (Committee on Appointment and Tenure) had actually solicited for the file, or whether answers had come, or what they said. The very outrage of expecting him to flout confidentiality! The effrontery.

"Fine, just fine, Armin. I've been on a roll, actually." Myron fixed his eyes at Fishbane's belt buckle, frightened of his controlled power. "And the Fielding Letters will make my book unique, more than just another 'contribution'."

This was the last hurdle on the way to tenure. The Letters would yield the book Fishbane seemed to want from him; it was just a matter of more time. If only Matthew slept through the night, if only he could get a fellowship at the new Center already in the works, nothing would stop the Fielding Letters from turning into a book that would completely revolutionize Fielding Studies.

Only seconds, and Myron Wiener's conference time was up.

"See ya, Myron," The Harvardian Bronx baritone receded toward Pelfe Hall. Fishbane made sure Wiener clearly saw him bound up the ten steps; he even gave a jaunty little wave. But there would be no letters, no inquiries, no answers, no file—or at least, nothing but dummy letters in a mass of worthless paperwork. Redfern still had plenty of people to see to that, budget crunch or no. At this moment, Fishbane's affection for the process closely approached romantic love.

He fondly watched Myron trot home, diminishing as if into some black hole. Then his dapper arms threw open the heavy doors and held an empty embrace as the doors thwupped closed behind him.

The "meeting specialists" were the first to arrive, the ones who had elevated meetings to an art form. Today they were really in business. The specialists clutched party favors consisting of Fishbane's agenda stapled to copies of memos.

The precious ten minutes before meetings began provided a rare occasion for assistant professors to attempt the staging of accidental meetings with the senior members. Since the little warren of rooms and anterooms that embraced Fishbane's office was intimate and self-contained, you could never see who was coming until they were almost on the spot, seeming to leap out of some doorway you hadn't cased.

It was part of the junior faculty game to make sure you never stood alone, so nervous little bouquets of strivers would form, only to reform around any senior member who turned up early, everyone preening with frantic unobtrusiveness. The entrenched sycophancy at the heart of these occasions was always overlaid by scrupulous egalitarian manners. For assistant profs this requirement meant working extra hard at being casual; obsequious camaraderie was an everyday paradox, a tightrope they trod without a net.

The boyish blue eyes of Tony Banter still avoided LuAnn Rossiter's when they met. Even though she would hail him with a cheery "Hah theah," waving and grinning, he couldn't get past "hello LuAnn" without wishing he could turn female just for a second. The right kind, of course

Tony, a savvy upper class Brit turned lower class, had nothing to worry about. His lightish hair curled into a cute cowlick. His build was slight but not puny. His smile could look shy or mischievously bold as the occasion demanded. The tried-and-true outfit, a double-vented tweed sport coat and a regimental tie in clashing colors, complemented his faux-naïve persona. His flair for moronic conversation would eventually sail Tony through the professorial ranks right into the arms of the Dredd Manikin Chair. Right now, though, the Comp Lit rabbit warren in Pelfe Hall was still

Versailles' Gallery of Mirrors to him, a setting for complex intrigues. Caution ruled.

Half turning, Tony saw Mumtaz arrive with Chris Hargreaves, his fraternal twin. The two set each other off perfectly. Chris had a state-subsidized education, so he caught on like wildfire as a tame beast of the snowballing Oxford Left. Where they came together was the hospitable terrain of political correctness. Banter had been raised on foppish Rococo art, so he became expert in Gender Studies. While Hargreaves picked up the Oxford specialty of impersonating an Angry Young Brit, dressed up in his Yorkshire dialect, growling greybeard, moth-eaten sweater, Leftist clichés. Trolling for new horizons, Chris had decided he could get richer promoting socialism.

Both were held in awe for being British. Since no one around them had a handle on the minute social distinctions observed among Englishmen on their own turf, they cheerfully exploited their bookended relationship for mutual benefit, each backing the other in a silent duet whose notes they alone could read.

Angry postcolonial Mumtaz represented the British Chickens Coming Home to Roost, and accordingly rated a supporting role with Tony and Chris, who had no reason to fear her as they did LuAnn. Now the three formed a whispering bouquet outside Fishbane's office door.

Bonza Leier (Video Studies) lollops in hugging a clipboard, her yellow Afro properly standing on end, a chain heavily loaded with keys dangling from the elastic waistband of her pull-ons. She and Mumtaz fall into a paroxysm of embraces and giggles, like reunited lovers. "It's practically eleven, did Armin really want us to be on TIME?"

"You KNOW Armin," Tony Banter grumbles, "he's got us all lined up here just to man—I mean, mind the store, so he can decide everything without us." He smiles the smile of a former Head Prefect and brushes the lock of blond hair out of his left eye.

"Tony, you incorrigible ingrate," LuAnn Rossiter lays a hand on his shoulder, causing a tremor. "Ahmin is the only chairpusson who INSISTS on havin' the whole depahtment come to meet'ns an' express theah views."

Tony swings into his act. "Ever heard the one about the student demonstration that turned out to be for a course?"

"No-oh!" LuAnn is caught a little off guard. "Whatevah–"

"That is absolutely correct," Maxime-Etienne Lamamba stands before them, a natty little figure in that day's dress-up, a fiercely tailored dark blue suit, starched white shirt and lustrous silk tie with a pin shaped like a boomerang. Maxime-Etienne's eyes are completely concealed today by cat-shaped frames that reflect whatever you want to see. "There is now such a sing at Redfern. My own innovation."

"Maxime-ETIENNE!" Everyone always pronounced his name in explosive French. "That's absolutely priceless! From the horse's mouth! What next! Take me along next time! On to Gorellick!! Down with the Huns!"

"There is nossing to laugh at in ze practice of individual responsibility," Lamamba reproached them, "or in strategic radical action. Ze students here, filled with a prejudice zat zey can learn somesing weezout paying for it, ha! Learning is supposed to come by magic though empty language, from me to zemm—but it is not so simple. I am fighting zeir stupide belief in language. What can it communicate anymore? As I 'ave said before—'ow many times!—reading is nosseeng but a technologie of control. NO more language mania, NO more tyranny of ze book!" Applause from Tony and Chris.

"Down with the book!" shouted Bonza. She held up her hands in mock embarrassment as Knox Lydgate showed up and took a seat. A little chill went through the group. Knox was known to have accepted the incentive of a lump sum payment from the Administration in exchange for early retirement. Knox carried with him into the seminar room a leathery feel of books, and was about as welcome there as the Ghost of Christmas Past.

"Zere is too much to do again," Maxime-Etienne complained, "I 'aven't seen my petit ami for one entire week ."

Chris Hargreaves had outed him from the gay closet only months ago at a Tell-All. At first he'd put up a certain resistance. "Why should I have to tell of ziss, which no one reproaches me of now, when I have, profoundly, no word to tell it? I favor discretion, it is all."

But Tell-Alls brought rewards of prestige and privilege to all who contracted to open up, share, speak out. And Maxime-Etienne had been hailed since his outing as an "insurgent" among the profs. The baptism by talk had loosened his tongue for good, and he was now a fount of intimate confessions.

They'd start the Tell-Alls with everyone linking arms, holding them up as in a mass game of London Bridge, swaying back and forth to the humming of the Tell-All song. A session could feature, for example, a student who had been assaulted by an alien,—"So now whenever I get up in the morning I just wanna SHOOT myself!"—or one who had used a word from the Index of Forbidden Terms, or even a prof who had suddenly glimpsed the light of Value-Free thinking, say, after a memory loss. At one Tell-All a student underwent "rebirth" in the arms of Hargreaves, who cried out, "It's okay! Mummy's here!"

"A worse shitload all the time," Hargreaves sighed now. "No end in sight for the worker."

The junior members arranged themselves in three sides of a rectangle at the seminar table, leaving the places near the head for the tenured faculty. Mona Blessing, the department's Head Executive Administrative Assistant, materialized, unnoticed, with her trusty shorthand pad.

Mona had recently celebrated her thirtieth anniversary with Redfern, and there now hung above her desk Chavadze's smiling photo with his signature and the salutation, "Congratulations To Ramona." How could the President have known that no one, not even her mother, ever called her by that name? It was the personal touch that counted, compensating as she kept it in her field of vision for the day-in-day-out solitude of the Comp Lit office block.

"Okay, everyone," Fishbane's voice surprised no one, it was more the fresh scent of the outdoors he brought with him, as he bustled in preemptively. "I do apologize for my lateness. Back in a twink."

He ducked into the adjoining men's room to allow Ricci and Van Geyst their concertmaster-and-conductor entrances. First Ricci thrust his way in past an invisible adversary, belly first, then a brownish Van Geyst was suddenly visible at the long seminar table.

A look of special concern played about the Tefflahn Professor's soulful eyes. In addition, a raised TV stand no one had seen before loomed at everyone above his chair.

He remained standing with his head bowed. "I have to tell you of a tragedy, if you will, that took place last night on our campus. Selena Fenn, formerly a Comp Lit concentrator, died under mysterious circumstances in the Underground University."

"We will have to compose an official statement." Ricci pursed his fleshy lips. His neck overflowed its starched white collar. "There will also be police interviews... no doubt."

"Bu...but we 'ad nozzing to do wiz it," Lamamba protested, an attack of the sulks coming on. "Who, but who, may have been engaged in somesing like zees, of our department? Ha! I can imagine some brutish officer concluding immediately zat it must have to do wiz zat outcast of a black professor."

"Come on, Maxime-Etienne; you know that you are one of our most valued colleagues. I'll just get to the point, if you will, so that we can go right on from here to the rest of our agenda. A very demanding one."

Ricci puffed his lips at LuAnn. "There was, if I am correct, a dissidence between signorina Fenn and your FAM. Per'aps something financial."

"Whah, Berto! Selena had the raht to change majors if she felt like it. Ah hardly knew her. Anyhow, she was a loyal FAM."

"No she was not," Ricci persisted. "She told to everyone that FAM no longer 'ad her telephone—no, that she 'ad got their number."

"It would not be a bad thing for your FAM to increase its financial position through a little in'eritance." Maxime-Etienne again, from outfield.

'Do you dare to implah... that Ah, an' mah colleagues...'"

"Do not be absurd. I speak no more than the truth. The Generale made it plain before now that the university was the next beneficiary after 'er. There will be contestations, that is all."

Van Geyst favored LuAnn and Ricci alternately with his attention as if he had to choose between two dubious objects in a shop. Then his voice from the grave etched itself against the air. "I heard that Miss Fenn came to see me once at my office but I was not in."

"Sita, you knew her, didn't you?" Armin persisted. Then he noticed the extra dark satellites outlining her eyes, and moved on.

"LuAnn?"

"Whah hardly, Awmin." But Selena's last words—the offensiveness of it all!—had embedded itself in her guts. "Y'know why I never have to be scared of people like you, Professor Rossiter? The reason is money. And you know it, and that really bugs you. Of course you want in...you and the others in that phony FAM thing, trying to look like you're for women and independence and free choice...when all you want really is room to grow more clones of yourself. Those fake courses you teach, those victim sessions make me sick....Wanna know who's really pro-woman around here? Professor McFarquhar, in History." LuAnn flushed with anger, just remembering it. "Or my friend Hilary Slocombe. I...I can't believe I talked like that to a professor. But you're ...you should be kept away by force from anyone who's seen less of the world than I have!"

LuAnn brightened. That WAS all she'd ever see of the world, but FAM would be alive and well for a very long time to come.

"Bonza? Palter? Anyone?" Fishbane appealed. They shifted in their chairs, studied their agendas. Palter Van Geyst's eyes trained themselves on the clouded picture window.

"Well, we're gonna expect to hear from the Eleventh Precinct. The investigator is a certain Simon.... Blank, as it were." A pause for giggles. "He'll want to hear from her teachers and friends."

"Ah, certainement, but if this Selena was black, what zen?" Maxime-Etienne broke in. "It would be assume that she 'ad no friend. No ONE would interest themselves."

"Wot's the use, Maxime-Etienne?" Hargreaves growled. "Troy, troy again, they just don't get it. Syme thing every time, can't fight the system."

"Now, everyone. The next item on our agenda, please...There's a rumor of more ridiculous hiring cuts to come, right across the board."

"Except for FAM," a fearless Ricci put in, one last time. "They grow like the pumpkins in the field. These pumpkins also are needing money constantly."

Armin took it as a joke. "Shame on you, Berto. You know how hard the Administration has been on us lately. Never mind that we have the largest student enrollment by far; never mind that we selflessly offer ourselves, never mind that our scholarship is internationally praised to the skies—" Banter and Hargreaves caught one another's eye. "Gorellick keeps talking about beefing up the SCIENCE departments, and we know what THEY are." He paused again for the laugh track.

"Isn't that what Gorellick was, some kind of a scientist," someone asked, "Or Engineering?"

"Who remembers?"

"Economics, not engineering," said Knox Lydgate. "The right subject for a moneyman." (Seymour Gorellick had in fact taken his father's far-sighted advice: "Study Economy, Seamy. Someone will always need you.")

"Anyone here speak Carpatho-Slovak?" Tony Banter chirped. "We'll send you right to Gorellick for negotiations." So much for the savage "Hun".

"So far all Gorellick and the Bear Hug seem to want from us is our new hours for next term," said Fishbane. "So I've put it first on our agenda: decide now what teaching hours we want."

"Ah nevah go home anymoah," LuAnn lifted off. "If it isn't the Womancentah it's a committee meet'n, what's moah I've got my ovahload, bringin' it to moah than fahve ahs. Ah manage, but what I ah'd like to ask at this time, Awmin, is some relief as to the ahs. Ah get heah by eleven, that's fahn, but ah real-ly need to be home bah two. That way my office ah can be Thursday from one to two..."

"Eleven to two are the most coveted hours, LuAnn." Fishbane whiffled his fingers through his silvery coiffure. "I've had the same request—if you will—from just about everyone in this department. That rather affects the total picture."

"I do not insiste," Maxime-Etienne said, "but you are of course aware, Armin, of ze fact zat my courses call for a considerable degree of activity outside the classroom, for which I do not charge ze Department. It would be only right for me to share ze eleven-to-two hours."

It was quickly determined that LuAnn and Maxime-Etienne would team-teach the same course, which meant cutting the hours of each by half. Next year the privilege would rotate to another twosome. Fishbane whewed and went on with the agenda.

"As you know, we need to invite a new Special Guest Lecturer for this year. You all remember how we scored last year with Fifi LaGrange. Can we top that?"

"Strippers are a tough act to follow," Knox Lydgate chuckled, reminiscing.

"EX-strippahs," corrected LuAnn. "Let's just open this up and ask for names."

"What about Michael Jackson? His sister went to Redfern."

"Too expensive. I tried to approach Cosby," Fishbane admitted, "but it's no go."

"Let's get Aldrich Provender," suggested Lydgate. "Aldo would always interest everyone. A great storyteller."

"Too academic," snapped Fishbane.

"If we really made it worth her whahl," LuAnn said, "Megan Mehan would speak on witchcraft. Or Aviva Har Shalom on The Madonna Perplex. I heard it at the MLA, she was incredible."

"Har-Shalom is very dogmatic," said Mumtaz. "An unreconstructed nationalist and for my money, a colonialist."

LuAnn persisted. "Susan Schlimazzel. This year's Codependency Survivor Prize. IF weah lucky."

"A panel discussion: The Panoramic Palter Van Geyst," suggested Maxime-Etienne Lamamba. Simpering at Palter. "I'ave consult Guillaume Mastroianni already, to settle the problem of whiteness...it is all right if only for once." Palter shrank even further into anonymity.

"Our poet, Abu-Badder..."

"We already have a poet here right now," the Tefflahn Professor reminded them severely, "Garsevan Yashvili. We'll have to tackle this at some future date." He had already slotted in an old pal from Princeton for the Lecture, a chairman who'd manufactured the phony offer that had allowed Fishbane to extort the Tefflahn from Gorellick, and there was less time than usual for appearances.

"I would turn now to a matter that is one which is unusually grave. I can't tell you all how much... real pain this is causing me."

"Myron?" murmured Sita Amanpuri. "Perhaps it concerns Myron."

"At this time, I'm going to show you a tape. I would hope everyone gives it his or her fullest attention, if you will."

All eyes now went up to the hovering TV set, and the mood switched to high expectation.

"I'll explain. It's a tape of Myron teaching, made by a couple of the Media and Massage kids."

"Did he KNOW?" Tony giggled.

"Armin," said Knox Lydgate. "I must remind you that we made it an absolute regulation not to violate academic freedom by visiting classes."

"Well, we didn't visit, did we?" The assistant professors wriggled in their chairs, rediscovering inner space. "This is the only discreet, tactful means, if you will, that we could think of to make a realistic assessment of what Myron is doing with his time."

Lydgate stood up tall, his eyes tearing slightly under the specs. He tugged at his knitted wool tie.

"I must protest. In my forty years on this campus I have never heard of such a thing. It may be my last month here, but your—unprincipled—action calls for nothing less than—an honest attack."

Knox pressed his thin lips together like a child refusing his oatmeal.

"I find it difficult, if you will," Fishbane went on the offensive, "I find it difficult to take an attack by Knox very seriously. Why not save it for retirement, Knox, give you something to do. Write in."

Lydgate got up stiffly and left the room, Fishbane raising his eyebrows in mock surprise.

"Who wants to see the tape now?" Fishbane grinned.

"We all do, of course," said Tony Banter. "Silly Armin."

"It's only our duty."

"Run it, Armin."

Fishbane turned the invalid table so that the TV set eyed everyone about equally. He inserted a tape into the VCR below. The Comp Lits saw a light-grey screen. Then came wild zigzags followed by snow and accompanied by the introductory quacking of empty tape. The Department was taken with out-of-school giggles.

"Sounds just like Myron," Tony quipped.

"But where's the picture?"

Myron Wiener appeared in pinched full face, staring past his colleagues. His little figure was arched over a lectern much too high for him, so that only his round cheeks showed on either side as he stood on tiptoe.

"We know of texts that are pregnant with meaning. But how do they give birth?" On the tape, voices erupted in laughter. "It lays an egg, Wiener," someone called out.

"What is the matter with this class?" Mumtaz spoke indignantly. "Wiener is quite right. He has framed the question perfectly."

"There's more, Mumtaz," Fishbane said, repressing mirth. "Keep watching."

Myron's tenor developed a tremolo "To even attempt an answer" ("Split infinitive," from Tony), "to even attempt an answer you have to look to the past. Every work of fiction inhabits a context that is determined by the race, the class, and the gender of the producer."

"Right on, Wiener," said a student voice.

"But I want to say," Myron swam into the waves, "that this is not the only past we need to seek. It is important, yes," he squeaked, "but we must always remember that aesthetic experience exists also for itself. The aesthetic experience of art is the only kind nothing else can replace...replace...replace..." The tape had jammed. Anyway, people were getting bored. Fishbane turned off the TV.

"Nuff said,"

"Is this turkey for real?" Chris Hargreaves shook his head in wonderment and caressed his beard, wondering whether Sita Amanpuri, opposite him, had black pubic hair to match her chignon.

"There's not much going for Myron on the plus side," Fishbane observed pleonastically. Reva's husband Benny...."Do we feel ready to consider alternative solutions? Do we want to? No. Must we? The sooner the better."

LuAnn tossed her head in the direction of the assistant professors, telegraphing to Fishbane, Not in front of the children!

"It's OK," Fishbane responded, palms up. "I want everyone to participate. None of us above any of the others, as it were. The floor is open."

For Ricci, VanGeyst, Lamamba, and Rossiter, neither food nor sex would have been half as much fun as this delicious foreplay.

But the assistant professors were terrified that someone might play the filthy trick of seeming to consult them. As one they unfocused their eyes, like people sitting on a New York bus with a raving maniac aboard. The tenured faculty nattered on.

"What about this file here, says she has five books?"

"Too academic."

"Dull—all historical."

"Someone not dull, not that Myron was really..."

"Someone more flexible."

"Maybe this guy here: the file looks promising. Works on Jane Austen..." Knox had come back, determined to see his last meeting through.

"Isn't he Mortmain's student? Mortmain's so old hat." Chris Hargreaves had been dinged more than once by Mortmain and was determined to take it out on his students. "Not someone of his."

"Here's a corker, would be just right for a little balance in the Department." Again Knox, squinting at a resumé. "A First in Classics from Oxford, already published a lot, rarin' to go. A little more historical than some of you. But Greek here, AND Latin. How often do you see that these days?" He brightened. "I really like this application."

He earned cool stares and lifted eyebrows.

"If you need to apply, let's face it," said Fishbane after a silence, "you don't deserve the job."

The tired regulation that you had to advertise all jobs publicly was getting as hoary as Knox. Everyone still in touch knew it only meant more paperwork, more files, more stuff for Mona Blessing to manipulate. They would have to advertise the job in professional newsletters—call for brilliance in teaching, commitment to research, leadership qualities, the usual—and then proceed to eliminate anyone who had them.

"Before we come to a vote— " the Tefflahn Professor turned to Van Geyst. "Palter, I think you actually quite liked Myron's deconstructions of Fielding."

Van Geyst's mild countenance regarded the group together, then each in turn. "Myron was full of good intentions," he said, so softly you had to lean forward to hear, "but to tell the truth, he isn't really very good."

"That's it, then," Fishbane said with obvious relief. "I won't ask for a show of hands. Confidentiality. Just write yes or no on a slip of paper. Mona will collect them and read us the result."

They passed the bits of paper to the secretary. Ms. Blessing, glad of this walk-on part, read out the results with an air of suspense. All but one said NO. She clipped the ballots together and put them in a manila folder.

"Image Enhancement will be grateful to us."

"And not a single procedural violation."

"When are you going to tell him, Armin?"

Fishbane paused, inhaled, and looked even more serious. "I would think it best," he said, "not to tell Myron at all, just yet. No, listen," he made a gesture of benediction, beating down imaginary protests, "he still has a whole semester of teaching before him. You all know perfectly well that it's going to take us longer than that to find just the right

person. Do we feel Myron should be replaced? Yes. Do we want someone around who's become—demoralized? Consider carefully..."

"Well... I can see there might be complications..."

"He has four courses to do..."

"It would be like firing a Teaching Assistant."

That clinched it. Telling Myron would have to happen at the very
last moment. But wasn't there some guideline or regulation about that,
too?

"Who's got time for petty beancounting?" said Fishbane.

The delay would also provide the Tefflahn Professor with the
time he needed to do what he really had to do.

The new project he had in mind wasn't really plagiarism—more
like borrowing. A borrower can make new combinations out of old shreds.
And Myron had something Fishbane needed to borrow—those Fielding
Letters. In fact, he had already developed a proprietary feeling for them.

It was all very well to blat it about that documents were dead, that
facts were what you wanted them to be, that history didn't matter. Palter
would understand the necessity for this appropriation despite his contempt for grubbers. This was actually a Palter-like idea in its way: a bold,
fast move that canceled petty objections out—a manifestation of pure will.
The beauty part was that Myron wouldn't be able to touch him with a finger, since Myron would always need Fishbane's help—his recommendations, his connections—in those ceaseless job searches. No one but Armin
even knew Myron had those Letters, and even if he went bonkers enough
to accuse Fishbane of theft, no one would ever believe him.

The meeting was declared officially adjourned with everyone
basking in the sun of concord. The younger members felt infused with a
holiday spirit and took off together for the Campus Can. Van Geyst went
missing, growing smaller and smaller like a genie stuffed back into the bottle.

Redfern's Culture Wars had already been showing signs of age,
but when spurred on by the promise of a Center, the debate swirling
around Old versus New firmed up into a serious turf war. It was rumored
that Chavadze and Gorellick might come to a decision about the Center

any day now.

The whopping Minamoto bequest jumpstarted the whole thing: Akira Minamoto, the silvery CEO of the conglomerate of the same name, had never forgotten over sixty-five years how Redfern U. had once been the only institution of higher learning in the Ivy League that would accept a stammering Japanese youth blighted with shyness. Minamoto misted over as he drafted the language of his will in his own words. The bequest was conceived in memory of respected teachers, most of all in grateful return for their gift to him of epic heroism, Italian painting, Shakespearean drama, German symphonies, French style—in short, for all that Redfern Humanities had done to develop his fine ear and connoisseur's eye.

How could he discriminate among the bounties he had brought back from Temperance to the succeeding years of work and duty? Akira Minamoto worked all his life like a Japanese but enjoyed like a Redfern alumnus, and since all the Humanities opened his eyes to the West, all would be included together in his gift. American Universities were enamoured of buildings, weren't they? So the language of Akira Minamoto's will stated broadly that five million dollars awaited the taking of "the Redfern departments of the Humanities, for the building of a Center."

But the news hit hot buttons Minamoto could not have even imagined. Comp Lit was the first department to hold his letter in its hand and lost no time hitting up Sakulin for matching money. Fishbane immediately went on the offensive to plan the future: endless conferences, lectures given by clones and cronies at places he needed to visit himself, the award of certain prizes that would eventually redound to Fishbane's credit.

But Comp Lit was divided within itself, or so it seemed, into rogue contenders like the Diversity Curriculum, FAM/BREW, and Radical Rereading. These were "interdisciplinary programs" which meant that they sucked in faculty and students from other departments for strength. The factions grew horizontally like ink blots so that the "inclusiveness" boasted by each one made it look more independent of the others.

Being "interdisciplinary" was in itself an idea with a respectable pedigree. It was driven by an impulse to grasp the relations between subjects, and to offer students a panoramic view of whole periods of culture. In short, the "interdisciplinary" urge was historical in a way. But for survival's sake it had to mate with its opposite, the drive to know nothing, to shake off history. The never-never land of the American dream.

This mating produced litters of lazy petulant children. The old Humanities emerged from it as stunned as sledgehammered chickens. And the monthly bills were growing faster than inflation. The Humanities were looking like a less and less affordable frill. Learning less felt like spending less. And a leaner, meaner life meant stricter counts of enrollments, the only way to monitor whether profs were earning their pay.

Since the '60s students had always been intrigued by professors whose style portrayed the institutions that fed them as dark, inhuman, Kafkaesque. Affluent middle-class kids liked nothing better than a snide snub to their elders. The Comp Lits were first to understand the profitable link to be forged between fantasies of rebellion and being permanently out to lunch. After all, why did almost all demos happen in the spring? Standards that had stood the test of time up to now could be discarded as irrelevant, for the greater good of survival. Budget cuts meant rationing the value of profs according to their body counts.

Not everyone took this lying down, though. Waste proliferated as before, though it took on a new spin. Good old pork was now called investment in the future. Fuddy old subjects got chucked or dressed up as professorial salaries ballooned. For the profs had learned enough of the oppression theory they were teaching to claim THEY were being exploited no matter how much they wrung from university administrators. In return, University Presidents became CEOs, administrators proliferated, flak-catchers multiplied, all claiming the kind of money you associate with big business while ceaselessly crying poor. Victim rhetoric had been a lesson well learned: if you applied it to the young they were often easily satisfied to go teacherless. Applied to their elders, it gave better bullshit to the pursuit of a purely commercial relationship.

Throughout the disturbances of the sixties and seventies Redfern could still float its paunchy Humanities departments on the assumption of a culture worth learning about because it belonged to a shared imagination. But as successive decades tightened that iron cinch, Redfern made "relevance" a practical mandate. Interdisciplinary came to mean non-disciplinary. Anything went as long as you could deliver enough warm, paying student bodies—with certain exceptions when the prof had an inside track.

Then a new wrinkle appeared in the social fabric: even body counts stopped mattering. The elders discovered that you could deal more efficiently without students. If it still looked bad not to have any, you could always rely on enough of them to take the easy road to an easy credential. The slogans of political correctness were easier to learn, so there would always be enough names on those printouts. But the beauty part was that the profs were cutting loose, by and for themselves. Like any industry that polices itself, this one was unchaining itself from its last responsibilities. First they taught students, then they taught each other. Now...who knows? Obligations were history. And new generations of academics had already trained themselves to think of "Lit" as detached from history, which was not difficult because they'd never had to learn much anyway.

The time and place were therefore just right for the deification of Palter Van Geyst and "theory." This strategy alone licensed people to do nothing and STILL PRETEND THEY WERE DOING SOMETHING. You could read not at all if you knew the right words to pronounce over books. The verbal gadgetry and mechanical moves of "theory" were even getting media attention for the first time ever—real celebrity! SO WHO NEEDED THE BOOKS?

Other professors.

Were the books too learned or difficult for students? Of course not, and they often displaced Homer, Austen, Dickinson, Shakespeare on the lists, contributing to the royalties of their living authors. Their main reason for existing, however, was that they reaffirmed group identity. Whether this meant conforming to Left or Right, Diversity or Monotony, to Sexist Pig or Feminist views, Humanities books totter down the assembly line without surcease because to this very day, candidates for lifetime jobs have to get rushed, then hazed, then initiated. But storage space is giving out, libraries vomiting old paper, so some new plan must be in the works that will probably have to be voice-activated. One step in that direction is the idea of a Center.

The bequest for a Humanities Center sharpened the conflict between the two real contenders, History and Comp Lit. There just was not going to be enough money for a high-rise building. This made simmering Redfern animosities boil over so high that the Historic Past and the Future could not hope to live together under one roof. Controlling the center meant you controlled the faculty positions that would fill it, that in a time of retrenchment you could bay for more —more staff, more conferences, more office equipment, more and more and more.

The Comp Lits did have their little vestigial differences but were farsightedly building bridges. A constipated civility was the order of the day. Radical Rereading and the Writing Program discovered their synergy. Maxime-Etienne Lamamba greeted Marvella Jilkes effusively on both her Redfern visits, sweeping aside his contempt for females. Ricci morosely complied with the prevailing spirit and stopped cutting LuAnn dead in the hall. Fishbane collaborated with LuAnn on the Tell-Alls, while Sita and Mumtaz learned to moot their crypto-nationalist-post-colonial disputes.

For all that History looked like a defiant stepchild, it was still a healthy one. Headed by Willona McFarquhar, the History Department lived in a cramped, though elegant, genuine Federal house that creaked all over. Its floors slanted. Students sat on classroom floors and spilled into the halls. Books were stored in broom closets; professors shared tiny offices in threes, edging their way around each other.

Willona showed up weekly for a sit-in at the offices of Chambers, Gorellick, and even Chavadze. You could hardly drive a black woman off your premises, but you could at last avoid answering her memos. Chambers would send word through Sypher, Garnix, Nill, and subdean of Values Clarification Marlayne Sorley that the Center was a "high-priority issue that would soon be determined." Gorellick would assure Willona via his deputies that the decision was "on the President's desk." From his stronghold about fifty yards from Willona's office, the President sent her formal letters telling her she was doing a great job and should be proud of her achievements.

In his last hours Akira Minamoto had remembered a smile for Redfern and its spirit of harmony. But the outcome of his generosity so far was an exacerbation of hatred. The crocodile-smiles of old turned into sneers. People who had once been dead scared of causing offense now made snooty faces at each other. The History Department had cheered for the new President, Chavadze, an historian by trade, wasn't he? But he was already turning sour in a puddle of evasions and empty pronouncements.

He had laid down the line of least resistance, which Comp Lit quickly translated into one of the academic boondoggles they had come to specialize in: the New List, mother of the New Curriculum.

The Department took the lead in squelching the Great Books at Redfern.

"People, people. Let's PLEASE come to order. We've only got a few more minutes left, and there are just five books on the Reading List."

"Come, Armin. We 'ave accomplish an enormous sing. Eliminating fifteen books from the liste."

"Ah think we've done wondahs. Now Ahmin, heah's what we've got so fah: we turned down Vuhgil, Homah, Dantee, the Bahble, Dideroh, Vol-tayah, Play-to, Ass-tottle, Mon-tayne, Milton, Suh-VAN - tees, Oona-moono, Proost, Fawkner, an' Man..."

"Especially Man."

"All in three hours, too. By the way, you're a pet for letting Chris and me sit in, Armin—untenured and all."

"Oh, now look, you're part of us in all but name. A matter of a few months. Tony, let's have you read out what we've got on the list."

"Mm, well. SHAKESPEARE AND THE BLANK PAGE, by LuAnn Rossiter. Hold the applause, please. LIVERPOOL LAD, Chris Hargreaves. Maxime-Etienne Lamamba, FAITES VOS JEUX: Gay Perspectives on the Black Square. Bonza Leier, Video Studies: O CAMERA, O VOYEUR. And last but never least, IN A SHEEP'S EYE by Mumtaz Mahmoud, to appear when it's finished. Our backup, by unanimous vote, will be YOUR DISEASE IS MY DELIGHT. Okay?"

"Shakespeare. I am not entirely convinced that he should appear on a list that has multicultural aspirations."

"LuAnn and I thought about that, Sita. We thought about that. And we decided that the general principle sometimes has to be overruled by the special case. And LuAnn severely indicts Shakespeare not only for rampant sexism but for writing in a language no twentieth-century non-specialist can understand. So..."

"It isn't as if Shakespeah's PLAYS stayed on the list. Oh, um, Sita: Ah was gonna mention it, but all this work—Ah haven't done that recommendation for travel money yet, jus' need a tad moah time."

"I must raise another question. It has come to my attention that students are taking courses Outside the Department because they want to read some of our Erased Books. They say they have no time to do both."

"But ouah Rule, Sita. No Outside Courses."

"Except Bonza's Film Studies. Anyway, the English Department picks those people up; they've got that course called The Wrong Way to Write a Novel. It's got a lot of our Cancelled Authors. Like Tolstoy. Eliot...Dickens."

"Win some, lose some. Well, if you all approve I feel entirely comfortable with this Ph.D. Reading List. As a basic reference source— terse and to the point. This gives our grad students the chance to stay on top of their teaching without getting overloaded with petty obligations. Innovative, pathbreaking. We've exploded the status of those musty no-impact masterpieces, haven't we? Now, as far as the Index of Forbidden Terms... our new additions, "beauty," "truth," "goodness." Yes? Then let's move on to the schedule of this term's Tell-Alls."

"I hear they're a scrumptious turn-on."

"Tony, shame on you."

"Do we AWL hafta be theah?"

"No, no. Certainly not. Laurie Lee, Emil and Yat Pang have already split most of them up among themselves. Given has notified me that he will not be present. Planning for the Diversity meetings, you know."

"We COULD get off our arse and have an 'eart-to-'eart wi' Barker about Marvella. She listens to him... Maybe he could persuade her to make a quicker decision."

"Mm well, right, Chris. Very true. Marvella should make up her mind VERY SOON about the Rumpe Professorship. There's still time for Given to put in another word for us, though. Good thinking, Chris... now if there's no unfinished business, will someone move to adjourn?"

Launching the New Curriculum had been as easy as that.

Police Business

Just as Simon Blank had feared, the heat was on from Chief Killifer. The Temperance sky still showed only dark windows waiting for dawn.

"It's decided, then, Chief? Are they certain she was strangled?" Simon gained a few seconds, sat up in bed.

"The mayor's office has made its involvement clear. These people are not like everyone else. I'm being straight with you. We've done everything we can so that the story doesn't hit the news."

"How can I work without showing myself, sir? Sooner or later it's gotta come out that we're looking for a strangler on the Redfern campus. I've gotta have help. I'll be talking to a lot of people. I can't see any way out."

"Just be a Blank, Simon. I mean it."

In the dark, Simon pulled on underwear, correct shirt, dark suit. He turned on the black and white set, expecting the weather forecast.

"We bring you this morning a story from the heart of Temperance," chirped the local newswoman, her pleasant features looking slightly asymmetrical between the inverted commas of blond hair. "Louis Gonsalves WILL walk again. In a tribute to the people of Temperance who saved their pennies to pay his insurance, Louis stated that these are the greatest folks in the world and we live in the greatest city." Simon went on splashing himself with cold water to get his memory back. He had dropped a few coins into a Gonsalves jar only yesterday morning. The weather was coming on, but: "We interrupt this broadcast to bring you a news flash straight from the Eleventh Precinct. Selena

Fenn, a twenty-year old senior at Redfern University, was strangled to death last night on the Redfern campus. According to sources close to the tragedy this was a sex-related killing... We have not been able to reach the victim's next of kin, her grandfather, General Ethan Fenn, who is a prominent Temperance citizen. Now this!" A commercial for over-the-counter stimulants came on, with a smiling woman who looked a lot like the newscaster.

Simon was thrown into a zinging headache. He lurched back into the bathroom and switched on the bar of fluorescent light to look for aspirins. The set was still on, the No-Som commercial now giving way to a plug for the 7 p.m. network show, More Gore. He heard a man's voice; unlike the woman's it did not carry a smile.

"Rock Video Stars for Political Reform" had run into trouble with the President's communications advisers. "Several are under investigation by the Internal Revenue Service, but now the inquiry will be extended...." The throbbing in Simon's head turned into a dull computer clack. The phone rang again like an alarm you couldn't stop.

"Blank, I've got no more time for you. You can't discover how this unsubstantiated story made the news, you can't stop it from going national, at least now you can goddam go out and find out who did it."

"We were on land lines, Chief, no one could monitor our transmissions."

"You got a sex murder here, Simon. Wrap it up and get it over with, fast and neat. You got a good man with you; Granita has the experience you want. I don't want one more person calling me about this—slipshod, goddam lazy work. Do it, Simon." The click of the phone sounded like an in-flight ear pop.

The way to the morgue was through the emergency room at County General. As he went through, Keith could hear antiphonal moans and whimpers against a noisy background that sounded to him like a disgruntled theater audience. He looked neither right nor left, following arrows scrupulously, seeing nothing but one orderly with a mop and three Hispanic women lined up unexpectedly in a narrow corridor on hard chairs, saying nothing. He took the special elevator, and for the rest was guided entirely by a relentless stench of formaldehyde.

"They started about an hour ago," the man at the desk told them, "you're late."

"That's not what we were told," Keith said stiffly.

The walls and the floor of the tiled room were spattered with blood—carelessly, Keith thought, in complete neglect of death's dignity. A doctor in immaculate whites worked without looking up at them. Beside him stood an assistant in a white jacket over suit and tie, taking pictures.

As the policemen noted the doctor's quick, neat movements, Keith's fastidious mind battled with last night's version of the dream of the Guard Dog—always a female, pursuing Keith through viscous red tunnels. At times he would awaken in a state of astonishment with no recollection of the cause, but now the atmosphere of the dream ambushed him again with quaking fear. The whole sequence of events, from Sita Amanpuri's repugnant advances to this very moment, threatened the very dissolution of his being.

"Maybe you can tell me," said Dr. Miles, "why the pressure on this case. The Mayor and the Chief of Police both call me and say get it done pronto. I said okay ten times. Almost everything here is obvious. Look," he tapped the body impatiently. "These bruises on the neck, this separation of the blood into separate hemoglobin products just where the bruises are, mean strangulation."

"Is there any sign of a struggle?" Simon asked.

"Certainly. These abrasions." Dr. Miles pointed deliberately at the jagged rough areas on top of which congealed blood was still clearly visible: one at a time, on an arm, over a rib, a leg. "And the face."

The two raised their eyes by force to Selena's terrible bared teeth. Keith Chambers tucked in his gut and swallowed.

"What about the sex?" Simon asked.

"That's what's still kind of mysterious. You will note that, um, there has been lubrication of the external vaginal labia."

"You dare—" Keith began, then stopped.

"What you're saying is," Granita put in, "that she was liking it."

The doctor looked embarrassed. "Roughly—probably."

"But you said that she was fighting him." Granita was puzzled.

"There is uncertainty," the doctor answered evenly, "concerning the time factor. These abrasions occurred just before the girl's death. You can tell that from the swelling of affected areas. If death occurs soon after an injury, blood flow stops, so you get only limited swelling, or even none. In this case you can see a good deal. But the sperm," meeting Keith's glare evenly, "is old. They're having some trouble analyzing it at the lab. It's gone with all the usual fluids but had to be kind of scraped off."

Simon asked. "Does that imply we could be talking about two separate actions—a sex act and a killing—that took place, that is, with elapsed time between them?"

"It does. This is not going to make your work easier. What I'm driving at is this: your Casanova and your murderer don't have to be the same person, though they could be. You get a lot of women here who have been gang-raped, then killed. The whole sequence took maybe twenty minutes. Enough to make identification a problem, even with DNA analysis."

The doctor wiped his hands energetically and took in the threesome through his magnifying spectacles. "Mr. Chambers, I respect your feelings in this matter. I want you to know that I've done nothing to assist the news people; we threw some out of here already. Just the usual morgue hounds. But something or someone concerned in this case has gotten past the proprieties. I work right next door to the pathology lab, but that doesn't entitle me to target their every move. Still, I can tell they've been able to work faster than me."

A flash from the assistant's camera made him and Granita blink. The doctor placed Selena's liver in another steel tray and went on without looking up. "Everything makes it look as if the deceased was having consensual sex with a person who strangled her afterward."

The pathology lab next door would always remind Simon of the Underground University—same fluorescent lighting, same clanging door, though the instruments gleaming in their rows gave it a special character. They looked for the white coat that had hunched over the body last night, but the technician on duty was a heavyset female who did not fit the coat.

"All we can do," she said, wasting no time after introductions, "all we can do is conjecture about the time of ejaculation. Dr. Miles has less contact with us than you might expect, but it looks like the ejaculation and the injuries to the body cannot be medically related according to what we have. I had the blood tested for alcohol. The results were negative. The urine screen for drugs—cocaine, morphine, marijuana, amphetamine, and PCP—was negative."

She turned away, busied herself with a microscope. As far as she was concerned, they were gone.

With Granita driving, the brown unmarked car plodded through sluggish Temperance traffic. Granita felt tethered. How long was it since anything had happened that called for speeding with your siren on? The campus streets seemed more meanly narrow than usual.

Simon was reading Selena's pocket agenda out loud. "You'd think she did nothing at this college but crash for the night. Look who she spends her time with: Beane Jeffreys, he's that old fag designer. Mucky Muck, the punk who gets his picture taken in underpants. Party at Malvina Fredrix."

They pulled up at Blight House. Simon blocked the path of a Chinese Physics student rushing to class who turned out to be Hilary and Selena's neighbor.

The door had no name on it. A rangy girl answered, who looked as if she had never had a night's sleep. She had an unruly mane of dark hair that made it hard to see her face, but when she pushed it aside Simon was surprised to think it a handsome face despite its sullenness. She stepped aside from the barely open door to let them in and sat down heavily at her end of the oversized bed.

The room had almost no other furniture. On the wall opposite, a Redfern calendar (OUR PRODUCT IS EXCELLENCE) and two enlarged photographs side by side. One displayed Selena in a long white dress leaning affectionately against the side of an old gent in full General's uniform. The other, less clear in outline, was a frontal view of Hilary's "Victory" statue in an intermediate phase. A long narrow desktop showed an array of student paraphernalia, loose-leaf books, stacks of index cards, a computer with keyboard and mouse neatly stored, everything in perfect order. They had made optimum use of their cramped space. The policemen glanced, shamefaced, at the single bed with its huge pillows and oversized quilts. Then Simon's eyes moved to Hilary.

She had pulled a crocheted afghan around her shoulders. Elbows braced against her waist, clenched fists, mouth closed. She stared before her at something nameless, waiting for something she could stand hearing. Fear thrilled through her, to the very scalp.

"Hilary Slocombe?" Granita broke the silence. "You're Selena Fenn's roommate, right?" A nod. "I'm Sergeant Granita and this is Lieutenant Blank. Hilary, we've got something you need to know. Your friend was murdered last night on campus, we hafta get your help."

Simon looked away. Leave it to Granita.

The scream started like the warning signal of a miniquake and opened up into the sort of bellow you get in Greek tragedy when the heroine hears the worst. The policemen had never heard anything quite like it, not even Granita last year, when he'd been stuck with reporting the Dionigi murders to Mrs. Dionigi. Phil began mentally running through pacification procedures.

At least this one didn't break out crying afterward.

"You must have been very...." Simon began.

"We loved each other," she said, "Selena was my whole life." She might have said instead my illusion, my nightmare. An almost palpable anger filled the room. Hilary's arms now tensed at her sides as she crouched in defiance of her grief.

Granita turned away, disgusted, to his own private world, and Simon took over.

"Miss Slocombe, as I told you, or hope I did, we are investigating the murder. We can't keep you out of our procedure but we can try not to waste time. Miss Slocombe, please... tell us anything that can help. Say, about what kind of person she was. Everyone who keeps quiet is an obstacle."

Hilary's voice seemed to come from the grave. "Not like anyone else. I can't talk about it."

"Is that her?" Simon asked, pointing to the picture of the sculpture in the making.

"She was much more beautiful. And she changed all the time. What's that saying about running with the hares? She could be so many different people. That was part of how hard it is to sculpt her. I'm supposed to exhibit this in June, it's nowhere near ready." Now Hilary's eyes filled with tears. "I was always learning something new about her. Sometimes I only found it out from the Style section. But she does a lot of work here too, takes it seriously and all, raises money. Nobody really knows her. I can't explain what I mean," her voice broke. "Leave me alone. You said she's gone, leave me alone."

My Moon Goddess. Inconstant Moon.

"Who did she spend her time with besides you?"

"Practically no one important. She went to class—pretty much, I guess." She would have to tone it down, keep her words casual, even.

"Same teachers all the time? Anyone a little weird?"

"She changed majors—this term, from Comp Lit to History, so the profs are different ones now. I thought she'd started with Comp Lit because they require hardly any work, and she was almost living a double life, here, New York, nightlife, daylife. You can imagine that the Comp Lit's., you'll get to talk to them—weren't too happy about the change. Selena has great connections." She smiled grimly at the thought of the professors, helplessly bowing obeisance before Selena's friends. "There were people in New York, she stayed in touch with some people in Europe. But here, she was mostly with me." It was still oddly pleasurable to think this, to say it.

"Who else around here knows her well?"

"No one, I said so. NO ONE. Not that they didn't try. The others in this entryway happen to be mostly science people, that means Asian, and it means keeping themselves to the science side of the campus. They work all the time, don't even say hello when you see them. We thought it might be more private living in Blight House. But still you can't hide if you're someone like Selena. Oh God..." She stopped talking to grope for a tissue in the empty box on the bed, the reddened rims of her eyes elliptical as she looked down. It helped to keep on talking, keep the unbelievable at bay.

"It was really a joke how the Comp Lit professors courted her. They really wanted her to help move their PR machine. Because no one around here can bring themselves to admit that they know you're a blatant fake, they thought she was the same. Admitting someone is a fake might even call for an open challenge. It would lead to UNPLEASANT-NESS. Can't have that, 'specially when your bunch of fakes is a big-time money eater. You probably know already that Grampa Fenn is a big donor. That's the first thing they'd tell you here. And she was coming into a huge amount of money. Now it will all go to Redfern." Why can't I stop babbling? Anything, just not to understand, not to see.

"YOU look like you could use the money yourself," said Granita, feeling shocked and affronted by the dyke's outspoken admission of what she and Selena had been up to. Simon took up the questions.

"Miss Slocombe, I know you had nothing to gain financially from your friend's death. Did you, do you have any reason to think that maybe Selena had... other close friends beside you?"

"No one who could possibly count," she snapped. Again a hint of mirth in the deep-set dark eyes. "Once in a while, though, she'd go wild. At first I couldn't stand it. We'd have these enormous scenes—"

"Did YOU ever threaten her physically?"

"Don't be stupid... do you think I'd ever have to tell you? Anyhow, I loved her and I knew I always would. I'd have killed anyone who hurt her with my own hands." She folded them tightly in her lap, molders of clay and wielders of the hammer.

"Give me a name or two, Miss Slocombe. That may turn out to hurt them even more."

"You could never begin to imagine what we were to each other. We were like one person. For her to leave for a day was like ripping off a piece of me."

"That's your own business, you don't have to tell me that," Simon answered, mortified. "You said she changed sometimes. That she went wild."

"I thought of it like that because it was so different from her usual. Then I understood that it was her way of showing contempt, of exercising power." She tossed her hair behind her back again. "If it makes any difference to you, Selena loved the effect she had on people. Men didn't matter to her; she didn't even care who it was. She called it sex-slumming. You picked the most ridiculous man you could find—there's quite a selection around here too. Then you had sex with them, and they got really hooked on you. On her. She said it was just playing," the tears welled up again. "That shut ME up, anyway."

"Didn't this—sex slumming—make you jealous?"

"Not really. You should've heard the laughs we had about it. You should've—"

"You probably couldn't stand it." Simon's voice rose. "I'll bet she made you miserable enough. I can see where this would drive someone like you crazy." He felt unaccountably angry. "You could have strangled her yourself, just from being fed up."

She smiled as if correcting a child. "You don't have the slightest idea what we meant to each other... I'm sorry for you, stuck in the middle of this mess without a clue. But you're not going to profane the way we were together. And I'm not afraid of you. So get this: men didn't matter. It's the last thing they ever understand, just look at you now."

"SHE had fun with them, anyhow, didn't she? I guess she needed them around somehow. Look, you and I aren't going to be friends, but you'll want to do everything to cooperate with our investigation if you really cared about Selena. Right? Now who were those men?"

"There wasn't anyone trailing Selena these last few months. But she really found a humdinger on the faculty to sex-slum with. Professor Ricci, Berto Ricci! She used to sneak off with him slavering behind her into one of the underground university rooms where they kept things like boxes and files. We used to wonder when Mrs. Ricci would ever notice something had changed at home! But THEY probably never did it, ever."

"Did Selena Fenn and Ricci 'do it'? Why would a beautiful girl like that—" the mermaid hair, the torn adhesive black dress surfaced in his mind, "why—"

"I always thought of them as Beauty and the Beast. Why does anyone at all pick a beast, I ask you? To watch it beg and bark for what it wants. To have the pleasure of giving or withholding. Ricci was a great choice—in his way—because he's the ultimate raunch. A blob, an inkblot, the waste from a pasta dinner. Look into his face and you'll find nothing but want. He wants all the time; he stands for filthy appetite. And it all comes dressed in a starched shirt and dark suit, with a self-important smirk written on it. Ricci is a notorious lech even on this campus, where he's got enough competition to make it tough. But he seems to have been really soft on Selena. Most people were." A note of pride showed in her voice.

"Do you happen to know," Simon asked out of the blue, "what she was going to tell Professor McFarquhar? There was a note in her diary; they were going to have an interview in a couple of days. McFarquhar told me about some huge discovery Selena had made. Do you have any idea what it might be, Miss Slocombe?"

She sat down and concentrated. "She did tell me that she had a new subject for her honors thesis, and she'd just picked out McFarquhar as her adviser. 'This is going to break up Redfern,' she said. That was exactly what she said, 'break up Redfern'; I didn't ask how she meant it. Then she said, 'It's irresistible, darling. And it's important in another way, too. The History Department needs me. My honors thesis is going to make history.' But I don't know what it is, what she had, nothing."

Hilary fell silent, dug her nails into her chin and pressed her bent fingers to her lips, unmoving until they left.

🎓

"I'm out my depth," Granita voiced the main thing Simon knew about him. "There's no way, we can't get close. You take Chambers: all he wants to do is cover up for everyone. The dyke, what does SHE know? That spook Van Geyst sits there lookin' like he's gonna burst out laughin' but wouldn't bother. An' all the time it could be some crazy student."

Simon turned the car. "We need to talk to anyone who knows her. It looks like she didn't have any professors, just those Teaching Assistants mostly."

They confronted a harassed Chambers. "Where's the Complete Literature Building?"

Keith gave a self-deprecating smile, and a hint of cynicism played about his lips. "I'm rather a deficient guide this morning. To get to the Comp Lit side of Pelfe Hall, say you're coming from Blight House..." He drew them a precise diagram on a piece of graph paper. "Then you make a sharp right. It's the largest department in the humanities so you can't miss it. Take these new card keys. You'll descend three flights of stairs for the Graduate Assistant Offices. Do you carry flashlights?" he asked them. "It's quite a handy thing to have when you're down there."

"Mr. Chambers, we also need an interview with President Chavadze."

"Time is of the essence," Keith said sententiously. "President Chavadze has been advised of the urgency of this matter. I've been authorized to slot you in for two thirty this afternoon, even though there is a Trustees' Meeting, an Emergency meeting of the Oleaginus Rumpe Professor Selection Committee, an Admissions Crisis Meeting, and a Human Resources Settlement meeting. I'll be looking out for you then, gentlemen."

Keith breathed a sigh of relief and fixed his pale-blue gaze at the

Redfern diplomas that hung side by side on the opposite wall. One in Latin, for the B.A. The second newer and larger in its thin silver frame, for the Ph.D. They'd long ago stopped doing them in Latin.

"That Chambers bugs me more every minute," Granita confessed on the way to the underground campus.

"Everyone bugs you. Chambers is important; he's practically our only contact here, kind of a shadow President. And he doesn't need to be—persuaded—to spend time with us; he WANTS to keep an eye all the time."

"He's an old woman," said Granita. "He's like the Chief's wife. Prissy and neat. Proper and dignified." Granita's feet hurt. "Don't they have any more students in this college? Everyone you see works here."

"Well, we're gonna see some now, Phil. We're almost there." They had heard the steel door clang behind them. As their steps sounded on the empty concrete, Granita said, "This is a lot like Green Mansions or Flossy Mill—or any other jail. Except there, you hear guys shouting."

"I just hope there's someone home," said Simon. The softly sloping lawns of the quad were now at eye level. Otherwise you saw nothing through the gated windows but feet, just up to the ankles. Simon felt up to his waist in some dark viscous matter that had no temperature but made him cold. They turned another corner, then another, and found the door with its card set into a little rectangular slot: "Graduate Teaching Assistants, Comp Lit"

Everyone was home. The three inhabitants peered out at him through the vacillating light of their subterranean office. The room held four desks and chairs, a set of steel bookcases painted army green, a few slumping ranks of dog-eared paperbacks. There was an unframed poster, curling at the four corners, whose subject they could not decipher. A cold damp draft entered through unseen leaks in the wall.

"Can we help you?" The nasal tone came from a lanky woman in her late twenties with lackluster brownish curls. On the desk in front of her were three mountains of student papers. Her glance was bored and cold, and her whole being exuded a tired sense of duty.

"We're in the Grad Student office, right? This is Sergeant Granita, I'm Blank."

"You don't need to advertise that, Officer." This was a man's gravelly drawl. "I'm Given Barker," said the man, as if that was going to explain everything. He oozed contempt for everything and everyone. "This is Laurie Lee Talbot. And Emil Wahnsinn."

A thin guy about his height, wearing magnifying lenses, Emil shot out of the greenish dazzle and jerked a hand, fingers spread wide, at the policemen, as his head moved forward on his neck. Given Barker, eighth-year holder of a Diversity Training Fellowship, touched his reversed baseball cap in a mock salute. The biker shorts he wore were snug enough to outline the veins in muscular legs, and his biceps bulged significantly from the leather vest. A body builder for sure. It was a shock to the policemen to notice, when he stepped into a better light, that he had to be over forty-five.

"I'm helping plan the Diversity Curriculum," he said. "Laurie, coffee."

Laurie Lee Talbot was the unofficial Head Feminist of the T.A. section. She was supposed to be writing a Ph.D. thesis called PROSTI-TUTION AND THE SUBLIME. But teaching routinely consumed eighteen hours a week, draining her of energy and push. The prescription for her contact lenses grew stronger as her will to work trickled away and even the weekly schedule became harder to remember. This one was usu-ally off campus on Mondays, Tuesdays, and Fridays because he had to feed his dog; that one would forget to send the library their reserve book-list so she automatically did it herself, signing the professor's name. There was always the biweekly get-together of FAM when she could make it, to brighten things up. But the four-year Financial Aid cutoff, which applied to every grad student except Given Barker, was now only six months away.

"You making the coffee, Laurie Lee?" Given asked, and the Head Feminist busied herself around a wheezing little machine.

They had all heard and were taking it pretty calmly, as if the only thing they had in common with Selena was the basement. "You have already found somesing?" Emil demanded. "You have found the crimi-nal? brought him to the justice?"

"Not even close," Granita assured him.

A sinuous trail of smoke issued from Given Barker like a saved soul.

"Aren't you kinda old to be students?" Granita said.

"We are student TEACHERS." Laurie made a show of forbear-ance, waiting for this to sink in. No one Outside ever seemed to understand about university procedures—but that was sometimes nice, too, especially when they addressed her as Professor.

"You mean you teach, too?"

"We each do two courses of our own and then some sections of other courses. Except Given."

"What's a section? Did Selena Fenn have a course or a section with any of you?"

"Sections are when classes split up into discussion groups. All Comp Lit courses have discussion sections half of the week. There really aren't enough Graduate T.A.s to go around any more," she sighed, "so we have Undergraduate T.A.s also. It kind of frees up the professors for more important things."

"You're saying that these students end up teaching each other?"

"The students are a pleasure to teach," Laurie Lee said stiffly. She did not look pleasured. To make things worse, the Office of Students Teaching Students was threatening her with obsolescence.

"The kids get paid too, by any chance?" Granita asked.

"No they don't," Laurie Lee said, unsmiling. "There's one more T.A., Yat Pang Shih. But he's either teaching or going to the class he's taking on English as a Second Language. It meets every day."

"You're saying that this Yak is a teacher who's still learning to speak ENGLISH?"

Laurie Lee was thin but her printed shirt, in the body-hugging cut of twenty years ago, strained against her breasts and creased at the back. "He does much more than his share. And he's getting much easier to understand."

"Did you know Selena? Was she in your classes?"

"Practically all the Comp Lit students were," Laurie Lee said. "All I know is that she handed in her papers on time, or someone did it for her. I heard she was going to change her major to history."

"Did she tell you that?"

"Professor Rossiter did. She acted like it was my fault." Her voice showed a guarded bitterness. "She chewed Emil out about it too."

"Guess I'm next to be grilled," Given suddenly spoke up. "Now lemme jus' in-ter-cept one line of questioning I SOMEHOW have a feeling you might take. Listen VERY VERY carefully. No fewer than FOURTEEN people can tell you EXACTLY where Given Barker was

EVERY SECOND, understand? Above ground, fren', above ground for once." He jabbed suddenly at Granita's waistline. "Five to five twenty, call it first period, I'm hanging out waiting in the lobby of Blight House. I know, 'cause I remember you hangin' out right there an' made you right away. Finally at five forty sharp I take off, with Professor Maxime-Etienne Lamamba with whom I have important business on the Diversity Curriculum, but he has to make a very special appearance at that party. An' before you even... so much as try..."

"We'll be talking to everyone on this list, Mr. Barker. No need for any tantrums. Just the questions you would ask yourself."

"Black means you'd never have a chance to do it yourself." At this Laurie Lee felt a thrill course right through her scalp. "You better know what you're into, the two of you. Hey...you understand? That Selena was rea-l-ly bad. Ba-a-ad. Maybe not as bad as she thought, though."

"Was Selena in your class? Your section, anything?"

"Nope. Not ever. That's on the record. She was all signed up with Laurie Lee so's to give Laurie more students. Rossiter and Sita worked it out that way 'cause Laurie's in FAM."

"You ever have sex with her?" Granita asked.

"No such luck, Ossifers... Not ever. Course I'd've been perfect, black enough to spook all her racist watchers, an' still tame when necessary. But no, sorry to say. I never even got to do her a favor as an empty suit. So before you get around to Mirandizing me for murder one, show me some PO-lice restraint. Oh, we've come further than that, Mr. Barker, sir... s'now show me, how far HAVE we come? The second ANYTHING happens you come to ME, and did you ask me my OPINION, my FEELINGS about it?"

"What are they, Mr. Barker?"

"They are as follows, that you're a couple of blundering Keystone Kops tripping over your own huge feet, trying to turn this sad and dismal...tragedy...into a divisive, POLARIZING race incident..."

"You fuckin' unbelievable...."

"...and swearing at me, and doing what you can to frame innocent people as long as they're BLACK. One last thing. There is no way you can get from this side of the Underground Campus to the Admin side. Check it out by your clumsy selves. Not me, even. And certainly not Emil or

Laurie Lee. Bubbeye, Ossifers." Given smiled and waved, swaying lightly on his Nike hightops as Simon and Phil turned away without a word.

Mizz Marvella would really love this one.

The above ground portion of Pelfe Hall was hexagonal, with rounded corners to make it look like an ancient mausoleum. The external walls were granite; the inside lined with imitation marble. Three stories ran around an open balcony, so that if you sat on one of the ground floor benches that were set into the corners every sound was magnified by the height of the domed ceiling.

Simon and Phil noticed the Comp Lit bulletin board near the entrance, a mass of overlapping campus notices, lost-and-found appeals, offers of employment to prospective assistant professors from Alaskan and Taiwanese Universities, ads for rents and sublets. Some had been removed and stuffed into a big trash can nearby. Simon stopped to read a couple of colored-paper notices: one, elegantly printed in medievalistic script advertised an upcoming talk from a Gambian scholar ("The Semiotics of Corn: An Adventure in Cultural Studies"). The other had been hand lettered and mimeographed by a student organization: Students for No Bullshit (SNOB) promised an unforgettable event, to take place the following evening under student sponsorship—the one and only campus appearance of Carlotta DiSalvo, no introduction needed.

"Some bimbo? In a college?" Phil wondered how students got the money to sponsor shows.

Berto Ricci was waiting for them in his spacious office, which occupied almost the entire second floor of a Redfern mansion. Berto's walls were a maze of Renaissance reproductions, his desk littered with ornate bric-a-brac. Even his wastebasket was dressed in a repeating design of black and white Italian prints on which Cupids chased nymphs. From its own ornamental shelf, the head of Dante Alighieri wearing a bathing cap topped by a wreath of laurels stared grimly past them. Ricci's bookcases held rows of the sort of untouched gold-tooled leather bindings lawyers assemble in their front offices. Simon was reminded of the booklined walls that showed up as backgrounds for TV talking heads.

'So, you have your work cut for you," Ricci began, taking charge.

'Sit down, signori. 'Ow you like your soda water? It is all I have today," he apologized. "Ice or not? I must to tell you also, I 'ave very little time. It is good that you come early."

"Mr. Ricci, I don't want to waste time either," Simon said. Ricci without his title suddenly felt like a naked civilian.

"I see. I see. Very good. We will talk like just three men, in a frank and honest way. After all, an urban policeman 'as certainly seen more of the world than it takes to be surpris-ed by the interest of a student in a professor. It 'appens wherever there is a student and a teacher. Even Dante, he understands this," gesturing toward the bathing-capped head, "he writes about love between scholars, between teacher and student: it is not always good but it is natural."

"I guess the interest went both ways.'"

"She could 'ave done much worse, I believe, than to choose a person both rational and experienced." The tip of his tongue ran slowly around his upper lip. "Of course you know that I was not alone, alas. It would have been of an absurd conceit to think so." His thickset body swayed back and forth from the hip. "I advise to you consult also the young lady's special friend, the sculptress. See what she has to say."

"We have," said Simon. "Where were you, Mr. Ricci, during the donors' party last night?"

"I had my duties there so I hardly moved at all," he said. "There were all the trustees, the donors, the President's visitor from Georgia, the gathering afterward. Was there the chance for me to record this in writing? I confess I am gravely offended by your question. No doubt already they are making a plot against me. Ha."

"No offense meant, sir. Please continue."

"What, continue? Has anyone watched me go out of the room last night? Perhaps once, to relieve myself. Per'aps I should 'ave written it down."

"Mr. Ricci, Selena Fenn had sexual relations during the party. We have been informed of your—relationship with Selena, you don't seem to hide it yourself, and we are simply asking you if you had sex with her last night. That isn't a crime."

Ricci produced a mountebank's grin. "You will not leave off about this, I see," he said. "Simple erotic satisfaction," here he paused reflectively, "is a crime, even if you do not say so. Very well. All right. Although I find it unthinkable that even in these times, Americans... Yes, then. We left the party for about, I would say, ten minutes. Selena was most willing, I can assure you."

"Where did you go?"

The grin drained away. "You know this so-named Underground University we 'ave? Well, there are a number of open rooms. The university does not possess the most efficient campus security police, as no doubt you know. We went to one of the open rooms. ...Tenente—Why do you want to censure the private behavior of a beautiful young girl? Boccaccio already deplored this cruelty in the fourteenth century."

"That's obvious, sir. Anyhow it's not just her behavior that we're, as you put it, 'censuring'. What time was it when you left, and when you returned to the party?"

"About five minutes to six, and we were returned to the party by ten past, so if you count the five or six minutes it takes to ascend to the ground floor again..."

"That would mean it took you less than ten to fuck her," Granita put in helpfully.

Ricci put two more ice cubes into his soda, added a lime twist without offering them any. "Selena was a very, how shall I say it, highly appetitive young woman."

"What then? Did you see her again at the party?"

"No, absolutely not. I had to escort my wife home before going out again, to Alan Sakulin's house."

"Mr. Ricci, how long have you been on the Redfern faculty?" Simon asked.

"It is growing ten years now. Ten very fast years."

Simon consulted his hastily compiled little list of Redfern dignitaries. "You seem to have risen pretty fast yourself."

"Everyone 'as 'is use."

"You were previously at Texas Megatech. Is that a place where students learn Italian? I would have thought more, science, technology."

"That was the principal reason to leave, tenente. There was little for me to do at Texas, even though I must say that it paid as well as Redfern. But a man 'as also other needs, of the intellect. These are well cared for here."

"Maybe it helps that President Chavadze came from Texas Megatech also," Simon suggested. "He probably helps look after your needs too, like any old pal." It seemed to him that just about everyone at Redfern was personally concerned with Ricci's welfare.

"Chavadze is a most extraordinary 'uman being," Ricci expanded. "'E is a megalopolis to 'eemself. Of course, now he is crush-ed (two syllables) by the disaster that 'as taken place on 'is campus."

"Is he normally on campus every day?" Simon asked.

"Chuck is completely dedicated. Of course 'e keeps 'is appartament in the city. But he works like a dog, so does Keith Chambers, whom you now have met. There is constant work these days, and especially for 'umanists. The whole campus is in one of those peculiar American turmoils. Who is left to defend normal study if not people like Chavadze, and—with apologies—me?"

"Whaddaya mean defend?" asked Granita.

Ricci stiffened with self-importance. "I refer to humane letters, sergente. The study of the classic books of the Western world This 'as been the affair of students since the first academies. Now you have a—gaggle of females, of blacks, of every sort of man, each one pushing out in front, each one selling his own very doubtful merchandise. The women —you will see that soon for yourself. The blacks imagine they can recompose the past with themselves as its inventors, the Indians are fighting for the return of land that was taken from them in the time of Cristoforo Colombo. Meantime, no student is obligated to follow any course at all. It is virtually impossible to get a moment's relief from worry, what we will do just to keep the peace. In fact, you will not be amazed if it transpires that some pazzo took his revenge on Selena—a beautiful, rich, privilege-ed young lady, only because he is furious."

"There seems to be some pretty heated controversy about a Center."

"It is a tremendous nonsense. Funds have been donated for the construction of a Center for the Humanities. Suddenly every faction on the campus wants to 'ave this center for itself. It would be much more reasonable to divide the Center so that every one is appeas-ed. For example, as in Italy. The law specifies," clearing his throat, "the relation between all administrators: if a mayor of a city is of one persuasion, the controller of finance must be of another, and the chief of police of still another. So—political life is peaceful because everyone gets some-e-thing. But no, not 'ere. A reasonable man is left alone to fight the mad."

"Some responsibility, huh?"

"But you know, tenente, passive resistance is som-e-time the most effective. Just wait. That is all."

"I hope YOU'VE been doing no more than wait."

"Why do you wish to be so persistently offensive? What has the so tragic death of a young girl to do with campus troubles? On the second thought, per'aps it is not so far away. 'Ave you yet encountered la Rossiter? Ah, now that is a road to take. And speak with that Lamamba, or the creature Bonza Leier, and Mahmoud and the rest. They had no reason to like this little signorina. You can imagine well 'ow much such persons would try to gain 'er confidence, but so far as I know, they did not get it. She 'as stood firm against their uncontrollable demands for money —I know it from her personally. The Generale her grandfather is one of Redfern's most respected donors, but besides he brings others, especially supporters who are not all, let us say, from New York."

"Are you, sir, also connected with Redfern donors? I know the party last night, that's why I'm asking you..."

"Ah. Well. I am a firm friend of the university, yes certainly. I 'ave participated in fundraising, together with the President. May I ask what is the connection with your investigation?"

"There is no clear connection just now, sir. We appreciate your cooperation 'til we get our bearings."

"And I must express to you frankly my resentment of your suggestion that I am invol-ved in some kind of...privileged relationship." Your ball now, said his pugface.

Simon had one foot out the door when he turned and asked his last question. "Maybe you could tell me, Professor Ricci, what happened to your file?"

"File? I know of no file. What are you talking about?"

"The personnel file. From the file room in the Underground Campus. Yours is missing, or rather, the whole contents. Except for the empty manila binder, which was on the floor last night. "

"You mystify me. I certainly don't want my file, if that is what you imply. Your question may be completely illegitimate for all I know, but I tell you without 'esitation that I have no purpose with any file. You must to know anyway that all information about personnel exists also in computer form. Why some pazzo dropped it on the floor is less a worry than how they got in. I marvel that the police is not interested in THAT."

Ricci saw them out in a rush of fleshy handshakes and assurances that he had no intention of stirring from beautiful Temperance. The spring, after all, was crucial for the welfare of his tomato vines.

Work never stopped. Once assured of the healing solitude that conduced to noble thoughts, he picked up the phone and dialed Bisticcio Morituro, his counterpart and crony at Ringside View State.

"Time to come across with that dynamite young man you're always telling me about. We are going to have a change of personnel here. A certain Wiener is departing."

Bisticcio was abashed. "My young man's not quite finished yet, Berto. I told you NEXT year. Is there a trouble about holding down the job for him? Just turn everyone else down for a while."

"It is moving faster than I thought. No matter if he's not through yet, we need him now. Just now the Committee will give the appointment its most superficial attention. What importance has a degree, anyhow? It's ability that counts. Send him on."

"Ability, well... yes..."

"Is this a young man who understands how the world works or not?"

"But of course."

"Out with it, Bisticcio. What's wrong?"

"There is a visa problem, some political mix-up... Berto, maybe a word from you to the Governor, etcetera..."

"I am going to Rome in just a month to pick up my Italian salary. Well yes, one lecture a year. I will give it, and then I will attend to this difficulty. You have nothing to worry about, the position will keep. Just in case, how does his resumé look? There are the Committees, etcetera."

"You know how it looks. Empty. Just school, etcetera."

"We will manufacture him a new one, with all the books he is writing and all the achievements, etcetera. A whole new past. The people here will be delighted."

"And I will not forget, Berto, I promise you that. Until very soon, dear friend."

He sat back a moment. If these stupid policemen were going to target simple human friendship as their enemy, they would never find out anything worth knowing. How can public business be conducted without incentives? Americans and their moral pretensions, their pathetic faith in systems of free choice. At least some Americans—yes, like the Rossiter— had some idea of the way politics and business intersect here without smearing the process with meaningless ugly names.

Still quagmired between sloth and fitful restlessness, Ricci turned to the computer on its own steel desk and swiveled his chair up to it. He hooked up to the mainframe and summoned up his E-mail messages for the morning. A windy message from some conference organizer in Pisa, his hometown. On the way from Rome to a few days on the beach at Viareggio, one might as well detour a bit in order to collect another free trip home, care of Redfern. So Berto had offered the conference a paper, which consisted of a title page followed by an efficiently stapled stack of thirty perfectly blank pages. The message expressed its enthusiastic reception.

Next came a piteous appeal from Myron Wiener for an extra letter of recommendation to the Department, preceded by URGENT and ending with NOW. Berto's plump smile dwindled to a twitch.

The last message made him sit up, raise his eyebrows and retract his chin. It was clear, unadorned, and unprefaced. YOU SWINE, the computer said, I KNOW EVERYTHING ABOUT YOU. IT'S OVER, CREEP.

SNEAK PREVIEWS

At eight-thirty that morning, Armin and Graziella had little to say to each other. Graziella had maintained the impersonal patience of a well-paid call girl for about an hour. But again, nozing!

Their sex life had become a casualty of Armin's developing Self. For one thing, she had turned out to be the wrong kind of Italian. An inexperienced Armin had been swept away on a scented wave and had proposed marriage to his vision—a vision of an angular, high-tech Antonioni woman driven by sex and Lancias, fueled on a peach and a sip of Chianti. But what had fallen to his lot was a cruel joke: the sulky, southern, spreading Graziella who was still growing more and more like his mama's mah-jongg pals.

THEN followed the complaints: when was the next raise? when could she get on the faculty as lecturer in Italian? didn't he remember his promise? Ten years, and his Self had zoomed right by her, a stranger to the gawking boy who once believed he'd brought Monica Vitti back home as his own personal toy.

Now she pushed the hem of the black lace nightgown down to her ankles and yanked up one of its straps, lifting a creamy shoulder to her cheek.

"Armin, tesoro," she crooned. "It is nozing. What can mean just one time?"

"It's going to last forever. Ever."

"How you can say so? Every married person knows thees can 'appen. Especially married persons. Nozing to do with us."

"It's like—not being able to move at all. I can't explain it."

"Do not disturb yourself any more, amore. There will be count-less ozzer times."

"I know," he said.

He got up, brushed his teeth for the third time, put on his plaid vicuna bathrobe. The thick bedroom carpeting, in a screaming magenta shade Graziella hadn't bothered to run by him before ordering it, swallowed his steps. Just beyond the master bathroom with its Jacuzzi, double sinks, and twin bidets Armin's home office beckoned.

There on the desk sits Armin's work-in-progress about plagiarism. Palter had loved the idea. Fishbane was explaining what it was that "problematized" the act of stealing someone else's work to represent it as one's own. Just as Palter says, the thing that makes plagiarism a theoretical problem is the death of the author—not that any actual person has died; that would make it somewhat less problematic. The Death of the Author was a special literary-critical way of denying the idea that once a piece of writing ("text") exists, the person "through whom" it has come into being is its author. Now if a book doesn't belong to its author, why should it not be "repeated" by another person? Aren't words infinitely repeatable? So they enter the public domain, which means that to put a piece of writing to your own daring new use is only to realize its destiny.

Palter had thought Fishbane "on the right track." The trouble was that when he sat down to write them, the words vanished into thin air. When did he have time to think about a lot of books anyway? It was more than ever obvious to him that the Fielding Letters were the only things that could rescue him from impotence. The computer screen, which he had forgotten to turn off, flashed emptily at him like a blank TV set. His mouth tasted bitter again, and he retreated to the bathroom to brush his teeth a fourth time.

The door chimes struck up a Mozart rondo just as he flushed the toilet.

"Tell them I'm out," he shouted. "I don't have to be here, do I?"

Shaken to his pacifist core, Armin plopped into the one comfortable chair left in his living room and watched the two pairs of pant legs recede down his front steps. His dad's old recliner was still angled just the way Abe Fishbein had liked it. Still an hour before the Department meeting. He spent it mired in cheap nostalgia, feeling indefinably sorry for himself.

Seymour Gorellick has toiled for a straight week at his charts and graphs, riding on his assistant vice presidents with a stick in hand and a whine in his throat. Seymour feels both aggrieved and flattered at being known as the Hun. He wants to be liked, really. But it comes with the turf for him to play the upfront perpetrator of the budget cuts and bruises while Chuck remains The Bear Hug.

Seymour reaches for a desktop Maalox and chews it down to a little white pellet. There are only a few dead minutes left before the hour of one strikes, the one hour of the week that makes the rest bearable.

The Maid For Love Motel, only ten minutes' drive from campus in his '78 Chevy, is the local take on a Japanese "love hotel": an institution created for trysts of more or less than an hour, plastic flowers included with the towels. You can even check in by computer and punch out when you leave. But why does the machine need to know your name? Seymour is always annoyed by the check-in.

"NAME," it inquires stolidly. The computer is connected to the only post-lobby door. "NAME PLEASE," it insists, politely.

Today Seymour taps in "TONY BANTER."

"WHAT, AGAIN?" the computer says. "ENOUGH ALREADY," Seymour complains. That's not how you treat a steady customer.

The door swings open with a complaining bleep, closes almost noiselessly. In two minutes flat Seymour is tucked into a pink double. His pyramidal little bulk tenses with sexual readiness, all systems go. He's got a reliable erection, a healthy, almost ruddy overlay spread across the greenish face. The dragged-down eyes, nose, mouth point upward, settle at medium. Seymour can feel himself breathe again, drops ten years in a few seconds. He dismisses the fear that waiting might be the best part.

LuAnn gallops up the fire stairs, slams the bedroom door. Her clean brown pageboy is brushed to a high gloss, and she's wearing that clingy black turtleneck and pants that stick to her all over, making her look from the side like two facing chests of drawers, one open at the top and the other at the bottom. What a magnificent figure of a woman. The vitality, the—abundance. The height. Turtleneck folded over chair. Black pants now peeling off. Those huge knockers just for him, that globular ass, the whole incredible package, the energy, the bounce. Seymour stares mesmerized. All the flow charts and sad nicknames in the world would be worth a few seconds of this wowser.

Alas. No sooner has this galumphing, scented magnificence thumped into bed than something goes awry: he can't hold it, can't stop, can't... It's over, folks, no money back. They sit there like Papa and Mama awakened by the little ones, cheated of the act of love, Seymour's eyes slit with suffering.

"You're so voluptuous, too." he sighs.

"What do we do for the next hour?"

All University decisions involving funds have to go through Seymoah, or look like they do.

"I have some ideas but I'm not sure you'll like them."

"That's a bore, Seymoah. It could take longer than an hour."

He runs a slow hand around some of the most luxuriant curves. "Not as long as that. Oh c'mon... I'll drive you back to Pelfe Hall or Womancenter or wherever, if we run late."

"Seymoah. We need to talk." Two-handed now, sort of coming together at the center. She twists free. "About the Centah..."

Gorellick is a crestfallen eight year old again, Mama standing over him with the math homework, no sweets.

"LuAnn, you know this is a problematic matter. We can't decide anything now; anyway it's going to depend on a vote. First the ad hoc committee, then the vice-presidents, discussion with the trustees, then the Executive Committee, and that's not just me and Chuck, either, then the trustees again... I have practically nothing to say except maybe make some recommendations."

"You know how important the Centah is. FAM has no room, the Womancentah is swamped all the time." LuAnn's full lower lip quivers. "An' I have to waste my time teaching things just anyone could do. An' I even have to teach offensive books, like, Milton, or even Shakespeare..."

"Offensive...Milton? Oh, I see, he's a man. Yes, that IS a problem. But we're all doing things we don't wanna do, this is 1993. There aren't maybe so many really important women writers for you to teach about..."

"Not enough? Whah, you...impohtant...that's just how it is, Seymoah, when anybody wants to innovate. Put together a book list that means somethin' in this world of today. Ah jes' don't see a way for a woman to teach Shakespeare." LuAnn had in fact been getting foggier and foggier about Shakespeare's language. It was looking like Chinese to her these days, not only those ole words but the way he had of putt'n 'em together so you can't unroll the mess. "So what Ah'm doin' is makin' him the subjeck of one of mah Sensitivity Seminars. That's the only way it works. What we do is take Shakespeare apaht for traces."

"What traces?"

"Sexist words. Racism. Classism, the worst. We consult the Index o' Forbidden Terms. Then everyone repents."

"Why everyone?"

"Because they're ALL paht of it. Ever'one that accepts Shakespeare as gospel. Or even likes him very much, the hateful word-mastah... An' those Seminars, by the way, need more room. Like in a Center."

Visions of Megan Mehan pouting, of Aviva Har-Shalom's defeat, appear to her on split screens. The Center itself, of course, would be a mere baby step toward what was really coming—the global FAM network. The Vision. The Search.

"Sensitivity Seminars need circular spaces for contrition, confession, an' absolution... Mah three steps. Somethin' really different, right?" She brightens a little, flashes the dimple in her cheek.

"Sounds kinda familiar to me LuAnn." Gorellick frowns now, interrogating the ceiling. The hand resumes its roving. "Only I thought religious confession was sorta private. But I think it's very exciting and eye-catching, right for Redfern. It's only that just now..."

"Now Seymoah." LuAnn mostly knows when to fold. She dislodges the index and third fingers that are acting more than usually unruly now and gives Seymour's hand a playful slap. He puts it slyly to his nostrils, trying for a coy glimpse out of one crossed eye.

"Ah'm doin' somethin' life-affirmin' here. An' if you didn't see it mah way, you wouldna let on about the Fenn money, now WOULD YOU?"

"You mean the special bequest..."

"You DID tell me, 'less I'm very, very mistaken. A li'l twit of a child, spoiled rotten, to control those millions. The ideah of it. We-a-ll, guess that's not awn anymoah."

He brushed a yellowing hand over his eyes. "I know. I didn't come here to drag myself through it all over again. Look, what's all this talk anyway? I've only got..."

"Seymoah. FAM is expandin' an' needs..."

"Dance," Seymour said.

"Wha..."

"I want you to dance for me naked."

"Ah mos' certainly..."

"Do it." A dumbfounded silence broken by slight pants. "Maybe you'll be glad you did sometime."

LuAnn slowly rises, a plump, rosy Juno sacrificing her will to the home fires. She turns on the little portable radio on the bedside table, her breasts swaying, hair falling over slightly reddened face. The radio blares out a rock beat. She turns it down, explores the dial for Easy Listening. Every station brings up a rock beat. Her glance darts right, left, center. The little pink room with its pink bed holds nothing but a waiting, grinning Gorellick, one sagging shoulder framed in the ruffled floral print of the sheets.

LuAnn gets up out of bed, stands, does a couple of shimmying warm-ups, not yet giving in to the rock beat, staring into the middle distance. She tries thinking about Richard Nixon, which she sometimes does during sex with Gorellick, but concentrating on Nixon only makes things worse, much worse.

However, LuAnn is a born optimist who doesn't shy from crises. The globular equipment on each side of her body comes to separate life. She braces her elbows against an invisible barre and swings into a series of vertical disco moves. The bass booms on, a whiny electric guitar riding on top. Chin up, she bops along, two scoops of snow-woman on those mile-long legs. Gorellick can't believe his luck. He pastures his eyes on a gyrating LuAnn like a first-time tourist at the Eiffel Tower. Everything is perking up again. When she swings into the final high kicks he has to stop her. His puny arm reaches forward and snags her around the neck like the cane old-time vaudeville managers used to hook a bad act off the stage. She plops back into bed on her back, Gorellick levitating on top, arms flailing.

Five minutes later. "Fenn is against us too."

"Wha..." Gorellick was floating in a benign sexfog.

"Selena Fenn's grandfather."

Recess over, he clears his throat. "I hardly ever get to talk to Fenn. He's Chuck's job if anyone's. Even Alan Sakulin doesn't deal much with Fenn, even though he's putting up so much more. It's no good my trying."

"Now Seymoah. None o' that New Yawk alarmism an' defeatism. It would be only raht for people to wanna memorialize Selena. Ah'm not thinkin' only of her love for FAM—it's the lyin' Ah can't take. The idea that she was hostile to us."

Stupid, stupid little shriveled man. How they'd all eat her dust. And after that—the Search would take its course. No more little green men, evah.

"LuAnn, you people in Comp Lit are doing something very exciting, and you're drawing impressive enrollments. But sometimes I think... you're politicizing maybe more than you need to. We have to hire more and more people just to do the teaching. What about the TAs who hardly speak English at all?"

"Ah'm surprised an' dismayed, Seymoah, to hear you of all people cast aspersions on the efforts of ouah foreign students. You of all people."

"I guess you're right. Half the science Ph.Ds in this country in 1991 were foreigners. Smart. Meanwhile WE have to be worrying about you Comp Lits all the time. Take Marvella. She's playing very, very hard to get. She missed all of last term but the hundred thou we agreed on had to be paid. The rent on the Mansion doubled, putting in the hot tub meant the glass terrace. She hated the BMW 735 so we got the 840. Everything looked okay at first, then before you know it these other campuses raise the ante to where I don't know how we can meet her new demands anymore."

"She'll be back from Oxfawd for tomorrow naht?"

"From Roanoke, the plantation house. Oxford was LAST week."

"An' jus' think, us FAMS have no li'l refuge atawl."

"What about the Bolingbroke-Redfern Womancenter?"

"That's a teensy little redbrick hole in the wall."

"You mean we could cut down on the budget there?"

"No way!" She wriggles her caves to fit his vexes. There wasn't that much cause for downheartedness really; with Selena out of the picture it would be a matter of jes' stayin' the course. Somewhere in her head a Texas revivalist hymn peals its call to vigilance.

He nuzzles back over, a wrinkled grey child. "I'll talk to Chuck about the Center, keep it alive with him. But it's gonna take time for me to even get to him, after everything that's happened."

"When you do, don' forget 'bout mah Sensitivity Seminar."

The Seminar and Tell-All was LuAnn's special invention, and an instant Redfern success. Like many startling innovations, it drew generously on tradition—the evangelical revival meetings her folks used to work. Every session, someone confessed their past failings and sins of insensitivity and was forgiven by the entire assembly... Passing by a Sensitivity room on his rounds, Marston Hall could almost swear he was back in church. Students loved the option of doing the Seminar instead of a course.

And Seymour had never seen himself as a stuffy old-line academic. Wasn't Economics itself a new science compared with the crusty old subjects he himself had snored through at college? This is America, and America means forging ahead and going forward and all that. He sighs, wishing he'd videotaped the dance.

Showered, turtlenecked, black-panted and back in the roomiest of her three offices, LuAnn makes a quick call to Chavadze, gets passed right through to the inner sanctum.

"I can get it for you wholesale," Chuck quips, eyebrows raised à la Groucho Marx. "Seymour is a good man, we understand each other like one family. He will not get in the way of The Search. I can promise you that."

Hilary Slocombe knew with the certainty of her twenty years that she was in for perpetual mourning. Yet the same physical energy that propelled her weight-lifting, furniture-moving, metal-hammering, and clay-moulding activities seized her with a furious need to act. The "Victory" still waited, and now it would be a monument. Now entering the second green quad, she picked up a rock and aimed it at a tree, hitting the trunk with a TOCK.

Loping into the Art Center, Hilary passed the classroom where the eleven o'clock mass course in Marxist Theory of Art that had been her best gut choice for this term was assembled.

You needed one or two guts or micks if you were going to concentrate on an important project of your own, and once you signed up for something like Hargreaves' Theory of Art you didn't need to come to class at all, ever.

Chris had decided after years of trying to catch up on his reading, desperately tossing books in the air, that he liked looking at pictures better. He had one and the same message about everything he taught. Everything was always and only a product of the classist colonialist capitalist system of the country it came from. You didn't need to know which country that was, which made Chris' course a natural for the Diversity Requirements. And the format was the most like TV, even though the pictures didn't move.

The room was a midsize amphitheatre, the steeply rising tiers of molded-plastic seats marked by rows of thrown-back heads seemingly aimed at the dark ceiling. The students in the top row, closest to the doors, had braced a complete semicircle of feet against the backs of the necks in front of them. The professor standing at his lectern, off to one side in front, was just a disembodied voice in the morning twilight.

Hilary's sometime seat was taken that day by the guy down the hall. She recognized his reversed red baseball cap even in the half-light. For a few minutes she stopped, enjoying despite herself the darting motion of the flashlight Chris Hargreaves was using as a pointer-scepter. A huge color reproduction of a painting flickered on the screen in front, which was not so bright as to interfere with the students' morning snooze. Like the kind of movie you go to when you're on a featherlight high, an adventure trying to reach you from afar.

Hargreaves' Midlands-accented voice was now tuned to a grumpy snarl. He directed his scepter to the midpoint of the painting on the screen, which showed a pair of entwined female nudes on a mussed bed, one dark-haired, the other with an auburn mane spread about her shoulders. The pointer rested where one woman's hand was poised at the genitalia of the other.

"It is inevitable that we examine the issues that Courbet himself was intent on examining here," he said, his words measured through the filter of unkempt graybeard. "Hierarchy. Power. Dominance. Authority. And in our examination of these issues we cannot avoid the close reading of that which comprises the question of status quo. How far is Courbet working from a perspective to conserve the status quo? How does he do it IF he does it? And if he's cleverly creating a diversion in which he merely utilizes the semblance of adherence to the social conventions of his day —while at the same time espousing an insidious subversion of the social order—how is he doing THAT?" Hargreaves stopped to let the few note-takers catch up, then turned his back on the painting and began again: "To what extent is Courbet openly contesting the trivialization of sex as play? Look at this," pointing to the same spot on the painting, "This is the site of authority, dominance, and submission. Courbet is doubtless projecting alternative possibilities of living by play—note the teasing gesture of the hand here—in order to imply a refutation of existing conditions. This painting is NOTHING BUT a tissue of refutations."

"Excuse me, Professor Hargreaves," another disembodied voice spoke up, "Doesn't it say that this painting was commissioned by the Sultan of Turkey? It seems to me that if it was, the artist probably doesn't have the chance to be thinking about alternatives to authority and submission, you know...'" the voice trailed off uncertainly.

"That's ethnocentric of you." Hargreaves turned blind eyes out to the audience. "Nothing less. You're assuming that European Man is the only animal by whose standards a just society can be measured. What if a third-world mind did exercise some influence on the subject matter? Your assumption is completely out of line. This, then, is the point," he went on at once, tapping the lectern with his flashlight. "Courbet is looking into a future that transcends his immediate surroundings, and his work is valid today because we are just beginning to catch up to his thinking."

From the shelf beneath his lectern top Hargreaves picked up a fat little volume entitled ALL PURPOSE DRASTICALLY ABRIDGED SURVEY OF WORLD ART, glanced quickly at a page marked by a yellow post-it note, and summed up: "Gustave Courbet, eighteen-nineteen-to-seventy-seven, painter to the aristocracy and the bourgeoisie of late nineteenth-century France. But a courageous traitor to his bourgeois roots." He slammed the book closed and strode over to the light switch. Everyone blinked in the fiendish green dazzle. "Next week, then. Picasso. That will be all."

Hilary ducked the sluggish bunches of her classmates shuffling out of the amphitheatre and took the three concrete flights down to the studio where her "Victory" stood draped in its tarp. Uncovering the statue was like undressing its beautiful original. She did it slowly and almost reverentially.

The fact that Selena would never come back was making its way into the area of her brain that controlled linear reasoning. There would be a great hullabaloo of a ceremony over the dead young woman's sterling qualities of character, a body to view, speeches. Hilary studied her work with growing criticism, backing up to see better, crouching forward again. The sinuous torso formed a long S-curve around its axis according to the classic contrapposto principle, which brings the body back to its point of origin.

Not too bad. Even in its unfinished state, this work should have been enough in itself to earn anyone the President's Fellowship. If anything about the process had been fair.

Knowing that helpless anger about the Fellowship could paralyze her work, Hilary was still incapable of banishing it at will. The recollection would mow her down whenever it surfaced, but she gave way yet again, replaying the two scenes in alternation.

The first showed Hilary, electric mane, blazing eyes, storming into Professor Rossiter's office, not the Comp Lit one or the English Department one, but the double office at BREW headquarters, with all the fussy little dried flower vases and stuffed cats. Hilary was clutching a crumpled letter dated March 31, signed "Chuck" (Office of the President) in the childish hand of an Executive Administrative Assistant.

Rossiter at her big pink desk consisted of a large pageboyed head, bent over a piece of pink knitting. Rossiter held the needles stuck out like elbows, as if elbowing anyone who tried to get closer to her. Moving in on her, Hilary knocked down one of the vases. Blue china fragments shot out of the impact. Rossiter's smile turned to open displeasure.

"Ah know you'll wanna pick that up right away, Hilary."

Bending to do so, Hilary had felt Rossiter's bored, desultory stare like the touch of a cold hand. She straightened up and looked her in the eye, or so she hoped. Knitting, knitting, with a satisfied smirk at the growing piece of lacy pink wool. Hilary tried her most controlled voice.

"I came to talk to you because of this letter..."

LuAnn needed no time to counterattack. "Ah'm afraid youah in the wrong place. You need an appointment with the Committee, an' I think that may be hard to get just now. Youah aware, Ah think, of the approachin' New Campaign. This is no time for peevish complaints about decisions made by the Committee."

Hilary swallowed. "Professor Rossiter, I'm in the right place facing the right person, the one who forced the President's Fellowship to go to a FAM student. I know damn well what was going on and I want you to understand that."

"Ouah Committee was entirely impartial, and in any case, every choice involves a subjective element. Neither Professor Hargreaves nor Professor Leier nor Professor Fishbane nor Ah mah self, and certainly not the members of the Administration who gave theyah valuable time to makin' this decision, have anythin' to apologize fo'. Ouah procedures were flawless."

"Professor Rossiter, you're saying that someone with no creative background, no work to show, and a project like...OUR COWS, OUR SELVES, whatever that is, has beaten people like Paul, and Karim, and me. In a fair competition." The President's Fellowship would fund two years of work in any country in the world. It came with a slew of exhibitions for an artist, performances for an actor, or readings for a writer. LuAnn's brain called up the moment of awed silence that had greeted Hilary's portfolio at the first meeting. She knitted on, leaving Hilary to reconsider her outburst.

"As if Ah had to infoam you," LuAnn finally said, "Professor Lamamba gave the winnin' project his highest recommendation. The fact that it is feminist and multicultural and accessible," she paused, "works for it, that goes without sayin'. We live in the world of today, not in Renaissance Italy... Really, Hilary, Ah'm left to...to question youah sensitivity. An' by the way, Professor Ricci added his voice to our unanimous vote..." Turning her rectangle of pink wool to start a new row, she turned down her mouth and tripled her chin.

"This was all fixed." Hilary took a step toward LuAnn's head and shoulders ensconced behind the pink desk. "By you, Professor Rossiter."

But Hilary had had her special boosters too.

"The Committee's just stupid, but I'll fix it for you, darling," Selena had assured her. "Something's come up that's going to work. Not that you actually need it, but you know how you are.... I'm talking foolproof, no-lose, in the bag. We'll be off to Italy right after commencement."

So confident, never in doubt of getting what she wants. Hilary felt a frisson of resentment.

"People like you never understand...when the party's over. Or that not everyone gets to go. You just have no conception of difficulty—the height, the weight of it, the dimensions.... How? What can you do?"

"No need for you to know. Fact is, it's better for me not to tell you right now. I only want you to know you're the next winner of the President's Fellowship so's you don't waste time worrying. The family stuff you have to get through with will be over by Monday, right? That waiter job at the party is going to be the last one you'll have to do in a very, very long time. Leave it to me."

"It's something to do with your grandfather," Hilary speculated. "But he despises me. He pretends not to know about us but he looks right through me when I'm at the house."

"If you only just let me give you the money. You know there's going to be a lot, and all coming up in a month. Your trip and expenses and everything, wouldn't mean a thing to me."

Hilary flushed red. "You know about that. How many times...You know that's the one thing I can't let you do, why keep asking me?"

"No use ever trying to make you understand about money—God, you're impossible. Anyway, it's nothing to do with Grampa, so let it go, sweetie. You're not going to hear anything from me, except congratulations from Chavadze by mail." The Gioconda smile, that detached, indulgent show of patience.

"You never tell me anything."

"I simply don't tell you EVERYthing. Or anyone else. That way no one, but no one, has a piece of me."

Hilary recalled the sex-slumming with Berto Ricci, the uncanny ease of her own conquest. "Are you really that safe?" she asked. "Beyond anyone's reach?"

"You come the closest, just remember that. I'm doing this no-fail thing for us both. We'll do Italy right after school is over."

"Don't you think your grandfather or the Dean will get in the way?"

"I can do whatever I want with my own body."

"That's such a dumb expression. It always sounds like you're talking about something outside you, not a part of you."

"You know what I mean. Grampa and Keith just go right on barking, never bite. And you're a shoo-in for the Fellowship anyhow; no one deserves it as much as you. Just stick to the things you're good at. I'll do my part on my own." A quick hug and she was out of the room again, calling over her shoulder, "Turn the computer off, REMEMBER!"

Rossiter's slitted eyes were now fixed on Hilary. "You'd best understand this, and not pursue your complaint. Ah imagine that Karim and Paul will show the same good sense an' spohtspuhsonship. An' with a tragedy on our hands, too. How anyone can take it on themselves to, well, just push themselves forwud at a tahm like this..." She emerged from behind the desk and stood at the same height as Hilary. The knitting dangled from one hand as she waited for Hilary to leave, eyebrows raised, mouth slack.

The furnishings of Rossiter's office looked even more unreal, the sunshine glaring on those stuffed animal faces. Like a weird pink bedroom. Getting out of here, waking up anywhere else, anywhere.

"You are not having a reverence problem, are you, Chuck?"

Palter Van Geyst's docile face opened in a rare smile. "A feeling of awe in the presence of the self-styled authorities?"

"Chuck" Chavadze, Seymour Gorellick and Palter Van Geyst were winding up their late lunch in the President's Dining Room, a hushed little oasis of brass and mahogany that was always kept scrupulously polished.

"I'm trying to be a maid-of-all-work and jack-of-all-trades, since you ask." Chuck pushed aside his dessert, signaled to the waitress for more coffee. "Not to speak of being expected to do the rabbit-out-of-the-hat trick again. I am not a universal Money Man. And you have to concede that McFarquhar is very, very persistent. I have managed to put her off up to now about the Center. There are staff members whose only work it is now to deal with her letters, her calls, her memos. It doesn't make it any easier for me that she's..."

"Black," Van Geyst said in his soft voice. "One of the most peculiar things about her is this woman's fixation on the War. It is not, I think, a general preoccupation of black history." Seymour looked scandalized. "Well, is it?"

"McFarquhar doesn't do Black History, Palter, you know that."

"Very well. But whatever it is she does, it is a complete anachronism." Seymour tried to focus, as if reading Van Geyst's lips. "I mean quite simply that she is superannuated, out of date, a dinosaur. That old-time learning—don't you Americans have a song that goes something like..."

"Gimme That Old Time Religion... I'm with Palter, Chuck. I had a conference just a few hours ago with LuAnn Rossiter. She says the same sort of thing about Willona. It sounds a bit harsh to me, but all this raving about the War, you know, the Moral and Intellectual Decline of the American Mind... it WAS a European war more than ours, after all. But you're the historian, Chuck—or you were."

"Maybe it takes an historian, as you so kindly call me, to see how right you two are. The time for a new slant is here. Comp Lit is eating up the university, more power to it."

"LuAnn says Willona won't speak to her, cuts her dead whenever she sees her."

"You sound like an injured husband, Seymour." Van Geyst teased him gently. "Standing up for the maltreated spouse. Would not perhaps a quiet oblivion be equally effective? How did Mrs. Reagan put it—Just Say No. Correct?"

They are silent as the waitress pours their coffee. Seymour absently watches her departing backside nod right, then left.

"Imagine seeing the specter of the swastika everywhere. THEN she calls US Victimologists!" Chavadze gets an easy laugh from the other two. "But you know, I sometimes feel as if having a sense of the past is like smoking, or eating red meat, or having voted for Nixon. I wonder sometimes if I've signed up to be the President of a School of Self-Esteem! One that's run by the Department of Comparative Literature, for instance."

"Bottom line is Comp Lit's huge enrollments. What deserves a Center if not the product the consumers want? Let's face it," Seymour pleaded. "The kids don't WANT musty old books that are hard to read. They wanna be turned on. Her memos—I've seen enough of them—are full of 'discipline' and 'restraint' and 'make them do complex thinking.' To me it looks like what she wants is to turn the clock back to where students learn nothing but empty facts."

"As far as I can see, they are not so clever at any form of thinking, either simple or complex," Van Geyst observed.

"They're some of the best this country can offer, Palter, and that's saying pretty darn much." Gorellick measured his indignation carefully with a teaspoon. "My concern is that education should be more than facts alone. YOU probably share that, right?"

"Indeed, yes. May I remind you, Seymour—with all due respect —that the decision to abolish the old tests was at my suggestion?" Van Geyst smiled self-deprecatingly. "Remember my example of the continents on the map? It was only about a year ago. Instead of trying to remember what the seven continents might be, I suggested, or the names of the seven dwarfs, I said that students must look at a globe. Look, and count the continents for themselves. And what would they see? How many are there? If Australia is one, very well: what is Greenland? Do not North and South America look like one to you? Europe and Asia too? You were born in Georgia, Chuck: are you European? What is a continent anyway but a mental construct?"

"Yup, I remember," said Gorellick. "Continents are political constructs just like countries." He took a swig of Maalox for emphasis.

"For god's sake," said Chavadze, "They should know what the continents are by the time they get here; that's not our job. But look, Palter, anyone who needs to mail a letter to a foreign country has to know how to write an address on it, political or not. Of course, they'll phone, very likely, or E-mail, or fax—but even then... can you quite dispense with continents? Not only that..."

"Continents are nothing but factitious divisions of political power."

"Not only that, but if the terrible inequities that divide the world come to an end, and the new divisions are better, no one ignorant of the old ones is going to understand the new ones, much less take part in the new order. They won't recognize that there should be any order at all."

"The most important thing, Einstein said, is never to stop questioning."

"Palter, that's fabulous." Gorellick perked up.

"And he also said that imagination is more important than knowledge. I have the impression, Chuck, that your Willona has yet to learn these things. It is unfortunate, in a subject like history... for there is no authority up there in the sky; there is only now, and everyone who lives in that Now has a separate, historically based peace to make with that Now. It is not morally suspect not to be dispassionate. The imperative becomes more and more clear. History cannot be at the Center."

"LuAnn says..."

"Enough of what LuAnn says. If you will excuse me, Seymour. She is not yet the president of Redfern. I'm sorry." Chuck hastened to apologize. "It is very, very difficult to think clearly about such abstract things in the wake of our own tragedy."

"The figures are on our side." Seymour calculated roughly that every third Redfern kid will be doing a Comp Lit major by two years from now. "They want skills, not facts. HOW to read, not WHAT."

"Soon there won't be any What. But I hope you're taking care of the How, Palter. By the way, I confess that School of Self-Esteem was her phrase," said Chuck. "Willona's. You know how steamed she gets."

After a year and a half in office, did Chuck lean more toward leadership or coalition-building? It looked as if, sensitivity-trained and consciousness-raised, he had nothing left to say today. The three fell silent for the benefit of the busperson clearing away last things.

Phil Granita's patience was laboring through the severest trials of his career. His head was a swirl of useless, fancy information. "One thing I've decided. My kid is going to engineering school. Period."

"Phil, it's the only time in your life, those four years, when you can study something because you're interested in it, read, think, decide what kind of person you're gonna be when you get out."

"I just watch the sports. An' that means only basketball. An' THAT'S just when there's no NBA game."

"You think Chavadze can help at all?" Simon asked.

"As much as that scumbag Ricci anyway. I thought you lose your professor job for fucking the students."

"Only if they complain, remember? Remember the case that

made the Rumble last year? It was six years old and still 'in committee.' I don't hafta tell you what that means. Besides, Selena didn't mind, it was some kind of fun for her."

"Why do WE hafta think about that?"" Granita was scandalized. "The only word we have comes from that lezz."

"Because right now it's part of the case, everything is."

"Chavadze, he's the college president. How come a place like this picks out a...foreigner for president? I never hearda that."

"Nobody woulda thought of anyone but a native American as the right guy. Maybe not even as far back as the War."

"Native American means Indian now."

"Whatever. What war d'you mean? Vietnam?"

"World War II." It came back to Simon how Willona McFarquhar was always talking up her specialty, The Big One. "Before the war you probably couldn't find Jews or Italians or any ethnics at all who were students at places like Redfern, let alone running them."

"That's us," Granita said feebly.

"It's YOU. By the way, as far as Chavadze, remember he's from Georgia. Not Georgia Peach or Georgia on My Mind: Georgia in the Soviet Union, I mean as it was. Like that Poet-in-Residence-for-a-Week, Yashvili."

They entered the Admin building, waved at the dozing campus guard, pushed through the turnstile to Chavadze's private elevator. The carpeted interior with its mahogany Greek-key motif running around the top muffled their voices though it made no sound of its own. It disgorged them right in front of the Chavadze suite. Two large secretarial pools full of Human Resourcepersons lined the corridor leading right to Keith's sanctum.

"President Chavadze has more on his plate than ever, but he insists on giving you as much time as you need. Just use it judiciously, will you?"

Chavadze opened the tall double doors himself. As he stood aside to admit them his arms remained extended for an instant, taking in all three. The Bear Hug, Simon remembered. The policemen were motioned into black leather Barcelona chairs gleaming with chrome. Simon realized that he was going to be forced to relax, sit back, and enjoy the ride.

The president eased into the same kind of chair a couple of feet from them, leaving his desk vacant. Chavadze immediately revealed himself innocent of any attempt to shield Redfern from the investigation. He leaned forward with an intense expression as if he were trying to convince them of something.

"I've even sent Garso Yashvili off to a bunch of Creative Writing classes. He would have been my responsibility for the last hour or so despite the demand for him all over campus. Anyhow, Garso is hitting on all fours with the alumni. If he were able to stay longer—you know he's only here till Friday —the program would be extended and everyone would get a fair chance at him! I can't offer you any smokes, you know, that stopped ages ago, but how about a sweet substitute?" He extended a box of chocolate cigarettes.

"No, thanks," Granita said. "What can you tell us, sir, about a professor you have here named Roberto Ricci?"

"Well," Chavadze, not at all taken aback, munched his chocolate cigarette, "Berto's been here for about as long as I have. Berto is—a towering, distinguished"—searching for a final term—"One of Redfern's stars."

"How long have you known him?" Simon asked.

"Simply forever, my dear Lieutenant. We go back a very long way, back to our days at the same university in Texas. He was instrumental in our joint effort to bring the Humanities to what was predominantly a science campus. Berto is very, very persuasive."

"Seems kinda windy to me," Granita remarked.

"So that's about ten years?" Simon said.

"That's right. We have been friends ever since. May I ask why you're especially interested in Berto?" He knitted his eyebrows. "Surely there must be so many aspects to your investigation. Berto wasn't even one of Selena's teachers."

"You noticed that already," Simon observed.

"You can imagine how anxious we are to get to the bottom of this. Everyone who knew Selena is involved."

"More like a boyfriend, Ricci was," Granita said.

Chuck's take-charge face turned sour. "I'm not sure that I understand you," he said.

"I mean they were having sex, sir. Sorry to be graphic," Granita said, "but it was even going on last night. Maybe even just before she died."

"Keith Chambers has not included this information in his summary." Chavadze became even more grave. "Perhaps he thought it did not qualify as fact."

"Don't professors get fired for sex with students?" Granita asked.

Chavadze raised his eyes to meet Granita's. "Nothing is that simple or sure. If you were stuck at the top of a huge pyramid with a better view of the sky than of the earth, you'd have an immediate idea of what I'm up against. If there is no complaint, if an affair goes on tolerated by the participants...then a valuable member of the faculty is able to lead his private life without interference. Of course I will personally reprimand Berto. He will learn to understand the anguish he has caused by becoming involved with one of our students. It almost makes you wonder if you know your own friends anymore." He seemed absorbed in some unrelated thought. "Do you think right now," he asked, "that this affair, if it existed at all, could be directly related to the—tragedy?"

One of Chavadze's telephones emitted a tentative trill. As if it had not invaded his concentration, he went on talking to Simon.

"To think of Berto that way is offensive to me. And yet, you can't know anyone completely, not even a member of your own family. I'm at a loss; I need to take in this terrible possibility. Berto—well." He sighed. The red phone trilled again, insistently. They heard the even voice of Keith Chambers, then the call was transferred to Chavadze.

"If I've told you once... we will absolutely not tolerate any cheap profiteering from employees. You'll have to let the Teaching Assistants know that we are fully prepared to treat your strike with a firm hand, believe me... You haven't seen anything yet. The Administration will break you."

With a hand on the mouthpiece, he murmured, "T.A. Union, strike... So what if you picket the Campaign? How many of you belong to the Union, anyhow? Perhaps half? Do you think anyone's afraid of a so-called university boycott? You have more thinking coming... This is my final statement for the Rumble and you can take it as applying to yourself: the rise in teaching hours and the decline in fees are no more than a part of our reality. That reality is DECLINING RESOURCES."

Chavadze reached for another chocolate cigarette and shifted his feet on the desk. "Let me remind you...let me remind you that Redfern was among the first campuses even to recognize your sort of union... We said all right, have your union. Now this pathetic fraction of graduate students—that's right, I said a fraction—maybe eight percent..."

The policemen waited patiently till he hung up. "The graduate students here picked this moment to express dissatisfaction with their terms," Chuck told them with a troubled smile. "We LIKE these people. We RECRUITED them. We don't want to give up on them—but we can't give them the whole store, you understand. We're all in this crunch TOGETHER. We ALL have to wait every year for the budget to be approved by the Trustees."

"You take a salary cut yet, Mr. Chavadze?" Granita asked.

Simon thought of the dark, humid, airless Underground Campus, where he had to use a flashlight. "Must be hard to negotiate so many demands," he said to the President.

Chavadze raised his eyes to the lacquered red ceiling. "A campus is like a department store," he said. "No—a hotel, health club, psychiatric clinic, employment agency, all in one. You can't imagine."

"Mr. Chambers has been filling us in on your campus security system. He says campus guards aren't enough for the job anymore, that their equipment is inadequate."

"Our first concern has to be avoiding liability. I have already called for improved lighting and emergency phones in the Underground Campus."

"No one outside could have been responsible for this one, sir. The electronic keys work efficiently, and we know they change all the time. Doesn't anyone log people in and out?"

"It is a civil right for every person on campus to move about as she pleases."

"Unless SHE goes wild and destroys some property, right?" Granita hoped he sounded sarcastic.

"Or commits assault." Chavadze finished for him.

The doors opened and Keith Chambers looked in anxiously. "Mr. Chambers, what specific provisions has Redfern made for the safety of women students?"

Keith snapped right to it, his discomfort showing only in a slight side-to-side movement of the shoulders. "To begin with, we are justifiably proud of our self-defense programs for women, including martial arts. There is our Take Back the Campus program, which brings speakers from all over the country. Then, the crisis therapy group, all managed by Human Resources. I could go on and on..."

"Don't," said Granita. "You coulda maybe just got more guards, more lights, and more rules... Save you lotsa crisis speakers."

"What is more," Keith droned on, "like all colleges and universities receiving Federal funds, we publish annually our security policy and our crime-reporting policy. We make public the exact number of on-campus incidences of sexual assault, robbery, burglary, motor-vehicle theft, and so on..."

"God forbid," Chavadze spoke from inside his own blue funk. "Suppose that someone in the...community is responsible?"

"I am not ready to concede that possibility, Chuck. Femicide on campus is a national problem. The most recent studies have shown that it is not usually committed by teachers or students."

"My God, if someone like Berto..." Chavadze fell back in his chair, sighting new storm clouds.

"Now, Mr. Chambers. You knew Selena longer than anyone else here. You were practically part of her family, and you could have been with her, or at least looking out for her, at the party. Did you see her go anywhere or do anything unusual? Did she leave the main room?"

Keith hesitated a fraction of a second. "No-o," frowning, "not that I could tell. But I was very busy." His mind's eye summoned up the image of Selena, stalking out through the archway with Ricci just behind her, the wretched slavering in his face.

"Did you and your goddaughter have any misunderstanding lately? Was there any reason for her to do something foolish just to defy you?"

Keith gave a bitter little laugh. "No one needs to go to any special lengths to defy me!"

"We talked to Hilary Slocombe."

No response.

"She says that Selena and Professor Ricci were having sex together. Maybe not then and there, but..."

Granita said, "Were you in the party room the whole time, beginning to end?"

"Yes—of course, except for a few minutes, to search in the wine cellar for the Romanee-Conti '85. Then..." he stopped. "I called the police about four minutes later."

The policemen found themselves outside the Admin. Building, blinking under a jagged piece of sunlight. "Why couldn't it be Chambers?" Granita said. "He knew her since she was a baby—but that doesn't exclude a suspect. He was at the party, he's a big strong guy, played football, he's not exactly coming up with answers for us. He found the body. He probably had it moved, could've done it himself."

"I'm not forgetting that. He's funneled us almost everything we know about the whole case. And he has no watertight alibi for any of the time." Simon's body felt heavy, drained. "I just think right now that all Chambers wants is to put us off the scent of any Redfern person. He probably wants to make sure Redfern gets her money."

"An' now on top of it, with her dead, no one has to ask her how she wants it split."

An early dusk was coming in; above them a cloud heavy with moisture edged across the sky. They had just left behind them a very worried Chambers.

FROM THE DIARY OF SITA AMANPURI

I greet the demise of the Fenn girl with mixed emotions. There is so much more going on as well—more hiring in the Department to come, since we have terminated Myron Wiener. Too much for me to do, particularly in view of my Beloved's inexorable reserve. Of course I have forgiven him, as only a free and empowered woman can have the generosity to do.

Yet I fear for you, Beloved. My God, I tremble to write this, but I see you in my mind, struggling with her as you did with me. I see you as you suddenly throw off all restraint. How you frighten me. But I will never, never let on. I know nothing of this Selena except that she was a nuisance to FAM, especially to LuAnn—perhaps to you as well? Then we are only even more firmly agreed. Are we not truly as one?

No wonder you left the horrid expanse of the Underground Campus so precipitately. Do you feel the telepathy? It comes from my whole body itself. And I have already forgotten your abandonment, my

Beloved.

📭

"There is no direction back from a fiction to reality: there is only a dialectic—a coming and going—between self-destruction and self-invention." Palter Van Geyst was winding up his weekly teaching hour. Hundreds of students had wedged into one of Redfern's biggest amphitheatres, the lucky few who'd managed to have him sign their program cards months ago. Heads supported on chins, pens scratching, not another sound. Even some other members of the faculty scattered around. Fishbane usually makes it to the big class. He rearranges Palter's sentences for his own weekly appearance.

"Sanity can exist," Van Geyst is saying in his perfectly even voice that makes everyone strain forward, "only because we are willing to function within the conventions of this self-doubling, even self-multiplication. We are willing to dissimulate and pretend that we have one true identity. Just as the languages of society dissimulate the inherent violence of the actual relationships between human beings. That is what all our written texts are about—how to make power or violence look like something else."

Sighs, nods, frantic scribbling. If nothing means anything, you don't have to read so many books. Why waste the time? To hear Palter get it all out of the way is a thrill in itself.

"In other words, we have to pretend that responsibility exists, so that the bus driver will drive his bus, the postman deliver the mail. That is a possibility I will never exclude." He bestows his shy smile on the whole amphitheatre, taking in the cracks in the cream-painted walls, the rows of metal chairs, the bowed heads. "For a thinking person, however, there is only one truth to keep in mind: everything that you know...is...wrong." A ripple of delighted laughter. School's out.

"For there is no transcendental and lasting truth as you once hoped. Some call it the Death of God. I call it the Death of Man." Every eye on him now, no one writing. "The so-called ideals by which we supposedly live are not inevitable, they are not even natural—but are merely artificial constructs that might just as well have no power to command us." A hand rises tentatively, drops. "It is only that buses need to be driven, letters delivered.

"What makes one reality more substantial than another? What is the use of substituting one kind of piety for another? Power exercises itself without bothering about those few individuals who choose to persist in not understanding it." Van Geyst turns one color with the cream wall behind him, his head mischievously tilted. "We can only approach the abyss without fear—and come away smiling. That's all for today," he ends, swallowing his voice.

Applause, scattered then gathering steam. Fishbane gathers up his empty alligator briefcase. To conceal his chagrin at being ignored, he strikes up a conversation with the nearest departing student.

"I for one, read Van Geyst as saying that, well a creative like, say, you, supplies a product—like a novel or a poem. Then the reader or receiver refashions the product to his own use, see?... Well, yeah, Van Geyst is teasing us as usual. I see that as integral to his fascination. Gotta go."

Palter slowly made his way out of the amphitheatre. He picked up speed on his walk home, which took him uphill and then along cobblestone streets, by trees and houses that matched his waning energies. Fences needed paint. An abandoned red ball lay in someone's yard. He felt like giving it a playful soccer kick.

A sudden screech of brakes, but when he turned toward the jarring sound, the car had sped off. He noticed a small dog, which had evidently been hit and was lying on the pavement close to the gutter. Its crushed body was twitching with the last signs of life; its eyes were open. Palter approached it with some curiosity, bent down slightly to get a better look, and then kicked it into the gutter with a swift but powerful movement of his entire right leg before continuing the approach to his house. He did not turn to see it quiver, its eyes close. A man in an entirely unRedfernian outfit was approaching the house from the opposite direction. He arrived simultaneously with Palter at the doorstep. He had on a wide-brimmed hat that conjured up the Pampas and a creamy white sharkskin suit.

"Professor Van Geyst," he said with an indistinct Hispanic accent, extending his hand, "my name is Natanson, Ricardo Natanson. I am an attorney, now representing your family. May we speak? It's about Anne-Mieke. Professor, I think the name of your Dutch wife is sufficiently familiar to you."

Van Geyst's distracted expression remained unchanged as he spread out his left hand to usher the stranger inside. It would have been unseemly to send him away, and besides, he knew something about persistent visitors. Better to get things clear from the outset. He retains his air of not being much interested in his guest, but polite enough to remain present.

Carol Van Geyst, a tall, stoop-shouldered, quiet young woman who had been a graduate student of Palter's, was just coming down the scuffed maple staircase as the two men entered. "This gentleman and I have some business to transact in the study. We won't be long."

The study door closed behind them, and Natanson looked around him at a completely colorless room. The huge amount of books that had been packed into the shelves, two tables of heavy dark wood, some indoor plants shedding dusky brownish leaves on lace covers. No pictures, no photographs, not a single imprint of a character or even a personality, yet the whole room was almost too light and airy, its thin curtains pulled back to admit the chill breeze from the north.

"As I have said, about Anne-Mieke, and about your sons."

"I was under the impression all of this had been settled," Van Geyst said. He did not loosen his tie or remove the beige suit jacket. His impassive, friendly gaze assured Natanson of his full attention. He gestured toward the little bar that stood at the end of the small living room, topped by a heavy lace tablecloth. Natanson's raised palm moved rapidly from side to side.

"You must at least make good on the financial commitment. Anne-Mieke still bears the name Senior Van Geyst; the divorce has taken its course in a completely normal way. Yet she has received absolutely no assistance for herself or her children. This cannot continue." Natanson's mournful eyes tried to connect with Van Geyst's mild, even benevolent gaze. "The...fluidity of your American life prevented me from coming to you sooner. But the situation is urgent... Anne-Mieke is completely without any other means. You know she suffers from the old wartime ailment, she cannot breathe easily. Of the boys only one is old enough to go away and live on his own. For months they have existed only, in despair."

"But apparently they are not without friends," Van Geyst observed, smiling slightly. "After all, you yourself..." He shrugged, palms up, prompting Natanson to go on.

"I have found help for them before. But now it is dying. Public assistance is not possible because it is known that a father exists and is easy to find." It had in fact been oddly simple, not only to reconstruct the entire history of the unhappy family but to identify and confront its former head. Van Geyst had never bothered with any of the concealment strategies, was always available for the asking.

"Is it possible that you have no compassion at all for your own boys?" Cast-off wives consigned to Limbo formed much of his practice, but practically never sons. His dark brows formed a pointed arch.

"I have not had a chance to see my sons since they remained in Paraguay," Van Geyst reminisced. "Simply put, Mr. Natanson, life chose different paths for them and for me. The pre-American days seem many ages away. Don't you yourself have a similar experience?"

Natanson looked nonplussed. "But this is the emptiest of talk. You cannot seriously believe it that simple to step aside from your own history. What do you take me for, Professor Van Geyst?" He seemed to take on several inches when angered, and his voice rose proportionately. "I have consideration for the present lady of this house, fine. I warn you it is not endless. As for your earlier life, it is perfectly documented by a very long series of unpaid bills, bankruptcy violations, and—as you readily will see—more. A veritable paper trail, sir, if I have the expression correct." The staccato Spanish accent jabbed at Van Geyst's impassivity.

"You seem very angry with me." The choirboy eyes seemed to reproach a stern, invisible taskmaster. "But I have simply renewed my life, in a manner that had to entail a refusal. And that refusal—of stupid encumbering errors and their dead consequences—is no more nor less than my own embrace of America. True, I intend to leave nothing behind me except some written texts..."

"You already have," the lawyer grumbled. "As I told you, among them, certain unpaid bills..."

"Some written texts that people in my line of work have generally felt...to be examples of a fresh start in the field of literary studies. A fresh start is the essence of American history: now isn't that a curious paradox for you?" Van Geyst smiled benignly. "A tradition of new starts. It is the glory of our new country, is it not, that it offers a new life to the veterans of old disasters? America takes people at their word. You probably noticed that in YOUR line of work. And that is no more than correct."

"You have contributed exactly one hundred dollars to the life of your family for the past five years. And I urge you to do more before the machinery of justice compels it." Natanson's voice had lost its whining edge. "The lady in the kitchen will not like to hear the result of our conversation."

The study door opened softly to admit Carol Van Geyst. accompanied by mixed aromas of cooking. An early dusk was growing around her.

OUR PRODUCT IS EXCELLENCE

Keith's evening shift is under way. The shower, the half glass of pale sherry, the two-minute consultation with Chuck, the choice of blazer and tie. Keith is happy to be back at the Admin Building, turning corners sharply, facing front.

Soon he will stand shoulder to shoulder with his faculty ("my faculty") welcoming Redfern's most elusive celebrity professor back to town. Then drinks with the Old Redfernian, now a Stanford mover and shaker.

Marvella's trip from the former plantation house just out of Roanoke, thirty rooms, with antebellum Greek columns and ballroom staircase, to the Redfern campus, would be a matter of only two hours. No chance of Marvella being late if she made the flight.

Everything had gone so well so fast. With Harvard, Yale, Stanford contending for her, Chuck could still pull his rabbit trick. True, it may still be relatively rare for anyone to collect a six-figure salary from an employer who doesn't care whether you show up for work or not. But how great it looks on the charts, on the Affirmative Action Compliance Reports. And in the Rumble, when Marvella announces that she will audition students for class openings. Redfern even caught a mention on the Tomorrow Show the other day. What if we couldn't quite nab Cosby or Eddie Murphy, what if Toni Morrison and Maya Angelou were busy for the next ten years?

Marvella has it all: the operatic six-foot height and five-foot girth, the tell-it-like-it-is, sock-it-to-'em delivery. The pedigree: former madam, multiple welfare mom, heroin addict, everything. Even the right teeth, maybe sixty of them lined up in all those rows. Marvella had the Force. Wherever she went, incidents followed.

Keith runs through the latest incident, something to do with one of her auditions, where Marvella sometimes "acts out" to capacity crowds. Some asinine student asked a ridiculous question when she'd given the assignment: write a poem about a madam, an addict, or a single mother.

"But I don't know anything about...what you said, being a single mom and all," the guy objected, blushing. "Maybe we oughta be free to pick out a subject by ourselves, something we know about."

"Well I don't know anything about being a rich, spoiled, lazy, quarrelsome jock either," Marvella answered, her grin opening wide, like the golden curtains of an opera stage, over the brilliant rows of dentures. Everyone just laughs it off, but then Marvella warms to the subject. Her six-by-five bulk heaves out of the special red satin chair LuAnn has had brought in. She is exuding flowing garments which she now gathers around her, holding up one end like a train.

"What's all this knowing? You think you know 'bout freedom? Freedom is MY beat, you 'member that! Why, I'll put my own foot on yo' neck an' THAT'S freedom!"

The way Keith heard about it, in the dead silence that followed the kid actually went up to the front of the amphitheatre and confronted Marvella.

"You really wanna put your foot on—my neck?" the kid asked, hesitating.

"I say handsome is as handsome does!" Marvella suddenly bayed, breaking into epic laughter. "Yay—uh." She faced the kid down from her towering height. "How yo'ever gone pass yo' audition? Jes' you 'member: SPACE to PLACE," she proclaimed. Everyone staring now, some frowning with concentration, others with mouth slightly ajar, friends turning quickly to each other and back. "Ian' no place for YOU." She pointed a twig-like three-jointed finger at the kid. "I'm offerin' you new space to place your steps. If you sayin' you patron-ize this academic course so you can parade your same old whitey-white sayin's an' get a charge out of it too, you got more thinkin' comin'. You unnerstand? More thinkin' comin', mm-hmm. You wanna talk 'bout some magic place, some safe castle wheah nothin' evah happens, you got more thinkin' comin'. That has to move on, see? Has to move on to new spaces, new green places of promise and fulfillment. You gotta be suitably apprised. Nevah mind youah ignorance. Nevah mind yo' cries of ignorance from beneath the rock. Nevah mind what your elitist mastahs have to say to us. The resta yall, come with me to the riverside. Come with me to be sold and stolen on the wave of a dream. Don' hide yo face. Let darkness break out."

Applause broke out, crescendoed, as her expression grew trance-like. "You—arrivin' on a nightmare but praying for a dream. The night-mare is you snakes in the grass. But the doom of the ex—tinct is here, nevah you mind."

She stepped down from the platform, grinning into the crowd. To this day no one is sure if they've been admitted to the course. The lit-tle mothah who'd started the trouble never came back. But Marvella has made herself even scarcer since that day. Students trying to communicate with her aides have reached a phone number that turns out to be in a broom closet. The message on the machine in the closet has a man's voice saying he will relay the name and number, but he never does. Voices are sometimes raised to express resentment. Four-page single-spaced memos show up regularly on Keith's desk.

He has already promised to quadruple minority representation on the Redfern campus. He has already quadrupled the junk mail in everyone's box. The parents of the offending student have been notified of his suspension. Because hurtful talk causes a pain Chuck cannot abide, Keith's major memo-of-the-week is powered by moral outrage against verbal violence.

To All Members of the Redfern Community:

A Bias Response Panel, which will respond to those incidents which dishonor cultural identity and provide channels for education, reintegration, and forgiveness has been proposed by President Chavadze. The panel will handle complaints of alleged bias behavior that violates Redfern's community standards. The panel will be able to implement a full range of disciplinary actions including social probation, removal from college housing, suspension, or permanent separation from the universi-ty. A further memorandum will define hate crime and describe how insensitive speech cases will be handled. It is absolutely clear that freedom of speech will be protected at all times. It does not, however, include stig-matizing remarks, misdirected laughter, or exclusion from conversation. Strong and immediate steps will be taken against offending students and departments.

But Keith, not Chavadze, fends off daily attacks on the Redfern peace; it's Keith's job to keep the dam from bursting, for assault by hurtful words is just like assault and battery. Now students who steal and throw away whole printings of the Rumble whenever it contains something offensive feel that they, not the paper, have been trashed.

Because you cannot forbid physical violence and permit verbal violence; they are now equally intolerable, in fact one and the same,

Keith and his band of PR people now have a sideline in speech control. But Monitoring the Racial Atmosphere, as Keith privately calls it, is a piece of cake compared to the Marvella Question. Will she yield to Redfern's courtship? Meanwhile, she is stringing it out, the humble suitor stuck with finding the money for Marvella's twelve research assistants, her Bahamas vacation, her no-interest mansion. With hot tub. Sure, she was entitled to these perks and more. Hadn't her ancestors suffered untold, untellable calamities at the hands of people just like himself? But she sure seems to like keeping people just a bit off-balance.

Knox Lydgate drops into the Admin Building to bask in the chandelier's light and see if anyone has noticed he's leaving forever. Knox is wearing an especially self-effacing expression; he stoops slightly in keeping with his years. He meets Keith's eyes in mutual nostalgia and sympathy. But by the time they consider unwinding, Fishbane and Graziella join them, and they clam up.

"You're sure, are you, Armin, that you are making a truly excellent appointment?"

"Got a litmus test for excellence, Knox?"

Lydgate passes on, bemused.

President Chavadze stows himself in front at the airport reception area, surrounded by a craning wave of reporters. Image Enhancement has managed to muster up more from the local news channel; their cameras pan the little airport. Clutching his coat around him, Chuck waits behind the glassed-in walls of the airport waiting area, the little phalanx of media types keeping their bored distance. There has been nothing new about the murder since morning. This airport assignment is no fun, no fun at all. It reminds Morgan Broadside of the time she had to cover the campus Candlelight Vigils Against Hate last year.

The flight's in now, the little commuter plane only five minutes late. Passengers ricketing down the little folding stairs, a few clutching attaché cases, no one with any luggage. The media types sluggishly move to the glass door like passengers entering a bus.

They're almost all off now. At long last a tall striking black figure descends like royalty. Soon she'll be there for hugs, kisses, photo ops. But what's this? The silhouette is thin, stringy almost, withdrawn. And it's not Marvella, but a man. A subdean materializes immediately at the President's side.

"Apologize instantly to the media for this interruption. Go call Image Enhancement immediately, the emergency number, tell them first. Then have the car brought right up to where we are, RIGHT UP CLOSE." The aide runs to follow orders. The towering black figure is coming through the automatic airport doors, right into the waiting area, his biker cap looking vaguely familiar. His jersey is striped in three-inch horizontal yellow and black, like a nineteen-twenties bathing suit. He carries a red attaché case to match his biker hat. He stops at Chavadze. Morgan Broadside and her little band straighten up, approach. People drinking beer at the cocktail bar wonder who everyone in the group is. The man selling boxed lobsters leaves his stand, ambles closer with his pal from the newsstand.

"President Chavadze?" A hint of mocking stress on the title. "I got a tape to play for you here. From Ms. Marvella Jilkes. Here's what she says." The man—vaguely familiar to Chavadze—takes a tiny recorder from his case, inserts the tape. Morgan Broadside fluffs the blonde commas of her hair.

"Havin' gone through a great deal of mental anguish," Marvella says in her unique bass, "I have come to the conclusion that your institution is STRUCTURALLY RACIST," the tape bleeps and whirrs now, "an' holds no space for my place. You people in your safe castles, buildin' up your own police state. Muffy and Binky will jes' have to get their education from someone else. Your shared values are my share-croppers, YOUR gentilitee is MY brutalitee. So I regret to say that I will not be returning to Redfern this term. I ain' goin' from Massa Harvard to Massa Redfern, no-suh. Accept the onion," she winds up, "accept the onion: you will be peeling away layers of racism all your lives. That will be all."

Chuck reacts at once; stops pacing like a landlubber on a pitching deck. Taking Morgan Broadside by the waist, he steers her front and center with cameras following. "Do you have anything further for us, sir?" he says affably, watermelon-seed eyes creasing into his special grin.

The tall black looks disarmed and regretful but isn't. "I'll be turnin' right aroun' again. Mizz Marvella needs me back at the Plantation. Toodles, Chuck."

He melts off in the direction of the security check, clutching the red attaché case with its gilt monogram: GIVEN BARKER.

Laurie Lee Talbot is exhausted. "What do we have to read for tomorrow's lectures? It just never stops."

Yat Pang looks up from his English primer. "We will obey our teacher."

The thin fluorescent bar highlights Laurie Lee's eyebags. "My last year, and everything still out of order." She takes a battered apple from her brown bag; bites off a mealy munch. Laurie Lee hasn't added a word to PROSTITUTION AND TRANSCENDENCE in a very long time. But Yat Pang's English is getting better every day. He covers Given Barker's classes now as well as Fishbane's.

"Let us go home," the longsuffering Emil Wahnsinn decides, three books falling off his desk as he gets to his feet like a ruffled flamingo. "The office heating has stopped long before."

The three empty Pelfe Hall, leaving the entire Redfern campus bereft of adults except for two security men who've just come on and promptly gone to sleep. Students going back to their dorms, one with a ghetto-blaster he's clutching like a suitcase. A guard shudders awake, turns to face his intercom as if he'd asked it to dinner, then falls asleep again.

Keith Chambers has wondered several times during this first terrible day whether Selena's murder could have occurred under the old rules and decides yes—but probably not right on the goshdarn campus. Imagine a strangler signing in and out of buildings, introducing himself to housemothers at entryways. ("Why, ma'am, that's real nice of you. Sure I'll have another cup.")

At night Redfern belongs to the very few who just can't stand to leave. They share the campus with the sleeping guards and the few confused birds of early April. No one wonders what becomes of the students any more than a performer would think about where his audience goes after the show is over.

But Myron Wiener can't bring himself to go home. Something terrible has happened; something to make matters worse than ever. The Fielding Letters are missing. Not the Originals, of course: they repose snugly in the archives of the British Library. But the facsimiles he'll be working from—the proof that he'd found them himself—gone.

The contents of Myron's desk are now hurled every which way on the grey linoleum floor. His stuff looks pathetic under the ruthless stare of the fluorescent light. Student papers for the four courses he teaches, memos from deans demanding instant response, memos on the Diversity Curriculum and the Index of Forbidden Terms, old Redfern Rumbles, photos of Jason or Melissa, jottings for the Book, yellow post-its with frantic reminders to consult Mortmain's bibliography or bring more milk home, even a five-year old Valentine from Vera. He feels shaky, has an impulse to double-lock the office door. But the damage has already been done, cannot be conjured away.

No one knew about those Letters. They are Myron's big surprise, something he'll spring on the Department the very moment the recommendations from Dilletont and Meinfield are in. The clincher for promotion and tenure. Myron can hear his own rusty hoarse breathing as his search goes on, and on, and on. He has covered every inch of the place now, even opened closets and cabinets meant to contain nothing but mice. His life has unaccountably flown out of the office. He is as wretched as if someone had poured ink eradicator over him and left him for erased.

Myron slumps into the caved-in swivel chair, his whole frame shaking. He stares and stares, the sickening thoughts succeeding one another. He had tucked them into the back of the file drawer in his desk for a last goodnight two days ago. So when did it happen? WHEN?

He paces the office on his little size sevens. No use pantomiming a useless search again. Myron understands that this is the time to confide in Armin, his chairman, to tell all about the letters and enlist his help, should some careless idiot of a janitor or guard have accidentally... he has to tell Armin, at least, about the "find" and assure him that he was on top of the job, "working on" the letters. Surprises will have to wait.

It's six thirty, and Myron mechanically circles the middle of the floor as if one of his legs were nailed in place. Should he go home and tell Vera? It's well past dinner time, she must be putting Jason (Melissa?) to bed. Myron pictures her harried face, her quilted bathrobe, her hopes of a better apartment, time to work a half-day, dinner out once a week. That new life is as good as dead. Because the alternative to getting tenure this year is getting fired—no, terminated. If you get terminated there's no hope of another job for at least a year, and by now.... this could be his last chance. Or maybe a move as a temp, scrabbling hopelessly for the privilege of year-to-year probation. A job has opened up at Icebound Poly, and Myron has heard Armin say that whoever gets landed with this one is gonna be shoveling snow off his stoop for the rest of his life. Off his stoop.

Vera couldn't take this. He'd only have to deal with her crying and reproaches. Myron ducks back into the chair, straightens up with his chest still aching from the tension, dials Armin at home. Graziella answers in her husky smoker's voice.

"But of course I remember you, My-ron. My 'usband unfortunATEly is not at 'ome. But you seem so preoccupied, I will transmit 'im whatever you wish. Tell me." She crosses her legs on the little aquamarine velvet footstool.

Myron's mouth opens, but his vocal cords give off only a strange whistling sound. The dazzling flicker of the fluorescent office light hurts his eyes. "I am sorry," Graziella was saying, "please speak higher..."

"It's something I've lost, some manuscript letters. Armin has to know. Because they are an important discovery, a major contribution." Hyperventilating, revving up again: "The letters —came into my hands last year, it was all going to be a surprise, for the Department. My Fielding book will be the first to take them into consideration." He swallows; the letters are gone now, vanished. Why, even at this moment, can't he help talking academese?

"But I have to let Armin know they're missing so I can—gain—some—more time. More time, right. A longer period of consideration for my tenure case. I mean, if I can just find the letters, they are the only ones of their kind..." He is overtaken by nausea. Every time he says this feels like the first, and he hears Graziella's voice as through a wad of cotton wool.

"I understand," Graziella croons. "The work will take a little longer than it seemed before, until you find your letters. I shall of course tell Armin. Per'aps 'e can even help you loCATE them." She spatters a few cigarette ashes with a long red index-talon.... "I mus' tell Armin as soon as 'e comes 'ome, it should be 'alf an hour." She replaces the receiver in a contemplative frame of mind. She has already forgotten Myron's problem, caught up in her special preparations, and lets a film of turquoise drapery float across her line of vision.

Graziella expects Armin home any time now. Since the Marvella party is suddenly off—crazy American manners!!—he'll be early and probably hungry. She has acted quickly. Caviar, paté, and freshly sliced prosciutto, charged to Redfern, are already displayed on little crystal plates. A bottle of champagne in their silverplated wedding night cooler, riding on ice. Graziella herself is also giftwrapped, practically bursting out of a sheer turquoise negligee received long ago from the Victoria's Secret catalogue store but making its debut tonight. It is loosely tied over its matching bra and lacy garter belt. Even the stockings—he 'as always loved stockings—are a paler aqua. Abundant red curls spring from the bit of aqua chiffon she has used to tie them back. The outfit is a killer, down to the turquoise-tinted false eyelashes, batting like the fins of a tropical fish in an aquarium.

Tonight is going to work not only because of the surprise element but because Armin himself is lately a so much 'appier man.

The key in the door, briefcase flung down on the vinyl parquet tile, Armin is home. He doesn't look all that happy, not even at the sight of his wife in her fluttering aquamarine getup. His eyes move right to the eats.

"God, what a great idea, Graziella."

He scoops up a gob of paté, spoons caviar generously on a toast point. Swallowing loudly, Armin pours out two glittering goblets of iced champagne, downs his in a gulp, and sinks into the velvet sofa, Graziella right on his tail.

"You can't imagine what an exhausting day I had today." Armin picks up the paper, scans expertly. Not far to go: the story splashes over the whole lower-right quarter of the Tribune's front page. REDFERN STUDENT BRUTALLY SLAIN ON CAMPUS, RAPE SUSPECTED.

"But it is not your affair at all, darling. No one can involve you." She hands him two more toast points bent over under generous little mounds of caviar. One drops from between his fingers, staining the velvet. Armin scowls, emits a pfff sound. She dabs at the stain with an ice-watered napkin. "'Ave some more to drink. Everything will sort itself out in time."

The empty champagne bottle, dumped upside-down in the cooler of melted ice, the food nothing more than a stale whiff, Armin and Graziella sit up in bed again. A lot of turquoise lingerie litters the magenta broadloom. Fishbane blinks at the violent, juxtaposed colors.

"I told you I was tired, didn't I?"

"It is not all. You cannot put it past me."

"You mean GET it past you."

"Put, get. Chè importa. An' I thought you were so much 'appier lately." She tries to soften up. "Somesing you 'ave discover, darling. Only now. Remember?"

"You mean the manuscript, don't you? Well, there are problems with it."

"You are not to publish it? with references, as you say, an' everything?" Two bits of information start swimming toward each other, toward a mating in the foggier reaches of her brain.

"I will of course publicize my textual discovery. The question is only when and how," Fishbane says stiffly. "You must know by now that such rare documents are not presented to the world without some thought."

"Certainly not, amore, certainly. It takes patience, presentation. Why do we not just forget it now?" She lifts a plump white hand to his cheek. "Relax. We try once more. What is only one time?"

Armin shakes her off with another pfff sound. "I can't." Graziella removes her hand from his cheek. She sees his fleshy lips and mournful eyes hardened into a bureaucrat's blankness.

"You cannot conceal what is taking place. You 'ave to confess to me, Armin. Why does nozing ever, ever 'appen anymore?"

Fishbane contemplates the scattered evidence of failed intimacy on the hot-pink carpeting, the decimated newspaper, the rumpled pink sheets, then faces up to his wife's consternation.

"I simply think it might be over for us, Graziella."

"'Ow is it possible?" Her hands outstretched before her in a tragedienne's suppliant gesture.

"We're simply not the same. That's all."

"That is absurd." The hands fall expressionlessly; false lashes sweep her cheeks.

It comes out in a childish blurt. "And...besides...you sort of...smell."

Graziella freezes. Nothing else in the room moves but the coquettish little gilt clock, which suddenly strikes a bell-like half-hour. Husband and wife listen in silence to the neighbors through two sets of thick stucco walls, noises of dinner getting ready, children being called, a television set turning off. Fishbane glances sideways at Graziella but decides to stick to his guns. He gets up, puts on his striped satin dressing gown, makes for the bathroom, closes the door firmly.

She sits motionless, a tragic queen by Euripides. Evening grows and gathers around her. Though her white flesh takes on a golden hue under the soft bedroom light, her face is as dark as Medea's. But even as she moves over to accommodate rage, fury, and humiliation, they begin to melt away, because the two bits of info fighting for life in her brain have finally mated.

So! Graziella reaches for the slimline aqua bedside phone, dials the number she had taken down less than two hours before.

"Signora Wiener—Vera, I am Graziella Fishbane 'ere. No—no—NO. I am 'appy also to speak with YOU."

Keith Chambers, early for drinks with the Old Redfernian, folded himself into a burgundy leather wing chair in the lobby of the Multi Stillwater. A wise corporate decision to restore the ground floor to its original nineteenth-century mix of styles had helped bring the old hotel back to its former grandeur. The ballroom was gilt and cream again, its draperies swirled and festooned in soft brocade, the musicians' balcony picked out in polished wooden lacework. Opposite, the archway leading to the dining room was almost hidden by a profusion of palms and exotic flowering trees. The polished, burled woods of the reception and concierge desks contributed to the warm glow, diffused by a great brass chandelier, reproduced from the original. A generous number of sofas and armchairs were spaced throughout the lobby and grouped in conversation formats that invited people to linger, while waiters circulating with silver trays and order pads ascertained that undesirables would not make themselves at home.

The one thing that seemed lacking was human life. The entire sweep of public space was empty except for the waiters and two check-in clerks who were slacking off, trading jokes, and glancing occasionally at the gilt banjo clock that hung not far from Keith's chair.

As he waited, Keith pondered his reserves of stoicism. Entertaining the Old Redfernian was actually an escape hatch, a time-out that would help him regroup and retool. The man was late, of course; that was only to be expected. Dinner would be leisurely, too. Keith hoped that the Federal Room would still be serving at nine; if not, it would have to be the less posh Thetford's—the corporation's one concession to the eat-'n-run nineties.

A rush of air through a side door he hadn't noticed made him turn around and peer beyond the shelter of the chair. The burgundy carpeting muffled the steps of a young woman, an overweight version of Selena, wearing spike heels and a loose coat that flared out behind her. She was in a hurry but impeded by the spikes, which sank with each step into the dark red pile. Keith noted disapprovingly how they shortened and tensed the calves of her otherwise plump legs. Hadn't those gone out of style? Over her shoulder the girl had slung a book bag that proclaimed OUR PRODUCT IS EXCELLENCE in gold on black. He could see that it wasn't full. The soft light contents made the bag bounce a little as she walked.

A Redfern bag. Keith's eyes wandered aimlessly about as he tried to conjure up who this might be. As soon as she pressed the button, an elevator opened and swallowed her up.

She was followed at five minutes' interval by a fragile brunette, her hair cut like a boy's, wearing faded jeans and a worn leather jacket. Despite the aviator glasses that folded around her head and eclipsed her small features, Keith recognized her immediately.

He never liked the effect of embarrassment that too often came over students he knew when he ran into them unexpectedly off campus. Most students had never had any personal contact with him, and even the few who did might easily walk right past him without registering his identity, as if he were the neighborhood mail carrier out of uniform. Borne on an impulse for once, Keith sprang forward and beat her to the elevator.

"Dean Chambers, how nice to see you." The preppie greeting, a hearty smile. "Going up?"

"Well, yes." He rationalized his move instantaneously: the Old Redfernian was running so late, perhaps it might be a good idea to go and fetch him. After all, they were old pals; it wouldn't be like just barging in... Although the guy might be on his way down this very minute... "Yes, I am. Just visiting. Nice to see YOU, Tasha, very nice."

"Aren't you coming?" She held the elevator door for him and he got in, concentrating on a pattern of interwoven lilies carved into the mahogany ceiling. "Floor?" She pressed eight and smiled at him, her hand still poised near the buttons.

"Eight for me too. Right. Thanks."

"We're in sync, aren't we?" She laughed, this time a little nervously. The elevator noiselessly deposited them almost at once on the eighth floor. They were obviously headed in the same direction, left ten doors, then a sharp right, Tasha looking over her shoulder at Dean Chambers with ill-concealed anxiety. The hotel was bigger than it looked, reached way back into a square block. It seemed to radiate tentacles, like the Underground Campus. They were now in the rearmost wing, almost as far as the fire exit. The ceiling in the corridor became two feet lower, the carpeting worn and dusty. Why would a substantial man like the Old Redfernian want that sort of economy-class room?

The sounds struck him first. A cacophony of grunts and cries, punctuated by a whistling slash of air and a crack. Keith's impulse was to pretend he heard nothing. He was even more mortified by the presence of the young girl striding comfortably ahead. What could she be thinking? The noise took on rhythm, a horrid predictability. Tasha was unmistakably waiting for him to catch up, pass her, say goodbye; she'd been headed for that room.

Now she paused and took a breath. "Dean Chambers, I've forgotten something downstairs." She rummaged in her bag for credibility. "Nope, not here...maybe if I talk to the desk clerk...Please excuse me. It was REALLY nice to see you."

Keith's head swam into preconsciousness. Unfocused, he followed her turn and wave, her deliberate walk down the murky corridor. He went on standing stock still in front of 823, the Old Redfernian's room, from which no sound emanated. Two doors away the grunts, cries, and lashes continued rising and falling. Amid the horrors he could discern something artificial, oddly controlled. At last Keith knocked at number 823. He heard scuffling, the creaking of bedsprings, someone getting out of bed. The Old Redfernian finally answered the door, hastily wrapped in a paisley robe, his remains of white hair tousled and his kindly cheeks flushed red, making an obvious attempt to breathe regularly.

"Good to see ya! Heavens, am I going to be late?" Keith could see beyond him that the bathroom door was not fully closed.

"I'm so darn sorry, meetings all day, y'know? A little time by myself, a little relaxation." The Old Redfernian was affable, accommodating up to a point, being on the giving end. He waved a hand outward to invite Keith in. The room smelled like a zoo fully occupied by ancient animals.

As his fog lifted Keith could see quite clearly a girl hovering in the peach-toned bathroom light. What he saw first were the boots that rose all the way to the white columns of her thighs, which made her resemble a legless person on black stilts. But the white walls were punctuated by a dark triangle that made him almost reel with disgust. The rest of her body was naked except for a shiny black contraption that encircled her waist and ended in flapping garters. As she moved unconcernedly about, Keith also couldn't help noticing the slight movement of her small breasts, topped by thrusting dark nipples. A mass of brown hair partly shielded her face in the mirror, but he was, again, condemned to recognize it—the third one that evening.

"I'll...just go back downstairs and...wait," Keith stammered, wishing for the leather wing chair. "Near the desk."

"In a while, then." The door shut matter-of-factly behind him. Keith heard whiplashes again, the same grunts and cries, from the room two doors away.

He stepped back against the corridor wall, turned his right shoulder forward, and with a running start hurled himself with all his strength against the door, a first then a second tremendous shove, before the people inside could even move apart. They looked up frozen in position, an animal machine come to a sudden stop.

The plump girl Keith had noticed entering the hotel had her face hidden in pillows, which she held over her head while her buttocks soared into the air. He was appalled to recognize her by her legs, which he had noticed straining to keep her balanced. The feet were still wearing spike heels. The head of a man in his forties, standing at the edge of the bed, swiveled at Keith in astonishment. The rest of him, represented by a large artificial member made of wood, or was it plastic? had evidently been thrusting into the girl and remained perpetually poised to strike. Two other individuals completed the tableau, one a thin, greyish man brandishing a horsewhip, the other a woman on her knees before him. At least, it ricocheted through his mind, Keith did not know them from Redfern.

By the time they even turned around to their door, which was lying smashed and face down on the carpet, Keith was in the elevator, his face showing nothing more than annoyance and a certain absorption, for he was weighing and measuring the next move. In the long term, the scandal would all come out, enraging the parents, but safeguarding short-term profits would have to come first, especially now that panic was on about Selena.

Keith had to wait for the Old Redfernian another forty-five minutes, but that was part of his regular assignment. The rest of the evening passed uneventfully and cordially, no more than two convivial Scotch-and-sodas per man. Keith liked his drinks very iced, anyhow, to kill the microbes of taste.

His decided to do nothing.

Half an hour later, Keith had visitors. When the door thundered and pounded he supposed it might be some mistake, for he had no name on his doorbell. They heaved into the jerrybuilt campus apartment like a wrecking crew, making the floor shake.

A mountain of a man crashed in, wearing a Hawaiian shirt unbuttoned to the third button, faded chinos wrinkled around the hams he had for thighs, and hightop running shoes. His neck almost as thick as Keith's waist, his eyes like glass except when the pupils flickered, making them seem human. He looked at Keith as if he were yet another obstructing door that would have to be knocked down as part of the wrecking job.

The other man was tiny, maybe five feet—slim and trim, wearing a bright green Lacoste shirt and pants with creases down to his shoes, like exclamation points. He had a wide triangular Hispanic face on a head too big for his little shoulders. A garish platinum and gold Rolex watch gleamed on his wrist. His puppet-like figure advanced in fits and starts, toppling books, a sherry bottle, the five-pound exercise weights Keith used every morning. He seemed perfectly resigned to his own jerky movements, as if they were those of a troublesome but lovable child.

They sat down on Keith's two hard-backed chairs, as if reassuring him that any accommodations would be fine with them. The hulk crossed his arms, training the glass eyes on a point somewhere on Keith's chest. The puppet took out a pack of Camels and a big gold Dunhill lighter.

"Not expecting us, right? Maybe we should clue you in, why we came." The hulk's voice sounded perfectly relaxed as he creaked in his little chair, primly crossing his legs. Keith stared down at him, wondering why the building superintendent had not heard them break in. His hands were cool, but he felt faint, and the sheer absurdity of this faintness wrenched his stomach.

"The point is," the little man took over, "that you could be standing smack in the way of free enterprise."

"Who the hell are you?"

"By the way, a piece of advice. Sherry is not a man's drink. I know everyone's got their weak points, but honestly, sherry...." He puffed on his Camel. Keith fanned away the curl of smoke. "Look, maybe there isn't so much time for socializing." His reedy voice cut through the lateness of the hour and the fear. "Like I said, or maybe didn't say, we saw you at the Multi, thought you might like some company on the way home." The partner grunted and looked around the spare, neat apartment for something to crush. "You could upset our young lady colleagues, just by being. Do you know that? Our mission is to explain why you need to be very, very discreet about the Multi Stillwater."

"I have not thought about my reaction," Keith said. Then, "How do you know who I am?" This was still Keith, brushing his teeth with his right elbow jutting out, Keith neatly rotating his eggshell on the spoon for the last fastidious bite, Keith putting back the first tie he selected and taking a second from the rack, every day.

"You PR people get on TV more than the junk you sell. This new gimmick, that new campaign. A person would think your precious Redfern was American Airlines or Merrill Lynch."

The hulk grunted again, looked at Keith more speculatively. For all the noise they had made breaking in, not one person had intercepted them. What were they waiting for, what was all this blabbering? He got up on his feet with a complaining groan, as if the world were conspiring against him, and began to circulate around the two rooms, punching at the funny little things standing or hanging here and there. Nothing to do. The hot pink aloha shirt bulged over his gut as he sauntered into Keith's bedroom, and for want of anything better, smashed a couple more bottles, hit the floor with a glass lamp, totaled the bed.

"Would you mind telling me exactly what you want?"

"We only want to make a point." The little man climbed almost all the way into Keith's refrigerator and came out with his nose wrinkled. He consulted his Rolex as he stood rooted in the middle of the floor like some cleverly made doll... "Discretion is the order of the day." Rather an educated turn of phrase. "Your college doesn't know a thing about the situation, but if they did they might decide to give the young ladies trouble. I figure the odds for your peace and quiet are better with us."

"Sooner or later the university IS going to find out what's going on."

"If all goes according to schedule, they won't. Now don't look so sad. We two are just helping out for a while—until the young ladies are completely independent. We explained it to them; they need friends in the business. They seem to understand. Now YOU need to." The puppet looked at his watch again and then at the hulk, who immediately came to life. He grunted out instructions.

"On your knees. Now."

Keith knelt, like one of the prayerful donors who appear at the edges of Renaissance religious paintings. He looked up at the hulk, who suddenly swooped behind him and pinned back his wrists. Keith also felt his ankles come together, firmly between the massive legs. He knew he could not even try to move. Meanwhile, the puppet extracted and gently caressed what looked like a six-inch blade, gleaming white in the sickly illumination of the tiny living room.

"I hope this doesn't hurt," the puppet whispered, a bad child in his miniature Lacoste outfit. He lifted Keith's shirt out of his belt, just a modest two inches.

Then all he did was raise the blade in the air, making lightning jags, then painted another gash, thin and sure as a calligraphic flourish, on Keith's flat stomach just above the belt line. Keith couldn't understand why it didn't hurt at all, then suddenly so very much. He couldn't help a sudden intake of breath.

"This is not an instance of wanton violence. I hope you can see that. We're going to leave you now, as peaceably as we came." The little man's quiet voice sounded almost reassuring. "Think of us just like any of your other university business connections."

Keith surreptitiously put a hand to the wound. Oddly it wasn't bleeding...how had this spastic made such a clean cut?

"That's right, I do clean work, you should appreciate it," the puppet said proudly. His grin showed uneven, toppling mounds of fang-like teeth, like those of a wild dog. "Sometimes I can't help myself, though. I get out of control. So this had better be our one sole rendezvous. Remember: business first."

He looked the little apartment over with contempt, shook his head slowly. Then the hulk nearly sent Keith reeling with a companionable hand on his shoulder. His long torso pleated, oozing a few drops of blood onto the campus carpeting.

They didn't even bother to close the door or make sure no one was around on the way down. The sound of their shoes on the concrete, like the clanking of an empty can, leaped down the two flights of front stairs. The pain was worse now, a huge stiffening hand spreading its fingers within him, so that Keith had to wedge his body into the chaotic bed without bending an inch. He became a stony tomb figure lying heraldic and still, arms at his sides, ankles pressed together, marble eyes fixed on a steadfast God.

'I told 'em if they got rough with me to forget it. So all he did was put a hand on my neck, maybe to get better leverage. But there was something about the angle; I couldn't move my legs at all. The way he held my hipbone, that was like doing pushups. You know, the usual. I don't know why I couldn't move."

"Probably because the others were watching."

"He wanted me to scream so I did, and it really did hurt. But then another one put it in my mouth, and I...it felt like I wasn't there."

"You aren't. They would have to pick the smallest, skinniest one of us."

"I think that was sort of the point. They did pay double."

"It was probably worth the investment to bring in those two monsters, we're in the black anyway. They should wear jackets around the Multi, though. I wish someone could tell them."

"No one at the Multi cares as long as they have money."

"I dunno... the chandeliers, those nice palm trees and everything. It's a shame."

"Sucking 'em off is better. I know a way you don't have to swallow it."

"No, it isn't."

"Yes, it is."

"I read in an article about the Japanese that men think swallowing it is the ultimate sign of obeisance."

"This sounds like one of Fishbane and Rossiter's Tell-Alls."

"Those sound worse."

"No they don't."

"There's one who only wants me to talk dirty. Wanna know who? You'll never stop laughing. Then he just does it and leaves. Don't you wanna hear who it is? You all know him. Or you know about him."

"Sure. Who"

"Hargreaves. From England. Beard, old sweater. Art History."

"He's Comp Lit."

"Everyone's Comp Lit. What the hell do they do in that part of the world?"

"Does he have a prick?"

"A really small one, like three inches top. Then he promised to refer me to friends. Refer!"

"I don't see anything funny, word of mouth is how you get a reputation."

"It's the professor's way of putting it that's funny."

"How can the professors. I mean, don't they feel sort of like substitute parents or something. Like they're fucking their own daughter, or... Good thing most of 'em don't have the money."

"I know. Only one of mine was a prof so far. Ricci, teaches Italian. He showed up just like you said he would. One card was enough."

"Hey—he's the one I had, too."

"You mean the one who had YOU."

"What's he like?"

"I...can't tell you. You know, a lot of 'em fall into categories; you've got your spanking, your filthy talk, your masochists, they're almost fun...your multiples, certain things you just get to expect. But some of what he wants...really, really twisted. I'm gonna pass him on."

"He makes me want to blow the whole thing."

"You CAN'T!"

"I just said I want to. The upside of Ricci... very funny... the upside, as I was saying, is that he poops out and can't do it. That's when he calls you all those names, right? Doesn't that happen to you?"

"Well, no...except maybe once in a while. He calls me Beatrice, pronounces it in Italian, Bay-a-TREE-cheh. I think it's sort of nice, actually. What I really have a problem with is the outfit. Just try and do what he wants with a waist-length blonde wig on, under that tent of a velvet dress with gold ropes all over it."

"Sounds even worse than your dumb idea of being literary characters—remember?"

"Can we all be literary characters? It would be great for the profs."

"Like who?"

"Madame Bovary. Anna Karenina."

"WHO?"

"They're all the same. I mean, they all LOOK the same. We need variety."

"Virginia Woolf."

"She's a writer, not a character."

"Penelope. Molly Bloom."

"WHO?"

"Dido."

"That's a THING, dummy, not a PERSON. Anyhow, we're not gonna need those."

"Are we including gay people or not?"

"We can figure something out. Emily Dickinson. Murphy Brown. Well, she's cultural, isn't she?"

"This is dumb. You're just trying not to talk about what we'll REALLY be doing. Nobody wants to fuck literary characters."

"That's what you think. Some people ONLY want to fuck literary characters."

"Then they're not about to try us, are they?"

"Look, if you've got a problem with the plan, admit it here and now. I've already made up my secondary list. You five are my first list because you're fabulous, but this is almost opening week and I'm not gonna tolerate waffling. Just speak right up."

"Are we gonna do gay people or not?"

"How can we justify doing this if we believe that equal relations between women and men are impossible in this sexist society?"

"Hey. Does a person not have relationships just because society is hierarchical? Boots, you're talking ten percent. That's too high."

"I'm in, as long as we have certain rules. Like, no students."

"Of course not. They'd never have the money. Where was I? Men are socialized to take sexual pleasure from the hierarchical disparity of submission and dominance. Well, we can handle that. Tasha, ten percent is what I get."

"Forget it. The Furrie Foxe pays as much as six hundred a night just for topless dancing, and you don't fuck anybody."

"We have to limit the hours. Time for classes and reading and the rest."

"Don't be silly. Four of us are Comp Lit majors."

"But I'm Engineering. Stephanie is History. Marie-Claire is Chem."

"Okay. Nobody can work more than three hours a day, split any way you want. That includes nights."

"That makes, say, two clients at two hundred, minus twenty each. And that's if your calls are in the same place. Give me the Furrie Foxe."

"Let me remind you that the Foxe makes you show up every

night except Sunday, and you get to work five hours. The six hundred you're talking about come at the end of the week. AND you could get recognized at the Foxe. Tell you what, I'll consider seven percent."

"Has it occurred to you that we could just as well do this as a co-op, without this hierarchical element of you as our leader? I know this was your idea, sort of, but face it, who hasn't thought about doing it themselves? We could have absolutely even shares."

"Bad, bad. That's naïve socialism."

"Hargreaves would think it's great."

"I bet he's one of our first customers, so you better get used to the idea."

"Ricci, the Italian prof."

"Aaaaaagggghh. Muurggggh."

"Are we gonna do gay people or not?"

"Seriously, what about the co-op? We could take turns on the line. Look, we'll have to trust each other. No one else allowed, 'cause it can't get too big; the bigger it gets the more administration you need. Seven people counting Boots and Tasha, same goals and aspirations. No parasitical superstructure."

"I guess you trust yourselves to do all the screening, right? Keep the calendar straight? And that's not all. What about supplies? You trust yourselves for all that?"

"That's right, Boots, we do."

"God, all that money. NO jobs anywhere, not even the food service. They're cutting more all the time. No more dorm crew. Bookstore firing people."

"I just think it will add a little spice to life."

"Make a change."

"Are we gonna do gay people or not?"

"You dilettantes don't deserve a piece. There are people starving, who'd want in on this. You privileged characters who always get everything for free, classist, racist rich bitches."

"I need this money more than anything. 'Til last year it was 'ask Daddy.' Now suddenly the world ends..."

"It's still 'ask Daddy', only he'll expect something in return. And with the co-op, you can get out whenever you want, 'cause you won't be in debt to Boots."

"Whenever I want?"

"'Course. Don't you see the beauty of it? Everyone who goes with us will have the same secret. Like a bond. And you walk away with whatever you make, it's a hundred percent yours. That's the only way I'm in."

"Me, too."

"I'm gonna try literary characters. Maybe change into anyone they want, on the spot. I mean, what else DID most of those women do?"

"D'you think this is a costume party or something?"

"Three hundred, not two."

"We have to pay someone for protection. You get attacked in this business, people even get tortured and murdered...."

"The Multi Stillwater bar has like bouncers, for free. It's the perfect place, right on the border between Redfern and downtown. You can almost see it from here. Straight downhill."

"My mom stays there when she visits."

"My parents too."

"Well, isn't that ever so nice and cozy? My Auntie Vanderbilt stays there too. Rich bitches."

"We'll have to have a backup place."

"Maybe a package rate."

"What's to keep a hotel from turning us in? I'm not paying them off, too. Boots would still be better."

"We can't just use the Stillwater. We'll have to hang out there sometimes but use this place."

"The DORM?"

"Use your brain. No other place is safe."

"For sure."

"We'll be a model of Redfern enterprise. You know, OUR PRODUCT IS EXCELLENCE. Kind of managed competition, but non-hierarchical. Three hours a day top, three hundred an hour. That'll lock in a worthwhile clientele."

"Carlotta DiSalvo wrote good stuff in ALL THE WORLD'S A SEXUAL STAGE about this kind of a situation. To fully express your sexuality, let your allure hang out, is...like exercising your whole persona. We're being progressive, putting our own selves first."

"That sounds like Fishbane's course. The SELF and sex, the

SELF and...creamed peas, etcetera."

"Maybe he'll call us too. He must have a shitload of money, always dressed up like that."

"I'm scared. Aren't you?"

"Who's gonna hurt us? Not the profs, or businessmen from the Stillwater? You don't have to do it if you don't want to."

"You've just gotta remember it's not you, just your body."

"I'm scared. And you're crazy if you think you can say it's just your body. Being sex slaves is..."

"Good business. We'll be the meeting place of Redfern and the business community."

"Why are women always PLACES?"

"Because...we're where it happens. Then they walk away."

"You're always so bitter. What about the Statue of Liberty? What about the Allegory of Peace and Quiet, or whatever Hargreaves was talking about the other day? All female."

"See, just like I said. Women are places and things and abstract qualities. MEN are human beings."

"I'm not sure you belong in this Group. Maybe you wanna think about it some more."

"Leave her alone. Some guys will always want someone with an attitude."

"I'm scared."

"C'mon, get the lead out. We've got work to do."

Wednesday, April 7, 1993
TELL ALL

Simon and Phil know Ricci will not be in his office this morning. It's the hour of Ricci's special class with only one student in it, which he keeps on the roster so that the Administration thinks he's teaching the usual two. The policemen have a clear field. Granita sighs with contentment at being able to do an old-time search He feels for the warrant in his pocket and smiles.

"We won't hafta deal with anyone else. They won't show up till practically eleven, if at all, and then they go to lunch. So let's get to it."

"Why the fuck do they get paid?"

"It's called tenure, Phil. You're a professor, you have a lifetime job. No one can fire you for anything—used to be that screwing the students was the only thing you could get fired for. No more. And not working is the least of it."

"Maybe they're never missed."

"See—if you get tenure you have, like, limited liability for anything that happens. It's not your fault, it's everyone's, because they're stuck with you. Whether it's stupid or unethical or maybe even criminal. Every department is independent. And now they're all involved in turf wars like in a corporation. But try an' interfere from outside and they close ranks. I mean, did you notice anyone wanting to help US?"

"Mebbe it's not such a bad thing to have employment security— I mean, s'pose one year nobody signed up for somethin', the teacher could get fired. This way at least they hafta wait 'til things pick up again, the poor guy isn't out on the street..."

"You got a point, I guess. That's good, Phil." Granita produced a sarcastic teacher's-pet smirk. "I mean it. I haven't got an answer. But the way they work the system, it's clogged."

"Aw, the hell with it," Phil grumbled. They bent to the task of ransacking Ricci's little office mess, which would prove utterly funless— no smokes, even, not to speak of bennies to help get through the day.

A pile of photographs showed up first. Some featured a grinning Ricci with his arm around the scraggy neck of a sickly-looking middle-aged lady in a print dress. Others showed Ricci with his cheek pressed to another, almost identical one belonging to an old woman, her white hair parted in the center, fleshy lips, black mourning dress. The backgrounds were sidewalk cafes, squarish buildings with columns. Simon recognized the Leaning Tower of Pisa. A long blond hair had gotten wound up in the pile.

It did not take long to shake out each volume of the instant collection of gold-embossed books that gleamed in the mahogany bookshelves, though they had to stop at times to separate clumps of newly minted pages. They lifted the carpet with its entwined designs of grapevines and evil-looking human masks. Nothing. The file cabinet took longer.

"Remember how the contents of his file were missing from the Underground stash? We'll have to dump everything out of all these files, just to find papers about things he must know already."

They scrupulously returned everything to its place. "Wish I could get into that computer," Simon answered. "He must have everything important in there. And here we are playing with his silly home decorations." They eyed the Macintosh PC on its black steel table.

"Hey look, dirty pictures!" Granita held out a sheaf of photos, each displaying an image of copulation. The positions of the writhing figures depended on whether you held the card horizontally or vertically. A few solo nudes were mixed into the batch, nakedly lying in provocative poses, all young and attractive in some individual way. There were also two or three business cards. Granita took a pack of Marlboros out of his pocket and lit up, giving the cellophane a bit of flame before putting it out.

"From this little table here. Just one drawer, nothing else in it." One of the cards said Maid for Love in an inky scrawl on the message side. Simon imagined Ricci ogling the pictures over and over, though they didn't look much handled—more like advertisements for a purchase under consideration.

"Maid, that's pretty corny," Granita said.

"Saying corny is corny enough." Simon grinned. "Maid. It's that Japanese love hotel, they call it, on the other side of the campus, down just a couple blocks."

"You'd think a professor could remember that without havin' ta write it down."

"Some people just write down everything, don't trust themselves."

"Handmaid," Simon said all of a sudden. It was the word from Selena's diary. He booted up Ricci's Mac, logged on to the Redfern mainframe, and input RRICCI, then HANDMAID. It was Ricci's password all right. There were several e-mail messages on the screen. The one from SELENAF@REDFERN, dated March 31st, jumped out at Simon. He pressed F2 and a split-second later it was on the screen: "The Texas business is boiling over. It's now or never for you."

Phil looking over Simon's shoulder let out a low whistle. "Well, lookee here! What did Berto's little piece of ass mean with that?"

"Be nice if you could put that in a fancier way." Simon felt that he'd like to get outdoors for a bit and chase some fly-by-night dealer down the street. The Texas Business, whatever it was, might take them pretty far afield eventually, but first Chavadze might know something about it.

Simon dialed the President's Office and heard the nasal tones of an Executive Assistant accompanied by the clacking of computer keyboards. She rerouted him to Keith Chambers' office suite, where two more secretaries passed him through. Chambers was definitely busy, but hearing a new resonance in Simon's voice made no attempt to brush him off.

"We really need to reach Chavadze," Simon told him. "No, I'm not at liberty to tell you the reason. He's the only one who can fill us in on a couple of key points."

Keith's frown deepened as he scrutinized the orderly square of sky framed in his picture window and picked up his special phone. Chavadze's warm hello came on immediately.

"At your service as always, Lieutenant, I never eat or sleep anymore anyhow. Would you like me to join the Force? Well, fire away."

"What's the Texas Business? It's something that came up accidentally during our investigation. The Texas Business, that's it."

The president sobered up as if he suddenly found Simon a more interesting man than before.

"I was the provost at Texas Megatech for some years. Could this special Business have something to do with that?"

"This seems to be about Professor Ricci. What could Texas business have to do with him?"

"This may refer to some problems Berto ran into at Texas Megatech," Chavadze offered. "I told you before that Berto sometimes behaved intemperately. He was still quite a young man, foolish in the way of young men. Apt to get carried away by the eternal feminine. That's how it was with him. Well, at Texas he somehow got a reputation for awarding high grades to certain not very deserving young women in exchange for—sexual favors. An old peccadillo. All clouded over. Nothing came of it."

"Is that what someone would have to mean by the Texas Business? Could there be something else? Maybe something to do with business, I mean finances?" Simon floundered a moment. "Well, what happened that time, sir? Did Ricci get fired or have charges filed against him, or what?"

"It's true, Berto played the heavy on that occasion, Lieutenant. I think the parties all came to a sane agreement. As I said, no more came of it."

"It's a serious thing, anyway, if he was charged with it at Texas. It could certainly ruin his reputation here."

"I know I have to be as candid as possible, Lieutenant." Chavadze's unseen face almost crumpled with the burden of what he was about to say. "Well, there was one more thing... As head of his Department, Berto was responsible for the budget. It was said that he yielded to temptation there too. Those accusations, naturally, were completely unfounded. How many times, when a man seems to have made mistakes in one aspect of his life, people start accusing him of everything! But whoever referred to some Texas Business could also mean something like that. This had to do with Teaching Assistants. The graduate students, some of them known malcontents, who were teaching in the Italian department, accused Berto of skimming a percentage from their salaries."

"Sort of a rogue chairman, then."

"If the accusations had had any force, yes."

"This is bad stuff, sure. But it's also old news, sir. Why would anyone want to bring it back now, all these years later?"

"Character assassination is the only kind available to some people, lieutenant."

Emil Wahnsinn wonders again and again this morning, with mounting panic, why so many students are staring at him like that. What is it they know, or think they know?

Covert looks are traded the minute he says anything. This book, *Miscarriage of Justice*, is full of words that make him look down and try to avoid their eyes. Still he can see through the magnifying lenses that distrust, even contempt, are writ large all over every girl's face. When he happens to meet their glances they swivel away. More coughing than usual too. No one even wants to argue with him, or corrects him when he says a word from the Index of Forbidden Terms. They just sit there waiting for something to happen. Maybe it's part of a new rights demonstration, or are they impatient for another teacher?

He felt wobbly on the way back to his cubbyhole in the Underground Campus. The Redfern Rumble, turned to page three, lay on his desk. He sat staring at it in shock, reading and rereading his name in the lead story. The same black on white every time. His head swam, consciousness now restricted to his visual field.

The article explains how Emil's name had appeared there. It seems that girls are writing the names of sex maniacs up in the women's toilets. That's what it says. But this is the last thing that could ever be true of him.

Emil comes from a line of people who have bequeathed him a lively sense of justice. Since he was a small child, "That isn't fair!" was his war cry. Emil has a fund of physical strength to help enforce this idea and does not scruple to use it. But now there is nothing to be done against this feline campaign of innuendo. Even the simplest words won't come. Denial means concession, not to speak of the ridicule: Emil senses, besides, that people who believed him incapable of rape would be the cruelest of all.

The worst part, though, is about Selena. Humiliation and ostracism are bearable, yes, but not this... If anyone really knew of his, his feeling for her, then probably the scribbler of his name wants to plant suspicion in the minds of the policemen. Could it be a student? But he gave everyone an A last term just as it was understood he would. And certainly the scribbler is not a professor, if only because the professors need Emil to go on teaching all those classes for them.

The Temperance Chief of Police, John Killifer, hangs up on the Governor's aide that morning with a very red face. The thing to do now is transfer the burden of this humiliation at once, shove the hot potato right at those blunderers Granita and Blank.

"The two of you better get it NOW: you're not investigating REDFERN. You're not investigating every goddam person who was at the donors' party. Do you guys know that I'll be cleaning out your shit for years, trying to reconstruct my relationship with the university? Governor Pelham seems to think I'M the dimwit running a keystone cop movie, doing slo-mo car chases between the Admin Building and—wherever you get to when you're through. I got complaints here from just about everyone who counts, down from Governor Pelham to the campus security."

Simon is not too dense to know that there are basically two kinds of investigation: one that seeks to uncover information, and one that seeks to cover it up again. In one day he has met many of both kinds. Who complained? Are they people who get up at five and don't sleep 'til two, people who have to sweat a whole system in a matter of days, badly fed and with nothing real to drink? Where does anyone get off being OFFENDED?

"I want to do my best, sir." Simon controls himself. He has actually just heard himself praised by the Chief on the afternoon news... "Can you give Phil and me some idea who's that mad at us?"

"You might as well know SOMETHING about it. You two seem to be pestering the hell out of some professor called Ricci who's plugged into big Redfern donors. I don't know what you're holding against him—"

"I'll tell you, sir; he was..."

"And I don't NEED to know. Governor Pelham's office mentioned Win Biscottini in connection with Ricci. Biscottini Stadium, got it? THAT Biscottini. He thinks you're giving the good professor much too much attention." The Chief's voice relents now, takes on a little wryness. "Biscottini is very determined. He wouldn't talk to me personally, but he told the governor's aide that Professor Ricci feels persecuted, especially since there is not the slightest evidence against him. Blank, listen: if you keep leaning on this Ricci we're gonna be mending fences the rest of our lives." The voice mingled with static, crackled off.

It came back again minutes later, a shout that left Simon and Phil gaping in shock. "Blank and Granita, get over to Redfern NOW. It's General Fenn, the grandfather. We got it from the *Tribune*, dammit. The papers had to tell US; he's called a goddam press conference. Just GO."

Ever since he had taken over the Tell-Alls, moulding them into reasonable facsimiles of TV talk shows, Fishbane had felt secretly bemused by the oddity of the topics at hand. He never resorted to mean-spirited barbs or bashing, but it was hard for him to hide the resentment he felt at having missed so much in his youth. However, he did his level best to welcome every Teller with an open mind and ready praise.

To a Teller who confessed his need to expose himself to campus passersby from the billows of an oversized raincoat, his reaction was, "I just love you. And I love that... upstanding defiance of yours."

To another who confessed her astonishment at campus cross-dressers, he brought the comfort of parental chiding: "Well, go with the flow. Be peaceful and life-affirming and some great fashion ideas may come. Try it maybe. Expand the reach of your SELF."

However, the Teller who confessed to a dislike for Indian food was harshly reprimanded and directed to spice up his life. Recipes were subsequently handed out to the entire assembly.

"People say this is all fluff," Fishbane once told the Rumble's feature editor, "and not educational. But I, for one, have learned a lot.

You learn different types of things than those you would pick up in an ordinary plain-Jane—I mean a simple course. It's an eye-opener, a wake-up call for more diversity and change."

LuAnn put it more emphatically. "When Ah heah that no one's sayin' anythin' 'bout ouah Tell-Awls, it's almost like, Ah wondah what's wrong with 'em."

Anyone who attacked the idea on rational grounds was subject at least to veiled ridicule. And sometimes hurtful adjectives were openly used, like "stuffy," "antiquated," "academic." Students who declined to appear and stuck to the course option were made to understand that they were not doing the whole job, "but that's your choice, your own self-expression, and you need to stand by it. Have a nice day."

The Tell-All group would always form up into a circle so that the leader would not look like a leader. But today had brought in a record crowd, which overflowed onto the floor and into the corridor. The news of the murder had propagated an almost festive need for togetherness and free discussion.

The featured speaker today is a pretty senior carrying, Fishbane estimates, about twenty pounds of excess weight, but more cutely distributed than Graziella's. He's pretty sure that she's not a Comp Lit major. She has a stuffed brown manila envelope in her hand, business-size, not the kind you use for memos or student papers. Her hair a little thin, a little sandy. Where from? She is tall but her body sags the moment she straightens up and faces the room.

"I'm not a Comp Lit major. I tried to talk to Dean Chambers first but he wouldn't see me." Total quiet rules. "I can't take it anymore." This was a very usual Tell-All opener, but her face told more. "My name is Stephanie," she said on a questioning note. "I'm in History?"

"Well, Stephanie?" Fishbane's voice had a note of brusqueness. But maybe the Tell-Alls were getting a new convert, so he brightened.

"I...joined the ring this year. But it's four years old. It's been going on ever since I came to Redfern."

"Tell us, Stephanie. What ring?"

"I had to tell. If this chance hadn't come up I would have gone to the police."

"Stephanie. You know this could be very serious. If there's something you can say about the...tragedy, you owe it to yourself to..."

"No. It's not that." Tears flowed hazily now. This was still standard Tell-All stuff, a definite enhancer when the Teller was attractive. "Selena Fenn, I mean, none of us hardly knew her. At least I don't think so." She was momentarily diverted by the possibility, then burst into audible weeping, mostly the last stage before the delicious facts hatched. Some members of the audience looked away shamed, in the spirit of the childhood years when crying out loud meant giving in.

"That's okay, cry if you need to." A maternal Fishbane leaned forward. His right hand twirled a Mont Blanc fountain pen between index and third fingers. Stephanie bit her lower lip, torn between the demands of performance and the import of what she was about to tell.

"It's that...I'm in the ring, only not any more? A prostitution ring? It started with just seven people and now it's...enormous. Four years ago, in my freshman year? Lots of dorms have members. It's all over the campus and outside too." Stephanie fumbled for a crumpled Kleenex in her jeans pocket, blew her nose hard. But then her entreating breathing grew more labored and the watchful attitude fell away.

Fishbane stopped twirling his pen. She hurtled on, straining to get it All Told.

"There are at least twenty Redfern people in it. Mostly we see clients at the Multi Stillwater or a dorm room. The rooms rotate. They have to be singles. It used to be everyone knew each other, but now that it's big...Most clients pay two hundred dollars because with the recession, y'know, they couldn't raise the prices."

An experienced Tell-All member was the first to react. "You mean someone here is running a sex business? Are you gonna tell?"

"This IS telling, isn't it? I mean, you know about it now. You're supposed to bring something to a Tell-All, aren't you? So I brought some of the pictures."

No one wanted to be first to express an interest in the pictures.

"What caused you to decide to share this with us, Stephanie?" Fishbane kept bravely to his role of moderator/host.

"WHAT? It's something that's happening, right here, I couldn't take it anymore." Jolted out of her weeping, Stephanie segues into wild chatter, as if someone were about to cut her off. "Someone came to my room, they didn't care if anyone even heard, and they made the proposition, they said the group needed me because I'd be great for...certain things they wanted to do, and they also needed someone for multiples, they said that was easier mostly, and you could split the work better, like an assembly line, she said, and she knew I needed the money. She said about how it would be okay to pretend you'd been raped because some people liked that as long as you didn't really start believing it. She said that a lot of clients only wanted someone from Redfern because it's an elite school and that everyone here was getting so busy they couldn't handle the volume, she said the volume. She said a lot of stuff about free enterprise and combining your university experience with something more practical... I didn't know...what I was getting into here, please...help me." She finished suddenly, blowing the rest of the lines, waiting for a prompter.

Fishbane spoke slowly. "Has anyone else here heard about this alleged ring?"

"Someone knows, some grownup, because when I tried to get an appointment with Dean Chambers he had no time on his calendar for weeks. I tried to hint what it was about without saying everything. Maybe that was just a coincidence, or something to do with Selena. But Ms. Truhart sounded so...mean... on the phone. It seemed like no one even cared." Stephanie's eyes opened wide with surprise, remembering.

This was not the Redfern Student Power she had believed in. Should she have gone to the Student Government? Hadn't even occurred to her, somehow. And the Rumble? That would have been incredibly disloyal. But what if someone from the ring were right here now? Now she felt the danger, or maybe it was someone speaking through her—brain in perfect control, body going to pieces. The obligation to avoid silence won out.

"The pictures...are of members of the ring. The clients get to pick who they want from the pictures. Then you meet them at these two rooms the ring pays for at the Multi Stillwater, in the back. No one hardly goes there, the hotel is half-empty anyhow. Other times we used the dorms—"

"Perhaps this is not the place and the time for all the details... " Fishbane began. Heads turned toward him, puzzled by so much faculty interference. The students took over.

"We have a right to know!"

"Why do they do it? To support a drug habit? To pay tuition?

The damn tuition is so high, I mean twenty-three thou just to live here, take courses..."

"They did mention that. I mean both," Stephanie faltered.

"It's just so...shitty. I don't think it's even ethical, I mean is it?"

"Doesn't bother ME," someone else contributed.

"But the effect on the school's rep is gonna be amazing."

"Doesn't bother ME."

"Right. But the morality aspect. It shouldn't be Redfern's place to interfere with your rights. I mean this whole paternalistic thing, we're all fighting that, aren't we? They're making their own free choices. If you felt you didn't want to stay in, Stephanie, well that's YOUR own free choice. I mean isn't that right?"

"The clients want an elite school, they should try Harvard. We're not Harvard."

"It's not a misdemeanor if they don't solicit, and certainly not a felony."

"Look: are we just gonna sit there?"

The last voice, too emphatic for a Tell-All, broke the momentum. Fishbane would have loved to know more details of Ring activities, but held back, forcing a sexual twinge back into the Tell-All mode of sensitivity and tolerance.

"We can neither affirm nor deny the validity of desire," he began, "or pass judgment on the marketplace. That is a lesson we can get out of this—"

"Hey. They're prostitutes. People beat up prostitutes. Rape them. They could get killed."

"Professor Amanpuri says prostitutes are sexual conquerors. Heroines—I mean, heroes, I mean heroines... Haven't you guys read ANYTHING?..."

"Professor Leier says the prostitute in *The Blue Angel* has the power of life and death."

"Yeah—over wimps and perverts."

"Right on our campus."

"Doesn't bother ME."

"Maybe you can find out the number. Heheh."

"You're disgusting."

Stephanie was recovering. "She said it costs too much for students. Like two hundred, didn't I say? More if you need supplies."

Supplies! Fishbane remembered playing hooky from a conference in Los Angeles, a sex shop in a pink stucco building, the leather and chains sold with videos in individual Ziploc bags. He'd never found out what it was all for.

'Stephanie, I feel...that you are putting yourself in the classic position of a guilty spectator, as if you, yourself, are besmirched by what you know. Let it out. Let the group know what you are feeling. If you went through any...degrading encounters, you owe it to yourself to..."

Her eyes filled again, this time with sheer frustration. "I've told you everything I know. You can pass the photos around if you want." Stephanie handed the envelope to the nearest person. He began a minute inspection, repeated it, meticulously replaced the photos, and sent the envelope in the opposite direction from Fishbane.

"Who do you answer to? Who runs everything?" The overemphatic voice from before.

"I can't tell. I can't snitch on her, on them. It's not their fault that certain things happened, I should've known. I'm so confused." She was stuck in reverse, babbling now. "But still—someone has to know... So when I heard about these Tell-Alls—where it's really happening—I thought...but I can't take it any further. Dean Chambers wouldn't even.... I forgot to say that I tried Dean Sorley too. She said she would not accept my evidence and that it would be discriminatory anyhow, to intervene. I thought maybe a woman. But that didn't work either. Nobody wants to even talk about it."

Fishbane struggled with a sense of outrage at having been chosen for this moment, he himself, out of possible hundreds. This person—not even a Comp Lit major—making a travesty of the Tell-All. He stood up, knocking the Mont Blanc pen off the arm of his plastic chair onto the floor, his outstretched arms tamping down the unease that filled the room.

"Unfortunately we must wind this up for today. Let us meanwhile take our cue from those who work in the trenches, put themselves on the line like Dean Sorley. Meanwhile, I want each and every one of us to look deeply into him-or-herself, come to terms with it. And I mean each and every one, ALONE. Let's at least give everyone their own space to solve this in, that's right, their own privacy. This calls for sensitivity to the max. Stephanie, I want to thank you for coming forward today. That took real guts. By the way, I'll try to arrange for course credit with the History Department. To me, personally, Stephanie deserves a supportive round of applause. Now give her a big hand."

Stephanie's reception by the Tell-All left her dazed. She had had no clear idea what to expect, but surely some sort of deliverance would come that was well worth the risk of breaking out of the Ring. It had turned out to be a spotlighted performance in some kind of weird circus. She paced her dorm floor, feeling trapped. Maybe some people, especially profs, had dug themselves so far into fiction that they couldn't tell the difference. Maybe the people at the Tell-All saw fit to interpret what she said as just another story, good for half an hour of batting around. But she has forgotten nothing about how it really happened.

There had been plenty of occasions to show her that what she was really involved in was hardly subject to misinterpretation. She stopped pacing and considered: Health Services, or Values Clarification, meant a direct line to her parents. She grabbed her jacket and bookbag and slammed out of the dorm to Willona McFarquhar's office.

POLTERGEIST

Whatever it's about, Fenn has obviously given Image Enhancement, Public Relations, and Values Clarification a fair chance. In the same reception hall that had hosted the donors' party only two days before, two camps have formed up separated by an aisle: Redfern on one side, the Media on the other, like the his and hers sides at a big church wedding.

Human Resourcepersons waddle about, arranging extra little folding chairs. A podium has been brought from a lecture hall. There are two chairs on it, two glasses with the water pitcher on the table.

The President creates a stir as he ambles in, looking about him as if he had personally built this room, raised the chandelier, and laid the carpets. He has with him Yashvili, an updated Valentino in his one same Soviet-style rusty jacket, which he wears like a proud uniform. Chuck swallows his mortification at having been called by the press rather than by Fenn himself.

There's Keith Chambers, always manages to look detached from the others as if his flock of vice-presidents, deans, and subdeans had come from J.C. Penney and didn't fit. His second-in-command, a flabby, sandy-haired man with a tie clip and features like buttons, whispers in his ear. Between them they've managed to keep the Old Redfernian entertained, despite everything. Last night Keith, his arms stiff at his sides even in sleep, dreamed of the Guard Dog again, of her slavering mouth and stinking drool. But he has fought his way out and banished the memory.

Simon and Phil, in gray windbreakers, melt against a dead-end staircase. Simon recognizes Palter Van Geyst sitting with his chin cupped in one hand, lounging a little, legs crossed. Palter nods pleasantly to the room in general. Fenn comes into the reception room looking impatient, with a single sheet of typed paper and his glasses in his hand. As if he were taking orders from a higher power. The guy following in the General's wake is a lanky blond six-footer in an oversized tweed coat, must be about thirty-five. Like one of those new Europeans in sports car ads, who never have to fight in wars anymore, he reminds Simon of ten-week vacations and too much aftershave.

As Fenn adjusts the mike, holds his paper up to the light, and puts on the glasses, Simon can see that it has been typed on an old machine. The little black points on the reverse side looking like Morse code. The general skips the press-conference openers that put the media at ease. His fine white hair is combed back, his clear-browed, symmetrical face has the brooding grimness of a longtime judge of men and events.

"I'll get right to what I need to say. I've been a Redfern man all my life. Redfern was my intellectual home, and I have believed it to be an embodiment of our idealism and our rationality, of all that is worthy and sound about our country." He coughs, irritated. "I took the measure of what I have to say. It will stain this institution for years to come, but it has to be said, for the ultimate good. It is this: you have among you, on your faculty, a Nazi criminal and collaborator, an individual who continues to dishonor his calling with a complex tissue of lies and pathetic ruses. It has often been my misfortune to come face to face with people like them, and yes, even to tolerate them in exchange for the talent, work, brainpower needed by our government. That is not the case now, Van Geyst."

The crowd breaks out in sound, media people craning for better angles. No one on the media side knows who Fenn is talking about. Keith Chambers shoots the General a look of acute resentment.

"Palter Van Geyst." Fenn stabs a finger right at him. Now the cameras dolly up to the sixtyish beige man. His mild gaze has turned to an indurated stare. "Your ignoble war crimes, and your masquerade as a member of the allied Resistance, are not the sole reason for this press conference. I am here to accuse you publicly of murdering my granddaughter, Selena Fenn, in order that...."

Traffic noises from the distant streets are clearly audible. Fenn coughs, wipes his glasses.

"In order that the facts we will present at this time might remain concealed from public knowledge. These facts make a sufficient case for the removal and deportation of Van Geyst from the United States."

A cameraman and a soundman attached to each other by a sinew come apart.

"I am hereby making available to the police everything that my granddaughter uncovered about Van Geyst. I have chosen this public forum because I firmly believe that my granddaughter's death is in danger of being wallpapered and varnished over by persons who would do anything to preserve their reputations at the expense of the truth. I have not been innocent of this error myself." He says all this as if reporting a change of orders.

"My granddaughter was doing research for an honors thesis in literature when she happened on crucial material proving the involvement of Van Geyst in Dutch Nazism. She found items of virulent propaganda, composed by Van Geyst, which he published in Nazi-controlled newspapers. Subsequently she made the discovery that Van Geyst infiltrated the Dutch underground so that he might turn over downed allied fliers to their death by torture at the hands of the Nazi occupation."

Van Geyst looks sympathetic, more interested than before in the outcome of this speech. Willona McFarquhar, trim in a black suit, is seated in the second row. Her eyes are fixed on the back of the head before her as at a movie so crowded that you've given up trying to get a decent view of the screen. To Van Geyst she seems to be concentrating rigidly. Yet it is more than she can put together on the spot, it will take time, especially because this news is competing with what Stephanie told her just an hour ago.

Could Van Geyst be THAT old? Fishbane wondered. Where did he publish? Is Fenn still living in the days of UNCLE SAM NEEDS YOU? But the media people seem to think this is news.

Fenn points to the young man on his right. "This is Marcus Houten, currently the chief executive officer of Dreizehn Electronics in Amsterdam. It is from him that my granddaughter acquired the materials that were at her disposal when she was brutally murdered. She was going to make them a matter of public record, and I intend to do so in her stead. For there can be little doubt that despite scurrilous rumors which impugn her personal life, she is dead now because she wanted to tell the truth..." He takes his seat, frowning at Houten like a coach waiting for a rookie to perform.

"I am a businessman, as you just heard," he addresses everyone equably. "So was my father, of whose company I am now in charge. But first he was a member of the Dutch underground. For all Dutch people, for us who remember, it was a natural thing to ask one's father about. But he spoke very little; it was always old friends who filled me in. I made the decision to do my own research about my father's life. This meant facing anything I found without looking away. It could have meant learning of terrible crimes or idiotic failures. But you must know this... I will come to my father's story."

Palter tilts his head a bit to one side, a good listener.

"But first I will immediately make available to you," the young man says, facing the press, "copies of ten of the approximately one hundred eighty newspaper articles published in Dutch and later in French, which I found in our Archives. They uniformly, and I might add, rather boringly, urge the deportation of all Jewish people from Europe. One or two, as you will see here, refer particularly to the idea that Jews have polluted European culture, especially literary culture. Those pieces turn up on the literature pages, so they may be of special interest to professors. All are the work of this man who is now a celebrated member of our—of your faculty. All are signed POLTERGEIST."

Dressed in top-to-toe intellectual black, Selena leans both elbows on a tipsy little white metal table. "I can't believe it. Marcus. I can't. Are you sure it's the same person?"

She sips the straight gin you're supposed to drink in Amsterdam, makes a face. This meeting is unbelievably lucky. You never meet anyone interesting at that kind of party, but Europe is still different. And of all things, he turns out to know a lot of stuff that will help. She could cut her library hours in half just by listening, and still have more than enough to say in the thesis. The new subject looks more like history than like literature, so she'd have to switch. Even though Professor Van Geyst himself is a lit "person." Deconstruction theory is so boring, especially compared with news like this. Too bad for Professor Van Geyst, though. Redfern probably wouldn't want a real Nazi on the faculty. Would they simply fire him?

"No question. This page of Het Land even has a little biography of the writer: look, Palter Van Geyst, born Utrecht, member University choir—of what importance?—Doktor Phil., age twenty-five, and so forth."

"And I'm twenty already myself, two weeks ago." She frowns, pushes back an unruly strand of hair. "A Redfern professor, just think!"

"He wasn't one then," Marcus says, downsizing her with an indulgent smile. "Or anywhere." Marcus adores Selena the way a collector adores a serendipitous, once-in-a-lifetime find. But can she be trusted with so much information? "Do you understand the meaning of what I've told you?"

"Sure. Van Geyst a Nazi; it's as clear as can be. I always thought he was a pretty hateful little man, always acting the great professor. Now I can see I was right even if I didn't know why."

"You Americans are always so occupied with what you call personality. I'm not talking about someone because of his funny manners. The newspaper articles are intended so that human beings will be lined up, piled into freezing freight trains with no windows, and taken away anywhere no one sees, to die. So that other human beings, the lucky ones, will have no country to live in, will lose their home and their dignity. Try to see, will you? The Nazis practiced human vivisection, they..." Such stupidity is a kind of armor, and he concentrates, frowning, on possible methods of penetration.

"Do you think Professor Van Geyst really believed those horrible things? That he was a murderer at heart? Hated so many millions of people?"

"No, not necessarily." That superior look of angelic patience again. "What he believed does not matter to me. If this comes out, I do not doubt that people will keep asking that. They will wish to know what sort of person he was, whether he wanted the Jews to die or just be deported, whether he felt himself a member of the master race. If the things he wrote here get republished," he waved the thick batch of yellowed papers, "more professors will perhaps take them apart for analysis, just to try to understand who would think such things. He will therefore become more of a celebrity than ever, with people digging into his psychology. He will end up to be a victim of circumstances. And of course a very fascinating personality. Why is the fellow so famous if not because people get mesmerized by these types, like rabbits under headlights? Can one begin to imagine how many of these collaborationists believed nothing at all?" Marcus turns even more intensely European. "They were just being—how would one put it?—politically correct. Making the clever career moves."

He thinks I'm stupid, right? "You're just saying anyone could have done all this writing. That intellectuals had to save themselves first. Frankly, Mark, I don't think the pen is mightier than the sword; that's crap. Once you're dead it's obvious nothing can help you, but where there's life..." Now I've done it, two dumb clichés in one. But keep going, show him. "And as far as P.C., that's just ridiculous, nothing but. Redfern is a P.C. place too, but I just ignore that." Another sip of gin, her eyes flirting above the rim of the glass.

Marcus can't quite get at the summary language he needs to bring the horror home to her. He has to give her more.

"Look here, look at this." He hands her a worn red notebook no bigger than two by three inches. "It was my father's. He gave it to me the day he died."

She flipped the little dog-eared pages, all empty. "No, here!" Marcus got up, leaned over to point. Several inner pages, once wetted and now curling, were covered with the faded names of men, American, some maybe English, identified further by military rank and serial numbers.

"My father was in a pipeline that funneled airmen who had been shot down in the Netherlands back to their units in Britain. In fact," Marcus says stiffly, "he was the liaison between these men and the British high command. It was his job to see that they got out of Nazi-occupied territory through a network of safe houses. He did well. These five, and also others, owe my father their lives."

"Your father must have been incredible." Selena gazes into his eyes. "Are you named for him?" Soon she will have all the newspaper articles to work on for her thesis. What would Grampa say about her "flightiness" now?

"In a way. My father's given name was Kies, I thought I told you." He tries not to look irritated. "But since there were twelve men in his organization, they used the code names of the twelve Apostles. The organization called him Mark."

Bicycles went past them, bumping on the cobblestoned sidewalk, edging pedestrians out of the way. The outdoor cafe was beginning to clear between late lunch and the next wave of pre-dinner snackers. Selena and Marcus' chairs grated on the pavement. Today's interview would soon end. As usual it was raincoat weather but unthreatening, the fluffy pale grey clouds portending nothing more than a drizzle. The scene gave off a whiff of sedate mourning for old Europe.

"There was one man my father failed to save. He never discussed it with me 'til the end of his life. It turned out that he had blamed himself unreasonably for years, without cause." Mark thinks of his father's game seriocomic little face, freckled under an oldster's suntan. "It was not his mistake but the crime of a traitor who had recently infiltrated them, namely your Palter Van Geyst. And the flyer Van Geyst escorted to his death was the last man, this one."

Selena, for once in her life silenced and confused, cups the little notebook in her hand, reading. Her big myopic eyes squint a little at the three names on the bottom of the page: Harry Boganski, Lloyd George Burt, Will McFarquhar.

"The last one," Marcus says.

"Writing propaganda is not a crime in itself —like infiltration of the Resistance, like base treachery. But in a number of cases writings like these have constituted sufficient grounds for the deportation of the author. As does lying to our Government on immigration forms. Van Geyst answered all questions pertaining to Nazi membership and activities in the negative. And as if that weren't enough, he claimed to have been a member of the Dutch Resistance. I urge anyone with further knowledge of Van Geyst's wartime activities to come forward. But it is plain enough that he must be removed—first, from any responsibility in this institution, and then, from the temptation to evade further the consequences of his actions. Therefore I have persuaded a representative of the Immigration and Naturalization Service to come here and to act on what he has heard."

A small dark man in the last row wearing an odd Panama straw hat and a cream-colored suit shifts his crossed legs. Another, taller man, leaning against the far door, stirs as if to intercept a runner. His face wears the respectful menace of an executioner.

"To save your life," Selena says to Marcus, "you'd do worse than that, wouldn't you?" Devil's advocate, she puts on a devilish little grin.

They sit on the floor surrounded by piles of Xerox paper filled with columns of news copy. From the top of a pile, a snapshot of a fair-haired, square-faced young man wearing an expression of profound innocence smiles modestly up at her.

"All he had to do to save his life was move. Paris proved to be a less dangerous environment than Amsterdam. La Nuit Blanche, Van Geyst's next paper, belonged completely to the occupying Nazis."

Marcus riffles in another pile, pulls out two sheets clipped together, and reads:

"'It is not art and culture alone that can flourish only under our new leadership. We are at the frontier of nothing less than a total revolution, one that will organize the whole of European society. Resistance is fundamentally pointless: we are entering a mystical era, a period for faith and belief, with all that this entails in suffering, exaltation, and rapture.' What do you say now, dear child?"

"I hate it when you patronize me with this 'dear child' stuff. I still happen to think that a real Nazi is more dangerous than an opportunist."

"I'm trying to explain. There wasn't any clear difference. Because the person and the ideology were one and the same. As an American of your age—I can't help it—you do not want to understand how people were thrown right into the midst of the action. The struggle is happening on your own street, in your own house. Not something you only read or think about, but something which is transforming your life. And also, I have found that it is more possible to convert a Nazi than to convert an opportunist."

General Fenn is reading a sample, too:

"Hitler's new doctrine is far from an aberration in history. On the contrary: the Hitlerian soul and the German soul, close together from the start, will bring about the union of a Europe, which eagerly awaits its destiny."

"What a bunch of clichés, can't be Palter," Fishbane hisses to his neighbor, Maxime-Etienne Lamamba. "Terrible writing," he repeats, this time audibly. Across the room, Van Geyst's eyes meet his in reproach.

"'Whatever is to be done, it must convert the inertia of the masses to one unanimous will.' This article was written when Van Geyst was eighteen years old. He kept the pen name, 'Poltergeist,' throughout the War. But the date on this one is significant: May 14, 1940, the month Holland fell to the Nazis. That will certainly draw the attention of Van Geyst's Jewish colleagues—and of course, all the rest of us." He harrumphs, ready to wind up.

"Maybe he was small potatoes to the postwar tribunals that tried war criminals, for apparently no war crimes tribunal bothered with him. I'd like to think that retaliation has come directly from the Resistance."

But it really started with a bad check and took more than fifty years.

Asuncion, Paraguay, a sweltering summer night in '54. The little patio is surrounded on three sides by a boardinghouse whose every room teems with sweating life. Palter Van Geyst has lived here four years, one month, and five days. His daily schedule is so methodical that the efficient Senior of the house knows just where to find him all day: perfecting his chess game at the Tuileries Café, ever since the dawn of his new life.

Today was no exception but for one small thing. The Senior has delivered a message for Palter, fulfilling a secret hope to which he has long bent all his patience and effort. More than a message: a large thick envelope full of the papers, stamped and restamped with official seals. On the way home, his steps barely skim the rough cobblestones. The bedroom is tiny and cramped, with little room for anything but three tents of mosquito netting stretched over beds: one large, two small. How to get through the hours? Neither Palter nor his lady seem able to live without each other, although the little boys certainly tire them out—hungry, thirsty, wanting to play. Most fortunate, that a tutor here can make enough money to feed a whole family. There are very few kinds of work a lady could get, especially one so delicate.

Anne-Mieke Van Geyst turns in her sleep, sighs, gives a start or a sob. Recently she has noticed a new uncertainty about her husband's greeting, certain changes of mood, gaps in his memory that seem odd for a man still young. Yet she knows these are signs not of mental decline, but of a return to the caprices of childhood, away from the life here.

For so attractive a young family, the Senior believes, things are sure to take a good turn They are strong and fair, like Germans. True, the real Germans live a fair distance from here in the best part of town, or in their green villas. Yet these people are somehow the same breed of cat. And today she has brought the young father his important papers, undoubtedly containing a fine surprise.

Palter swings open the shabby blue shutters upon a squat little patch of airless night sky. The turbulent house has finally turned quiet. Old people and children snore through the papery partition walls. Outside, a few non-sleepers seek relief from the day's heat, aimlessly strolling as if in the elegant parade of the late afternoons. The odd drunk goes by right under Palter's eyes. One, dressed in a fine white suit much too big for him, lurches along in bewildered pursuit of his dignity.

The room is almost black, but the forms of everything outside are clearer than by day. A squint at the three motionless forms under the mosquito netting. They've forgotten to turn on the ceiling fan, which now creaks reluctantly to life under his switch, its whirring camouflaging any accidental sound. Palter Van Geyst takes his necktie out of a pocket, meticulously knots it. On a table, his hair lotion, quickly smoothed on. He rubs white hands together to get rid of the residue, as if concluding a deal. A check for the Senior should keep things going for a while. Too bad she's not such a sound sleeper.

He picks up a fat brown leather briefcase, calmly throws it out of the window only about two meters from the cobblestones; it thuds lightly, wadded contents safe. There is no balcony, but Palter is agile enough to hoist himself onto the waterpipe that runs the length of the building. His legs hardly swivel at all, just a shimmy right down with a little swing to the pavement. He lights a match, and suddenly two rows of tumbledown houses right themselves, a clump of dry bushes creeps close to the flame. Right behind the boardinghouse, the shortcut starts through an overgrown lot dwindling to a dirt path. He walks unhurriedly, noiselessly, and steadily without looking back.

Fenn was taking questions.

"General," said an embittered young woman with a wash-'n-wear face, "did your granddaughter speak to you directly about her research?"

"I thought I said so. Next, please."

"General, you're leaning a lot on the propaganda writing. Don't you think it was a more serious war crime to infiltrate the Resistance so as to lead allied men to their death?"

"I do. Next, please."

"How do you think Professor Van Geyst found out about Selena's discoveries?"

"That's simple. I faced him with them myself." A murmur passes around like teacups. "Last Friday morning."

"One way or other, Van Geyst, this is going to come out. Be smart, make a clean breast of it; at seventy years of age you can end your career with some dignity intact."

Palter neatly replaces his glass on the Faculty Club coaster (OUR PRODUCT IS EXCELLENCE). "I would go so far as to admit, for the purpose, that I reinterpreted the existence of my time according to the drift of power."

"That is arrant nonsense. Now look, Selena is a thorough worker. When she gets down to it. She means to do a complete job on your treason—though she connects it with some literary tishtosh of yours."

"Treason." Van Geyst looks mischievous, the flat surface of his face warding off harm.

"Do I need to tell you what that is?"

"Against what, please?"

"Against our Allies, against, well, the Jewish nation, against democracy."

"Democracy, General. Why should we assume democracy to be intrinsically superior to totalitarianism? Think about it."

"I have not called you here for a frivolous dispute or a riddle session. Look, Van Geyst, as a trustee and, let's say, an old-timer at Redfern

I could probably have upset your applecart by myself. I held back only in order to protect Redfern from the ruin of its reputation. Has none of this come home to you at all? Ah, Van Geyst..."

Palter seems to feel compassion for the old man before him, with his old connections. He waits patiently, hands loosely folded in his lap.

"You could save some measure of your reputation by saying, 'I was young, I made a mistake.' Yes, even about the counter-Resistance treachery. Because there is already sufficient documentation to produce a connected biography."

"No, General, not a 'connected' one, no." Van Geyst sighs, as if rejecting all mankind's usual displays of disbelief. "Nothing is ever connected to anything else: no event, no fact, no so-called 'reality'."

"You are adding impudence to your sanctimonious lying."

"I am merely pointing out that confession, as you put it, amounts to no more than self-exoneration. And there is nothing to be exonerated from."

"That's crazy too. Confession is a plain, fair accounting and nothing more. How dare you go on talking this rot?" General Fenn inhales a large sip of his Glenfiddich, feels in his pocket for medication. "Next time I call you will be the last. You still have a chance."

"No, General, not at all." A demure smile of apology. "No chance."

The crowd had dispersed but Palter Van Geyst still occupied his chair, absorbed in some conundrum. Holding his Panama in both hands, Natanson approached the INS representative in his relaxed grey suit. A third, burlier man joined them, and Simon and Phil slouched over too, a friendly little bunch.

"Just a short conversation, sir," the INS man said. "We don't have far to go."

"I'm sorry to keep you waiting," Palter's voice was even and civil. "But will you gentlemen excuse me for just a moment? Or you may accompany me if you like. A moment's retirement."

His face darkened almost imperceptibly as he turned back to the group.

"You know the severity of the charges you are considering. The public will clearly see the accusation as an attempt to blacken the name of a world-renowned scholar. You are making damaging allegations without proof. You have no witnesses to anything that may allegedly have occurred. You do not understand in the least the consequences of your actions."

"Wasn't it you givin' it to us, Van Geyst," Granita asked, "that actions don't have no consequences?"

My father was the third flyer. I never knew what to think about him when it was over and other kids heard what their dads did in the war because mom would just hush me up with that hopeless look on her face. She only repeated and repeated he was a hero. But he was a victim, not the same.

The smile on his picture, his face a little heavier, more square than it would be if he were twenty-five now—a war movie face. But I can't really see it. Only remember what it felt like to get a real bear hug when he came home in a rush of outdoor air, everyone really glad to see him.

He had to trust there was no other choice out in that field. A chance in how many that a paltry Van Geyst would be around that day? So he trusted that Apostle too. A personality for our time—a blank face where you can draw whatever features you long to see. People agreed about him all the more because everyone could read him a completely different way. That's how you get elected, keep 'em guessing till your term is over.

I regret only that however justice comes to him, it won't be masquerading as compassion and help, the way he came to take my father's hand when he was lost.

And they dither on and on about a lot of writing.

Palter calmly approaches the window of the drafty lavatory. He can hear the reporters outside laughing and joking in knots, comparing answers, a few feet from the police. No one would notice if this window were opened, what with the cold. A pity that Professor McFarquhar did not return his goodbye, but unsurprising in view of her obvious limitations.

An Administrative Executive Assistant holding a clipboard approaches the policemen. "Is one of you Lieutenant Blank? The Chief of Police is calling you. Take it with this." She hands Simon a cordless phone.

"Yes, sir," Simon tells the Chief. "Yeah, there's something of a delay." Then he sees Granita and the INS man go to the lavatory door and put their heads to it.

Palter Van Geyst moves quietly, his self-possession unwavering. To everyone waiting outside, an indistinct turning, a change of pattern appear in the air. The policemen hear something that sounds like a chunk of plaster wall falling on the tiles. Then the first shot explodes, one cracking report. And a second. Simon drops the phone.

"SONOFABITCH..."

Van Geyst has contrived to drop in a modest posture, lying on his left side, right leg slung over the other as for a spy movie poster. A red pool is spreading under him, fed by a redder spring from his forehead. His left hand, perfectly relaxed, points politely to the gun. Simon picks it up, turns it around and around. It looked age-old like everything about Van Geyst, down to the set of his choirboy face. A nine-millimeter Beretta. On its mother of pearl handle, a name engraved in spidery script: PIETER.

"There's comfort in knowing the worst, anyhow." Keith sighed. "I got something out of Sakulin, too. He's more shocked than angry, but he hasn't really understood everything yet."

No one home in the vast suite now but Keith Chambers and his President, chewing over the dry bones.

"Palter Van Geyst was Sakulin's pride and joy, his lodestar, as if he had discovered him." A dreamy look scuds over Chuck's face. "Do you have any idea of what this will mean to the Campaign? It is so painful it is almost pleasurable."

"I've thought it all out, Chuck." Keith leans forward, hands on knees. "There's only one way to go. What happened points to the most sensible conclusion: that Van Geyst would have done anything to keep his secrets."

"Mmmmf. Maybe."

"Obviously there is no way to save Palter. He did himself in twice over. Three times if you go with the idea that he should have 'fessed up. I'm convinced that Fenn would have forgiven him if he had made a 'clean breast' of everything, as he puts it. With Fenn, lying is worse than Nazism."

"But it is all so oddly comical. Look, now there is a wife and a second family, the trail of unpaid bills. Someone will undoubtedly come forward soon and accuse Van Geyst of cheating at cards. I'm just waiting for that." Chavadze looks like a sitcom star with troubles heaped on his head. "For something like this the New Campaign loses everyone. Alan Sakulin alone gave us over fifteen million in the last three years. And his friends. Their contributions are as of this instant a thing of the past. Fenn can be happy about that if he wants. This stupid, empty snobbery of his is going to win after all."

"Look, Chuck, we hadn't a Chinaman's—a chance in hell of knowing. Maybe no one will blame us. More important: we can cut our losses. It seems pretty clear that we have Selena's murderer."

"You mean you actually think the investigation stops here?" Chavadze snorts, almost. "Wouldn't that be nice? Does anyone still believe that an accusation of anti-Semitism is so terrible that a person would murder to avoid it?"

"You're not Jewish, Chuck. And forgive me, but you don't seem to be concentrating. Palter Van Geyst made his career as an arch-skeptic —someone who didn't have to believe in anything except chance and power. For some people, the Nazi journalism will soon be just a part of his radical appeal, like that dumb fashion of Nazi souvenirs. But he also proved he could act to kill, that he's capable of murder. Think how neat it will be to put this all behind us."

Chavadze is not convinced. "You want to get your paperwork done, this I understand. Send memos around to everyone in the world saying we hardly knew the man. Fenn has gone out of his mind because he is not used to tragedies striking close to home. People listen to whatever crazy thing he says. It is not the same with us."

"I think," says Keith, ignoring this display of volatility, "that the key back to Sakulin's good graces is to ask his help. The guy never gets tired of being reminded he's a big boy now. We then make sure the case against Van Geyst is pursued with all possible vigor. The police will be happy to close it down early."

"Look, let me ask you as my friend, as a man. Are you personally convinced that Palter Van Geyst murdered Selena Fenn? Are you yourself convinced? Does no one else come to mind? Keith, much as I dislike to reawaken this possibility, what about Berto? You know how much he means to me, to us. But..."

"It's perfectly self-evident that Berto had nothing to gain by murdering Selena. He's completely in the clear."

"Ah-ha! but how stupid." Chuck's foreignness is gaining on him. "The sexual evidence, too: do you seriously imagine Van Geyst as a sex criminal? I would laugh if only I could."

Keith takes a deep breath, running the same clip: Selena exiting the party, trailed by rotund, stunted Ricci. The viscous red tunnel, like open tonsils, like the gates of hell.

"I thoroughly believe Van Geyst would do anything he felt necessary. If the crime had to look like a sex crime he would deliver that too. Chuck: we're the custodians of a two hundred-year old institution..."

"Two hundred years seem awfully long to you, don't they?.... Fine. Get hold of Image Enhancement and Values Clarification. Accuse and defend at the same time, unpack our whole bag of tricks. Anyhow, we're not the police."

When Keith was gone, Chavadze perked up, drank some white wine and cassis, munched a cheese puff and made his last call for the day, to LuAnn Rossiter His special phone redialed ceaselessly until LuAnn finally answered. Her upbeatness proved reassuring, though there were still plans to be implemented. The Search was progressing even as they spoke.

MINUTES OF DEPARTMENT MEETING, DEPARTMENT OF
COMPARATIVE LITERATURE, APRIL 7, 1993

Present: Professors Fishbane, Lamamba, Lydgate, Ricci, Rossiter;
Associate Professors Amanpuri, Leier; Assistant Professors Banter,
Hargreaves, Mahmoud.

The Department of Comparative Literature, supported by
Professor Leier (of Video Studies), voted in this unscheduled session to
recommend strongly that the position of Professor occupied to date by
Professor Palter Van Geyst remain within the Department and that a
replacement be sought during the course of next semester.

This search will have no bearing upon the current search for a
replacement for Professor Myron Wiener, whose contract will expire
next year. The Department resolved that a very strong case can be made
for its need to maintain (at least) the current number of its faculty, since
it is known throughout the university for outstanding teaching, tireless
service, and energetic scholarship. Professor Fishbane expressed his full
confidence in the continuing unanimous support of the University
Administration. The progress of the Departmental campaign for a Center
was also discussed, and an optimistic forecast prevailed.

The subject of Professor Van Geyst's wartime activities was
briefly discussed and a resolution passed to the effect that his secrecy
concerning these activities was morally bankrupt.

Professors Ricci, Fishbane, Rossiter, Leier, and Lamamba each
stressed the absolute requirement of confidentiality regarding the pro-
ceedings of the meeting.

ROGUES' GALLERY MINUS TWO

Just to be on the safe side, the thief dialed Hilary Slocombe's dorm number. No one answered. The next phone call, to the Art Center, produced someone who promised to get Hilary out of her studio corner. But the thief, bunching a handkerchief around his nose, respectfully declined the offer. Next he had to check the whereabouts of the Chinese student chemist who lived next door to Hilary. The chemist had a cot in his lab; should we wake him up? No, I'll catch him later. The thief paused to admire his own new cool.

The heavy metal rockers were harder to raise. It seemed to the thief that he could hear the music even before he was connected. Against the relentless boom and screech, a nasal voice told him that Neal and Cadd were out forever and not coming back, as if the stupidity of the message needed emphasis.

Speed was everything—even though breaking and entering was known as the commonest of campus crimes. Despite the increase in reported Redfern assault cases and bias-related attacks, the leading category remained petty larceny. The Administration insisted that students brought these crimes on themselves by sheer negligence. Image Enhancement and Student Life routinely blamed "such student carelessness as unattended book bags or student room doors unlocked." Campus robbery had been dumped on spin doctors because the whole hierarchy found it easier to sigh that it was intractable, here to stay, though a nuisance. It had taken its place as just another sign system that broadcast the feelings and grievances of the sign-producers.

A few cars and bikes were parked on the little asphalt square near Hilary and Selena's entryway. Inside the old brick building the air was cool and damp. The thief stood in the tiny foyer a few minutes, lounging in his Redfern T-shirt and reversed baseball cap, a Harvard crimson jacket tied around his waist—an incongruous outfit for him, but as good or the job as camouflage fatigues in the Black Forest. The shades were just right too, granny frames that lent him a scholarly diffidence. A guy taking the steps two at a time said "hi" without even a glance.

The doors and interior walls were built more than a foot thick, so the thief had to strain to hear any sounds of activity from any side. He quickly gauged the distance between the entrance and the side he would have to explore. He was at the south end of the building, Selena Fenn having rated for herself and Hilary a room with two sunny exposures and hardly any miasmic drafts. This meant, however, that the privileged corner would intersect with another, stupidly unexplained row of rooms. He figured he'd lose about fifty seconds crossing it.

A door opposite Hilary and Selena's opened a few inches as the thief loped by. The head that looked out belonged to a slim fairish young man who seemed older to the thief than most college students. The young man had a towel draped around one shoulder over his shirt and a striped zippered case of toiletries in his hand.

"Oh, sorry—" he mumbled, "just arrived, have to find the bathroom..." and ducked quickly back. What was he so afraid of, the thief wondered contemptuously. Or could it be...no, it was very, very unlikely... The university didn't have the money to set up decoys wearing pajamas.

For his part, the svelte young man was too tired and nervous to register much of what was around him. He frowned and then passed a hand over his eyes. The fellow in the baseball cap looked vaguely familiar—but maybe it was a type they just happened to have a lot of at Redfern.

So many campuses, so many rooms for one night, you could hardly keep them apart sometimes. At every campus you inevitably got the full tour—gyms, libraries, everything, as if they were selling you the place. The svelte young man had an hour or so before the dinner. His shower could wait. He plopped down on the narrow bed and closed his eyes.

Selena's door yielded at once. The thief tiptoed into the room as if his steps could have raised its occupant any second. He saw that the room did not run to order, as he had been told it would. So much the better. Approaching the file cabinets the students had improvised from three-sided red plastic cubes, he discerned no identifiable filing system. All the arrangements in this room seemed to give way easily, even voluptuously, to the slightest application of force.

He picked up an unstudent-like scent of apples and freesia from the expensive clothes that took up more than three-quarters of the closet. A framed photo of two laughing young women, one willowy and blonde, the other grimacing against the wind that electrified her mane of hair, toppled from a plastic cube. His outsized hand in its black glove set it noiselessly upright again.

It cannot be long before the police, stupid as they are, decide they need to come back here and search. They will blame themselves for missing it the first time. But even the most obvious clues can be missed the first time around.

He untied the Harvard jacket, cupping one hand to receive the paper file that he had been wearing on his posterior. Ridiculous but necessary. The best place to plant this file was—any place at all, among the papers in these red plastic cubes.

As he waited to exit, the thief worried that he might not have kept his figure as well as he'd thought. He took an extra moment to remove the baseball cap, substituting a pirate's bandanna, which concealed the darkness of his hair. It was easy to tie with both hands free, and as right as the cap for the frayed T-shirt. He took off the gloves and stuffed them into the pocket of the Harvard jacket, now back around his waist. A shoplifter bringing back a piece of unwanted merchandise must feel like this, he sneered, and stepped up his stride as he left the deserted entryway, for once without the pretense of self-effacement.

Crude renditions of human cavities, organs, orifices, glands, limbs, excretions lie everywhere on the exhibition floor. They are a piece of "installation" art, branching out like a huge sea creature on the ocean sand. After the Redfern Artists' Collective had finally swept into the garbage all parts of their installation Annual that could give offence to ethnic minorities, to women, religious fundamentalists, and the disabled, this was what they had left.

Val Miro, the coordinator of the project, had complained at first about the quotas. The Diversity Stipulations were hard to obey too. An outspoken campus radical, she found herself, nevertheless, radically challenged.

"Being asked to present a good 'mix' of races, genders, ages, and disabilities is too irksome in cases where the text may not suggest such a mix," she had written to the subdean in charge of studio space. "I agree to remove the grassy lawn as a background, because it is true that many people do not have lawns. And I agree that it is old-fashioned to portray anyone going to a ballet class or riding a horse. I will substitute people swimming or working out at a gym. Since the Studio Manager experiences difficulties with our angels, we will not include the supernatural. But pigs seem to me a matter of individual preference, although the reactions of the Redfern Muslim Community will be taken into consideration. Do pigs have to be entirely shunned?"

The problem spiraled as far up as Sypher, Garnix, and Nill. Their answer was an unremitting yes: "Perhaps you think us a bit obsessive about our rejection of 'Pigs' as a title or theme for the upcoming installation. However, we have come up against negative reactions. There are really a lot of other animals to choose from, so we would prefer to take that option. We are afraid that you will have to rethink the pigs."

In former years, the Annual was a talk-generating marvel. Weren't shock and controversy the very essence of the "dialogue" the arts were supposed to generate? Like the time they presented the exhibition space itself, completely empty except for the captions on the wall—now, THAT was a "catalyst for dialogue." Having been there on the opening night still certified you as a free spirit, two years later.

"Exciting, exciting," droned Gorellick.

"More provocative than the Whitney Biennial."

"The THING as no-thing."

"Screw the visuals. Who needs them? Fabulous."

But the political stakes had kept on rising. Aesthetic issues were social issues. As representational art had done before, captions became a sign of elitist arrogance and "linguistic prejudice." They did mean you'd have to read to get the message.

That seemed to take care of everything but the senses of taste and smell. Val Miro and her coworkers affixed tubes of noxious gases to the walls, the floors. ("I mean, anyone can smell, can't they?") Attendance dropped to record lows. Then the Edibles show flopped because people kept eating everything. Some art lovers with bellyaches were even talking lawsuits.

Hilary makes her way past mounds of clay buttocks, breasts, sombreros, ankhs, skullbones, boomerangs, with her nose clamped between thumb and forefinger. She uncovers her Victory for the second time in only hours. The last freestanding sculpture on the studio floor. She exhales with relief—no one has touched it.

But she can't make a start, just stares at Selena's clay body, savors the paralyzing misery that is already as familiar to her as a cat to a witch.

The only way to bear it is to start over. There lies my freedom. Hilary grabs one of her knives. Her head tilted to take its measure, she begins to slash at Selena's left breast, was that like an Amazon? Globs of clay hit the sawdusted floor, making a satisfying squish, like throwing a steak on concrete. Which side did they chop off? Let's do the other one too. Now there's a scar on the face. Scars give instant character. Go right through the lip line, down the sweep of neck. You need both hands. Breathing so hard hurts.

Destroy, destroy the idol. Hilary steps back; where to strike next? Lop off the arms and you get instant antiquity. These have to go. Too. The knife carefully etches ankle bracelets and a matching one round the throat. Slashes on the right need to be balanced so...was strangling her even harder?

Right down the middle, like that old Roman picture of a man sticking his arms out like the spokes of a wheel so that his body is the center of the world. Hilary stops to admire the ruined Selena still pivoting on slender ringed feet. I don't know my own strength by half! We'll keep the legs as they are, but no more of this classical hipline. Off it comes, a hipsteak out of clay. There, and there, and there. She will always be mine alone now.

Out of breath, Hilary tosses the knives beside the pedestal at Selena's maimed feet, picks up the tarp, and wraps her reverently in it. She doesn't even turn around to make sure the sculpture—or its wreck—is as well covered as usual.

"You guys have a clear-cut choice." Keith Chambers addressed Treacle Morris of the Redfern Rumble in his most military bark. "To drop your unfounded speculations about Professor Van Geyst, or to get the paper suspended, and that's if you're lucky. In my honest opinion, that kind of slander calls for expulsion." Thank God, he thought, thank God Van Geyst didn't do it in the reception hall.

In fact Keith was going through the exact maneuvers he had foreseen the minute he laid eyes on the Rumble editor trolling around for information on the heels of the media people in front of the Admin Building. A tiny girl wearing glasses bigger than her face, she had inserted herself without difficulty into the thrusting knot of reporters. She was young enough not to feel that she had to display shocked feelings and had immediately set about assigning aspects of the story, to reporters, keeping the best parts for herself.

Keith now felt physically sick of Redfern girls. The dream of the guard dog had come back last night, only now the red tunnels expanded and contracted like the dizzying tracks of an amusement park ride, or, as it had seemed to him before, the deep canals of a human throat depicted in an anatomical volume. Strangely, the terrible knowledge he carried in his gut had managed to blend with the old nightmare, expanding and contracting. He kept his eyes courteously trained on the student before him without focusing them, so that the very mildness of his look irritated Treacle Morris.

"The staff is solidly behind me, everyone I could reach in the past hour." Treacle tried a more placating tone. "You shouldn't worry, Dean Chambers. No one's going to slander anyone. We just think reporting as usual isn't enough. So we're also going to devote the editorial pages to the crisis, explore the issues it raises."

"You mean you people are going to treat this in an evenhanded way? That you're considering the alternatives, weighing them carefully?" Keith began to ration out the phases of his retreat from the stance of censor. "You're all fully aware of the consequences to the institution?" But how could these student reporters, passing through college on their way to a life, have any care for the institution?

"We just want to get at the truth. And we want to try and understand Professor Van Geyst. He was definitely the most amazing professor at Redfern. If we ignored the story, we'd be a laughingstock. I never thought we'd be up against censorship, not here."

An impatient intake of breath. "You seem to think this story is just another journalism exercise."

"No, not at all!" Her intensity reproached his bulk and sloth. "It's different from anything we've ever had to do before. Because the story has so many sides, and it goes back to the war, and it implicates so many people, and..."

"If you really MUST, I'm not going to try and stand in your way. No matter who gets hurt. You better be sure of what you're doing, though, there are regulations against mindless mudslinging."

"Oh that's GREAT, Dean Chambers, that's great. I'm so glad, we're all so grateful, I mean they will be when they hear..."

Good job, Keith thought. Van Geyst murdered Selena to evade exposure and the ruin of his academic monarchy. Van Geyst would mimic his own death if he could, saying it was his last coincidence. Palter's usefulness to Redfern being at an end, Keith could finally vent his revulsion for this man, the embodiment of cowardice, decadence, fakery. Keith had found himself listening rapturously to Fenn and Marcus Houten as they unpacked Van Geyst's crimes and miserable lies. Salvation lay in exorcising Van Geyst and his decadent Euro-nihilism, which was still sending up clouds of rancid smoke.

The third phone on the left rang, the one for callers who meant business. It was the Surviving Descendant, Mrs. Slote. Keith spoke into the phone with a courteous smile, as if Mrs. Slote could see him.

"No, Juliana, not yet. No one has called to take their daughter home. Ye—yes, Sakulin wants his money for the Chair back. But he certainly won't get it."

Knox Lydgate is winding up the last lecture of his career, his kindly, bemused face aimed a bit over the heads of the class as if out to sea. He's actually looking forward to the sailing trip with grandkids that has been planned for months. Drinks at the Faculty Club with some pals from History have been scheduled for immediately after the lecture, but an old pro like Knox would never cut the hour short or slight his obligations in any other way. So Knox's FDR accents just go right on summing up Wordsworth's immense "Prelude" ("background, situation, and aims") to the usual diminished student audience, accompanied by light snoring from the back row.

"Don't wake him up," he cautions, "I feel the same way myself sometimes," and a tentative laugh ripples through the class. Why, all the upsets have probably tired the young people out too, as well they might. You hardly run into anyone who isn't being quizzed by a policeman or harassed by the kids from the Rumble or up to their ears in memos. In these circumstances you can't reasonably expect people to take much notice of Knox's retirement or even to try and speak agreeably. It's the right time to be leaving.

The speech Keith Chambers had prepared long ago for Knox's hastily scuttled retirement party bloomed with words like "decency" and "honor," as befitted the man. Keith had of course omitted the equally suitable terms "boredom" and "lightweight." Knox couldn't repress a start of emotion when he read the copy waiting in his mailbox, though it made him feel silly to stand there misting over a piece of sheer flattery like that. He had only done the modest bit of teaching that was in his power, and, well, some youthful writing on Wordsworth that didn't really deserve to be called "research." But old birds like me are now pretty rare, he thought, wiping his specs, so maybe they'll miss us in a while, yes they will.

"Now if anyone ever sics an exam on you people, you're prepared," Knox says, elbows off the lectern and at his sides. Another polite ripple from the class. Two students walk out, letting the door shut loudly. The sleeping fellow in the back snorts and awakens. A number of clockwatchers start picking their stuff up off the floor but make no move to rise.

"Professor Lydgate," says a woman student, "we heard that today is your last day. So we want to say thank you and give you this. We hope you enjoy it—once you're rid of us, heheh." She comes up to the lectern and hands him a squarish bottle wrapped in Christmas paper and tied around the neck with a big green bow. Knox straightens up with a what-have-we-here expression and clears his throat. This is a lot like a commencement speech, but then practically everything Knox ever had to say in class was like a commencement speech.

"Hope you got the right brand, scouts... I'm grateful for your kind gift but I probably don't deserve it. Teaching has always been a real pleasure for me, as I trust the poetry will be some day for you. Just try and respect the dates. They don't really spoil the poems at all." He clears his throat and turns the bottle in his hands. "Time's up. Whoever wants to see me, though, still has a chance at the office tomorrow. Thanks again, good luck, and goodbye." He picks up his neat little file and steps down from the lecture platform, taking a last leisurely look around.

On his way out past the Pelfe Hall bulletin board, Knox stoops to retrieve a fallen poster for Carlotta DiSalvo's student-sponsored appearance, COMING RIGHT UP. Something going on all the time, despite the troubles. He pins the poster back on the board, straightening it carefully. Good luck and goodbye.

To: Provost Grigol Chavadze, Texas Megatech University
From: Charges Committee, Texas Megatech
Re: Charges against Roberto Ricci, Professor of Italian, Chairman, Department of Italian, Texas Megatech

The Charges Committee met in executive session on fifteen different occasions to hear testimony relating to charges brought against Professor Roberto Ricci by four graduate students in the Department of Italian, all of whom were under the direct supervision of Professor Ricci.

Our report will summarize the charges as they were made in oral testimony and recorded stenographically, make a finding, and recommend possible courses of action by the Provost and/or the President of the University.

Since a copy of this memorandum will be made available to Professor Ricci pursuant to University Disclosure Regulations, the names of the complainants have been deleted.

SUMMARY OF CHARGES. All four complainants testified that they were Italian nationals who had been recruited as graduate students at

Texas Megatech by Professor Ricci on his visits to Italy.

"Whadda they need to bring people from Italy to America to learn Italian for?" Phil Granita is puzzled again, puts down the Ricci file, and stares in front of him.

"They need students," Simon said. "Just warm bodies to sign papers and pay fees, or maybe teach all the courses. Don't you remember, those Teaching Assistants in the basement..."

"Who pays for this bullshit?" Granita snorts and goes on reading the piece from the file.

Professor Ricci made it an express condition of their admission to the graduate program in Italian that all agree to serve as Teaching Assistants for the duration of their years as graduate students ("See?") and that, furthermore, they all agree to "kick back" to Professor Ricci a certain percentage of their monthly salaries, the exact amount to be negotiated upon entry to the program.

The four complainants further testified that they agreed in advance to the scheme of "kickbacks" just described and that they were admitted to the graduate program on the condition that they "fulfill their side of the bargain." Admission and continuance in the graduate program in Italian at Megatech was therefore contingent upon their agreement to the scheme.

"A little more here than usual," says Simon, no longer the newcomer. "Go ahead. Why did they decide to blow the whistle?"

All four testified that within a month after arriving at Texas Megatech and assuming their positions as teaching assistants they were approached by Professor Ricci and informed that they would have to increase the amount of the aforesaid "kickbacks" from a percentage of their monthly salaries to a uniform payment. It was this increased demand that triggered the filing of charges.

Professor Ricci appeared before the Committee and flatly denied all the charges. He claimed that all the complainants were "malcontents and troublemakers" who had concocted a "fantastic canard" in order to "retaliate" against Professor Ricci for reprimanding them about their unsatisfactory job performance. When asked for an explanation of the checks made out to him by two of the complainants and bearing his endorsement, Professor Ricci admitted that his signature appeared to be authentic but was in fact a skillful forgery. He denied ever having received the checks and pointed out that the complainants could easily have "doctored" them.

Since the Charges Committee is an administrative body with no subpoena power, it was unable to obtain bank records which would have definitively confirmed or disconfirmed the validity of the checks. Professor Ricci did not offer to facilitate access to such records.

ADDENDUM. Certified copies of checks made out to and endorsed by Roberto Ricci are part of the documentary record in the files of the Charges Committee. In two cases where cash payments were made directly to Professor Ricci, the file contains complainants' sworn statements to that effect. The same section of the file includes sworn testimony from a former assistant professor from whom cash payment was apparently extorted in direct contravention of university regulations for three weeks of maternity leave during which Professor Ricci had to engage her replacement.

"So Ricci had to hire someone to replace this woman. She had to get paid, too." Phil contemplates his store of information about Redfern financing. "None of these colleges have much to pay anyone with, so...."

"That's not how it's done, though. The institution pays. Not the other professors. Hell, that was just another way of pocketing more kickbacks."

SUMMARY OF COMMITTEE DELIBERATIONS. During the period in which the committee met to hear testimony, members also held a number of discussions of the evidentiary grounds underlying the charges against Professor Ricci, together with the possible consequences for him and the University in case the charges were deemed credible and sustainable on their face. The Committee invited the University Counsel to sit in on its deliberations as soon as the potential gravity of the charges became clear.

As a result of its deliberations and discussions, the Charges Committee arrived at the conclusion that Professor Ricci was in gross violation of university rules and of the laws of the state; that his denials were permeated by inconsistencies; and that this unethical conduct is actionable and could make both Professor Ricci and the University liable to lawsuits involving civil if not criminal extortion charges. The Committee considers the charges to be so serious as to warrant their formal presentation to the Provost and the President as grounds for Professor Ricci's separation from the University.

Furthermore, as an interim measure we recommend that appropriate administrative steps be taken by the Provost to make restitution to the complainants—if necessary, by withholding the amounts owed to them from Professor Ricci's salary.

"They let him off. Nothing happened."

"Not 'they': Chavadze. Take a look."

"I get it. Chavadze was the provost. Why the hell did he let Ricci off?"

"For chrissake, Phil, they always work together. They're doing it here too, at Redfern. D'you think Keith Chambers knows about this?"

"It's in the file, right? So he's gotta know."

"Straight Arrow Keith. Got a lot to defend these days. Now what I'd like to know is why Keith lets this material sit around in the file where anyone can get it. He did say, remember, that paper files are still the most durable way of keeping anything, that computers have breakdowns, blowouts? That they can't scan every kind of material. He told us all that a long time ago. Paper's user-friendly. So Chambers wouldn't want to keep this stuff around, not if he wants to help Ricci."

"Go 'head, let's see the rest." Phil sounds resigned.

"Funny how we missed all this the first time round."

"Well, let's go on." Phil and Simon turn over to the next section of the file, some impeccably cut newspaper clippings stapled together.

MEGATECH PROFESSOR ENSNARED IN KICKBACK SCHEME

Phil is just going to flip this over, but Simon stops him. "It's not the same thing. Look. Years later. This stuff is different."

Odessa, TX. — Roberto Ricci, Chairman of the Italian Department at Texas Megatech, has been identified as the mastermind behind an illegal scheme which caused university capital improvement projects to be awarded to a local contractor, Massimo Scambio, by leaking secret details of low bids.

Dr. Ricci's role in the scam came to light during a daylong appearance in court by Regina Dunque, a contracts officer at Megatech, who testified earlier today for the prosecution in the state's criminal bribery case against Scambio. Ms. Dunque has herself filed a lawsuit against Megatech, claiming that she was denied accumulated benefits after being fired from her job as a contracts officer when the illegal bid disclosures were leaked.

According to Ms. Dunque, Dr. Ricci came to her in 1965 with the proposition that she funnel information to him regarding sealed bids in exchange for a portion of the "kickback" that Ricci was to get from Massimo Scambio. Using the illegally obtained information, Scambio was able to underbid all contractors for capital improvement projects at Megatech totaling approximately $300 million in state funds.

"THIS is the real thing."

"Looks like he graduated fast," says Phil.

"But stayed consistent, with the kickbacks."

Responding to reporters' questioning after Ms Dunque's testimony, Grigol Chavadze, the university's provost, staunchly defended Dr. Ricci. "Roberto Ricci is a towering, distinguished figure at Megatech. You could not put a dollar value on what he has meant to our institution."

When asked about Ms. Dunque's testimony, Chavadze expressed his total disbelief in the truth of her disclosures and attributed them to "the expected sour grapes from a disgruntled employee who has been caught with her hand in the till." According to the provost, "this scurrilous accusation against one of Megatech's most respected professors cannot be allowed to stand uncontested, and I am absolutely confident that Professor Ricci will be completely exonerated." Chavadze went on to criticize the investigators' reliance on "bogus documents" in the case.

Despite the provost's strong support, however, the accusation that Dr. Ricci enriched himself at taxpayers' expense by means of the deal with Scambio has been echoed by persons close to the university's own internal investigation of the "Ricci Business," as it has come to be known on the Megatech campus. Speaking on the condition of anonymity, informed sources confirmed that the university's Charges Committee has been conducting hearings on the allegations.

"What, more?" Phil sighed as they flipped over the attached papers, a fat bunch of Charges Committee memos. "Shit, all this paper..."

The process is complicated by the fact that Dr. Ricci has other charges outstanding against him that were first heard before the same Committee. However, Ricci continues to assert his innocence of any wrongdoing.

"I am quite satisfied that my credibility with the public has been altogether satisfied," he said in a statement to this newspaper.

Palter Van Geyst, a professor of modern languages and vice chairman of the Faculty Council of the Humanities at Megatech, said the faculty was concerned that "the considerable amount of negative publicity percolating up through the administrative structure and into the public press" had damaged the public image of the university. As a result, he said, the Council has approved a resolution calling for greater oversight by the administration in determining the culpability of faculty members and staff whenever improper actions come to light.

"Busy, busy Berto."

"Busy Van Geyst too: snuffing the truth out all over the globe. No one mentioned that he'd been at this Megatech place."

"All one little family," says Simon. "How do they manage to bring each other along?"

"What's it got to do with us?"

"I can't see anything clear yet. Right now it looks like the important thing is that this file was in the room, that Selena'd gotten her hands on it. But it's also important, how she did it. And how's the Chief gonna put up with this, with what it really seems to mean..."

"Van Geyst is still the perp I'd put my money on. Maybe Ricci's lookin' bad, he was no saint, this kickback business and fuckin' the students an' all... but that ain't murder." Phil thumbs around in the file.

RICCI LINK TO CONTRACTOR CALLED "SEAMY" AND "CORRUPT" PROF EXPERT IN BRIBERY
MEGATECH PROVOST URGED TO ACT ON "CONSULTANT" PROFESSOR

"So Ricci was accused by this Committee. And THEY let the media have it all, even though there was no police action or legal follow-up. And Chavadze was the provost—the Gorellick, right? Chavadze went right on helping Ricci evade the law. And then comes Van Geyst, isn't that typical, and worries about nothing but protecting the Megatech image! So everything just fades away."

'Then why are all these memos and clippings and junk here in the file? If Chavadze wants the contracting scam buried why doesn't he get at this stuff an' destroy it, or have Chambers hide it? Someone made sure we'd find all this shit out."

"Ricci might've been scared of Selena. She wouldn't've stopped at anything she felt like, right? With this file in her little hand, she could've, maybe...but what would she or anybody else want from Ricci in exchange?"

"Look, if the guy can run a multimillion-dollar scam, manipulate a whole university in Texas, scare the shit out of the administration here, and—at a single bound—wipe out the whole idea of competition, he's gotta be a meaner sort of critter than most of the rogue professors we're getting to know around here."

"For my money," Phil said, winding up, "Ricci's too busy muckin' around to even CARE about just one Selena. For my money our man is still Van Geyst."

"He obviously needed expert help," Sita Amanpuri solemnly opined, frowning at Laurie Lee Talbot. The corrected harelip made her compassionate smile look asymmetrical. "Nothing less. The poor man had simply suppressed everything from himself. He must have lived an endless agony." She covered one hand with the other in a serene attitude and erased the frown, choosing instead to open her great eyes wide, a clear-browed goddess meting out impartial judgment.

They had arrived at Chez Minimal a bit ahead of time, Laurie Lee having run two and a half blocks—Commerce Street, cutting left at the dry cleaner's parking lot, right again at Bilge Lane—to catch up unobtrusively with Sita's sinuous walk. Anyone else following Sita that evening had ample opportunity to benefit from Laurie Lee's intervention.

Chez Minimal was still almost empty. They could enter side by side without bumping against the blackboard menu that usually blocked the entry.

Laurie Lee had long felt awed confusion in the presence of Sita, who liked to send her mixed signals. Was theirs a relationship of teacher and disciple (their closeness in age notwithstanding), or of future peers, or sort of elder and younger sisters? Sita was her thesis director. Laurie Lee often wondered whether the stymied state of her "work in progress" was really Sita's fault, for not providing clear instructions, bibliographical suggestions, "leadership." But at the same time she liked and admired Sita's "nondictatorial" indirect style, her contralto, her way of saying things free of the pedantry of clarity. Laurie Lee perceived this style as fundamentally a woman's, especially right for a woman student. And yet Laurie Lee's very gaucheness, her abrupt, mistimed responses were driven by the fear of offending Sita in her inexorable mystery.

Sita, her thoughts displaced by the quasi-military figure of Chambers, saw that Laurie Lee was simply a chore she would soon never have to do anymore, now that the post-tenure honeymoon was over. She had no instruction to offer her. But Laurie Lee right went on adoring Sita, together with all of FAM: Megan Mehan, Vassiliki Fink, Clara Bowl—the lot. Anyway, since they all kept saying the same thing it was easy to learn what to say. The trick was in the "how", and a stray word in the wrong place could mean curtains.

Like forgetting that prostitutes were not sex slaves but goddesses ruling over enthralled captives. Laurie Lee's sex life had been neither varied nor active. It could better be described as desultory, charmless, and dutiful. She brought to it the same conformity to instructions and hope for a favorable outcome that had made her a tireless daddypleaser as a child. Maybe things ran more enthrallingly for Sita, whom Laurie Lee often pictured entwined with an equally intriguing male in impossibly serpentine erotic positions.

As they sat opposite one another in Chez Minimal, Laurie Lee realized yet again how afraid of Sita she was. She tugged at the frayed collar of her brother's old button-down shirt and wondered whether she had really achieved the correct feminist style. If Sita could walk around in that adhesive but "pristine" suit, could Laurie Lee have been wrong all this time? Where was the key? Her best hope, she knew, lay in her ability not to be anything very much.

"Oh yes," she said, "Poor man... Do you think everyone will come to the funeral?" What she wanted to ask was, "Do you think he did it? Did Palter kill Selena?"

Sita got huffed, to vent her nerves. "How can you expect ME to know? It is all entirely a matter of chance." She shrugged, craned over Laurie Lee's head and shoulders toward the Chez Minimal entryway. In obedience to an old habit, her eyes also took in the rest of the empty restaurant just in case someone, anyone, was lurking in the shadows of a corner table. Laurie Lee, whose lanky presence loomed in her way, was like something once bought on the installment plan, now useless but still being paid for.

"I wouldn't ever have thought it of him," Laurie Lee said.

"Palter Van Geyst will always remain an unknown quantity. It was a life infiltrated by mystery and, I can only call it, wonder."

"The suicide, I mean. That he would kill himself."

"If, and I say, if," Sita said, paying no attention, "Palter Van Geyst engaged with the ideology of anti-Semitism, that error does not make him a murderer."

"No, surely not."

"And just because of a long-ago mistake, we will not unleash a senseless anger against him, some kind of lynching or bookburning."

How soon the collective "we" had come to Sita, Laurie Lee thought, picturing her now as the only woman justice in a preternatural academic court. But she's so irritable tonight, even for someone so fine-tuned, so infinitely complex.

"We would hardly wish to reproduce the exterminating gesture of the Holocaust, would we? Has the man not suffered enough? But if it is so, it is so. The picture does not look so very fine from his point of view, I will concede."

Mixed signals again, thought Laurie Lee. But it is all one with her fascination.

"Oh, Laurie Lee—I might as well mention that I cannot make our appointment tomorrow, unavoidable circumstances."

Laurie Lee swallowed meekly, overawed as she was at having been chosen the only graduate student to participate in this hiring dinner, and looking forward to a real sit-down three-course meal.

"Okay, we'll just take a look at the guy," Fishbane had promised the crony who was selling this Candidate. "We ARE going to need some-one, although how you could have known...send him over and we'll take him to dinner. No, the resumé can wait. That book he's doing—UTERINE ISSUES? LuAnn, this should be right up your... Sherri Tooley loved it? Sounds fine, fine... Gonna be in Venice again this summer? Scrumptious. Venice—Venus, venality, venereal...get it? Talk to ya after."

A cold draft from the dingy restaurant door admitted Bonza Leier, who banged against the blackboard menu as Sita had hoped she would. Sita repressed a howl of mirth and moved over for her, a tad fur-ther away from Laurie Lee. Bonza's Concerned Face was overlaid with a barely suppressed excitement. She draped two bulging canvas totes on either side of her chair, her pea jacket on its back and her briefcase under her feet, and lunged at Sita, her gooseberry eyes magnified by rimless specs, to execute the FAM embrace.

"Did you ever—could you imagine—what can I say?" They hugged, kissed on all four cheeks, giggled, hugged again. Bonza then noticed Laurie Lee. "Oh hello. Laurie Talbot, right? So as I was saying, Armin had to just PRY me out of bed with a major, MAJOR headache. I felt—like a rape victim. The students will certainly be too upset to come to class, so I thought it best to cancel tomorrow." She laughed the wild laughter that is the mark of humorless people. Sita nodded, her eyes melting with sympathy, the harelip receding.

Armin swept in, his customary bustle, a six-foot length of regimental stripes muzzled his nose and mouth and flared out behind him. Two others followed in his wake: Ricci, dressed as an undertaker, and a svelte young man who avoided everyone's eyes. None of these, to Sita's disappointment, knocked up against the blackboard menu. The last of the group to arrive, LuAnn Rossiter, finally brought it down with a mad crash...

The Search was getting her down. Things were less sunshiny than she had intimated in her last talk with Chuck. Plus you still had to keep on diddling Gorellick no matter what, just because he's completely dependable. Or should she take the next step...alone? Visions of a consternated Megan Mehan and a chastened Har-Shalom usually cheered her up, but now, what with the Van Geyst news, Comp Lit might be utterly defeated. Chuck might have to give the Center to Willona McFarquhar, and just because she was black, too! LuAnn reddened as she propped up the collapsed blackboard.

"We've kept you waiting," Armin said to the Candidate, looking hopeful. "Have we kept you waiting?"

The two scholarly waiters who had scampered over to the table when Armin arrived noticed a sudden rush of customers and took off. A pallid couple currently appraising Redfern as a potential roosting spot grumpily disentangled their dashikis. A heavy woman in her mid-seventies wearing a Grateful Dead sweatshirt and matching drawstring bottoms ground a piece of chalk under one old sneaker and waddled backwards in surprise. Three car salesmen had strayed from their usual dinner-time venue and looked sorry. The waiters began to work the room, scowling at the unwonted number of occupied tables.

The common humanity of the members of Comp Lit asserted itself in six seconds of miserable silence. Then all except Laurie Lee and the svelte young man began to talk at once like a TV sitcom family. Fishbane finally vouchsafed the Candidate a glance.

"We're kind of disorganized now, as you can imagine. I bet you're almost sorry about what you've walked right into today."

"Oh no...this looks like a wonderful restaurant."

Fishbane knitted his bushy silver brows. "I mean the...campus sensations. We really aren't like that at all; you'll see that when you come."

"I can hardly wait," said the svelte young man. "Redfern seems like the perfect place. If there is one," he giggled. "Of course there's my offer from Sunbath A & M to consider, but it's just no contest, really." There had been no offer from Sunbath or any other place, but it was a safe lie because Redfern would never talk to the likes of Sunbath.

"I hope youah settled quat comfortably at Blaht House," LuAnn put in. There had been no time to try and find a hotel room for the Candidate, so they had stuffed him into the dorms.

"Couldn't be nicer. Thank you."

"UTERINE ISSUES: The Emancipation of the Erotic." Sita read from the Candidate's resume. "What a marvelous research topic. Such a good title. We will await the book impatiently."

The svelte young man wriggled in his bistro chair. "I'll send you a chapter the minute I get back. I'm up to the part about Capitalist Slavery and its Denial of Sexuality."

Sita turtled up to him. "Could you elaborate on that, please?"

"Sure. I'm saying that obviously and increasingly, not everyone has embraced a discourse we have come to see as anti-feminist, pseudo-objective, adversarial. Not everyone, I'm pleased to say. Sherri Tooley, for one, has called that discourse a 'gender-based straitjacket.' What I'm looking at here is so-called literary-critical writing. Which thinks it makes use of argument. Which casts aspersions on orally transmitted knowledge. Which deifies the god of reason and denigrates emotion. DeNIGRATE—get it? The word itself not only debases emotion, but is a racist slur. To go on, I'm saying, in effect, I guess, that there were slaves to machismo in

Europe after the slaves in the Caribbean were freed...that European civilization refused to end slavery, they just made it endemic to the whole culture. Slavery to argument, proof, verification—all that silly cant. Professor Van Geyst had the last word on that, of course. The rest is history."

"Don't you say 'enslaved person,' not 'slave'?" Fishbane asked almost admiringly, letting Van Geyst's name pass unnoticed. But the svelte young man caught the nuance and stumbled for a moment, confused.

"Touché, touché," the Candidate laughed, jabbing a playful index finger at his chest. 'Now I'm referring, of course, to ALL who were enslaved to capitalisms."

The group brightened and shifted to attention in their seats. "Maxime-Etienne could work with you really well," Fishbane said. "The guy generates an unbelievable amount of work,—genuinely activist work too, if you will."

"That would be MARVELOUS. I actually go on to say that—uh, enslaved persons include everyone who has been subject to cultural racism, to a preference for one's own cultural heritage and values over that of another. For example, why shouldn't a recipe for stew be as important as a sonnet?" This sounded word-for-word like Marvella Jilkes, and was. "I have a rather novel way of tabulating, that is, graded instances of racism, sexism, ableism, and lookism."

"Lookism?" Ricci peered out of his private mudbath like a disgruntled hippo. "What means 'lookism'?"

"Well, that's discrimination against people on the basis of their appearance. Aesthetic discrimination. Do I appear to get a bit carried away?"

He took a babystep backward, a giant step forward. "Well, I'M going public anyhow. We can't put up forever with the cultural elitism we live in. It's up to us to move society into the twenty-first century. The idea of my book is to expose the distortions capitalism wreaks on our erotic heritage and to play with a new force of joy. Joyous pain. Joyous force. Joyous desire-like dessert after a boring dinner. I mean. Dessert, deserts, de-sert. You know."

"To protest repression..."

"Western metaphysics...repression."

"Repression, absolutely."

Ricci slumped in his seat, mentally undressing that ghastly old woman in the sweatshirt with heads on it and coupling her with Sita Amanpuri. The Candidate plowed on.

"Aristotle was of course massively elitist, racist, and sexist. Massively." Everyone but Ricci nodded and grinned, swaying like push toys, Sita enveloped in the embrace of her Dream Lover. "Requiring students to read him just robs them of gems like, well, Marvella Jilkes, for instance." The svelte young man had heard on the grapevine of her imminent agreement to join Redfern. Another moment of silence, as a delicate flush coursed over his face.

LuAnn wasn't about to let incidentals cramp her style. She feels pretty tonight, as much on show as the Candidate. "Ah've assahned all mah students Jilkes' work on Being-On-Drugs. Not bein' on drugs, see: BEING...ON DRUGS. But of course we've gone beyond that too. Theyah's the university-wide get-acquainted course—fust thing in the Diversity Curriculum—an' we're being included in that. Ouah Program in the Moral Superiority of the Third World has a powahful feminist emphasis. You could teach that next yeah."

"Well, here I am—a self-described P.C. Feminist," the svelte young man declared with a flourish, permitting himself a little laugh in which Fishbane joined. Guy's getting a little cocky. But nice, nice.

The table talk took an upturn. Laurie Lee, spellbound once again, devoured every word of Sita's little set piece.

"What does it mean—REALLY mean—to use a vacuum cleaner? To make yourself answerable to whatever it chooses to sweep up, in a situation where a gestural syntax always already means YES although to dispose of the sweepings means NO? Is this not a fundamentally affirmative force, above and beyond individual self-assertion?"

A waiter approached bearing the wine list, a grubby laminated card. "Whatever shall it be?" Fishbane flirted with the list. "The Mouton Minimal? The Louche-Bertrand? This little California vintage might even beat them all. Tellya what, let's have drinks first, postpone the moment." He turned to the future Ph.D. in Waitpersoning: "I'll have a Perrier with lime."

"Perrier watah fo' me ."

"Ah si', cameriere, a Perrier. No lime."

"Perrier."

"Perrier."

"Perrier," says Laurie Lee. "Thank you." All turn to the Candidate, who hesitates infinitesimally.

"I'll have a small pale dry sherry, please."

No one spoke. Fishbane moved his chair a precise three inches further from the Candidate's. He caught LuAnn's eye. LuAnn caught Ricci's.

What was the exact instant when chance and necessity intersected? What attack of nerves or failure of intellect prompted the svelte young man to choose sherry over Perrier? Had he read one of those self-help books on job interviews that tell you to show your superiors some gumption?

The Candidate was not going to fit in after all.

Dinner dragged on anyhow, course after tasteless course washed down by Louche-Bertrand: eggs mayonnaise, minute steaks, canned-peach melba, ending with flambéed international coffees. The conversation had turned even more feverishly animated just before it was to die.

Canceling this Candidate assured the faculty of lots more convivial meals to come at Chez Minimal and all on the Department, natch. A bigger high, even, was the promise of more creamy meetings, more gossipy interplay, more minidramas of power. And the actual hiring decision, which would eventually limp in flanked by the twin handmaidens, Vanity and Fear, could be put off indefinitely until the Bear Hug and the Hun began to make a show of impatience and threaten effetely to drop the new Comp Lit position or give it to another department.

Though the Chez Minimal fare tasted worse to him than American fast food, even Ricci perked up, rising to deliver the coup-de-grace.

"I am in every way delighted," he proclaimed to all the surrounding tables, "to 'ave spent this fine evening with you, young man. I wish you all the best in the world." At this the svelte young man caved in utterly, never to be heard from again.

They began shrugging into their peajackets and Irish oilcloths, adjusting sou'westers and folkloric headgear. For the admiration of a hovering waiter, Fishbane signed the charge slip with a certain modest flair, tossing his muffler rakishly behind him.

"Professor Ricci," a familiar policeman's voice said behind

Ricci's chair. "Would you mind coming with us, please? Just a few questions."

"C'mon, Ricci, let's go," said the other even coarser one.

"Serves him right for wearing that seal hat," whispered Bonza. But even she was taken aback by the shot of pure hatred in Ricci's glare. Ricci seemed to meditate for a moment, knowing he was free to refuse. Then his shoulders sagged as if he felt that in spite of any innocent protestations he might make he was not going to be believed by anyone

"You have a good night, now," the waiter said to Simon, Phil, and Ricci.

The shocked dinner party broke up, leaving the svelte young man to his own shattered devices. No two members left together.

Sita's serpentine progress through the restaurant's little parking lot was being hampered by the close-fitting skirt, which permitted less than optimal flexibility. A man holding an umbrella passed by her without even looking. Many matters weighed on her mind, a jumble that would need sorting out in private. Keith's spurning of her love goaded her to indignation, now spiked with fear for his very survival. Could those fleeting moments in the underground labyrinth erase themselves from memory? The steps, the strobe-like light, the swerving run—they were all apparitions of no consequence, to be accounted for by her own heightened emotions. Now it was the Monday night whereabouts of Palter Van Geyst that needed "clarification." And if the police were to question her about the Beloved, there was nothing to hide and nothing to tell, for she would never betray Him as long as the possibility could be said to exist that He would be hers one day.

But He was helplessly mired in emergency meetings, in the Marvella fiasco, in the Van Geyst riddle, and coping with the last disposal of Selena Fenn. Had the girl no other relations? We live in the twentieth century, these things happen.

Her bright blue Toyota awaited, looking optimistic in the midst of an atmosphere charged with electricity. Shafts of brilliant yellow light announced a distant snort of thunder. Driving in bad weather would remain a fact of her life until Redfern came up with a decent one-bedroom costing less than a thousand a month. Sita buried her face in the scarf that matched her "pristine" suit as she walked the twenty yards to the car.

Easing into the driver's seat, she noticed the jagged piece of closed umbrella protruding a little from the back—should've brought it along. At first her mind, shocked into a second's stupor, refused to recognize what her eyes now clearly saw. She put up a tentative hand and stroked the soft dark material of a man's jacket, and now there was only panic and exultant terror as he bent over her, and extended his arms to take her, and her last thought in this world was that yes, she would die for him.

Back at his magenta and aquamarine habitat, Fishbane is composing his speech for Palter's funeral. The mosaic of other people's words he is putting together now is going to have some of everything. The Tefflahn Prof's nifty way of putting words together is just the kind of postmodern thing that would have delighted Palter. It would also show what he called "Palter's Philosophy of Plagiarism" in action. No such thing as intellectual property—only words released into the void, to be rescued now and then by passing entrepreneurs.

It feels great to be rid of Palter, too. People deferring to him all the time, floating his myth. If Palter was right, then his death calls for an heir to all the success he milked from the idea that reason is a matter of opinion. And isn't it coming out the way he said? Like a raft on heavy water, academic fashion endlessly lurches between goofy extremes, notions you could knock down with a feather, only everyone who counts agrees not to try. After a while, some czar retires, dies, or the reins of power go slack in their hands.

Every Comp Lit fad rushes in on a wave, only to deposit its sediment of tenured quacks. That way you can count on the jolt of change to keep us interesting. WE'RE IT. We've come to represent the whole university. No one writes in *The Times* about anything except Lit departments. No one has profs of Geography or Engineering as talk-show guests. Who writes whiny complaining books about how Physics teaching has changed, or Microbiology? Hardly anyone remembers that most of the damn place is filled by people who just go around doing their jobs.

The media watch us because the idea just won't die, that you are what you read. That somehow you impersonate what you believe in. It's all a part of the Self, in a way nothing else you take at school could ever be—not yet, anyway.

Being Tefflahn Professor is fun, but not enough.

Tomorrow I'll go back to the Fielding letters, find them a better place to live. I could call the book, maybe, FIELDING: HIS SECRET SELF.

The first wave of unisex kids in black berets, black turtlenecks, black jeans and black caps try to look lost in thought as they flow into Biscottini Stadium. The Biscottini sound system booms. Strobe lights make the audience blink like moles. Bar Nun, whose first album reached No. 18 on Billboard's charts, is already rapping in the style that has moved Modern Media and Massage profs to compare them with Ice T and Fresh Prince. The crowd keeps snowballing. People are already wearing the $50 DiSalvo shirts on sale outside, heedless of the normal shirt-aging process.

Treacle Morris of the Redfern Rumble has left off persecuting Keith Chambers for tonight. "I think this hip revivalism is focusing on style as opposed to substance," Treacle says to the girl next to her, earning a blank stare.

"Mu-yam-mar!" someone bellows from the floor. A gangly guy wearing a pointy black beard and three layers of vests in leather, canvas, and hot pink nylon lumbers onto the stage to shift synthesizers and control decks—right in front of Bar Nun. Undeterred, the insinuating patter never stops. Hips bobbing, hair flopping over shiny foreheads. The music makes less sense than a bus-station schizophrenic. But the posters, which someone has festooned with swathes of gold lamé, look terrific with the nineties-hip crowd. A female student wearing a stocking cap and a housedress undoes the first three dress buttons to reveal her grandma's slip and toys with a burnt-out joint, never smoked. Her boyfriend has come all the way from New York just for the DiSalvo night. He is an assistant executive in a company that makes face gel.

"I love the lamé," says the boyfriend. "Looks just like a bordello."

"A what?" She yawns, gagging slightly. He's thirty but looks twenty, she the reverse.

Somebody no one can see starts reading out a catalogue of Reagan-Bush cruelties and tossing discarded pages of it into the front row. Earnestness prevails. The event is a Witches' Sabbath waiting to happen to a crowd still cocooned in a cloud of bonhomie and niceness.

Suddenly the music switches to a bump-n'-grind more insistent than the bongo, and the strobes leap into full action, making everyone blink. A yellow puddle of spotlight hangs waiting, and there sashays onto the stage a little thin ragamuffin in a tux with huge sharply cut satin lapels and a black lace top peeking out from underneath, swinging her lower half to the bump-'n-grind and balancing on black spike heels. Everyone screams and yells and holds up "V" signs. The front rows can see the cleavage under the suit, and Treacle recognizes the cover shot from Rakes Quarterly. The ragamuffin semaphores for quiet. Her introducer shouts into the hushed audience, backing away:

"Per-fesser Carlotta... Di...Salvo!"

And there she is, looking diminutive in the spotlight, loading up on attitude, left hand on forward-thrusting hip. The world's first Total Media Professor, of...of....well, most everything. Just goes to show you. Carlotta does her stripper walk right to the edge of the stage, wrapping her top half around the handheld mike.

"HAVING A NICE TIME?"

"YEEEEEAAAAAHHHHH!" The audience is basically sitting up straight but Carlotta can make out two solid back rows of feet and is not pleased.

"Then shuddup, okay? I want quiet, okay?" The sound system is doing its number so that her scrappy urchin's voice carries a booming edge. "You heard me." The noise dies like a fly. "And get those feet down or I'm gone." Most feet come down. "THAT MEANS YOU TOO, SUCKERS, OKAY?" No one except neighbors hears the defiant thump of the last feet.

"I'M NOT YOUR DOTING PARENTS. I'm not a part of this Redfern place. I don't owe you anything, okay?"

"YAAHHHHHH!" They're ecstatic already.

"But out of the goodness of my heart, out of simple goodness, okay, I'm here to shake you little mommies' and daddies' babies up and tell you to do the same for this college. No one ever did that for me!

Here's the benefit of my experience. My philosophy of edjakashon!"

A few yeas.

"You got a problem, okay? Here's what it is. You live in a country that hates brains. It's up to you to fix that. It doesn't matter what the current metamorphosis is, ME-TA-MOR-PHO-SIS, transformation to you. You lack a literate culture. Go read some real books. Don't listen to those sissies who call themselves your teachers. Cowards and poltroons posing as RADICALS!"

"YAAAHHHHHHHH!"

"Shuddup. They call themselves radicals, dress up as some kind of leftists standing up for the oppressed. You have folks around here who think that refusing to sign the Loyalty Oath—you don't even know what that was!—made them brave representatives of the people! The Loyalty Oath meant you swore to be faithful to this country and would not try to overthrow the government. Well, picture anyone here overthrowing anything!"

Some snickers. Carlotta struts around the pool of spotlight on her spikes, does a sharp about-face like a rock star.

"Real radicals have something to risk. Real radicals stand on principle when they make real life decisions. Bleating about the evils of capitalism is nothing but a DUMB POSE, especially when you have no idea what it did for you. So these frauds make out they're leftists. People who wouldn't know a principle if it sat on them, people who have never done anything, people to whom nothing has happened in their entire lives. Scared to go to war, scared to enforce a peace, scared even of their own privileges right into a weird fantasy of being oppressed and deprived. Wanna know what they are? EXISTERS. The ones Dante wouldn't even let into Inferno. Here's a free chunk of Great Book from me to you: third chapter of Inferno, where you'll find the wimp circle reserved for spineless, odorless timeservers who walked through their whole lives without being for or against anything.

"Well, maybe universities have always been holding pens for the young, the old, and the lazy. Maybe anyone with hormones could feel oppressed around early springtime...." A wistful little pause. "But now we're talking Big Big Enterprise. Your side of the bargain is to spend four years playing with Frisbees and looking oppressed together with the profs, and for your parents to pay for it. The administration calls the shebang a community, but make no mistake: a university is for teaching and learning, even if people-moving happens to look easier, okay? The essential ingredient is for parents to KEEP ON PAYING, to keep the wheels grinding so the wimps in charge make sure you get processed and the parents keep on paying. Courses on how to go shopping. Courses on how to masturbate. I mean, really."

How does she keep from melting in that tux? A buzz takes over, swells and dies off, as when the most determined players in an orchestra go on for several bars after the conductor's stop signal, then fizzle out.

"ACADEMIC FREEDOM SNUFFS OUT DISSENT. Literature and art are a hard sell—because they're complex, dark, surprising. You don't know a whole lot yet, do you? But still the teachers want you to have those touchy-feely sessions, rather than listen to the boring lectures they haven't even prepared. They want you to tell them how you FEEL because that helps the clock run out so they can go home free of you and your ignorance. The animals policing the zoo.

"Your mommies and daddies hardly notice you, they have their own lives to live—so of all people, the professors turn into vendors of instant junk feeling. Selling you a phony drama that looks like it's about finding you and your SELF, okay?

"So the Generals of Bureaucracy and Captains of No Enterprise go along with this boondoggle because they know you kids have to get your B.A. credential—the rubber stamp on your hand that says you've been here for four years and will always be welcome back as paying, donating alums. And this is your last chance to think till you're sixty-five."

Carlotta drops her mike and puts her hands on her hips.

"I've got one last thing to say, okay? If you're a woman, you've got all the power. You are the focus of longing and desire for the whole world. You're it. Venus, Mona Lisa, Madonna. The cause of man's lust to penetrate the unknown. How dare you complain you're being Sexually Harassed by the poor slobs who can't help swarming around you?" She arches her back to make the most of the cleavage she has managed to muster up under the black lace. Her eyes fill with sudden tears.

"BITCH!" The shout comes from a female student in the front row.

"Don't you even know what happened?" The student breaks into weeping. "YOU BITCH, isn't a sex murder enough for you? A fucking MURDER. Bitch."

The chant goes up, bitch! bitch! bitch! But Students for No Bullshit are prepared. Several appear and link arms onstage while Carlotta waits for the noise to end. At first jeers and incoherent noises prevail, then trail off as curiosity takes over, because she's primed to resume.

"I thought you were really brave," an admiring male voice says, carrying into the far reaches. "Confronting everyone like that. You're fantastic. Are you gay?"

A full stop and she explodes. "Of all the unbelievable nerve. How dare you. My private. The offensive.... Don't they teach you any manners... I'm out here." She signals for backup and the music starts again.

But the students are mortified, looking at each other in embarrassment because they've glimpsed the chink in her armor. Mortified, because they needed to express their cynical detachment from her tears, but didn't know how to go about it. Mortified, finally, because she was leaving them in the lurch. Magniloquent, raging Super Media Prof, gender bender extraordinaire... why'd she suddenly get so mad? what had they done to mama?

Sixties strobes redazzled the shell-shocked auditorium. You could catch the unexpected silver in her blond boycut, and a scandalized prop person aimed his white mask of distress at the audience on his way out. Cordoned off by her makeup people and her music, Carlotta's gone.

The whole crazy Carlotta performance reminded Phil Granita of the circus sideshows that were still permitted when he was a boy. As then, he got up reluctantly, still glancing around the empty auditorium, but you would think the disturbance had never happened. Coming here in the hope of a closer look at the Comp Lit "radicals" had been a dumb idea. None of them had even the weird kind of courage it took to kill someone.

Adjusting his belt, Phil heaved himself out of the molded-plastic seat and down the aisle and the stairs to the auditorium foyer. He was met by the last round of lingering students in search of someone to talk to about the event. He spotted the hefty woman named Rossiter, trading moose calls and high fives with a frizzy little dame and a third dark, pimply one. All three looked very, very happy with the evening's events. He'd never heard women keep saying "bitch" with such utter joy, and he wondered if these three had masterminded the show from the opposition. Three tacky-lookin' babes they were, too..."aesthetically challenged", he pronounced slowly. The one in the sari wasn't around, though; probably taking the night off.

Phil pushed his bulky frame in its nondescript grey upholstery through the middle of the group to get a better look, and thought he'd keep close on her heels for a while. Not much else to do, and he perceived something extra forced about her social cries and exaggerated gestures. At last the frizzy blond one and the pimply one took off together, and Phil fondly eyed his woman as she struck out solo into the green quad.

It was foggy and the straight angles of the campus seemed to soften and blur under a flat rain that was just starting. He kept about a dozen paces behind her and as her stride lengthened he felt the beginning of an old limp become more pronounced. He saw the absurdity of tailing this female professor as if any quarry were better than none, but he was smart enough to know that the solution could come from anywhere in the end. There was no such thing as a criminal class, a thought he had now for the first time. LuAnn stopped, twisting around for a moment as if to turn on her pursuer, and a big red umbrella shot up over her.

As she hoisted her slipping shoulder bag, a piece of paper fluttered out of her raincoat pocket. Just more paper, he thought, keeping well to her rear. But then he stepped on it and picked it up. Black arched squiggles on white—a big help. But then he discerned from the worn rim on top of the fragment that it was the bottom of a much-read computer-typed letter which had just torn in half on its fold, and that the squiggles were letters halved lengthwise.

"...delighted by your assistance," he made out, supplying the top halves of the squiggles. "...and look forward to your further participation in our search. Victory is at hand. Affectionately, Vassiliki." The signature was a handwritten flourish, no typing beneath. In the same handwriting, "hugs 'n' kisses."

What a name. This letter—no date, even—was probably useless, but nothing lost holding onto it. It might have something to do with a more important job this woman was jockeying for. It struck him that maybe LuAnn had been digging into Selena's money by way of persuading Vassiliki to give her the job. But "hugs 'n' kisses"? It could be Vassiliki was just searching out some book or other. Could she be interested in books? Supposedly a professor's business, but he hadn't been seeing much of it in this corner, where no one seemed to have the time to do much reading or writing.

LuAnn turned in the direction of the Admin Building, where he could see that a couple of third-floor windows were festively illuminated. Chuck's office, still open, probably working overtime these days. He walked on behind her, the echo of their steps blunted by the fog, closely enough to see the cautious expression on her face as she surveyed the empty campus from side to side. Her image thrust itself forward, confident of its path and urgent in its purpose, right up to where he could no longer follow, and in the glimpse of an instant the Admin door opened and she got into Chuck's private elevator.

No bugs allowed, as usual, but maybe soon no one concerned with this investigation would be so particular about what was allowed. When Simon heard, for once he agreed.

It's late, but Myron Wiener is his own man now. His legs feel longer than ever before, his eyes seem to pierce right through the dumpy rows of downtown Temperance façades as they rush by him on the way to an ending. His glasses left at home, he can't actually see much, but everything floats before his eyes as a harmonious whole. His senses scatter, but he has the power of knowing exactly where in the dark his footfalls are taking him and what he needs to buy...

Temperance has cut down even more on street lighting this spring, so probably no one will come along. The silent streets have no expectation of sound. If he had a shadow it would be tall and thin. No, Vera said, you can't, you won't do it. But there's time; Myron doesn't have to stop walking yet. With every block and corner the shop recedes. No need to worry, no one to listen to. And better: he stands tall, straight, sober-faced, ready to smile if anyone passes him, answers at the ready if anyone speaks to him. A gentleman of good will with nothing in his past to shame him. Myron wonders why he'd ever stammered or stumbled in his life, sailing the dilapidated Temperance streets, touching down lightly whenever he feels like it, aping Armin Fishbane's gait. Jason or Melissa would stop bawling if they only knew what a rock Daddy is, how they can count on me.

A brown car swings low on a turn, and Simon and Phil sight the little scuttling figure of a suit on his way from work, practically giggling to himself. They brake to a crawl as a long stretch of row houses ends abruptly in a roadblock composed of trashcans, Some of the cans have been upended, so they back up, then head left onto a block whose houses could have been sheds, shops, anything, they catch sight of the same little man again. "Guy can't wait to get home," Granita says.

"But practically no one lives here."

"This one does, why would he be on the run like that? Musta had a day today. Boy, I feel the same as him..." Granita looks back down at his aching feet. "Anyhow...Like we were saying: Van Geyst has to be our murderer. He was at the party. He circulated around like the others, maybe more because of being a star and everyone wanting to talk to him. The person who did it doesn't have to be the one who fucked her, so let's background that. Van Geyst obviously was ready to die rather than have his game exposed. Those European countries all have their penalties for his kind, so getting sent back would have been no picnic. The whole thing screams Van Geyst." Phil lounges in his seat, thinking of the Chief's latest diatribe and hoping the perp is a dead man.

"I can't believe you, after everything we just saw and heard." Simon accelerates with a stomach-turning lurch. "We don't even know half of it all yet. But at least we managed to keep our eyes open this time. Why was that evidence in Selena's room?" Granita looked blank and Simon waved his free hand back and forth in front of his eyes like a pendulum. "Evidence, papers, the file."

"Someone stuck it there, that's why." Granita said. "Someone who wants to try pinning it on Ricci."

"Phil, did Van Geyst strike you honestly as the kind who would get their nice hands dirty?"

"Their nice BIG hands. Van Geyst had paws like Mickey Mouse —and that's not all. That smile. He wouldna had a hard time."

"And the girlfriend? Selena gave her plenty of cause for jealousy. She was a lot less devoted. Nothing rules Hilary out. She could have snuck out of her waiter job for as much as half an hour."

"She wouldn't leave semen spots, Lieutenant. Sir."

'But it didn't have to be the same person," Simon sighed.

"There's even something weird about LuAnn. Did you see what a whopper; she has what it takes, and that FAM bunch wants the money—but she's got an in with Chavadze anyhow... Look, I think Chambers is being obstructive because he wants the killer to be Palter, so that we'll call the investigation off. The two of 'em—him and Chavadze both, want to turn us away from Ricci, just because they'd be embarrassed if it's him, the good professor. But he looks to have a dynamite motive. And it just fell into our hands."

"The file?"

"Sure. What I want to know is how Selena got hold of it and if she was planning to go public. What would that have done for her? She didn't need money, and if... how'd she get hold of that file anyway?"

They hear the distant wail of a freight train. On a billboard that juts against the low sky, they read MOTHER MARY SAVE US. An abandoned construction site covers a whole block. The car has plenty of room to stretch out in, and Simon suddenly wants to give way. But there is paperwork to do first, the day to wrap up.

"Simple—someone just put it there. An' one more thing. I didn't hear you say, all the time you've been busy with Ricci. CHAMBERS WAS AT THE PARTY TOO. He was every place that our perp needed to be. Or do you think only Italians specialize in crime?" He looked funny miffed, raising a grubby finger in teaching position, "Chambers hates sex, right? an' LOVES Selena, right? He was everywhere at the wrong time, right? So. Maybe he went berserk when he saw her with Ricci, or maybe he knew about that for a while an' couldn't take it any more. But he was talking like it couldn't ever've been Ricci. So was Chuck. So like I said..." Phil was losing the thread. "Anyhow it doesn't HAVE to be Ricci no matter what else he's done. Not even to shut Selena up, it couldn't be worth the risk. That leaves Chambers."

Simon grinned. "Some of my best friends are Italians. I know it could be Chambers too, they were all out of the party room some time. But remember—there's not only the paper file, there's Handmaid. The messages in Ricci's computer. She was out to get him and said so." He parked the car in the station lot.

"That little guy on the street just now, he's the only person we saw tonight. Maybe it's him."

"That's really, really funny."

Myron is almost there, passing by the Maid For Love and the adult movie house, smiling a shy, elated smile. Images and colors drift and fade before his eyes, but all he has to do is ignore them. He sticks his tongue out at them. The chill wind striking at his collar and through his sleeves passes through unnoticed. Tonight is a "threshold" night—a favorite lecture expression of Armin Fishbane's and the same one used by the rabbi yesterday, when I became a man thirty years ago. How easy the connections were all the time, why hadn't I seen it from the start? You need only stretch out a hand. He does this, delighting in the simple performance of the gesture. Concentrate: you can feel everything you do as if you were someone else, and still it's you doing everything. Amazing, the sheer force at your command, utterly under control.

Full steam ahead. I'm doing this for the institution, what will they do for me in return? Fame, fortune, and fun. Tenure, even, to be followed by Chateaubriand, Louche-Bertrand, and a lifetime of laziness, cowardice, and resentment, yeah. Not like years and years of pushing boulders uphill anymore. Hate LuAnn Rossiter, Bonza Leier. But always let them out the elevator first. Hate Hargreaves and Banter. Hate Lamamba. Lamamba talks like Idi Amin. Hate Idi Amin.

Myron ducks into a little alley, where? The dampness seeping even into the telephone poles and into Myron's clothing is a nice good wetness, protects him from sight and judgment, a milky fog holds Myron in its slipstream. Some volitional force is trying to catch hold of him, but it harbors no ill will or rancor.

Just a dim light inside the pawnshop, always open. They count on the neighborhood folks for all their business, no need even for a sign. He points to the gun he wants, sort of whimpering so that the guy behind the metal fence thinks he's drunk or coming down from some drug. But he must know Myron's money is no common paper. In fact it is a very special paper only Myron has in the whole world.

Thursday, April 8, 1993
KEITH RAMPANT

A dark morning squall disoriented the streets of Temperance, making the few faint smears of sky look like dirt. The blurred contours of trees and houses collected long grey raindrops that went on falling between showers. Simon has already taken Chief Killifer's early call. The first duty of the day is to deal with the autopsy on Van Geyst. Big news: you can almost smell the lack of fervor. Shit always happens early in the morning, Granita says: more people die, more women give birth, more autopsies.

In Simon's face, down the collar of his windbreaker and on his back squared against the wind, Temperance breathes a close, cold breath that has made both policemen button up all the way to the top... Their path keeps trying to turn away from them. Simon feels that he has come a long way to get run over by bad luck. He gropes around in the right pocket of the windbreaker, comes up with a curled-piece of lemon rind he'd stuck into the pocket at the donor party, flips it onto the pavement.

Phil's back is bothering him today so he groans as they get back into the brown unmarked, and it galumphs off, allowing speeding trucks to pass them. Simon feels that he might go back to smoking. The morning falls over them like a silence, broken only by intermittent barking from the radio. Wild theories grow in Simon's mind, taking various fantastic forms. To Phil he looks as if he were on automatic. "I said shut the fuck up," suddenly comes through the radio, and now Simon pulls the car up to the low building in its rectangle of brownish grass.

The moment they walk in, the policemen can tell that this is no ordinary morgue day. The usual rows of black and Hispanic people line the linoleum corridor, the usual two technicians work alone in the ante-room blazing with fluorescent bars. The usual bull-necked clerk sits parked right in their way, T-shirt under nylon shirt, and it's still fun to shoulder past him. The something different is a hushed, secretive atmosphere inside.

Keith Chambers sits jackknifed into right angles on a hard chair, brooding in the formaldehyde cloud, his eyes fixed inward, fingertips fastidiously steepled together. He looks extra pale today, and doesn't even stir when the intercom above his head barks out a message or the policemen enter.

"I got an idea," whispers Granita. "You take a picture of Chambers, an' we go right to the papers." He snickers. "That was a joke." No one in the tiled, metallically glinting inner room hears the huddle of dark people outside, the occasional squeak of their chairs. The room has no outside windows. Somehow that makes Keith look more at home.

"Speedy Gonzalez, ain't you, Chambers?" Phil grunts.

"We worked fast," Dr. Miles was saying, "in light of the urgency here. I think it unreasonable, Mr. Chambers, for you to pursue your argument. In these special circumstances, I would not object to your viewing the body yourself, if it helps." He moves as if to lead the way.

But Keith sits with his eyes front. "That will not be necessary."

Simon and Phil notice through the open door the shrouded gurney that had just been wheeled off to one side and the outline of shortish legs under the sheet.

"It's pretty straightforward," the doctor said with a hint of impatience. "There is a cancer here that could quite possibly have metastasized again. I could show you just how it's developed if you want..."

"No need," said Keith.

"He's been like this for years, on and off. That would be plain from his medical records. He's not in appreciably worse shape, though, than he would have been, say, six months ago or even more. Lots of people go about living in that kind of condition and doing their jobs."

Simon spoke up. "But why did he shoot himself? There would be no reason for Van Geyst to commit suicide because of just being unable to go on."

"That's probably right. Although it's possible that he did not take full advantage of chemotherapy. He has quite a head of hair." The doctor indicated the shock of fairish brown hair that flopped onto Palter's forehead.

"To return to my point," Keith said evenly, "Van Geyst shot himself with his right hand. He had a pretty steady hand too, there wasn't much mess in the lavatory."

The doctor answered patiently. "But the left hand, as I told you, has been severely incapacitated. It isn't withered, true," he waved Keith down, "and there's not that much to see, but the cancer had severely affected the hand, its ability to flex, for instance, to make a fist. The arm is in fact somewhat wasted. Any medical eye could spot what happened."

"You are quite certain that the arm and hand lost that much strength."

Chambers was being more than necessarily tedious. What the hell was he driving at, with this fuss about the wrong hand?

"I will not insist further, doctor."

The policemen stared right into Keith's face. but he contrived to avoid their eyes. Of course: if Van Geyst had a useless left hand, he could not have used it to strangle Selena. There would be no way for Keith to purify Redfern by pinning the crime on this sublimely detached sleeper.

"Doctor," Simon said, "We're going to need confidentiality about this. Because I have an idea. If we can only keep the truth about Van Geyst's left hand from the public, we can use the facts to flush out the murderer. I need to explain how important this is. Van Geyst was a suspect in the Selena Fenn murder. But now it turns out he couldn't have done it, the strangulation. Look: if the hand can be kept secret, if our guy thinks it's over. He'll do or say something to betray himself."

"I see," the doctor said. "Well, I have nothing to say to anyone else about this. No one has come forward yet to claim him. There is a Mrs. Van Geyst, but she seems to be taking her time."

"Confidentiality, sir," Simon appealed now to Keith. "The same as you university people apply to university doings. Like about the files. It's essential. Just don't let anyone else know what we know. Pretend it's over."

Keith looked bland. "Your curiosity about university files is quite a different matter, Lieutenant."

"Remember when you were showing us the underground university?"

"That's right: opening university files is entirely unwarranted."

"It may become WARRANTED in the near future." Simon was surprised by his own sarcasm. "Can't we forget that now, Chambers? I'm sick of snob talk and clubbiness. What's good for Redfern, what's bad for Redfern. You want the murderer to be brought to justice same as we do, or not?"

"I won't dignify that with an answer." Keith ostentatiously consulted his wristwatch. He had to meet with the Old Redfernian in half an hour. The New Campaign wasn't about to come to a stop, was it?

"This is a special chance. More important than just pinning this crime on Van Geyst because he's dead. If you can't keep quiet about this it's a warning, a tip-off to the strangler, unnerstand? DO YOU..."

"Lieutenant: I have an appointment this morning that can't wait." Keith spoke sharply but his pale eyes were mild, forbearing. In the archway, they all caught their last sight of Palter Van Geyst as a pair of shrouded feet.

Back in the car, the phone rang and Phil, picked up. "Sir, we just got it ourselves. Thassit. He could NOT've done it, no way. Her marks changed, she's been in the morgue days now, they can't search anymore.... Sir. Confidential. Sir."

Simon slumped, banging his elbow on the armrest, almost enjoying the pain.

"He's heard ALREADY. Maybe five minutes, it took. An' the pressure's making him crazy. Shoutin' at ME, to keep it quiet. Shit... Killifer wants to see it pinned on Van Geyst, same as Chambers and the rest. Makes you wanna...fuck the whole thing."

The phone voice crackled again. "Blank...and Granita...you will come in and tell me everything that happened at the morgue. Blank, you will not screw...innocent...people...for lack...of clues...dead or alive. You...will be here ...NOW if not YESTERDAY."

Simon hung up, keeping the receiver in his hand. . "That's fine," he told Granita, "but I'm calling General Fenn first. He's got a right to know enough to call the Van Geyst thing off. You check out the paper."

While Simon dealt with the General, Phil took in the story. He passed the paper to his partner with a snort.

CAMPUS MURDERS ASCRIBED TO DATE RAPE

Undisclosed sources have suggested that the murder of Redfern senior Selena Fenn in the "Underground Campus" of the University is the work of a "date rapist" who might easily have entered that section of the campus in the course of the party which both the rapist and Ms. Fenn attended.

Dean of Relationships Keith Chambers said in an early morning interview that he still believes "some youth who obviously had a different set of expectations than those of the young woman" strangled Ms. Fenn in the course of a struggle involving uninvited or unwanted sex. Attempts to link the murder to yesterday's suicide of Professor Palter Van Geyst, Chambers claims, are "feeble, raw, and futile." The Dean of Relationships stated that he is "ready to pursue vigorously any person who thinks he can get the better of Redfern, now or ever." He also expressed compassion for "anyone so disturbed or frustrated that he would sacrifice his whole future to one second of rage." Chambers admitted "the fact that date rape is a fact." The President of Redfern University, Grigol Chavadze, allowed himself to be quoted saying that he "means business" when the amended University Relationship regulations come out this fall.

The police investigation has established beyond any doubt that the sexual assailant of Ms. Fenn was a Caucasian male. No further information is yet forthcoming from the Eleventh Precinct.

"Fat lotta good that does." Phil tossed the paper at Simon.

"What I hate," Phil said, "is that the hair sample they finally got isn't gonna help, not even the DNA banding results when they come in. If there'd been TWO samples...shit. Some evidence collection."

"Barker had nothing to gain from killing her, plus we have no right to treat him as a suspect. The more you try the stupider we're gonna look when it's over and the more chance the Fishbanes and Chamberses have to scream brutality. Let's drop it for chrissake, at least for now. We've made our modest contribution to Given Barker's career already, right?"

The sheets of rain seemed to have swept Redfern clean of students too. Odd hunched-over figures ducked into side entryways, deliveries arrived, Human Resourcepersons could be seen lumbering in for the late breakfast shift, Marston Hall came on duty. Julius Redfern, rearing on his bronze horse, still saluted an invisible general in the middle of the larger quad.

Suddenly there appeared from the direction of Commerce Street, right across the quad, a sight Marston had never seen since he'd left Crown Heights: ten—count 'em—ten Hasidic rabbis, just shuffling single file down the street and into the quad as if they'd been allowed out for a walk.

Marston squinted, remembering how often he'd seen guys like that walking around in twos like nuns. Now twenty—and more!— Hasidic guys showed up with their long black gabardine coats, some wearing black bowlers, others huge red fox fur hats. Everyone with those long curly forelocks, and black lace-up shoes even in the rain. Some of them bobbed in those little back-and-forth bending motions like they make when they say their prayers.

They moved into the quad, shuffling and muttering, the long black coats dragging Chaplin-like on the wet ground, scraggly beards looking glued to their faces. For chrissake—they WERE glued to their faces! STUDENTS, nothing but students, up to some dumb-ass trick. And look! Some of 'em are girls. What the—!

Some of the rabbis took up a sort of ethnic moan "Aaaahhhh, maaahhh!" A few really inspired ones paraded shrugging at the heavens with upraised faces and palms. Even in the rain this display began to attract attention.

The rabbis turn in at the campus Arts Center, because they are rehearsing a superspecial Holocaust Installation: a joyous sendup of orthodox Jews. Jewish eight-branched candlesticks would line the runway for the fashion show. The latest see-thru fashions are waiting to burst out of the rabbi outfits. Manischewitz wine will be served. The finale will feature inclusive matzo-ball throwing at the audience. Invitations to the opening have been handlettered in a sort of Hebraic script. The production has been scrupulously monitored for signs of cheap comedy or disrespect.

At the end of the rehearsal the procession of rabbis, tossing the hats, makes its way out the back of the building since the front entrance is blocked with people coming to work. Each rabbi gingerly lifts the skirt of the gabardine jacket he or she is wearing as the group proceeds past the other Installations on the studio floor. One kid picks up a clay penis and absently puts it into her pocket; another stubs a toe on a crudely hewn inner organ.

"Hey, guys, c'mere, the installation in this corner." A couple of rabbis go over to look. A tarp on the floor like a furled parachute, around it the pieces of a beautiful young woman's body. One arm still has a hand; it beckons with thumb and index finger. A foot already has two stubbed toes just like a real antique. On its pedestal the torso on slim legs continues its invisible revolutions. Selena, head on floor, doesn't seem to mind missing a breast but goes right on gazing classically into the middle distance.

"This is FANTASTIC. Whose is it?"

"Aono."

"Hilary Slocombe. It's that sculpture of a woman. Don't you remember? Always covering it up."

"It's incredible. The idea of...just cutting her up. Better than the other part. To DO the sculpture first, THEN demo it, that's...wow."

A number of rabbis crawl among Selena's discarded limbs, marveling and exclaiming.

"She should enter it for the art prize. You get a trip..."

"She probably...needs the money too."

"Hilary. I'll call her and tell her.""

"You don't know her that well. "

"No one does."

"We'll call the Department and tell THEM. The way Hilary is, she'll just cart everything away if she knows someone saw it."

"You get a trip to anywhere you want, to look at the art. She'll be crazed."

"Call the Department and make them look."

"She has to give it a name."

"Remains of Woman""

"Survivors on Parade."

"Why should we help HER?"

"Because she's...financially challenged and because we need her installation."

A lower voice. "She was Selena Fenn's lover."

"Got a problem with that?"

Days later, a stupefied, red-eyed Hilary opened the computer-generated letter announcing her Art Prize. Sure she'd let them show the pieces of her Victory; what difference did it make? This wasn't the President's Fellowship, but a couple of thou would always help. What difference did it make what the reason was?

Keith Chambers lifts his six-four physique out of the camp bed with renewed vigor, oblivious to the rain. He hasn't even bothered at all with the evil distractions of sleep and the worse ones of dreaming. The pain and nausea even seemed to be reducing his vision. Outside everything looked white—a white sky to which the whitened pavements looked directly connected, He hauls his legs out first, then his unbending upper torso, out of the vessel of sleep.

Together with his morning corn flakes and milk the usual TV news drones on far away. Today, just the third day after Selena's murder, Morgan Broadside has already found something else to worry about. But sooner or later, if he remains idle, Morgan Broadside and all her ilk are going to grind the Redfern name into the dirt. OUR PRODUCT IS CORPSES. Keith has tried time and again to estimate something of the losses but found them incalculable—money, prestige, student applications—survival. It could take ten, twenty years for the institution to rebound.

All because of carelessness, nothing more.

Damn Van Geyst and his cancer and his withering arm or whatever it was; he has evaded his just deserts yet again—if not one crime, surely another. Never mind: after a decent interval, he will come out a martyr, with his choirboy face. Damn the repugnant Ricci and the amorous Amanpuri.

Awareness continues to drift in, like ice flowing together toward the middle of a grey sea. Okay, not Van Geyst—that leaves Hilary Slocombe, but that's sort of a stretch, and what of the sexual evidence? The police are bent on arresting Ricci. Professor Extraordinary Roberto Ricci with his string of Italian academic titles and Redfern honors, his line to Biscottini... Chuck is right, the man is essential, cannot be sacrificed, ever.

How would Keith go about saving Redfern?

Find someone plausible, someone from the outside world. A likely, transient character who would take the rap—in absentia, of course. The solution dazzled him with orange bursts under his closed eyes. Yashvili. The Poet in Residence, an even worse poet than Marvella Jilkes.

His slithering walk, like a big cat or a reptile. How long is that bore going to be around, with his nationalist verse and his toy soldier manners? Yashvili—the sort of guy Mother used to call a "lounge lizard." Yashvili.

Why not? He has it all: those polished dark surfaces, that way of challenging your eye, then suddenly evaporating. And in a mere matter of days, he'll dive into the indecipherable Caucasus and its civil wars. No magic disappearances called for here.

For in the wake of the defunct Soviet Union, Georgia is like the Middle East—the home of a frayed Russian army to the north and of wild paramilitary groups in the south. Keith knows that for months now, tribal struggle has been laying waste to ordinary life, that the demand for cultural independence has become a war cry for Mafia-like groups skilled in disinformation and "spontaneous" chaos-mongering. Culture Wars like ours, only theirs are for life and death. Yashvili will be swallowed up once he gets back.

Why WOULDN'T he have raped Selena, a wild man like that, a peddler of emotions? Even if the sex was there for the asking, all over this place. A splendid young woman like Selena, saying no, for once, wouldn't that suffice? Chavadze may be a man of the world and a pretty crafty one at that, but he has never taken in the full extent of Keith's sacrifices, and he is easily fooled by superficial manners and flourishes, doesn't know who his real friends are.

A murderer—would that fly? Keith inhales deeply and stares into the night. He has to mount a heroic offensive and manufacture a criminal who is calculating and deliberate but can break under the sway of vile appetite. But no one knows much about Yashvili.

The "drinking pal" of the University President himself. Yet Keith knows that even this serious a mishap for Chuck could be varnished over eventually by common consent. When your Presidential ratings start to slip— as Chuck's might do for a while—just rev up and start communicating. And no one can do it better than Chuck. He would come on very persuasively as a victim of deceit, of international perfidy. Together, they would answer attack with attack; why, just the talk shows alone....

One clean stroke. "If thy right hand offend thee..." How did that go? You cut it off, and the body is well again, immersed in the New Campaign. Chuck's negatives won't last: he will just have made an unfortunate error, thinking of this bastard as a friend.

Keith can already hear the speech Chuck would produce, maybe as soon as commencement. "I congratulate you," he would say, "for coming together in support of one another and for summoning the strength to move Redfern forward again. You have suffered the pain. You have surmounted the pain...You will heal the pain."

Keith still knew some people to call, could still pull some strings in the Soviet Politics orbit. He picked up the phone and ordered Ms. Truhart to cancel the day's appointments.

"Yes, that includes the appearance at the Sensitivity Seminar and the meeting with the Diversity Curriculum people and the Van Geyst Memorial Committee. Cancel everything; I have to go out of town." Chuck would immediately understand the necessity.

Perhaps Artex could tell him something. Artex was a foundation that handled academic and cultural exchanges between the United States and the former Soviet Union. Keith had taken no part in the preparations for Yashvili's visit to Redfern but knew that no poet, artist, ballerina, or mime came from the Commonwealth of Independent States into the United States without Artex's help.

The honking noises of a late-night traffic jam outside his window made him scowl, but he heard the racket as if from a great distance. The trip to New York would take a little over three-and-a-half hours. Plenty of time to put together the available facts and invent new ones. The lure of sleep swam before his eyes, an irresistible undertow, and though the digital clock glared at him with its red numbers, for the first time in days Keith found some peace. The thread that pulled his consciousness together lengthened into a plumb line through his whole body. No matter how tired the body, never let it intrude on thought. With sleep, his world foreshortened, flattening to the dimensions of a plastic card key.

Artex had its main office on Madison Avenue, on the twelfth and thirteenth floors of a building otherwise occupied by advertising and media companies. It never opened till nine-thirty, and then slowly, sleepily. Keith smiled as he remembered his dealings with the good-timers at Artex, who knew the better Georgian wines much more thoroughly than they knew just where Georgia was on the map.

Now he had to wait until opening time, which he did by scanning through the array of news accounts of the murder. Finally he dialed Artex. Cutting through the little flurry of secretaries who passed him along, Keith could hear the frantic cacophony of New York in the morning. When he looked at his watch only fifteen minutes had passed; it was close to ten already. Ten minutes later, exuding colorless, tasteless, odorless perfection Keith was maneuvering the grey Plymouth off the grubby patch that served as his building's parking lot.

The nearly four hours' drive from Temperance to Manhattan could have been a space journey in a hermetic capsule. Keith did eighty all the way down I-95 and a furious sixty to the FDR Drive. There, like all mortals, he sat beached in late spring traffic, thinking about biting his nails. Another standstill. A red sports compact had slammed into an eight-ton truck carrying a load of concrete blocks.

He had to go into an underground lot to park. Here too, lining up was the order of the moment. Even though he had gained confidence with each advance, he still felt uneasy in the labyrinth of trucks and cars and loading docks. For a moment he realized that someone could jump him there, and no one would ever notice. This together with the enforced slowness made him tingle with nervous energy. He ran up the one flight to the office building's elevator with more speed than he'd thought his legs had left in them since football days.

Thanks to old pals, in the little Artex reading room Keith was able to carry a sheaf of printouts to a table stacked with periodicals, one of the few places in the crowded suite where one could actually sit and read. The man on his left read *The New York Times* one word at a time, running his finger under the lines as he moved his lips. The woman on his right, large and dark with an imposing moustache, kept up an anxious commentary under her breath.

Blotting out the human sights as best he could, Keith began reading about the achievements of the Georgian branch of Artex. It was responsible for a healthy flow of academics, most of them specialists in epic poetry and painting. Last year it had brought to American acclaim the Georgian State Dance Troupe, whose show Keith had attended, admiring most of all the taut, contained moves of the male dancers who held their floor-length black capes around them like the wings of ravens as they glided, winged across the vast stage. Keith read through document after document, detailing passport and visa information for the use of the Immigration and Naturalization Service.

Then there it was, everything looking in order. Garsevan Yashvili, aged forty-eight, nationality Georgian, passport, visa good for a month's stay. In the appended bio Keith could read of acts of rebellion and anti-Soviet courage, mountain hideouts, everything seeming a bit too wetly permeated by standard-exotic landscapes and images. A land of towering mountains and legends, sure...but Keith knew enough Soviet Politics to be aware that there was more to them than bloody backdrops and stage villains. The material seemed more vague about Yashvili than similar bios of dancers, painters, archeologists excavating churches. Linguists had their research projects extensively described in an alphabet that seemed composed entirely of arching scallops.

But the real stuff on Yashvili, which HAD to exist, was nowhere to be found in the official file. Think, Chambers, think! Who could do it for him? It had to be somebody in the State Department or the CIA; no one else would have access.

Keith looked outside the Artex window, and just as his eyes were about to drop down for another look at the file, it came to him in a flash. Connor Ballstrup, his old student, had written him a Christmas card from McLean to tell him that he was still in the Air Force but permanently assigned to the CIA in the Soviet section.

"Look, I've got to make some phone calls without being disturbed. Can you find me an empty office?" Nancy Upham, the Artex secretary who had smoothed the way for Keith so far, looked up to see him looming over her desk, addressing her with surprisingly unconcealed urgency.

Two minutes later Keith was ensconced at a small desk with its private phone in a storeroom piled high with ancient application dossiers in bleached cardboard boxes. It took several telephonic crisscrosses before he succeeded in getting Ballstrup's number. They hadn't talked in several years, not since Connor had paid Keith a visit after his marriage broke up, but the easy familiarity was there as usual.

"Connor, I need your help with some non-standard material." Keith had come right to the point, making no allowances for the usual chitchat. "I've got to get the lowdown on a guy named Garsevan Yashvili. Does that name ring a bell?"

"A Georgian, huh? Nobody I know about. Give me the context, some background on him, maybe I'll be able to point you in the right direction."

Keith disgorged every possible scrap of knowledge from the Artex file on Yashvili. There was no sound from Ballstrup's end until Keith had almost finished. "And there's a letter of recommendation in Russian from some high-energy physics type named Artur Babashvili who seems to have known our poet at the University..."

"Stop right there," came crackling over the phone line, interrupting Keith's measured account. "I know exactly where to get the info you're looking for." Ballstrup had come through just as Keith knew he would.

"Keith, there's an ex-KGB operative living in Blackpool Beach in New York who'll help you make Yashvili. He's helped us out before and owes us a whole bunch. His name is Paolo Mdivani. You'll find him at a place called the New Tiflis Bookstore. It's not far from the last stop of the Brooklyn subway. Hold on, I'm just getting the address for you from my Rolodex. Anyway, I'll call him as soon as we finish and alert him that you'll be dropping by."

Blackpool Beach, Keith knew, was a community where Russian and ex-Soviet influence was so pervasive that it had been dubbed "Kiev By the Sea," a name coined in 1979. When the Soviet Union had begun easing the emigration of Jews and other minorities, it opened the gates to what was probably, in Blackpool Beach, the largest ex-Soviet settlement in the Americas. Seaswept and cleansed by the ocean air, Blackpool had never stopped thriving despite the capricious tides which often menaced life and property. While nearby Coney Island was blossoming into a summer playground in the mid-nineteenth century, what was to become Blackpool was still dunes and farm country. But when a former Union general bought several hundred prime oceanfront acres in 1878 for $18,000 and named them after the English resort, Blackpool took off as a more sedate but equally desirable summer colony. The Seaspray Grand Hotel and Pavilion was followed rapidly by the Blackpool Hotel, offering a park and open-air concerts. Success after success, capped by the arrival of the first train of the Brooklyn, Flatbush & Coney Island Railroad which stopped right at the steps of the hotel. The subway still ran, as did the concerts, now largely organized by Artex. And real estate values— from cozy little beach bungalows to rattling piles of frame—were on their way up once again, driven by immigrant verve and optimism.

Keith had never been to Blackpool. His only idea of it looked like the set of a movie about the Manhattan Lower East Side someone had once tried to include in a Redfern multicultural cinema evening. Crowded, dirty, unruly, streets running off their grid into byways and alleys. Glad of the nondescript look of his Plymouth, which would never attract thieves, Keith listened soberly to instructions, finally breaking down and taking notes. Something multicultural really was about to happen.

His arrival at the right turnoff was signaled by an enormous condominium development, which had nothing septic about it: monolithic and white, its two thousand units greeted him as one majestic mass. The development, with its four imposing towers, had long replaced the Seaspray Grand. So much for immigrant quaintness and grime. Keith could see terraces, ornamental pools connected by Japanese bridges, manicured stretches of greenery. Ocean panoramas wrapped themselves like huge posters around balconies. No vacancy.

But once Keith had passed the condo city he felt Russia everywhere. Not monumental St. Petersburg with its imposing boulevards and naval buildings, nor the stepped granite towers of Moscow with their hundreds of unseeing windows, but the teeming mess he liked to associate with Jews or mixed races. His car slowed to a creep. The scribbled instructions failed him at several intersections so that he kept returning to the same spot, whose landmarks were the Blackpool Board of Trade facing a public bathhouse across the street. Keith's elbows hugged his sides in disgust.

Street signs, many hand-lettered in both English and Russian, offered a hodgepodge of goods and services such as "A Bottle of Vodka at Every Table" of the Golden Cockerel Club, job placement, potato pancakes, nocturnal English classes for working parents. Presumably their kids spent all day speaking English at school. The rows upon rows of attached houses seemed to contain no activity, for everything was outside: a glut of vendors of Soviet army medals, food sellers, and lurking opportunists lined Keith's way. Though Russian signs prevailed, he began to note automatically the marks of many different nationalities. Like a compactor of nations, Keith thought. And it worked. In time they would find hyphenated identities, take root. Without a drop of blood lost, without ever taking to the streets.

As the car crawled along he heard the crude sweetness of a Slavic language he couldn't place.

"Right you are, mister," said a burly hot dog man, "we've got at least seven nations represented just on this street. We welcome all immigrants, all." He began to count them on upheld fingers. "Turkey, Hungary, Kuwait, Egypt, Georgia, Iraq..." Keith, who had double-parked, took off into the traffic leaving the astonished vendor staring after him.

At long last he turned into a narrow residential street that proved to be much longer than its air of intimacy promised. It was lined on both sides by saplings planted in neat rows, though far enough apart to make Keith think of starting a tree fund. What made it look really different was the fact that many houses sported little wrought-iron balconies, some with intricate designs of entwined flowers and leaves, looking too light to support the weight of most of the people Keith could see. His rusty competence in things Russian wouldn't help now, because he was looking for a neighborhood where Russian was unpopular. He thought grimly of Garso Yashvili's stage patriotism.

Keith stopped to ask for directions to the New Tiflis Bookstore. It turned out to be just around the corner, but those one-way streets meant a six-block detour. When he finally swung back to the store's entrance, he was relieved to find a parking spot just in front.

It was a narrow space lined on all sides from floor to ceiling with books of all descriptions, from leather-bound quarto volumes to ragged paperbacks in what looked like no arrangement at all. In one corner were a few little café tables, one with newspapers lined up in a wooden binder on a stick. The proprietor, a man looking for all the world like Frito Bandito without the sombrero, reacted with a wordless nod in the direction of the tables to Keith's inquiry.

Incredibly, the lone customer, looking erased in a black turtleneck and cords, turned out to be Keith's man. The first impression of an overweight hospital attendant dawdling over a newspaper and a smoke was immediately replaced on closer scrutiny by the reality of someone in top physical shape—a steel coil ready to be unsprung. He looked up as Keith approached, betraying not the least surprise at being addressed in the private haunts of the third-wave Soviet diaspora by a total stranger, obviously an apple pie American.

"You're Paolo Mdivani, aren't you? Connor Ballstrup told me I would find you here. My name is Keith Chambers." Keith extended a hand, even letting his elbow loose from his side.

Mdivani silently motioned for Keith to sit down, ignoring his outstretched hand. "Ballstrup called me," he said in an accent equal parts Middle Eastern and middle-European. "What can I help you?"

"I've come to find out what you know about Garsevan Yashvili. What can you tell me? It's important."

Mdivani was in no particular hurry without being evasive. He began talking, slowly and deliberately, choosing his words with pedantic punctiliousness.

"Yashvili is a man of many parts, my friend, but there are certain features that distinguished him. We were like brothers in arms, we served together in a number of postings."

Keith was making a concerted effort to assimilate himself to his interlocutor's leisurely rhythm, but it was evident that he was nervous, off his guard. .

"Have you seen him lately?"

"Oh, no—long time. Have you?" Mdivani smiled a semiprivate smile. "I would never be able to find him. He was one of the best we ever had. A poet also. So he was always invited to travel, visit, read his poems. He never had money, it simply wouldn't stick to him, went right through his fingers... So if you asked he was already leaving for somewhere else. There were too few men like him. Too few men, too many groups, and they all squabbled like children. It's known as cultural warring, I believe.

Ekh, you know." Keith smiled too.

"Two things everyone knew about Yashvili—his tendency for violence and his insatiable womanizing." Mdivani took a couple of deep drags on his cigarette, warming up to his subject. "We accepted it and just waited for him to come back because he always knew the moment to stop. He was always ready to take matters into his own hands, literally I mean. Powerful, the hands like a combination of karate and chicken plucking. Gamsukhurdia himself—our president then, that's right, he was crazy about Garso. He would say, 'I am crazy about that man, I love that man.'"

"What about the women?"

Mdivani had paused to snuff out his cigarette.

"Yes, I was coming to that. The women were always in evidence, although not in the foreground. Yashvili specialized in blondes, young ones, and he kept on finding them wherever the work took him. These encounters were not without their violent moments also, I must add."

"What exactly do you mean?" Keith's pulse was racing in tempo with the avalanche of thoughts in his brain. Selena's last moments. She could handle a Ricci, but this...

"You know," said Mdivani, as if reading out a papal encyclical, "we who take up the calling of our country's special services come to think of ourselves as the living embodiments of love and war. Yashvili took this idea to extremes in his personal life as well. His women friends sometimes suffered unexpected consequences, he just laughed and said it must have been worth it."

Keith knew that he had to get to a phone fast. Any further disclosures from Mdivani were superfluous at this point. He'd found the ideal scapegoat.

He looked around as if seeking response from the rustling saplings, the empty pavement. For once his mind veered counterclockwise. His breath came in heavy gusts, but he did not feel the usual gagging pain. Call the policemen, Blank and Granita, it's their job. I'm doing this for Redfern so that the cloud will lift, the calamities end. Redfern will get her money the way Selena would have wanted it herself, the way Tom and Nancy intended, and the General too, when push came to shove... the lesser evil serving the greater good. There has to be a phone around here.

He stands at attention in front of the only booth around, waiting for a talkative young woman to set up a date with several equally talkative friends. When he taps on the glass door she scowls and goes right on chattering and giggling. Crammed at last into the foul booth, Keith dials Blank's carphone. Not there. At the station no one knows where they are. Their beer joint, nothing. Nothing.

Keith redials the station. Mike Haley answers, remembers who he is.

"I have something essential to tell them," he pleads with Haley, who wonders at Keith's urgent tone. "Something that can't wait. A new line. They need to know. They have to know." His breathing sounds hard and fast like a crank caller's. Yashvili has only two more days as the Redfern Poet.

Haley promises to get Keith's message to Simon and Phil, but Christ knows how long that will be. Where the hell are they? "Tell them to meet me at the President's Office. Whatever they're doing. Five o'clock. The President's Office." Van Geyst's funeral would be over by then, the students would be off campus or crammed into the Student Union. The Admin Building would be empty.

There was only one course left to pursue. It was the hardest choice but ultimately an ethical one, and it called out loud and clear, so clear as to make Keith feel dizzy, hold on to the phone booth's grimy wall. Call Chuck and give it to him straight. No time to find the propitious moment or dither over the precise wording. DO IT. NOW.

"This is the last time. The last indignity. WHO DO YOU THINK YOU ARE?"

Berto falls back on that reliable Americanism, confronted by Simon and Phil so soon again under an unflattering light. He is sitting in front of a crud-laden, dilapidated desk in a rickety chair with one leg shorter than the others. It tilts whenever he moves.

The policemen have selected this site in order to be free of calls. Reporters, too, still hang around the station house for that last crumb.

Granita's idea of going to the county jail for Ricci's questioning was really smart. Not only did it offer maximum privacy, but the jailhouse setting could also work to put the fear of God in him. Up to now Ricci has shown unshakable offhandedness, but with the paper file and a perfect summary of Ricci's E-mail messages, this morning will nail him to the wall, the sonofabitch.

"Unfortunately, Ricci, we can't give you what you deserve. It's a pleasure to show you this, though." Simon sticks the file under Berto's face. "As if you didn't know... It's over, you creep. The Texas business boiled over. More than you could take."

"There is no possibility of my being found guilty. I 'ave restated my demand for an attorney."

"You'll have one soon enough. This is just a friendly get-together like last night."

Granita intervenes. "You better cool it, maybe that can help you. 'Cause you're looking pretty bad. Your friend Chuck isn't sticking his neck so far out anymore. He just 'deplores the tragedy'—just 'deplores', is what he said." What Phil is really thinking about is peeling off his tight jacket, the way a woman peels off a girdle.

"I will sue you for to the end of your life." Is that a frown or a pout on Ricci's bulbous face?

"Let's go back now." Simon perches on the desk as if dictating a letter. "We established that you were at the party, left with Selena Fenn, and finally, at long last, you shit, that you fucked her in the two minutes it needed. Must've been studying your feelthy peektures. The fact that you said so means nothing, just shows how arrogant you are. Thank God there finally was enough semen left to count as evidence. Do you think we'd invite you right back since last night without a reason?"

The jailhouse was so quiet that their words seemed to echo even in the eight-by-eight cubicle. Ricci's chair thwonked on the floor as he stretched and yawned.

"She was on to you, though. She got hold of your stinking file. You'd do anything to keep her from giving it to the papers or TV or Biscottini, who bought you your job."

"That is not a file. You yourself know this. It was assembled with the express purPOSE of providing reasons for me to perform a criminal act..."

"That's a laugh. Reasons."

"...and it was put in the way for signorina Fenn to find it. A crude, stupid trick. But for what? Sex is not a forbidden activity. And more: is not forbidden to be absolved of a misdeed—or an infraction of rules—by one's superior. There is such a thing as a system, a certain precedence of committees and of administrators, and if you 'ave studied the American university system, there are no surprises left 'ere for you."

Simon smiled, a surprisingly beatific smile. "No, I guess not... But the system let you go even further. Tell us how, Berto. Before this file goes to the media."

Ricci never felt better than under crude direct attack. He struck an operatic pose: Don Juan, unrepentant to the end. His smile was almost conciliatory, showing yellow teeth. Simon began to wonder if it was time to get out the whole list of party guests and search out the ones who had been acquainted with Selena—back to square one.

"I reiterate that there is no more to be said." For the hell of it he rooted among his unused concepts, pursing his fleshy lips. "Your slander of me is entirely political. Because perhaps I do not speak the same nonsense as certain of my colleagues, who knows. Gentlemen, you are impeding my schedule, and you are trespassing on my right of silence. And you are vexing my poor wife, she is exhausted. For nothing but politics, because per'aps poor Van Geyst 'as let you down by dying, and you must find a scap-e-GOAT. But it is YOU who will 'ear from ME. I shall endure, be certain. I shall without a doubt endure."

LuAnn sings in the shower to the tune of "Steam Heat":

"The swiiiiinnng—vote, she's—got—the—swiiiinng—vote!" She's so pumped up, so completely elated that the soap falls out of her hand, and she has to drop the showerhead too and grope around on the floor under a sudden shocking, scalding blast. But this morning she can hardly feel it because she is immune to obstacles. Moments like this are the most life-affirming of all—the delicious anticipation just before all the pieces fall into place. This morning the sun is struggling upward over limp fences and trees, finally breaking through to give some minutes of actual sunlight.

The New York Times lies on her bed, folded to the wonderful page six story about Chuck, with full-face photo, promising that strong and immediate steps will be taken to identify and apprehend, etc., etc., but LuAnn has skipped all that part because there's nothin' left to feah. Besides, Image Enhancement and Values Clarification doing their job isn't that exciting to watch. No, it's the signs of things to come, the splendid transformation that can't happen without her.

Comp Lit is about to get that Center. Even if Alan Sakulin went bonkers over the Van Geyst thing, and even if he manages to take all the other kikes along, there's nothing to worry about. The time with Gorellick was well spent too. Cheerleading experience actually came in handy. Weak men like Seymoah could come over all mulishly stubborn just to show you they're still alive. But although LuAnn hardly ever looks back, now she knows it was smart to hold out for a solid, continuing relationship—as long as it lasted. Chuck loves to make it look like Seymoah makes all the decisions.

The first step on the home stretch was getting Vassiliki Fink, Clara Bowl, and Sherri Tooley to endorse the nomination and put FAM to work. Dear, global FAM. The idea had to lift off with almost no one but FAM and some New York types to start, but then came Radical Rereading, Black Studies, Us Not Them, and so many more, everyone rallying round. LuAnn wishes it had been her own idea, not Vassiliki's, to involve some of the more advanced thinkers of Hollywood in the Search. Plus even this late, LuAnn has to go right on worshipping Vassiliki, fixed on her Vision. Planning is everything—planning, persistence, and context.

Context means that you can even make a murder work for you, why sure... You give it the right spin, and then you say it has to be "put behind you," that it has "brought us together in a common tragedy." You call it "unfortunate," not criminal. You show boundless sympathy for the "insanity" that caused it as well as for that snotty little Fenn girl who had it coming. All in it together, all in the same boat. LuAnn grinned ear to ear as she calculated how much Selena really ended up helping after all.

The wait for the full light of day, and for hours after that, was terrible. But neither FAM nor BREW nor the classes which were all taught by Laurie Lee Talbot ever needed any attention, so LuAnn could while away the time building puffy little cloud castles, sailing them on the brightest of skies.

She called Vassiliki the moment she could almost feel the California sunrise peeking in on her. And when word came, it was the right one, the only one.

That irritating person being propped up by the opposition was set up to lose. She'd never made a fit opponent for Chavadze—just didn't have the oomph. A woman, yes, but the wrong kind of woman. Even so, since a woman was a more formidable opponent, the sides had come out exactly even: six to six. But the swing vote finally belonged to a coalition—including Vassiliki just for one—that would make sure the players got shuffled around in a meaningful way. The whipped cream on top was that none of the other three frontrunners you constantly saw in the papers—people who'd spent fortunes blowing up rumors—had even gotten within sniffing distance. This outcome was a sunny radiance to distract her from any lesser thing on earth.

It took some time to get by all the Administrative Executive Assistants, only to find Chuck's special phone mysteriously engaged. But the news couldn't hold. Months and months of labor were flooded by success all of a sudden: the paper trail going on and on, the committees galore with their four-hour meetings, the cocktail parties, the sex with that kike Gorellick, the rubber chicken dinners, all the flights, with their jetlag, the special appearances—it worked! Even the Old Redfernian had cottoned to LuAnn, a fine figure of a woman and damn shrewd too.

Chavadze sounded worried rather than happy.

"But Chuck, the funds are in the bag. Ah mean, aren't they?"

"You know it isn't that. The stain on Redfern could be permanent. How can we ever recover? And then, we'll all be tainted with...don't you understand, we'll always have to live with it. It will take time and time, if ever."

That was just Chuck's way—always cautious, always sounding like an alarmist, putt'n' himself down. Even on the brink of dazzling success he would withdraw for a moment into one of his exotic fogs, probably to appease some watchful foreign gods.

"That is wonderful," he repeated later on, "wonderful," but LuAnn heard the forced edge of his voice. Maybe he's just overwhelmed. The Search is all but over. And the swing vote is ours. Steam Heat.

LuAnn crumpled up a Kleenex and tossed it into the toilet with a pitcher's flourish. There goes another History person. FAM has come through; now let's see Chuck deliver. Let's jes' see 'bout that Center.

"I'm sorry we're meeting after such a while under these circumstances, Willona." Keith sighed, the red line still bisecting his abdomen. "But you did the right thing, coming to me."

They sat in Chavadze's leather chairs, Willona's charcoal grey suit and white silk shirt a tribute to Keith's immaculate getup—two adults afloat in a sea of youth-wannabees. For once she was getting to him.

"I confess that I thought of going to the police directly, but the possibility that we could shut down the Ring without involving them at all seemed better. We've got the names of the Redfern students, so the Dean's office only has to take action, and it's over. There doesn't even have to be a record. All you have to do..."

Keith allowed himself a faint smile. "Hey, now...you're going too fast for me. That can-do spirit of yours, I really go for that...but let's take things one at a time. This Ring, now: was it operating on campus? To the best of your knowledge?"

"Twenty of our students." She had been precipitate, backed up a bit. The thin sound of someone walking outside the room was clearly audible.

"That isn't exactly what I had in mind. Did they meet clients on campus?" His tone was the usual one, patient and even, but he was shuttering his face.

"Stephanie didn't say much. It was mostly the Stillwater. She said that a lot of the johns were staying there, that they rented a couple of rooms. Rather than the Maid For Love, because they were afraid of being recognized by some member of the faculty..."

He frowned, irritated. "Did she say that? So it appears that no encounters took place on campus."

"I didn't say that." Already a crack in the harmony. "Must try and keep it low-key. "She said that some men came to the dorms. Only during peak class hours, for the obvious reason."

Keith appeared to see nothing remarkable in this. "Stephanie's allegations are very serious. What kind of student has she been these last four years, I wonder. You know how some young people get over-wrought under the pressure of Redfern expectations."

"We seem to be talking a lot about what she SAID. I'm holding the evidence in my hand. She gave me the lists and the pictures—here."

"I don't need to see them, but thanks, Willona."

She heard herself speaking in her controlled, standard Willona voice. "The facts will emerge in the course of investigation And that doesn't have to go further than the campus. At least the Ring was smart enough to do without pimps and...outside organizers."

That's what YOU think. Keith's stomach wound had healed just enough to keep him ambulatory, as the two visitors had planned, but it had been excruciatingly painful to slide into Chavadze's silly modernistic chair. He waited for her to go on, displaying fastidious demurral like a military order.

"I know it's unpleasant. But sometimes you HAVE TO TALK ABOUT UNPLEASANT THINGS, don't you? Is conforming to hap-pyspeak the only standard that means anything to you? Is yours nothing but an office of crowd control? I've suffered enough, here and elsewhere, for the sake of genteel appearances. Face up. Let the truth out. You can't ignore these young women."

No response, just the top-of-the-line bland attention.

"One has to tell the story as one knows it, first of all."

"I think you may be exaggerating the whole thing, Willona. These are young women of independent mind. They didn't ask for our concern. I sincerely believe yours to be an overwrought, over-embellished version of what really went on...."

"And then one needs to act on one's knowledge. You're not going to derail me with trivia, Keith. What if some details might be inac-curate? They're like... Dante's 'unfalse errors.' In the Divine Comedy."

"I'm not sure I..."

"Dante. He meant that the intention and the result can be right even if the means are imperfect. Look, Keith—" she paused for breath. "Some campus women started this Ring as a crazy rebellion against The Repressive Bourgeois Society or because they needed the extra money. They're too young to know that without inner restraints you're nothing but a slave."

Keith blanched at the word "slave," straight out of the Index of

Forbidden Terms. "I want you to know, Willona, that I approach this matter with undisguised anger. I realize we need to take a caring and responsive attitude. Has Stephanie seen Health Services? Talked to Values Clarification? We must consider our options."

Stephanie's face, Willona remembered, already had that motherly look abused wives have, the ones who are incapable of either escape or retaliation.

"You must not forgive," Willona had told her. She could expect no less of herself.

She rose. "That's just what Chuck writes to me when I raise the subject of the Center— 'we must consider our options.' There is only one option. These are FACTS, not attitudes. You need to answer them with ACTIONS."

"I apologize if what I just said was misinterpreted..."

"Is it bureaucratically correct to look the other way? Is it somehow heroic to pretend we know nothing?"

"...and the last thing I want to do is offend you..."

"OFFEND." It seemed that every encounter with Chambers would always and only replicate their very first one, the moment of mutual dogsniffing that had determined the outcome of all of their contacts from then on. He would always make certain that their meetings shattered on the rocks of some impenetrable protocol. Not much different from the job searches of her youth, as a freshly minted assistant professor, excluded from consideration on an inventive variety of pretexts.

"I think," she said slowly, "that being criticized is a sort of right. If it's meant fairly. No, more: being unmasked and corrected is a right. Because if you just play into people's fantasies, it means they don't matter, that they have no stake—except as deceived consumers—in any society you care about. We can save those girls from public humiliation if we handle it ourselves, but if they get away with any more of their Ring, they'll know for sure that it's happening with our connivance."

"Who or what doesn't matter?" Chuck Chavadze had appeared noiselessly at the door. Keith winced as he straightened up.

The President's white teeth flashed in a broad, friendly grin. "Can I tear you away, Willona? At last we have a moment together."

He steered her through the mahogany double doors into the smaller room that contained the little bar, poured drinks, and passed her the cheese puffs.

"I wish someone'd remembered about ice. Now, I have something to tell you personally."

She contemplated the Kirman rug, in warm shades from coral to orange, its interlaced pattern culminating in a knot of Arabic writing at the center.

"The Center, Willona. The Center." She almost jumped. "I'm glad I can spare you the account of all those godawful tedious discussions."

She could see her reflection in his eyes.

"There's something..." she began.

"The Center is to be not only a site for study and research but as symbol of who we are and where we're going. The major contributors have had their say, and I end up taking no credit for any part of the decision. By the way," leaning forward, "tell me: how old was your father when... it all happened?"

"Twenty-five."

"God. The past is many things, but one thing above all: it is irrevocable, except in memory. Well, here it is, for you to see first."

He picked up an office copy of a press release and slid it over to her, his fingers splayed and rigid. She chased the words down the page.

NEW BUILDING TO HOUSE LITERATURE STUDIES

Alan Sakulin, of the Sakulin Development Corporation, and Tetsuo Minamoto, of Minamoto Industries, have announced that a new building will begin to rise at the heart of the Redfern University campus by next fall, for the exclusive use of its rapidly expanding Department of Comparative Literature. The Center for the New Humanities, as it will be called, was made possible by a $10 million grant from the Minamoto Foundation and by generous gifts from the Sakulin Corporation. The architect chosen is Olney Mee, best known for towers such as the one added in 1987 to the New York National Museum. "It will be a limestone building, very contextual," Mee said, describing his plans for the Center. "The four corners will be formed of pools of offices, enabling small groups to work together more easily." Mr. Minamoto said that his gift to Redfern was the largest single award by the Minamoto Foundation and would be an "enduring memorial" to his father Akira Minamoto, like Sakulin a Redfern alumnus.

"And to Selena Fenn," Willona said.

Chuck went on as if he hadn't heard. He was smiling the especially warm smile he kept for refusals. "The Trustees met without even my presence at the session..."

"All those discussions..." Willona said.

"It was decided that Comp Lit so desperately needs space, as well as personpower, that there can be no expectation of sharing the Center. Because it is profoundly, comprehensively multicultural it will need to be divided into those marvelous corners... to promote better relations among the various dynamic groups on campus. Do you see?"

"Yes," she said, unseeing. Then, "Why did you invite me especially to come and hear this?"

"Why...what a question, discussion is the only way to understanding. Discussion and consensus." Quick figuring told Chuck he needed to give this situation about a quarter of an hour, top.

"Let me come to the next thing now. In consultation with the Trustees, I am prepared to listen very hard to what you have to say..."

"The Trustees need not be concerned," Willona said, more puzzled than defeated. "I told Keith about the Ring, and I intend to tell you as well, of course."

"The WHAT?" Chavadze pressed Keith's button, heard him out for about three minutes, then slumped at his desk. There followed an impenetrable exchange in a code Willona could not read, then Chavadze turned back to her, as if wondering why she was still there.

"I only want," said Willona, "to break the compact of silence. And I shall, no matter what has been precooked in this office."

"What nonsense, Willona, compact! This was a completely innocent scenario. This last—news fell on our heads like a—juggernaut."

Keith came in as if on cue and sat down, keeping his mild eyes on them like a chaperone. He showed the President a new sheaf of papers, his index finger helpfully pointing out an entry, and Chuck gave a nod to show he was grateful for being reminded. Willona felt a presentiment of disgust.

Chuck hesitated, like a musician doubtful about whether to give an encore. "We think it would be no less than you deserve, Willona," he said with an anguished grin, "to offer you the new chairpersonship of Black Studies—the plum of the Diversity Curriculum, which as you know is shortly to supersede the New Curriculum. The job carries considerable responsibility and authority, as you are surely aware. Therefore we believe it to be tailor-made just for you."

She was thunderstruck, the blood rushing to her head. "I can't believe this."

"I did rather try to work it into our conversation," Keith said, rubbing his nose with the back of his hand as if to still an itch. "We got this rather super idea only Tuesday, when..."

"When Given Barker showed up again as Marvella's aide and then just took off." Her chest ached with the sheer preposterousness of it all.

"I am not prepared to discuss someone...by name...in this manner...."

She might as well not have heard this. "I understand perfectly—me to replace a freeloader like Barker! And how? Presiding over a ghetto program you KNOW I despise. Teaching in some kind of groupthink that blacks invented fire and wrote the Bible. Of all the Black Studies possibilities, that's the kind you'd pick. A sop to black students, to shut them up and keep them occupied while the others get on with the business of learning how to make money, jockey for power. And my part is...what? Laziness, cowardice, and complicity. My part is perfectly negative—NOT to tell."

Her head in her hands, she felt a wave of weakness spread all the way up to her shoulders and down her legs.

"The program is very prestigious, high-profile, service-rich and of considerable merit."

"But doesn't 'merit' just perpetuate class and race differences? That's what I'd be supposed to say in your program, isn't it? Merit—isn't that on your Index of Forbidden Terms yet? Your program grinds down the whole idea of actually achieving anything in the world. It's Thorazine. It's stupefaction by lies. It's liberation from life. It's a sandbox for everyone who can't or won't cut the mustard, where they dole out bullshit about how blacks are the most noble of savages, and how knowing nothing is genuine Paradise. And it's feelgood nonsense for white kids—no, never you mind today's correct word—who need to feel just a bit guiltier than thou. That is NOT MY FIELD, as I think you know. And the whole bribe package comes my way just so that I won't bust those girls, so I won't bust YOU. You're the legacy of Van Geyst,

that's what you are." Or was it the other way around, had the moral imbe-
cility of these people produced him?

"All the ritual pronouncements about free speech exist just so
you can keep spinning your wheels and collecting for it... from these...
paying customers. Bigger business than ever, right? It's like you're paying ME for some kind of... protection; as long as both sides understand
each other, as long as the right hand doesn't know what the left hand is
doing. No one will care."

"I take it your response to our offer is negative."

Willona felt worn out, but anger brought its own clarity and
vividness.

"You can eat it, Chambers."

She aimed for slamming doors and pounding strides but her exit
was hopelessly muted by the carpets on the polished floors, and the
mahogany doors closed soundlessly.

"Nothing to be done about her, Chuck. YOU know."

"No. Nothing to be done." The president wore the look of personal frustration that comes when one seems unable to help a friend.

Ten minutes later Willona dialed the Eleventh Precinct.

BODY COUNT

The rain had finally given way to a metallic afternoon sun. The crowd of Executive Administrative Assistants, subdeans, office managers, and Human Resourcepersons who had been given the rest of the day off mingled for once with faculty around Palter's gravesite, greatly outnumbering his acquaintances.

Although a global contingent of intellectuals would have gladly mustered, given the time and the money, it had also been too late to scrape together the professor's literary-theory counterparts from other campuses. Carol Van Geyst had returned the same day to her home in the Midwest. Even Chuck had declined to come in a gesture of appeasement to Sakulin.

Amidst all the turmoil of his solitary hours, Keith had painstakingly earmarked the time on his own calendar and made sure that there would be healthy contingents from all the Public Relations sections and from the layers of subdeans. Though Keith himself stood at a certain distance from his minions, his muscular presence, charcoal grey suit, and clean-shaven funeral face gave the impression of a fastidious businessman on a flying visit. The newish cemetery, about ten minutes' drive from campus, also had a non-Redfernian, hybrid character, with a shiny young minister doing the honors. No one seemed really to belong, as if guests had been rented for a shotgun wedding.

"That's Catholics, silly," said an Executive Administrative Assistant to another, "'cause Protestants get buried even if they commit suicide. People in Holland are Protestants." But she wasn't really sure, and there were no other people from Holland present to explain it to her.

The media graced even this drab event, just for the free access it offered them to Redfern personnel; for the demise of a literary "superstar" can hardly compete with the Ring. A TV crew lumbered about now, lugging equipment like a hospital patient dragging an I.V. rack. Everyone was being blamed publicly in a pyrotechnics of accusations: parents, professors, the recession, unemployment, hotel desk clerks, television shows, night clubs, the Left, the Right—everything but raw masculine appetite and the high Redfern tuition. Sypher, Garnix, and Nill have been pressed into service, busy summing up Redfern's "position" to media and rubberneckers alike:

"We can neither confirm nor deny."

"Allegations that coercion on the part of students was involved."

"Therefore we won't discuss it at all."

"We believe undue emphasis was placed." Sypher ran a finger under his damp collar.

"On Redfern's role in the investigation." Garnix drew himself up in the manner of Keith Chambers.

"We do not perceive any connection at this time. Sorry about that." Nill extricated himself from a tangle of wires.

Sypher read from an agonized scrap of paper. "We must review the charges before commenting or deciding to make any comment on whether action should be taken in the university..."

Garnix read his scrap too. "It is essential that the two issues be perceived as separate..."

Not to be outdone, Nill piped up. "At this time there is no evidence suggesting Redfern's prior awareness of any wrongdoing."

Guillaume Mastroianni, lone Deconstructionist of the French Department and practically a salaried member of Comp Lit, shivers in his cramped intellectual leather jacket hoisted up in back by its tight armholes. He also sports a new Roman haircut with little grey tendrils radiating from a central bald spot and curling cutely on his forehead. Guillaume's cupid's-bow lips mouth phrases of his speech like a mantra. He's up next.

Redfern has requisitioned an unassuming but decent cherrywood coffin which stands near the open grave like a piece of Palter's home furniture, trying not to clamor for undue attention. It goes in smooth and easy because Van Geyst is a middleweight, well-behaved corpse.

Guillaume looks furtively around him and steps forward, with a face he hopes is all existential integrity but is really petulant sulks. The tiny armholes of the jacket lend him a slightly humpbacked stance.

"To recontextualize Van Geyst," he begins, "is my project and my task. Van Geyst—fearless assailant of the two sacred cows, memory and truth. Van Geyst, our wonder and our enigma."

Speaking of enigmas, where was Sita Amanpuri? LuAnn, as head of FAM and BREW, ought to have some idea—now, come to think of it, Sita has no classes today or tomorrow, not even on the official schedule. Passing up Palter's day takes some nerve, but not such a lot since tenure started.

Bonza Leier (Video Studies), stands bent over the grave like a stunted willow in a black granny dress, a big black witch's hat riding her yellow frizz. Lamamba, keeping a careful distance from Marlayne Sorley, wears a six-sided embroidered cap like a prelate's topping his snappy black blazer. He pouts and frowns like a petty dictator who has had to forsake a ransom of beautiful boys. Tony Banter and Chris Hargreaves, positioned at the edge of the crowd for a quick departure, ooze off before things get under way.

LuAnn is trying earnestly to compose her cheerleader's face into a decorous solemnity. She feels radiant, bursting with plans, galloping into the home stretch. She could have stayed home now that Van Geyst was no more, but had been finally persuaded to come by Aviva Har Shalom of Haifa U. Aviva dropped her classes immediately on the head of an Israeli Teaching Assistant, and flew the fourteen hours to Temperance at Haifa's expense on a wave of urgency.

She seems to be Palter's sole mourner from distant shores, standing encased in an assortment of blouses, skirts, and vests and flanked by shoulder bags. Her eyes brimming over, she too ("I, too") will address the gathering.

Armin Fishbane makes his peremptory rushed entrance with trailing striped muffler, rubbing cold hands together. Casing the crowd, he can't see anyone at first but cafeteria workers and Executive Administrative Assistants. For his part, Armin wouldn't miss this for the world. Catching sight of the group, he points to the ground near him and shrugs elaborately to show that he would love to stand close to them but has to stick to the dignitaries.

"But, Armin, as a Jewish—" Graziella had objected as she watched him buff his silvery hairdo for the ceremony. Armin had retained the masculine habit, picked up in Rome, of checking your profile as if it were your blood pressure. "As a Jewish, 'ave you not any sentiment at all for your own nation?"

She could always find the right size needle. "I am a member of the INTELLECTUAL COMMUNITY, if you will," She answered stiffly. "I owe Palter my presence at his ceremony, just as he would at mine. What has being born Jewish got to do with it?" He slammed the front door extra hard, like Rhett deserting Scarlett, but the gesture was lost on Graziella as usual. Now Fishbane accords a Queen Elizabeth wave to Mona Blessing, red-nosed and black-coated.

"...to bring the whole tragedy up to date," Guillaume is saying, with a moue at the recalcitrant God in the sky. "Vizzout Palter Van Geyst there would have been no intellectual existence possible in this country, and now he is lost to us. Van Geyst has shown us our path. We 'ave thought knowledge is power but we were wrong: power is knowledge. He showed us how all words—wonderfully and blessedly—lose their meaning. Their so-called meaning, I mean."

Guillaume pauses, uncomfortable with his own gauche repetition, to blow his pointy nose with its little red tip. As if an invisible index finger were jacking the nose up, his mouth lifts, rodent-like, to show tiny even teeth.

"He did not ever embrace a vulgar thought in all his life—in fact, I would put it that the arrogance of thought was actually of no interest to him at all—the juvenile hysteria of thinking that one thinks. Palter Van Geyst brought to our country, I mean zees one, the fact that facts are myths, metaphors—constructions. Zat ze world one sinks to live in is nothing but illusion. After ze texts of Nietzsche, zis was no less than a second coming."

The mourners shifted their feet and endured. A cafeteria lady wondered if the Professor was comparing Van Geyst to Jesus Christ.

"Van Geyst's whole effort is a silent trace—a trace of the reality of an event whose very historicity—borne out by his own catastrophic experience—has occurred precisely as the event of the impossibility of its own witnessing." Guillaume Mastroianni closed his mouth and took five courtly steps backward, cannoning into Maxime-Etienne, who goggled and fastidiously withdrew the hem of his garment.

A rustling began in the hedge that ran parallel to the burial ground. It came closer and closer, mingling with the steady steel dripping of rain. Aviva Har Shalom had taken up the eulogy.

Only the most trivial, guilt-ridden academic people who have always resented Van Geyst's intellectual power would want him to have inscribed himself in a confession! We will not participate in a—what you say, a witch-hunt. And only the collaboration of the mass media can account for the violence of the reaction to Van Geyst's youthful writings. What you expect, for a man to turn against the truth of his own self?"

At the mention of "self," Fishbane leans forward to hear.

"We know that there is a Hitler in us all. So, recognizing this, we will be magnanimous and not engage in senseless hatred. We will even try not to despise the press in general." She pauses to let this sink in.

I get it. Fishbane raises his eyes. It's newspapers everywhere that are guilty, not just the Nazi hate rag. What alternative did young Van Geyst have? Holocaust, sure, but hey, Palter didn't create the Holocaust all by himself, did he? He was just doing what he had to do, the correct thing, it was called for, the same thing I would have done myself.

"I have heard in the last two days only, abusive, arrogant, crude, degraded, ignorant, aberrant, indecent, murderous, obscene, obtuse, venomous, and yes, naïve armies mobilized against a piece of writing. What a number of fronts I must confront!" Aviva tosses off a bitter laugh. "Not from detractors are we finally afraid—but from censors! Uninformed, gross, uneducated, fanatical...."

It was Lamamba who saw it first, craning over the other standees, a tiny missile barreling forward, hurtling toward the funeral with tremendous momentum. But Maxime-Etienne made as if not to notice, grafting his attention onto Aviva's harangue. Closer, closer, and bigger, the steps could be heard thumping unstoppably toward Fishbane. His elbows stiff at his sides, his legs flying and pounding, a mass of air pushing him from behind, at five yards from his target Myron Wiener, contorted with fury, held a gun at his target in a two-handed grip. For the last time in his life, Fishbane squarely confronted his second self.

"Don't," Fishbane cried out at a jarringly high pitch, just as the gun exploded once. Fishbane stumbled backward, crashing into the tree behind him. The first shot plowed through his chest, and Fishbane tumbled down, his head slamming on the hard ground. As Fishbane seemed to reach languidly for the little revolver, Myron brought it down on Fishbane's cheek. Bone cracked. Fishbane hardly felt anything because of the shock, but as the blood spurted, energy drained from his body. He went blind for a second, then the gun dropped as Myron began to tackle him into the earth.

Keith Chambers fell upon Myron, wrestling his gun away from him with absurd ease despite the pain in his viscera. For a second Keith held the little revolver up in the air. Keith kicked Myron's short little legs out from under him, then without breaking speed moved in and planted a second football kick in his chest. He rolled over like a beetle too small to exterminate. Panting, they fought groveling on the ground, lips drawn back from grinning teeth, observing the strict silence of people wrestling. Keith grabbed Myron's shoulders and twisted them back as if he were teaching him to straighten out and kneed him in the small of the back, so that he arched forward, his gut soaring in air, and flopped disconsolately over on his back. The world spun for him once again as he wavered a second, then slumped.

Keith stood up, disgusted, the same red line of pain bisecting his abdomen. He brushed off his charcoal grey suit, straightened his striped red tie, and took the beeper out of his pocket. The campus police would have to make an emergency exception, anything but call the Eleventh Precinct again. But Myron stood up again, all five-four of him, and foam came from the sides of his mouth, drawn into a jack-o-lantern's grin, one hand still curled around a crumpled bunch of paper like a baby's hand around his mother's finger. The sounds that came from his mouth were the whimpers of a starving child.

Ten minutes later Marston Hall and the other available campus security guards had arrived. As Keith had warned, it took three of them to overpower Myron. As they carted him off they had time to see that the papers he'd been clutching were upstaging the people.

Some leaves were white; others weathered to the color of dead leaves. Now the papers came dancing over, not rising more than two yards from the ground, weaving and frisking between people and trees, catching everyone by surprise. Just as they seemed to be gliding smoothly over the surface, they suddenly flew upward, but horizontally, then some plastered themselves against a tree trunk or the side of a car, and finally they were no longer in view as they followed, puppy-like, behind faraway passersby.

On his stretcher, Armin Fishbane wore the saintly expression of the utterly incapacitated. LuAnn, Mumtaz, Maxime-Etienne, Hargreaves, and Banter clamored at first to get into the ambulance with him, then backed off as one. He looked terrible—bloody and twisted, spread-eagled in his own blood. Something had burst through a wound, and no one wanted to know what it was, or to get close to Fishbane's contorted face with that hole exposing bone. Even at a distance they could hear him making a sound like a kitchen sink draining. The medics had brought all kinds of plastic bags none of the mourners had ever seen the likes of. The ambulance doors closed on faint murmurs and twitters of concern. A small pool of blood was spreading and darkening on the turf where he had lain. They made sure to step around it as if playing a children's game.

Palter's eulogies, it seemed, had been unforeseeably curtailed. FAM, Radical Rereading, Black Powerholders, Postcolonial Revenge, and the rest never had the chance to pay their final respects to their benefactor—the man whose philosophy that truth was illusion had opened the floodgates and welcomed them into the university.

The squad of deans and flak-catchers began to disperse, Keith distancing himself from them as usual. Flabby, sandy-haired men wearing tie clips mingled with hungry-looking women in meeting suits, tennis shoes. They had long been inured to events like this. These days, it was just another Redfern day.

No one watched their boss, Chambers, as he fastidiously reopened the wrought-iron gates, which tried to swing closed behind every departing person. A few laggards, hoping something more might happen, hung out around the gravesite.

"Didya see that? I mean, didya?"

"Too fast for me. I mean, who was that little crazy?"

"A Comp Lit prof. I know because he kept calling up and asking me did some letters come in yet; he said who he was."

"Maybe he wanted the papers he was holding. They're all gone."

"What happens to him now? Fishbane must be dead."

"No handcuffs, didya see?"

"Because he's insane."

"No—because campus cops have no equipment. They were just damn lucky this time."

Keith felt old, overburdened, for once in his life. His hand massaged his wide forehead, his light blue eyes clouded over, almost closed. But he concealed his weariness as best he could, striding across the desiccated cemetery lawn with its rectangles of shrubbery that reminded him of the campus quad, never breaking his stride against the damp wind that struck against his face like a wet mop. There was so much to do, and the terrible dream, somehow, had passed for good—it would never be back any more than Selena would.

Even his own long footprints seemed to dog him, about eighteen inches apart, out of the drenched parking area, but soon to be free of its squelching, sodden earth. And in the opposite direction, under a brightening sky, came Simon and Phil.

"We'll catch up with Chambers here, look, they're just breaking up."

"What the hell was so important?" Granita had been dragged out of an untimely nap, his first in three days of practically no sleep.

"He called from the shore, that's all Haley said. It sounded urgent."

"Yeah, sure. Did his sweetheart Ricci lose a shoelace? Was Ricci OFFENDED?"

"Haley didn't say anything about Ricci. Anyway I got surveillance on Ricci's house since nine thirty. He's home reading Dante, his wife said. Isn't that nice?" Simon notices a few Human Resourcepersons in pastel-colored raincoats, one holding a child's hand.

"Chuck here?"

"Maybe. I didn't find out. So the sooner the better. He'll give input too." They quicken their pace. An ambulance siren wails at them, maddeningly loud as the vehicle whips by. Then another van—no marks, but the driver is wearing a lab jacket, and an attendant is holding down a little guy who seems to be trying to fly.

"Nice Temperance traffic, huh? Sorta heavier than usual," Phil says.

"I think it's time to let everyone who needs to know about Ricci in on the DNA," Simon said, with a side-glance at Phil.

"You forgot already what the Chief said? You... Will... Not... Smear... Redfern... Without... Cause," he barked, imitating the Chief's stentorian voice.

"Whether it's him or not in the end, if you only let people think it's Ricci and flush out the guy that way, the Chief would relax."

"Get real," Phil told his superior. Age, too, had its advantages. "Ricci's admitted the sex. We found out it was him that pertickler time. That whole sex-slumming, like the lezz called it, means nothin'. If we let it look like rape some more, the perp will think—no matter what—that we're after a rapist. Our guy—or gal will get cocky, think it's all clear for them. See?"

Simon wondered if Phil's soft spot for a fellow Italian was still getting the better of him, but had to agree. "It's better for Fenn to think it's rape—right now, anyway. General Fenn belongs to the same group of Redfern loyalists. Worse, so does Pelham—worse for us, I mean. From the Chief to the Governor... And they're right, we've got nothing on any Redfern person, just like Chambers and Chavadze want."

"Christ, if it's Chambers himself, if it's Chambers with his stupid wine bottle holdin' the door, Redfern explodes."

Subduing Wiene—imagine!—had been the work of a few seconds. But Keith Chambers still keeps before him the foreshortened view that accompanies emotion. Without letting up, Keith smartly skirts the few cars still parked in the weedy lot. Long strides, even and sure. The grey Plymouth waits patiently. Keith would never have exchanged the comfort and dependability of the Dowager Car for anything like Sita's little Toyota, or Guillaume Mastroianni's racing-green roadster, or Fishbane's vulgar Porsche. Despite the nearly unbearable pressure, he sighs with relief as he staggers into the driver's seat.

A white flash and a giant clap of applause, a geyser of shattered glass: which first? The next flash erupts like fireworks, catching Keith's face in horrified recoil. As the flash turns to orange, little stars dance in the daytime sky.

Running at top speed back to the lot, Simon and Phil see Keith Chambers in blackface astride a fiery steed, his hands frozen at the reins, brilliant in his own glow. He stays oddly motionless even though his whole weight is leaning forward. Now black clouds, whirling through its gutted windows, whip him from the inside of the car. Fountains of glass scatter festive crystals at the rider's feet, and as the interior of the car changes, slowly, reluctantly, he comes down, staying ramrod straight on the burning seat which turns to poisoned purplish smoke. Then the silence that makes normalcy a terror.

"It was a good car," Phil said. "So it took him longer to die."

The acrid smell of burned plastic was still in the air, buoyed up rather than quenched by the heavy gasoline odor. The skeleton of Keith Chambers' Plymouth sat on the singed brown grass, its windows hollowed-out eye sockets. The heat of the fire had exploded and then burned the tires, so the burned-rubber stench added to the bouquet. A forensic van had joined the police.

"The glass is spilled pretty evenly all over," said the head of the forensics team to her photographer and a note-taker as the three circled the wreck. "Doors both shut, hood shut, headlights out. Fuel tank blown. Muffler separated from exhaust pipe. The glass is interesting because it's sprayed so widely it must have come from inside the passenger compartment, not outside. Exterior paint peeled, chrome on door peeled."

The forensics expert got one door open, her hand wrapped in a large handkerchief against the smoldering chrome of the handle. "Interior gutted. Seats down to coil and frames. Steering wheel upped and gone. Rear seat burned to springs. Batteries in dash compartment. On front seat, metal rectangle approx two inches square. Look at these curved marks on it—maybe the back of a change or coffee tray? Ignition key turned on. Fragments of charred vinyl..." The voice went on and on with its autopsy on the dead car.

When it was time for the body Simon and Phil moved forward again.

"Can't see a lot," the photographer complained.

Keith was blackened and tiny, too badly shrunken to be identified as any specific kind of human being. He now suffered the indignity of nakedness, but his belt buckle marked the area where a belt had once been. It was still neatly closed. The policemen looked away as Keith submitted to the same treatment as that of his car.

"Gotta peel him out," someone said.

The camera snapped everything down to the molten coins that fell from Keith's pelvic bone, which had broken when they touched it. Of course Keith had worn no jewelry, nor did he carry keepsakes. There was no ostentatious gold in his teeth. But even without any metallic distractions the police and forensics people could find no remains of a timer or a fuse for the bomb. No prints either but Keith's own, which were all over, and which they lifted carefully, neglecting nothing. The lot had been emptied out long before, the campus cops having been sworn to shut up about everything tonight.

"Anyone could've done it," Granita wondered aloud. He had never before realized how easy it would be to torch half of Temperance if you picked the right time. He hitched up his belt with both thumbs, thinking of Myron Wiener. A little shitbird like that could've done Fishbane with a bomb if he'd been smarter or more willing to take other people along. Two clean bursts of flame, and now just look! "He died of the fumes first," the forensics expert said simply." That's how it'll turn out at the morgue."

Simon inwardly groaned. Not the morgue again, third time in as many days. "D'you think he had something in the car they wanted to burn, or what?" He didn't say it, but everyone knew he meant something connected to Selena Fenn. "We have to keep searching," he said. "As long as it takes." The forensics people looked at him with a mix of respect and pity.

He felt filthy, same pants and windbreaker all the time, barely changed underwear in three days, all sorts of crud in his pockets. In the midst of the putrid wreckage Simon thought of finding a wife, okay, maybe a girlfriend, maybe the first girl who'd help him change the outfit. Redfern might call him a sexist pig, and for once they'd be right on target. But they're not the ones who'll be here searching hours and hours, doing and redoing the car, sifting through brown grass and dirt throughout the far-flung area the glass had sprayed.

"He musta had somethin' for us." Granita straightened up and grimaced, his fists buried in the small of his aching back. "I'll go back to the car a minute and call the station."

The team went on working. Keith had apparently preferred to break rather than bend; lots of him didn't peel cleanly off. Everything that did went into what looked like Ziploc sandwich bags. A twenty-yard radius had been cordoned off and needed to be searched, as well as the car itself, for clues to the detonator. The "how" before the "why."

The sky began to change, and the team pulled up their collars, zipping themselves up into the last cold phase of the day's efforts.

"Whoever it was worked fast," Simon said. "This lot gets watched all the time."

"But there's no attendant here," said the forensics person. "I should know."

For a second Simon admired the person who had actually bucked the odds. Maybe a woman: who would care enough to notice her around the place? For instance, that professor Rossiter, or any of her pals. But why? Chambers had become their pawn, pretty much; they had no reason to want him gone. Hilary Slocombe? She had the guts, but what would Chambers have had on her? Could he have found out some clinching fact about her, was her grief just a show, or perhaps even genuine remorse? These days, anyone could find out how to make a bomb.

Simon estimated that they could get about six inches done per half-hour. With two hours max left before dark, just a couple of feet could get done. Because a detonator could be a tiny thing, a piece of metal or plastic no bigger than your thumb. Simon's beeper squeaked and crackled, but he tried to ignore it. This damn stench, the cold, the chilly sky. But a fresh wave of adrenaline had spiked his nerve.

"You are a born investigator," McFarquhar had said.

He bent again to digging and sifting for bomb remains with the rest of the gleaners in the killing field. Shards of glass and flattish clods of earth in rainbow colors. Ash floated around like paper. The bit of paper in Simon's windbreaker pocket fluttered out onto the hard ground, showing its blind pattern of black scallops and arches. He stepped on it out of habit, shifted his weight, and picked it up.

"I told the Chief we got everythin' bagged," said Granita, back from the brown unmarked. "He just said Chambers was calling from the shore, someplace like Brighton Beach he called it, that place in New York with all the Russkies. The inside o' the car's done. The outside's gonna take forever." He glowered at the forensics team with its harvest of rubbish. "Plastic lasts and lasts, dontcha know it? If he did it with plastic it'll be as good as new. Only..."

The inside of the car. Curves and arches. Something caught the right-hand edge of his inner vision. Piece of metal like a rounded-off square.

"WAIT!" Simon ran to the forensics van, elbowing Granita aside. "Wait, look!"" He waved his paper scrap at the head of the forensics team. She frowned at him, almost unseeing. "Those bags," he said, "there's something in there. We can get right to it before we pile up more. Please. One thing." He began to rummage in the back of the open van among the neatly piled plastic bags and found the one he wanted, no bigger than three inches square.

"This, look," he showed them, "has the same pattern on it. Like writing." He held the piece of metal out at them in his left palm, right index finger following the arches and scallops that snaked across it in line.

"There's more on it," someone said over his shoulder. Someone else brought out a jeweler's loupe. They elbowed each other to be first. Immediately above the scallops there was a fainter line of what looked like a combination of Greek and Latin script, followed by numbers, the last one broken off. "That's Russian," said the forensics expert, following the script. "But the other stuff, underneath—let's hold on to it. I'll get this blown up tonight."

As the forensic team and the police, bone weary, exited the scene for the day, they were brought up short by the figure of the University President. He was walking toward them, a brisk, dark, compact presence, as if to disclaim the slightest association with the long black car which waited discreetly where it would cause no tie-ups. He quickened his step when he noted them, stopping only at the periphery of the crime scene. As he neared, they could see the tears flow unabashed.

So much for police confidentiality: Chief Killifer had evidently lost little time letting Chavadze know this latest catastrophe.

Chavadze could hardly speak, searching their faces for reasons.

"Lieutenant Blank?"

A few seconds before Simon came forward. "Sir. This is all we found. We don't know what it is yet, but it's something that could have set off the bomb. It's got this Russian writing on it;" he held the little drooped square under a lamp post, "and something like this too, a design or some other writing maybe. That's all we got."

Chavadze bent to see, took the object in his hand. "It's Georgian. Oh, God, no..." Chavadze kept looking at it and away again. "It's Georgian writing." His grip trembled as he held out the little square like a child surrendering candy, and Granita took it back. Then both hands began to rake his cheeks, over and over. The New Campaign came to mind first, then Keith, then Selena. He put his hands over his mouth, covering it like a surgical mask.

"Yashvili. Garso Yashvili. But if it's Yashvili, it's me, too. I brought him here." Chavadze's thoughts began to wrap around the consequences of Keith's demise. Disarray everywhere, though the headless bureaucracy ground on. He had lost the university's most loyal servant and keeper of its secrets, the companion of his endeavors and his stalwart on-campus protector, the truest man on earth, the last old boy. He crumpled.

"No time for that, sir. We've gotta go get 'im."

They sprang into the old action mode. An APB went out as the real search began. No noise of sirens, only the radio static crackling, the brown unmarked cleared the disapproving streets of Federal Temperance to the campus guesthouse in minutes. The Poet in Residence was out, said the kindly lady who looked after the house, once a colonial inn. But she knew he had a reading to do the next day and expressed her hope of being able to attend. The room yielded a battered cardboard suitcase, standard-issue Soviet pants, crumpled shirts on the floor, moustache pomade in the bathroom.

The policemen got speedy reinforcements and the search fanned out, Chavadze continuing to ride with Simon and Phil. Dining Hall, Campus Can, Chez Minimal, Fulfillment Center, library, Redfern Bookstore, beer joints, Maid for Love—where the hell could they have missed? At Fishbane's house, a boohooing Graziella. LuAnn? The very idea! Then the station, the bus depots, the same mazes of streets and alleys from every angle, all in less than an hour.

"I saw him just this morning," Chavadze kept saying, leaning forward as if to be sick, head in hands. Then he began rummaging, first in his overcoat, then his jacket, for who knew what.

"Eighteen commuter flights a day to New York" growled Phil. "An' that's just New York."

The calls went out to Logan, Bradley, Kennedy, O'Hare, Dulles, Seattle, LAX. No Yashvili. He had quite simply vanished for good.

"It's all wrapped up, right?" barked Chief Killifer, holding his relief behind the barrel chest of his built-up Eurosuit. "Well, I must admit that you two lost no time. You did have me worried for a while though."

It wasn't a Redfern person after all. Thank heaven. As the phone rang, probably the mayor's office, he waved at Blank and Granita to stay on for congratulations and coffee. Raises and promotions, too, Simon thought, and none too soon.

"My men have done their best, and now Justice is gonna take it over, sir," the Chief said into the phone. "You know what they say, he can run but he can't hide. Sir."

General Fenn noiselessly replaced the receiver and leans his elbows on his desk, his eyes like ice. The General knew better: a pro like Yashvili can melt right into the gore and confusion of the Georgian civil war, turn the same color as the mountain soil. Tom's only child, the last of us, murdered by a pervert for his filthy pleasure. Fenn turned grimmer yet as he imagines how she died.

He looked up from the desk to see Hilary Slocombe looming above him.

She'd simply planted herself in front of his desk, got past his manservant, past the whole lot in the kitchen. Tired of scenes, Fenn wished for the bodyguards of old times. He looked right past Hilary at the opposite wall as she detailed her plan. Her voice carried an imploring note he wished he could not hear, but never wavered or stumbled.

"...because I loved her as much as you did, on my honor. And Redfern's out of it too, nothing will happen to Redfern," she finished on a sudden note of appeal.

"Doesn't matter that much about Redfern, young woman," he muttered, and was immediately ashamed of having answered. But he had spoken from the heart; he hadn't much left to do with the place. It was a different place now, alien and twisted, a vanity production for people like Sakulin, a hideaway for Van Geyst, a breeding ground for ignorance, waste, and fakery. Now he contemplated the silver-framed photographs of a dashing Tom with his bride, Nancy Mortimer, then a four-year old Selena, all gone... The current was weakening, the connection fraying, his personal world as he had known it easing away from him.

You had to admit that this Hilary was not without courage. He saw in her his own contempt for weakness as a defense.

"I will review what you had to say."

A fine pair they'd make. With his Intelligence connections, his weekly Washington sessions, what would he need HER for? Even if he could imagine carrying out this loopy scheme, she'd be nothing but a liability. Still, you could count on stamina and determination like that, and the plan is her idea. Only fair.

Dismissed, for now. But Hilary, her prize check burning a hole in her pocket, ran the miles back to Blight House like a rampaging angel in flight.

Monday, June 5, 1993
HOT PROFESSOR

The theme song and the New York skyline fade, and Larry King Live faces his audience of millions. Tonight, for once, he is also Redfern's choice. The trance-like boredom induced by the prospects of journalists, senatorial candidates, or the President of the United States yields to gleeful anticipation.

If the Redfern Murders had bid fair to ruin the University for the next half century, that was only how it had appeared to the more shortsighted. Values Clarification and Image Enhancement had worked out a new strategy to save the New Campaign that was to revolutionize the spin control industry. In a nutshell, you could call it The University as Victim. Because Redfern knows that the tragedy is really nobody's fault and everybody's at the same time. That's just how it is, this is America now.

An off-camera voice gives the cue, "Hee-e-ee-ere's Larry!" and there he is, saying that he's gonna do issues tonight not just individuals, and that the topic of the week is Survivors on Parade.

Three people share the platform with Larry instead of the usual one-on-one arrangement. The first is a dad whose divorced wife is kidnapping back their brood of kids, one by one, because he is now the codependent of a lover who eats only Mallomars. His gut swells under a pink velour warm-up suit. The second is Mrs. Betty Duane, mother of the cult leader and child torturer Tawfik Racha (the former Wayne Duane), shot dead two weeks ago by the FBI in a mass assault on religious freedom. Mrs. Duane adjusts the puffs of her giant yellow coiffure and smiles a friendly farewell right into the camera. The third is a Redfern U. professor sweating orange tears of makeup. A special squad from Image Enhancement has done him up and hauled him to New York.

Redfern has been on top of its game since the first glimmer of early summer. With the Ring broken up, its members sent home for a little extra leave of absence, the university ceased to function as a media HQ. The disappearance of Professor Sita Amanpuri, which had gone unremarked for several days after the dinner at Chez Minimal, still remains to be explained. Probably an effect of the shock to her delicate nerves.

Nevertheless, Redfern knows that from here on in, its fiscal health will depend more on sheer persuasion and public sympathy than on the loyalty of Old Boys—and Girls.

The Administration swung into damage control with equanimity, marking time in stately measures. First and foremost, time for the University Counsel to begin suing for Keith Chambers' retirement benefits in order to indemnify Redfern, should one of Keith's family members surface and decide to sue the Corporation for his death—just in case.

Time to cordon off Chavadze until he recovered from the shock of his drinking friend's crime. He was replaced at the Commencement ceremonies this year by Provost Seymour Gorellick and his special guest, Michael Jackson.

Time for the upended wreck of Sita's blue Toyota to be uncovered in the upper Temperance hills, carted off, meticulously scoured and pronounced a mystery. Thank goodness no fleshly trace of her has yet been found.

Then the warrens of little streets emptied themselves of vans, station wagons, and vintage wrecks carrying student belongings, and Old Crazyhorse and the rest of the homeless community switched to their summer places, closer to the campus green. Outside entrances to the Underground Campus were ostentatiously and jealously sealed, and the decision to do so accorded a generous write-up in the Rumble.

"Can you tell us how you felt when you heard the shot?" Larry

King Live is asking the professor, holding his breath.

"Can I tell you? Larry—I cannot, I should not and I dare not even try. The pain will take years to go away—the... scar... the nightmares, if you will, the sense that any day he could be back. The hauntings of memory. But I'm keeping busy, doing a book on the Fenn tragedy, if you will, which I would expect to finish this summer because... well, Fox insists on rushing it into production before the book even comes out. I've signed my life over to them for the time being." He sips some water and recrosses his legs. This is a civil conversation, just fine, not what they teach you to expect of TV hosts. "I'm not allowed to mention casting possibilities yet."

"Are you okay, I mean surviving the shock, getting better in your own mind?" Larry leans forward, anxious about his guest's physical wellbeing.

"It's a whole long process of healing, what can I say. A learning process, a trial of self-discovery. A trusted colleague like my friend Sita Amanpuri—gone without a trace. My wife is gone, too—off to California, leaving me like this." Armin rolls his eyes to indicate the rest of his body, which is swathed in mummifying bandages and topped with a robe like Lawrence of Arabia's.

"But the people you work with, I know they can't wait to have you back."

"They've been superb—all superb. Caring, supportive. And the Selena Fenn bequest is going to help fund an extension of our new building, the Minamoto/Sakulin Diversity Center for the Humanities. That's the way she wanted it. Even though we had other funding from..."

"That brings me to the students. How did they take the tragedy?"

"Students?... well, um, the students. I don't get to see too many lately. But I would guess that applications have not declined. The upside of the tragedy, if you will, the upside is that it has made everyone more aware of themselves. And isn't self-knowledge everything? Isn't compassion?"

"Do you yourself harbor any bitterness toward anyone?"

"Larry, this is no time for divisiveness. We at Redfern remain strong precisely because we refuse to become polarized, because we're supportive of each other. We took the short-term heat and went right on from there, and came out of it wiser, moving right on ahead, putting our house in order. Tellya, my heart goes out to that poor little maniac who only lacked a sense of self. He just had no internal compass, you've gotta pity someone like that."

Larry addressed the viewing audience. "That's Myron Wiener, the gunman." He turned back to his guest. "I understand that his wife Vera is suing Worldwide Foods...."

"She has not confided in me, Larry."

"...on account of the large quantities of the flavor enhancer MSG which Myron had consumed on the day of the shooting incident. It is known to produce aggressive behavior in certain individuals. Do you think Myron will make a complete recovery?"

"Who knows," came the mournful response. "In any event it is unlikely that when he gets out he'll find much of a welcome in academic life."

"What if he'd hit you one inch to the left? What if Keith Chambers hadn't entered the struggle? What if the Van Geyst funeral had happened at the wrong time for the Russian guy to get to the car and..."

"Georgian."

"The one who got away, huh? Basically I wanna ask you, whaddaya think would've happened if the university had actually given a guy like Wiener a permanent job, and..."

The professor lowered his head, peering upward reproachfully. "That would be a different kind of university, Larry...and a different kind of story."

"Well, that's the breaks," said Larry King Live. "Audience out there, I'm with Hot Professor Armin Joel Fishbane of Redfern University. We'll be taking your calls after this."

One Year Later
ON MY HONOR

General Ethan Fenn and Hilary Slocombe sat next to each other, rarely exchanging so much as a glance, each lost in a galactic stream of private thoughts. But they wore the same face, a staring mask of single-minded concentration.

The change of planes at Sheremetyevo Airport went without a hitch. Moscow was the only point from which to make the connection to Tigerskin Air. The airport looked almost empty, the day mercifully slow in coming. They had no trouble clearing customs and immigration. He was on a diplomatic passport, and she was traveling as his granddaughter.

The continuation to Tbilisi would take five hours, with a stopover in Erevan. The aging TU-104 was the identical one the old man had handled himself all those years ago. When the Georgian capital spread out before them at daybreak, both were just awakening from a fitful sleep.

This airport was a milling shouting chaos. People stood unhindered on the tarmac right near the planes on which they were haggling for space. Others were sensibly asleep, stretched out flat on what seemed to be their complete belongings. Hilary, shifting her bag from one shoulder to the other, had never known this wartime blurring of contraries. She saw men in groups armed with clubs, others with rifles. Fenn seemed not to notice anything so she made no comment.

The same customs ceremony, brusque and surprisingly efficient. The taxi ride to the Tbilisi hotel was a matter of minutes. She turned around in her seat to gawk at inlaid-marble buildings, a square with a granite Stalin still very much in charge, placed off-center. But there was no time to waste. They left the mystified check-in woman with two nondescript canvas flight bags containing the barest necessities and continued straight to their rendezvous.

Nothing out of the ordinary, just two American tourists waiting in line with a hundred others to ascend the steep incline to the amusement complex above the park. The funicular was just coming back down to the station when a nondescript figure silently emerged from the latrine to the side of the ticket booth and joined the pair in line. He was carrying a small leather pouch of the sort commonly worn by men in Europe. So was Fenn, despite his dislike of men carrying handbags. The exchange was effected silently and smoothly.

Back in their hotel room after the perfunctory promenade around the amusement complex, they examined the pouch. The Lugers were there as promised, together with the phone number of the contact man. Everything had been prearranged from Washington. They were to meet the following morning at the airport. Mtsyri was just a speck on their map. It was going to be an hour's flight in a single-engine Piper.

They had some trouble finding the plane. It was no regular service they were looking for. The pilot had been instructed to wait as long as necessary and to keep his mouth shut. This round-trip flightseeing job would be enough to bankroll a well-deserved fling in Venice.

The old man and the girl were both on the tall rawboned side, but they managed to squeeze in, scrupulously avoiding contact. Taking off into the morning mist the small plane broke fearlessly through the clouds, though Mount Elbrus, the tallest peak in Europe, rushed forward dizzily, devouring them in its shadow. Off to the right side snow-capped peaks alternated with rocky slashes, violent blue torrents careening down through treeless formations of schist. The little plane bobbed up and down with every gust of wind but plowed relentlessly on with its mute, motionless cargo.

Their descent into Mtsyri was a tricky bit of mountain-hugging that ended with a bump-and-a-half of landing gear on packed clay before the Piper taxied toward the shack at the end of the strip. The pilot got out first, then the girl, and last the old man. They were greeted by what looked like a uniformed policeman but could just as well have been a soldier or a border patrolman. He addressed the foreigners in passable English and barked a short instruction to the pilot, who went inside the shack and sat down to smoke his makhorka on a crude wooden bench in the corner.

The sun was making a vain attempt to pierce the fog that drooped over the mountain like some shapeless headgear. A cream-colored Lada of uncertain vintage could be seen waiting on the side of the road, and the odd trio got in, Hilary in front with the driver, the General in back. The local was in no hurry, and the car made its way slowly up the mountainside, past the occasional domed-roof house and barnyard. Scraggly vineyards soon gave way to mountain scrub and pine. It took no more than twenty minutes to the house that stood away from the road surrounded on three sides by a stone wall, on the fourth by a barren tumulus of a mountain.

They stopped at some distance, hidden from view by a stand of alders that shielded the bend in the road from the terraced patch adjoining the house. By the time the wisp of smoke began to curl out the driver's partially open window, the passengers had gotten out and continued their way on foot.

In the dry air a smell of baked earth and leaves, a raked path of yellow ground leading to the door. The sole occupant of the house, a man pushing fifty with an ex-athlete's frame, had just risen and thrown on a brocaded velvet bathrobe. It had been another night of wine-induced sleep. He took his time answering the knock but recognition was instantaneous.

The shriek of a circling hawk did not completely muffle the dull reports from two bursts of nearly simultaneous gunfire—one to the head, the other to the groin.

But no one who lived barricaded within the jagged skyline of those mountains gave any evidence of hearing. The cigarette burned calmly to its end on the dirt floor, its smoke lazily touring the room. Though no words had passed in those few seconds, the eyes and mouth of the corpse which now lay sprawled on the threshold were contorted as if to say that the man had enjoyed a private joke before dying.

He was traced as the origin of an evil smell three days later by the woman who came to visit him twice a week. Amid the carnage and holding around her nose the hem of her apron, she still could not help smiling at his death mask. Yashvili had been such a serious man.

No one ever found out where they buried him. He'd simply drifted away for the last time, into the dark.

July 5, 1994
EPILOGUE

"PRESIDENT GRIGOL CHAVADZE" looks too blatant in those enormous letters on my new door. But I like the way this desk is placed, this angled platform bisecting the corner. And I love hexagonal rooms. This is the perfect point of view for my panorama of the Stanford campus, just flowing out in three directions, all the way past the hills to the blue haze at the top. Silly, perhaps, but they remind me of my mountains.

The thirteenth floor sounded like bad luck but isn't. I feel as if I'd never been president anywhere else, as much at home as a world traveler making his way from one grand hotel to the next.

God, that Search must have gone on a year at least. Look at those Old Presidents on the wall. Like the Old Redfernian, what the hell's his name—a dear man but not so clever. Muscular Christians, all, militant and stern. One origin, one purpose. But a Diversity President for Now has to be different—has to be someone for everyone. I wish Chambers were here.

I miss Chambers so much.

But there was no other way. He left me no alternative.

Thank God Garso could come to my help. That I was able to pay him. Thank God for Garso's dexterity, his lion's bravery, his singleness of heart. And his lightning speed. Now Gorellick will take years to discover that any funds are missing.

The Fenn girl hadn't seen everything yet but she would've, given

Ricci's stupid extravagant boasting. Goodness knows I try to please. But that time, I simply couldn't produce the one thing she wanted, however I might try.

🎓

"It's simple," Selena says flippantly. "All you have to do is give Hilary Slocombe the President's Fellowship, she deserves it anyhow." She is wearing three gold bangles which run up and down her right arm as she admires their soft glitter under the chandelier.

"That is impossible."

"Don't be silly. What I've got is enough to make you think lots harder. Maybe you wouldn't have to leave Redfern, but your um, effectiveness, would be impaired."

"If you weren't General Fenn's granddaughter this insolence would not go unanswered. As it is, I can only feel sorry for you, that a young person with your—future would ruin herself by going out on a limb with mad accusations."

"President Chavadze, Ricci says he has the passbook with your joint account, millions, that he just walks around with it when he feels like it, any time at all. Plus I've got it all straight, living right here in my head. YOU were the Provost at Megatech, YOU wanted in on the contracting scam, YOU got rich on it, even more than he did. You're damn lucky all I want is the Fellowship for Hilary... if it weren't for her obstinacy about taking money from me, maybe it wouldn't have to come to this. But I happen to love her so I'm going to help her..."

The fingers of Chuck's right hand begin a steady drumming on his desk. Ricci yet again, and the man always knows just where to stop. Contingency plans will not work with Berto, because he cannot lose. If it all came out in the open—well, lawyers get disbarred, but not professors. And now the loose cannon is a silly child; what will she want next?

"Don't you understand about loving someone? But that isn't even... she needs the recognition, she's far and away the best artist here. It would be only fair." She stops for breath, adds in a lower voice, "And it was only fair exchange for Ricci to give me the info, and now I have it." Forever.

Her beautiful myopic eyes gaze reproachfully into his face, belying the terrible harshness of everything she'd said. He stops drumming.

"How much have you told Keith Chambers?"

"Absolutely nothing," she says, feeling more confident. "He can stay in the dark, dear Keith, why worry him? He frets about me too much as it is, and he thinks the world of you, he'd do anything for you. Remember???"

"He'd do anything for Redfern, not me," Chavadze says thoughtfully, as if he'd forgotten her.

"Same thing, as far as Keith is concerned. And what about everyone else here? Doesn't its reputation mean a thing to YOU?" Her voice trembles slightly with impatience, or is it uncertainty?

Now that betrays the child in her, Chavadze thinks. As if Redfern meant anything more than just a way station. But the situation is serious anyhow because of the Search—and all the future Searches. The same people turn up on boards of trustees all over the country.

Ricci has of course convinced her that success is in the bag, that just a little intimidation is the ticket to whatever she wants from me. But he has always underestimated LuAnn and sneered at FAM.

"I think we could come to some satisfactory agreement," Chuck says soberly. "But the Fellowship is out."

"Why? Why?" This child would have her way no matter what. Doesn't anybody, Fenn, or Keith, or this Hilary, anyone, ever say no to her? With a sigh, he swings into his explanation.

"Because I am going to award it to the most deserving student project of your class, as is my duty. You might as well be the first to know: OUR COWS, OUR SELVES, a multicultural and feminist mural system, which will be the first art-creating system to dispense with the necessity of a maker. Cows and humans will join limbs, attached to mechanically propelled levers, to create horizontal art spaces on fences throughout the world. This means as I understand it, the destruction of the fences separating human beings from each other. It means that arrogant notions of human superiority will be dispelled. It also means a powerful attack on the conception of the masterpiece as such." She feels the cold touch of ideology on her shoulder.

"FAM. That's what happened—Rossiter and company..."

"The project will do a world of good."

"It will do nothing but make you look Politically Correct and jolly up Rossiter." Why does even the president suck up to that bitch? "How would the True History of the Megatech Capers look in print, President Chavadze? I'd love to know what Professor Van Geyst would have to say about this one. Guess he'd have to admit that some things really do happen!"

Chavadze knows he could find no adequate excuse to LuAnn Rossiter for switching sides this time. On the other hand, any scandal set in motion by Selena would be enough to ruin his chances in the Search. At Redfern they might have snuffed the scandal or at least smoothed it over, but Stanford hasn't chosen him yet, and owes him nothing. His jolly face sours with the irony that Berto, thousand-time traitor, remains solidly beyond reach.

"I need a week to think this over," he says.

The same night, dawn across the world, I began the work of finding Yashvili. It was lucky he could be picked out like a Braille letter from the midst of the sightless chaos of the civil wars. From the moment we connected, speed was the watchword.

The daredevil part was that Yashvili had to await his chance. There was no telling when the moment would come. We knew only that he had a week as Poet in Residence. A good thing so many of us Georgians are poets at heart, but really, that thing about chickens... Too much!

He had only general orders, though as everyone knows, God is in the details. To seize the moment, he followed Ricci and Selena from the party. He certainly had to learn our Underground Campus in a jiffy. The coolest thing about Garso was his refusal to break his rhythm. If it wasn't the cleanest possible job, still he was thoroughly professional, a can-do man. When he moved her off the floor for everyone to see the effects of—her time with Ricci, that was mastery incarnate. So the first thing the pathologist saw, was that evidence of dear Berto. But you cannot inject personality or initiative into a pathologist, try as you might. The fellow just wouldn't help target Berto for us. You can bring a horse to the water—or the Chief of Police can order him up for us—but that's where our control ends.

Then he had to leave the device in Keith's car. Stroll casually away with a mourning face. Get into waiting car half a mile away. Activate the device with radio signal from transmitter in waiting car. Anything could have happened, for people are quick to forget solidarity under terror!

It must be admitted that Garso left a mess, but he did it with my reluctant blessing. There is no other way the strangling could have looked like something a sex maniac would wreak on his victim. So there it was. I might be nothing but a glorified office boy, but at least I did my errands to perfection. The money and the airline tickets were ready in a matter of a few hours. I was as efficient as Chambers.

Now THAT really hurts. Why did Keith have to turn detective? Probably because no one else was doing it. He loved the place like a woman, thought he'd found at least one evil knight he could slay for her. My poor friend—that was his undoing. Detective novels put competent investigators in charge, but life does not necessarily follow suit. He had to be sacrificed from the moment he reached me on that last day, just before the Van Geyst thing. What is the value even of my right hand, compared with my whole body? And Keith did well by Redfern, just as he would have wanted: was it not his death that exposed the outsider?

That was how we did it, working fast under cover of the New Campaign. The instant reflex of my brain and Garso's brawn. No, that's unfair—as further tasks made their demands on him, he showed his own special versatility. To think that Sita Amanpuri would take it into her head to dog Garso's steps. Some sort of stupid infatuation, I suppose—a bit sudden, and not much in line with feminism. Amanpuri must have chosen the very moment that would not permit of her continuance. And all this misery, because of one petulant child!

How many times will I sit here tracing over the old ground only to arrive at the same end? Alas—as long as Garso lives. A man of honor, he put me first, his friend. But he had a price—not cheap—and who knows how long it will seem enough? Garso, the only person on earth who could incriminate me—I pray that his honor may last, and his cunning.

If Garso stays far away and silent, then I have only one "Ricci" left. The genuine article, still with me. None of our efforts against him got anywhere. Not the messages I put into his computer from Selena. Nor the file dangled before the police. Naturally, as soon as I moved him here to Stanford, he proved as demanding as ever. In fact, his office here is even closer to mine than at Redfern. Wherever I go he is wrapped around me, his fangs biting into my neck. What can I do but return his fat, twisted embrace, hold it just enough away to keep from smothering? Ricci and I, locked as ever into Dante's partnership of traitors... at least it will end in this world, not the next!

Would he really break our bond? If the chance fell into his lap and he had nothing to lose. Someone in my line of work takes a false step every day. Look at Goldmonger, my good friend from Texas days, my counterpart at New England University. Borrowed a million from the place, bought stock in a company whose parent the U. still owns. Sells, makes a giant profit, "forgets" it at tax time. Oh, Doctor Goldmonger, bad boy. But they swallow it because he makes lots of money for them too. If that isn't simple business rules, what is?

I deserve no less than Goldmonger. But just look at the nuisance the Government is creating about my refurbishment of the President's House. As overseers of the contract between Stanford and me, they think they can butt in everywhere, in violation of the simplest business etiquette. Do they expect me to pay out of pocket, or what? The least they could do is restrict their inquiries to my office and stop bothering Peggy at home. Try and tell them that.

Everyone here likes me, though. More than anyone likes HIM. My New Ideas look like some of the old ones maybe, but each lifts its head into the air wearing a new nametag. To recreate the image and atmosphere of a new conversion is essential to every new man.

So now that the disturbances are in full swing here, let's do a Redfern and rid Stanford of the Old Curriculum. Just a stroke of the pen and all is made new. The demographics, the demonstrators, the textbook publishers, the media people, the load of newly credentialed ignoramuses who want the easy life, the retirements of the old—and the arrival of Marvella Jilkes, my Big Fish hooked at last! The hour is at hand; they're crying for change. I really have no choice. For good or ill, a new "justice" is at hand—of the heart, not the head!

Does it matter whose justice presides over our decline? Dear, inscrutable Palter Van Geyst, surely he would see it my way. What is justice? What deserves to be defended? What is courage? What is noble and what is base? Why do civilizations flourish? Why do they die? Most of the world still thinks it can find the answers in places like this, and in ideas that are European—not Asian, not African.

But over here we'll be flooded with the virtues of the "sun people"—who keep women in subjection and ritually mutilate them, who carry out tribal persecutions. We'll be mouthing the principles of religions whose purpose is war on individual freedom—two new dirty words. A composer, a painter, a poet will be remembered just for being gay—if anyone finally remembers them at all. People will once again compose odes to tyrants and despots in stammering dialects.

Survivors of the old guard like to accuse me of neglect, betrayal, even "pandering." Big words. They even claim that the New Ways do extra harm to disadvantaged students, who lose the chance to store up worn-out facts that the others can get elsewhere. Classist nonsense, I say: the so-called "knowledge gaps" will stretch right across the board! Thought police all gone, no one to preach conformity in the name of "standards." Out with spoilsports like Willona McFarquhar! No leverage for her in Fantasyland.

And Fantasyland is where everyone wants to be, as long as the music plays and the machines roll and there's lots to eat. But split into yelling factions, Fantasyland would run amuck... soda fountains spewing geysers, rollercoasters derailed.

So we'll do what it takes and keep on managing—piecemeal, like patching up New York potholes. One at a time, 'til hell freezes over. My Presidency will be yet another sacrifice to the groups; but on MY terms—human terms—they bid fair to agree. And agree they must, for the stakes are taking off, spiraling into the blue, at least for a CEO! Higher Learning is a Bigger Business than I could have dreamed myself—but at least I'll have done my bit to help.

For good or ill, we move with the times. Isn't the Computerized Home University just down the pike? NO MORE CROWD CONTROL—to think that I could live to see it! And meanwhile, Gorellick tells me that Redfern will soon announce the appointment of its first woman President, my colleague LuAnn Rossiter. A fine administrator if there ever was one.